Whimsical Dreams, Book Two
Whimsical Princess

Tiffany E. Taylor

Whimsical Princess
Copyright © 2022 Tiffany E. Taylor
Published by Painted Hearts Publishing

About the Book You Have Purchased

All rights reserved. Without reserving the rights under copyright, reserved above, no part of this publication may be reproduced, stored in or introduced into a retrieval system, or transmitted in any form, or any other means (electronic, mechanical, photocopying, recording or otherwise) without the prior written permission of the copyright owner and the above publisher of this book. Distribution of this e-book, in whole or in part, is forbidden. Such action is illegal and in violation of the U.S. Copyright Law.

Unauthorized reproduction of distribution of this copyrighted work is illegal. Criminal copyright infringement, including infringement without monetary gain, is investigated by the FBI and is punishable by up to 5 years in federal prison and a fine of $250,000.

Whimsical Princess

Copyright © 2022 Tiffany E. Taylor

ISBN: 9798828614363

Publication Date: April 2022

Author: Tiffany E. Taylor

Editor: Kira Plotts

All cover art and logo copyright © 2022 by Painted Hearts Publishing

ALL RIGHTS RESERVED: This literary work may not be reproduced or transmitted in any form or by any means, including electronic or photographic reproduction, in whole or in part, without express written permission.

All characters and events in this book are fictitious. Any resemblance to actual persons living or dead is strictly coincidental.

Publisher's Content Guidance:

This work of fiction contains a scene of disciplinary spanking and other instances of light BDSM that some readers may find triggering.

Acknowledgments

To my kickass, take-no-prisoners beta team who keep things in Whimsy real: Sam DeFiglio, Kim Gosselin, Juliet Pishinsky, Maria Lau, Tricia Potter, Ashley Ribeiro, and Mysty Ross. Kelly and Riley would be proud.

Author's Note

Several years back, I was binge-watching a show on Netflix called *Unforgettable*, starring Poppy Montgomery, in which Montgomery's character had a rare condition that gave her an incredibly flawless memory. She could recall places, conversations—her whole entire life—in impressive, exacting detail.

How cool would it be, I wondered, *if one of the femme protagonists in the Whimsical Dreams series had the same condition?* (My series has been living in my mind for seven years, incidentally).

And boom! Kelly Holland and **Whimsical Princess** was born.

Hyperthymesia, or Highly Superior Autobiographical Memory, is a very real thing (although I definitely took some creative license with memory recall when I was writing Kelly). If you'd like to learn more about hyperthymesia, look up Marilu Henner of *Taxi* fame—she's only one of fewer than 100 people worldwide who have been found with this condition. It's fascinating stuff.

In the meantime, however...I'd suggest you mind your p's and q's around the formidable Kelly Holland. Don't say I didn't warn you.

For all the femmes in the world who are as bold, badass, loyal, and fierce as Kelly is. You know who you are.

Prologue

Rowan's cell phone rang and she answered the phone. She had a quiet conversation until her voice raised, and the heads of Bryn, Riley, and the Seven whipped around, immediately tense.

"You're where?" Rowan's tone was horrified, her body rigid. Her eyes shot to Clem.

"Kel, seriously. You didn't have to…forty-five minutes? Are you freaking kidding me? Okay… I said, okay… Fine, I'll see you then."

She ended the call, then tossed her phone on the counter. A moment later, her head followed suit as she banged it down on the counter right after it.

"Rowan?" Bryn's voice was sharp as she moved to Rowan's side. "What the fuck is it?"

Rowan raised her head and stared at Clementine in disbelief. "That was Kelly. She landed at MacDill Air Force Base a half hour ago and she'll be here in about forty-five minutes."

"Oh, shit, no," Clem yelped, leaping up from her seat, her eyes wide. "Christ on a crutch, Rowan. We are so fucked."

"Kelly? Seriously?" Bryn raised her brow at their panic and stroked a calming hand over Rowan's silky curls.

"*She was upset when I talked to her on the phone yesterday and she was even more upset after she talked to you today, so it shouldn't be a surprise that she would want to see with her own eyes that you were okay,* dulzura. *Plus, whatever the hell is going on with this note, which scared the shit out of you. But why would you be fucked?*"

Clem groaned and dropped back down into her chair again. Nine pairs of probing eyes fixed on her unblinkingly, waiting for an explanation.

She looked at Rowan, ran her hands through her wild blonde curls in agitation, and sighed.

"*First, let me explain something to you all about Kelly. People meet her for the first time, she's wearing a dress and looking all proper, she has her company manners on… They think she should have her gorgeous ass parked in an enchanted cottage somewhere in the middle of the forest, cooking for fucking dwarfs and talking to birds.*

"*Bitch looks just like a Disney princess. She looks more like that redheaded Little Mermaid than Snow White, though, except Kelly's got more fucking sense than to give up her legs for anyone.*"

Clem rolled her eyes. "*Who fucking does that? Except maybe some crack ho who needs a fix and will do anything to get it.*"

"*It was her voice, not her legs.*" *Rowan closed her eyes and pinched the bridge of her nose in an effort to stay calm.* "*Ariel gave up her* voice *to have three days with the Prince, Clementine, she didn't have legs. She was a freaking mermaid.*"

Whimsical Princess

"Voice, legs, what-fucking-ever." Clem waved a hand in impatient dismissal as she continued. "What I am saying to this crew here is that Kelly *looks* like a sweet little Disney princess when you catch her in proper attire and in the right company.

"You see her *not* in the right company, however, and in her usual gear, a sight to which I'd guess you are all about to be treated, and what you got is a Disney princess gone badass. I mean... Bad. Ass. *Emphasis on* 'Bad.' My girl being a CIA operative and all, down with some pretty funky and scary-ass shit on a regular basis. Her showing up with no warning like this, someone fucking with her sister and sending that note, means Princess Spook is pissed and she is looking to wipe the floor with someone.

"And I am here to tell you that it might be us, collectively, that she wipes the floor with, seeing as none of us saw fit to tell her everything that jackass Coravani was doing until Rowan called her about the note. Add this note to all the bullshit been going down with Kelly over the past several months, whatever the fuck it is, and shit. Girlfriend is going to go totally nuclear on our asses. We. Are. Fucked."

"Shit," Nova echoed in a whisper, eyes rounded, as the rest of the girls froze in disbelief.

Rowan sighed and leaned against Bryn for support as Bryn wrapped her arms protectively around her. "Kelly is an information analyst for the CIA, not a spook, Clementine."

Clem snorted and rolled her eyes again.

"Yeah, right, the CIA constantly sends all their info geeks around the world at the drop of a hat. Guess most countries are still using a fucking abacus to count, they need an information analyst like Kelly to show them how to use a fucking calculator. Give me a break, Rowan. She has a MacDill Air Force Base pass, for the love of the Goddess. You trying to tell me, between that and her other huge-ass superpower..."

"Clementine." Rowan's voice cut her off sharply.

Clem clamped her lips shut and looked at the floor, avoiding some suddenly very interested gazes.

"What other superpower, dulzura*?" Bryn asked quietly.*

"Nothing." Rowan quickly dismissed it and frantically sought to change the subject.

"I told her I was fine, Bryn, and we took care of that piece of crap. He's dead, crisis over. At least for me." Rowan closed her eyes and pinched the bridge of her nose again.

"This other... I'm sorry, but I really don't know much detail. I just know that Kelly has always had a very *adverse reaction to that name and it scares me when it comes up, simply because I remember the* look *that's always on her face when she hears it."*

Riley looked at Clementine. "Her lover lets her run around alone like this?"

Clem shook her head no.

"Kelly had a fiancée, CIA like her. Couple of years ago, she got killed in an operation, think it might have something to do with the shit going down right now. Although, you ask me, much as I liked

Robyn the few times I met her and was real sorry when she was killed, she wasn't the right one for Kelly.

"Don't know there is **anyone** out there right for Kelly, since in my opinion, the Goddess has yet to create a butch with 20-pound balls, which is what she will need when she takes on Kelly and all the shit that comes with her."

"What kind of shit?" Riley's voice was level.

Clem snorted again. "Kelly is always ass-deep in some kind of mayhem. She's not like Rowan, who's calm and sweet and everyone's oasis. Kelly's bold and badass and only hell knows the shit she's either in or causing half the time.

"She's one of the smartest women I know, she's fiercely fucking protective of those she considers hers, and she has a moral code that is absolutely uncompromising, even if the path she takes to get to the truth is often…uh…a bit circuitous."

Riley had a considering look on her face as she looked at her twin, then at everyone else.

"Bryn and I have both felt there has been something off with Kelly for some time now." Riley drummed her fingers on the table. "To be honest with you, I've been doing some digging recently and things just aren't adding up for us. Kelly is currently off the CIA books completely, whereas before she was listed in their internal directory as a low-level information analyst. Now, there's no trace of her.

"I don't know much about how the CIA is structured, but I do know they don't make a still-active analyst just disappear from their books like that without a very good reason. I also found out recently they have a division called SAD, which stands for 'Special Activities Division.'" Riley looked at Rowan and Clementine. "Does that name mean anything to either of you?"

The two women shook their heads.

Riley steepled her fingers. "SAD is a special branch of operatives within the CIA. No one really knows anything about them, but they are apparently considered one of the most mysterious branches of operatives in the world.

"Think Navy SEALS or Delta Force." She nodded at the Seven, whose faces reflected dawning comprehension. "With SAD, however, one of the branches within the division is different from all the others in that it works more behind the scenes with covert operations, not with direct combat."

"This is purely speculation on our part," Bryn chimed in, "but it is conceivably possible that the CIA has created a new covert mission within SAD to go after Percutio and cut off the heads of the Hydra once and for all. And Kelly is neck-deep in it."

The Seven looked at Bryn and Riley, and then at each other with hard, unhappy faces.

Bryn stroked a visibly upset Rowan's back soothingly. "I don't want you to worry, dulzura. When Kelly gets here, we'll get to the bottom of this and find out what it is that's had your sister so scared. And I promise you, we'll take care of it and we'll fix it."

Riley's smile was cold as she crossed her muscular arms across her chest. "Kelly doesn't know it yet, mi corillo, *but she's now one of ours. And you know we always take care of what's ours."*

Just then, a car door slammed out front. Clem peered out the front door, blanched, then turned to look at the assembled APS crew in trepidation before she whispered anxiously to the room.

"Shit. She's here."

Chapter 1

Kelly Holland stalked through the front door of the Whimsy Arts Center (WAC), home of the Dream Creamery—the best ice cream shop in west-central Florida—and came to an abrupt halt about five paces inside. Her deep green eyes, lit up in sixteen different kinds of pissed, first swept over her sister, Rowan, as if looking for injury, then slashed sideways to assess the collection of badasses lounging at the rear tables.

Riley Armstrong, co-owner of Armstrong Protection Services and one of the head badasses, straightened up slightly as she caught her first glimpse of the tall redhead who was the little sister of Rowan, her future sister-in-law. Dark auburn hair fell down her back in a tangle of curls, framing a delicate ivory face with dark green eyes. Her body was generously showcased by the tight black T-shirt and jeans she wore, covered by an expensive black leather jacket.

Despite her height of 5'7" and her less than feminine clothing, Kelly Holland looked like one of those exquisite women painted by the Renaissance masters. Voluptuous. Refined. Fragile. Clementine, Rowan's best friend, had been right on the money when she had likened Kelly to Ariel, the Disney princess.

Until Kelly opened her mouth and shattered the illusion.

"Can you please get the fuck back from in front of the window, Ro-Ro," she gritted as she cut her eyes back at her sister, her green eyes narrowing.

Riley's lips twitched in evident amusement.

Kelly arched a brow at Bryn Armstrong, Riley's twin and the other head badass, who was standing next to Rowan.

"Jesus Christ, Armstrong. I would have thought you of all people would know better."

She pursed her lips and jerked her head toward Riley and the rest of the APS management team, with hands on hips that were beautifully rounded.

"Any more of your crew outside, Bryn?"

Bryn's brow raised right back at Kelly, then she flicked her eyes at Riley briefly. Riley shook her head almost imperceptibly, signaling that there was no way Kelly could have seen anybody from APS.

"What makes you think that, Kelly?" Bryn drawled, her calm eyes back on the irate redhead.

"Which means that yes, there are, and you just don't want to admit it. Fuck." Kelly started toward them, a single-minded purpose in her step.

Riley's pleasurable view of the beautiful femme as she strode toward them was brought to a screeching halt by the barely visible outline of a shoulder holster under her leather jacket.

Riley's eyebrows hit her hairline.

"Princess?" Riley's commanding yet seductive voice carried through the room and brushed down Kelly's spine like a caress, halting her in her tracks.

The fuck? Kelly hoped the tiny shiver triggered involuntarily by the sensuous pull of Riley's voice hadn't been visible.

It had already been almost next to impossible for Kelly to hide her unwitting physical reaction to Riley when she had first seen her and looked into her scorching amber eyes.

Like her fraternal twin, Bryn, Riley was extremely tall at 5'11" with a lean, yet powerful build. Her dark brown hair was cut shorter than Bryn's black hair, but the similarities between the twins were striking. Riley's next words, however, set Kelly's teeth on edge and pulled her back from the brink of making a complete fool of herself.

"I understand you are CIA, *princesa*, but I thought you were an information analyst. Are you experienced in covert or clandestine ops firsthand, by any chance? Before you start maybe firing from the hip and putting you or your sister at even greater risk?"

The slight smile that tipped up the corners of Kelly's mouth didn't match the warning chill of her eyes.

"Don't know that's any of your business." Kelly let her icy gaze drift slowly up and down Riley's body before coming back to bore into her eyes in unmistakable contempt. "Was *your* daddy a United States Marine Corps scout sniper and sniper instructor? *Princess*?" Kelly sneered, then turned her back on Riley in a dismissal that suggested she found Riley insignificant.

The identically incredulous looks on the faces of the Seven, the team leads of Armstrong Protection Services, conveyed the thought in their heads as clearly as if they'd shouted it aloud: *The redhead has some balls.*

There were few people in this world who would dare to dismiss Riley Armstrong like that.

Riley hadn't missed the all but invisible shudder that went through Kelly at the sound of her voice, however. Her face reflected the flare of desire that coursed through her as she looked at Kelly's retreating figure. Kelly's nature matched her hair, fiery and feisty, and Riley was clearly intrigued by the thought of having all that heat and passion in her own bed, under her control.

"You okay?" Kelly's voice softened when she reached Rowan and Bryn. The sisters hugged each other tightly for a long minute until Kelly stepped back to look into Rowan's hazel eyes, finding a masked unease that worried her.

"I'm good, Kel, truly." Rowan hugged her sister again.

"Mind telling me what the cast and crew of *American Sniper* is doing in here?" Kelly heard Riley snort from behind her but refused to turn around.

Rowan sighed, her arms still wrapped around her little sister. "Bryn and Riley came to the shop like you asked when you texted them about the note I got. It had rattled me a little bit and I was worried about you, so Bryn called the Seven and asked them to meet us here, too."

"Rattled you a little bit? You were fucking terrified." Bryn was blunt. She crossed her muscled arms over her chest and pinned Rowan with a look that gave the petite blonde the shivers.

"I know what Percutio is, *dulzura*, and there is nothing fucking good about *anything* that even remotely goes on near them." Bryn abruptly switched her laser beam glare to Kelly. "What the hell is going on, Kelly?"

"Nothing," Kelly answered, her eyes hard, her annoyance and a tiny bit of anxiety evident in her tone. "Nothing that is any of your business or anything you need to worry about, Bryn. I got this, so you and your merry little band of butches need to stay out of it."

"Stay out of what, *princesa*?" Kelly started at the dark voice directly behind her. She spun around and came face to face with Riley, who was standing less than a foot away from her.

Riley's equally muscled arms were also crossed over her chest, and her amber eyes were watching Kelly closely.

Kelly looked up, momentarily disconcerted. At 5'7", and even taller in heels, it was rare she ever had to look up to anyone. Riley still towered over her by a good several inches, even with Kelly in her boots, forcing her to tilt her head back.

Christ, she's gorgeous, Kelly thought, unbidden, as she looked at Riley's impassive face. She gave herself a mental shake and turned back to Rowan.

"If it involves your sister, you can bet your sweet ass it *is* my business, Kelly." Bryn's voice was cold. "She is *my* woman and her safety is *my* responsibility."

"Hate to break this to you, Ace, but eight weeks of acquaintance does not trump thirty years of sisterhood." Kelly's voice was equally cold, clearly unafraid in the face of Bryn's menace, and uncaring of the deathly silence that had fallen over the room. "Besides, this has nothing to do with Rowan. This is *my* gig, so when I tell you it is none of your fucking business, it. *Is. None. Of. Your. Fucking. Business.*" She arched a challenging eyebrow, then her voice softened again. "I appreciate everything—more than I can ever say—that you and Riley and your 'Seven,' or whatever they're called, did to keep Rowan safe while that motherfucking dickhead, Coravani, was on the loose." She waved her hand at them. "I'm sure you all will continue to keep her safe, which is one less worry for me right now."

Kelly turned back to Rowan.

"There's nothing to worry about as far as you're concerned, big sis." She gestured casually to Rowan. "You know how crazy my job gets sometimes, and I'm sorry some of the crazy has spilled over to you. Bryn will continue to keep you and your friends safe, Ro-Ro. Just listen to her like you've been doing, and you'll be just fine." Kelly rolled her eyes. "This particular organization couldn't risk sending any communications directly to me at the CIA, so they thought they were going to swing their dicks and reach out this way."

"Just who keeps *you* safe, Kelly?" Riley's eyes were hard and her voice was biting.

The corner of Kelly's mouth tipped up without humor. "I keep myself safe, Armstrong," she said, answering the hard look in Riley's eyes with one of her own. "Again, none of this is anything you should concern yourself with. Clementine." Kelly held up her arms, once again ignoring Bryn and Riley, the ghost of a grin crossed her face. "How the hell are you, my homegirl?"

Clem flew across the space and flung her arms around Kelly. "*Chica*, where in the *motherfuck* have you been? Ro and I have been so fucking worried."

"No worries for you either, short shit." Kelly laughed when Clem drew back and gave her the finger. "As usual, work has been insane, but what else is new?" She shrugged, seemingly unconcerned. "I'm going to have to head back to Langley in a couple of days, but I told McAllister if they couldn't give me some time off in light of what happened to Rowan, he could take this job and shove it the fuck up his ass."

Alan McAllister was Kelly's handler at the CIA.

Kelly slung her arms around Rowan and Clem. "I'm booked into a hotel in St. Petersburg and I have a rental car, so I don't need to be dependent on anyone while I'm here. Sshhh…" she soothed, rubbing her sister's shoulder as Rowan opened her mouth to object. "I work for the government, Ro-Ro, so I stay where they tell me to stay. Besides, I understand the hotel is less than ten minutes from here, so it will be just like I'm staying in Whimsy."

Rowan nodded, appeased. But Riley, Bryn, and the Seven all looked at each other impassively as warning bells clanged loudly in their heads.

There was so much going on under the surface here. If it was the last thing Riley Armstrong ever fucking did, she'd find out what it was.

Chapter 2

Rowan and Clem introduced Kelly to Brooke, Alyssa, Nova, and Delaney, who couldn't take their eyes off Kelly.

"Clem was fucking right," Nova blurted out in awe. "You do look just like Ariel, the Disney princess."

Kelly shook her head, sighing, then leveled her gaze at Clem.

"She's said that for fucking years, and I keep telling her: There is no one in this world less princess-like than I am," she informed Nova with a slight laugh. "I happened to inherit my mother's red hair and green eyes, that's all. I'm actually more like my dad." Kelly and Rowan exchanged looks, love and sorrow in their gazes.

"Kelly, I'd like you to meet the rest of the APS management team." Riley's voice reached her ears next. "We call them 'The Seven' because these are the seven team leaders who run APS along with Bryn and me."

Kelly turned around and nodded to each one of the Seven as they were introduced to her.

"Again, I can't thank you enough for looking after Rowan when she had to come down here by herself," she said when Riley was finished. "I know you've all clearly figured out by now how incredibly special she is." Kelly looked at her sister with a warm gaze and love in her eyes.

"That we have," Riley said. "However, you should know that, according to your sister, you are your own kind of incredibly special as well. She's been really excited for all of us to meet you."

Kelly smiled at Rowan. "With any luck, my current assignment will be over soon and I'll be able to come down permanently." Her voice was noncommittal. "I'm trying to work out the logistics with my boss as we speak."

Warning bells. More motherfucking warning bells that were resounding so fucking loudly in Riley's head, her ears were ringing. She, Bryn, and the Seven exchanged more sharp glances.

"Have you ever considered leaving the CIA and finding something in the private sector?" Bryn was nonchalant. "I can tell you that Riley and the Seven and I have been more than impressed with your skill set. We'd seriously like to discuss you coming to work at APS. We all think you'd be an incredible associate."

Although Kelly's face never changed, every single one of the APS management team caught the sudden acrid scent of fear that emanated from her.

"That's very flattering," Kelly said with a composed face that belied the unease they could still smell rolling off her. "We can definitely talk about that when this project of mine is over with. Unfortunately, however, I can't give you an exact end date because the timeline on this has been a bit unusual." Kelly smiled with a calm expression. "But I'm more than happy to give you a project status occasionally if you'd like."

She deliberately dismissed the subject and turned back to the girls. The Seven and the Armstrong twins regarded each other with a silent promise to discover what was going on.

Riley had no idea what the fuck was happening. The look on her face, however, made it obvious that she didn't fucking like it.

"Kelly." Clem's face suddenly lit up. "How long did you say you were here for?"

"Two days. It's Tuesday, so I'm heading back to Langley Thursday morning." Kelly jumped on the change of subject.

"Fabulous. Then tomorrow night, we're having an LBD night." When Kelly looked at Clem with raised eyebrows, Clem stuck her finger in Kelly's face…no small feat for a 5'1" woman up against her 5'7" friend.

Clem glared. "Girl, this whole moving to Whimsy thing has been nothing but a motherfucking shit show in so many ways since Rowan and I stepped foot into this town. There's been a lot of great stuff that's happened—like creating the WAC, and meeting the girls and the APS badasses—and Whimsy itself is an awesome place. But because everything was wrapped up with that dickhead, Coravani—may the Goddess burn his soul in eternity—we haven't had the opportunity to fucking go out even *once*. We need an LBD night, Kel." Clem was insistent.

"What's an LBD night?" asked Alyssa, intrigued.

"A Little Black Dress Night. It's the mother of all femme nights out," Clem enthused. "It's a night where we go out, all tricked out in our finest little black cocktail dresses, hair done, makeup done, come-fuck-me heels on, party, and drink cocktails until wherever we are announces last call."

"*Yassssss*!" Nova punched her fists in the air as all the girls started to chatter excitedly. "Outstanding!"

"We'll get an Uber so we can have a few cocktails and not have to worry about driving, in case we get a little tipsy." Clem high-fived Nova.

"I'll come and get you." Bryn folded her arms implacably.

"We don't need …" Clem began.

"I said, I'll come and get you, Clem. Rowan can text me when you're ready to leave, and I'll be there to make sure you girls all get home safely."

Kelly interrupted before Clementine could kick up a bigger fuss.

"It's a nice thought, Clem. Unfortunately, the only thing I have with me is a small bag with a toothbrush and some clean panties. I don't think jeans and a leather jacket will work for an LBD night," Kelly said wryly.

"And that's where I've got you, homeslice," Clem gloated. "When we packed everything in your house in Virginia, we separately packed the clothes we knew you wouldn't wear until you got here, like your LBD gear. It's all at your new house."

"I should have known," Kelly groaned and sighed.

"Fine. But I'll get an Uber myself since I'm staying in St. Petersburg and you all are here in Whimsy."

"I'll take you to your hotel." Riley was just as implacable as Bryn. "And before you argue, the only acceptable answer to that is, 'Why, thank you, Riley. I appreciate it.'"

Kelly drew back in incredulity, her eyebrows hitting her hairline, then her green eyes narrowed again. She had started opening her mouth when Riley placed her finger over Kelly's lips and shushed her.

Kelly, with wide eyes and in complete shock, let her.

"No arguments, Kelly," Riley said, her voice filled with formidable sternness. "I fucking know what Percutio is, *princesa*, and I'm already tired of playing this game with you." Kelly paled.

Riley slid her hand around to cup Kelly's cheek. Amber eyes met green eyes with severity.

"You're going to spend these two days with your sister and your new friends. You're going to accept the protection APS provides to you while you're here." Riley tilted Kelly's face up. "I can't force you to tell me why Percutio scares the ever-loving shit out of you, or why you even know what they are, but I can goddamn well make sure you're safe while you're in *my* town."

Kelly stared at Riley for a long time before she nodded.

Rowan's and Clem's eyes were huge.

"Have you *ever* seen her fucking back down like that before?" Clem whispered to Rowan, bewildered.

Rowan was equally astonished. "Never once in my lifetime," she whispered back to Clem, her eyes still enormous.

Riley addressed the Seven. "I'll need some associates on bodyguard duty both today and tomorrow, *mi corillo*. I have Kelly, Bryn has Rowan, so I just need coverage for the rest of the girls."

Kelly opened her mouth again to say something, but a sharp look from Riley shut her up.

She was beyond confused as to why Riley Armstrong was able to affect her the way she did. Kelly bent for nobody, she didn't follow anybody's orders—other than those given to her by her directorate head—and if anyone else had tried to boss her around the way Riley Armstrong just had, they'd be spitting through a new gap in their front teeth.

She huffed, sounding so much like Rowan that Bryn's mouth twitched in amusement.

"*Dulzura*," Bryn said to her fiancée, who was evidently still reeling a bit from Kelly's reaction. "Why don't we take your sister to your house? She doesn't have much time with us, so we'll definitely make sure she sees the important things."

Both Kelly and Rowan looked relieved.

"Since it will take us a little while to set up the bodyguard detail," Bryn said to her twin, "you and I can cover Rowan and Kelly while we go to their house. We'll meet everyone else back here when we're done."

Kelly arched an incredulous eyebrow before her brows then lowered. "Why didn't you tell me the Armstrongs were so fucking bossy?" she whispered to her sister.

"Brattiness is a spanking offense in alpha butch world, *princesa*," Riley, who had clearly heard Kelly, informed her. "Consider this your one free pass."

Kelly's eyes narrowed even further as she decided she was done with *this* game.

"You seem to have me confused with someone who actually belongs to you, Armstrong," she said coldly to Riley. "Last time I checked, *my* fiancée was murdered two years ago."

The room grew utterly silent.

"Now, if you'll excuse me, I'd like to see what Bryn needs in order for her to feel safe letting my sister show me our house. I don't believe your services are required any longer."

As Kelly turned her back on Riley, however, a tiny tear escaped from the corner of her eye.

Chapter 3

"Kelly." Riley's voice was incredibly gentle. Kelly looked back at her with hard eyes.

"*Princesa*, Percutio is no joke, though I suspect you already know that." Kelly remained silent. "Why don't you let APS do what it does best so you can enjoy these two days with your sister without worry?"

Kelly looked at Riley dispassionately for a long moment before she turned away in wordless assent.

"Starting tomorrow, your contractor is going to bring a crew in to work on the cosmetic changes and upgrades your sister said she wanted, Kelly." Bryn stroked Rowan's back.

"If I recall, Nia said it wouldn't take her any longer than ten days, maybe two weeks, to do everything Rowan wanted done. When they're finished, APS is going to install your security system. When that's done, you can get your stuff out of storage and have it delivered. I'm thinking it will be a month tops before the house is move-in ready."

Kelly nodded, still silent.

"Aren't you excited?" Rowan asked her younger sister quietly, suspicion suddenly growing in her mind.

"I think you've done an absolutely tremendous job managing everything, Ro-Ro." Kelly squeezed her sister's hand and smiled a bit stiffly. "You know I absolutely suck at doing this kind of shit. If I'm completely honest, I'd want to be back up north in our old house, with Mom and Dad still alive." Kelly's voice was matter of fact. "But that's a pipe dream. You're down here—happy and safe—and I can go back up to Langley, knowing you're in good hands."

There was a lengthy silence.

"You're not planning to come down here permanently, are you, Kel?" Rowan's voice was still quiet as she hit Kelly right out of left field.

Kelly looked at her sister for a long time in the deafening stillness.

"Believe me when I say I want that more than anything else in this world, big sis." Kelly wrapped one arm around her sister as she swiped the tears that were starting to fall down Rowan's face with her other hand. "What I do…It's complicated, Ro." Kelly sighed. "Sometimes it's boring, sometimes it's exciting, and sometimes, it's not quite as safe as I would like it to be these days. For your sake right now, Ro-Ro, it's better if I go back to Langley for a little while." She rubbed Rowan's back soothingly as a sob escaped her sister.

"Kelly." Riley's voice was as quiet as Rowan's had been. "I don't like what I'm hearing, *princesa*. At *all*.

"I don't understand why you just can't give the CIA your notice and come work with APS. Every single one of us here has already talked about what a fucking great associate you would be." A rumble of agreement swept through the Seven.

"I appreciate that," Kelly said, her anger evidently forgotten. "But that's not something I can do right now, and I'm not at liberty to divulge the reasons why. Someday soon I'll be here, I promise. But I can't be for a little while. So," Kelly blew out a big breath, "I think we should enjoy these two days and then see where the path leads us after that, okay?"

* * * * *

Riley stood at the edge of the outside bar at Seashells, a glass of unsweetened iced tea in her hand, watching Kelly with Rowan, Clem, and the rest of the girls as they laughed and talked.

It had been an amazing couple of days.

Kelly had absolutely loved her and Rowan's house and had also loved Rowan's ideas for redecorating it.

"Remember, this bullshit in Langley isn't going to last forever, Ro-Ro. That's *my* master bedroom, and I have every intention of moving in it just as soon as I possibly can," Kelly informed her sister firmly.

The first night, Riley and Kelly had gone out to dinner with Bryn and Rowan at the Pier House Grill, a local favorite. Kelly, Riley had discovered, was wickedly funny and as intelligent as her sister, and they'd all enjoyed a wonderful dinner.

When Kelly had learned both Bryn and Riley had known her father, she was quiet for a moment but quickly recovered and shared some anecdotes about her father's life and career.

"He was an amazing man," Riley said eventually. "I don't know anyone who knew him who didn't have the highest respect for him." She put her hand over Kelly's and squeezed. Kelly, after startling, allowed Riley's hand to remain.

When Riley had gotten home after dropping Kelly off at her hotel and finally crawled into her bed, she'd spent a long time laying there with her hands behind her head, thinking.

Kelly Holland, she'd decided, *was the most fascinating, aggravating, brilliant, beautiful, enigmatic, and feisty woman she'd ever met in her thirty-five years of walking this earth.*

And Kelly was hers.

Kelly didn't know it yet, but Riley had every intention of claiming Kelly for her own.

When Bryn had claimed Rowan as fast as she did, Riley had thought her twin had lost her fucking mind. You were seriously going to look at a woman and decide within ten minutes that she was the one who had been made especially for you?

That was some fucking bullshit right there.

Except…it hadn't been bullshit. Rowan had been so goddamn perfect for Bryn, it was as though Bryn had called some celestial bakery in the sky and custom-ordered a mate.

As much as Riley adored her future sister-in-law, however, she knew there was no way she could be interested in a woman like Rowan herself.

She would need someone who was way more of a challenge, who needed to be kept in line with a strong hand, who constantly pushed the envelope, and who made every day a contest of wills.

Someone like Kelly.

Kelly, Riley knew, intimidated the fuck out of ninety-nine percent of the people who encountered her. Rowan wasn't intimidated, because Kelly was her little sister and Kelly worshipped the ground Rowan walked on. Clementine was Rowan's best friend and was extremely close to Kelly, so she wasn't intimidated either. But the rest of the human population?

Outside of her and Bryn and the Seven, there were probably very few people in this world who could go up against Kelly Holland and hope to win.

There were also more than a few mysteries that surrounded the beautiful redhead Riley had every intention of taking for herself.

Riley had Drew Hollister, one of the APS Seven who knew where the bodies were buried in what APS called Purgatory—a shadowy place on the dark web—doing some digging.

On the surface, Kelly was listed as a low-level information analyst for the CIA, one with an unremarkable security clearance. However, her CIA profile had mysteriously disappeared in recent months, although Riley was as sure as she could be that Kelly was still a part of the CIA.

It also appeared as though Kelly had been directly targeted within the last five months by an organization called Percutio, a malignant crime syndicate involved with extortion, drug dealing, arms dealing, gambling, and stock market manipulation all up and down the Eastern seaboard.

The head of Percutio, Grigor Reizan, ran the Percutio operations from their main base in Miami, although his exact whereabouts were kept a very closely guarded secret.

Additionally, there was a mysterious division within the CIA called SAD, or the Special Activities Division. Little was known about them, only that they carried out world-wide top-secret missions. The vast majority of SAD's operations dealt with direct combat missions, but there was one branch within SAD that focused exclusively on covert operations.

Riley and Bryn were speculating that the CIA had launched a full-out assault on Percutio through their covert operations—most likely through SAD—and that Kelly was deeply involved. It would explain why Kelly had gone dark all of a sudden, without any warning.

Why Kelly had become the personal target of an organization like Percutio, however, when there were more than a few covert operations operatives within the CIA, was one big motherfucking riddle.

It was a mystery Riley was fucking determined to solve.

Additionally, Kelly had once been engaged to another CIA operative named Robyn Braswell, who'd been shot and killed while on a Percutio assignment approximately two years before.

Although Robyn hadn't been right for Kelly, as Clementine had insisted, it didn't mean the pain of losing her fiancée wasn't still affecting Kelly on some level. *That was a minefield she'd stepped on squarely*, Riley had admitted to herself.

However...

Before things went to hell, Kelly had responded to Riley's dominant alpha personality beautifully—until she'd suddenly realized she was at risk of losing the control that seemed to be so important to her. Then the gloves had come off.

Normally, that wouldn't have been enough to stop Riley. But it was that one tiny tear, which had traced its way down Kelly's cheek, that had stopped Riley from pushing Kelly any further in public.

Riley had turned over and gone to sleep, vowing with everything in her that Kelly Holland would be in her arms and in her bed before she knew what hit her.

Now, Riley casually observed the other patrons in the busy bar, occasionally making eye contact with the other APS associates there, and letting her glance linger on Kelly. In keeping with the LBD night theme, Kelly had on a fitted, black tank top-style dress with a low back scoop that hit her about two inches above the knee. Her dark red curls were loose and her makeup was dramatic—less Ariel tonight than a sultry, red-haired, green-eyed, fair-skinned Jasmine.

She was the loveliest woman Riley had ever seen.

Even with three-inch stiletto heels, which put her at about 5'10", Riley noticed Kelly had been a bit disconcerted to realize she was still shorter than Riley, who was just shy of 6'0" in her boots. Every time Kelly let her eyes wander over Riley's lean, deeply tanned, muscled body and blistering amber eyes, a bit of color would wash over her cheeks when she realized Riley had caught her staring.

The predator within Riley stirred.

"Riley. Well, hello there," a provocative voice purred, interrupting Riley's thoughts. "Fancy meeting you here."

Christ, Riley thought to herself in disgust. *Just what I fucking need.*

About six months before, Riley had hooked up with the niece of one of Whimsy's more prominent citizens, a woman who was supposedly just visiting for the summer.

As was standard for the Armstrong twins and the Seven, Riley had told her in no uncertain terms she wasn't interested in anything more than a brief hookup. This bitch, however, was completely ignoring the fact that Riley had zero fucking interest in pursuing anything further with her. Even worse, at the end of the summer, Riley had found out this chick had decided to extend her stay in Whimsy, with the sole intention of pursuing Riley just as hard as she could.

"Clarissa." Riley's voice was bored and disinterested. "Sorry. I'm here with friends tonight."

"I'm sure they won't mind one bit if I decide to join you all." Clarissa pouted, running her tongue over her shiny red lips as she tried to clutch Riley's corded biceps. "At the very least, you know you'd *love* to buy me a drink...wouldn't you, darling?"

"Riley." A familiar, wickedly amused voice reached Riley's ears. "Where did you run off to, babe? I thought you were going to tell the girls that story about the time we got caught skinny-dipping in my dad's pool?"

The next thing Riley knew, she was holding a lusciously curved body and kissing a pair of soft lips devilishly curled into an impish grin.

Kelly pulled back almost immediately, then turned toward a very pissed-off Clarissa. "Hi." Kelly beamed, pretending to be a touch inebriated. "Are you one of Riley's friends? I swear, it's going to take me a million, gazillion years to remember everyone's name!" She slung one arm around Riley's waist, laid her other hand on Riley's impressively hard abs, and pretended to be hanging on for dear life. "Riles, I think I'm going to need some help getting back to my seat, lover. Would you mind so awfully much?" Kelly giggled and rested her head against Riley's shoulder.

That little she-devil. Riley narrowed her eyes playfully at Kelly, letting the heat of her eyes say everything she wanted to say to her.

"Not at all, *princesa*. Sorry, Clarissa, it looks like my woman has had a wee bit too much to drink." Riley pulled Kelly firmly into her side. "Enjoy the rest of your evening."

"Toodles." Kelly beamed again and waggled her fingers over Riley's shoulder, leaving an incensed Clarissa behind.

"Seriously?" When they were far enough away, Kelly looked at Riley and rolled her eyes. "You have shit taste, Armstrong. I wouldn't fuck her with your dick."

Riley gave Kelly a lopsided grin. "Then it's a goddamn good thing I only fucked her once about six months ago. It was also so eminently forgettable, I think I fell asleep about halfway through."

Kelly burst out laughing as they arrived at the girls' table.

"I probably don't want to know, do I?" Rowan's eyes were suspicious as she eyed the two of them. "No…No, of course not. I definitely do *not* want to know."

"It's all good, big sis. Riley was just teaching me the finer points of how to avoid a potential landmine." Kelly looked innocent, as Rowan snorted and Riley smirked.

*****

As soon as Kelly had sat down and made herself comfortable again, however, she sighed irritably. "Oh hell, be back in a flash. I need to run to the ladies' room." She swung her long legs off the barstool and stood up.

"I'll come with." Clem stood up with her. "Apparently, I don't have the bladder capacity I once did." The pair headed off to the ladies' room.

As the two of them were washing their hands when they were done using the facilities, Kelly frowned when she heard a really odd sound coming from outside the bathroom door.

"Stay here a minute, Clem, okay?" she said in a low voice. "That sound was a little weird for me. It's probably nothing, but let me check it out before you try to come out, okay?"

Kelly raised the hem of her dress and withdrew a Beretta APX from her thigh holster, then laid one finger across her lips in a *sshhh* gesture, before tiptoeing quietly to the bathroom door.

When she yanked the door open, she surprised the hell out of two foreign-looking guys who were loitering with a surveillance device just beyond the entrance, clearly waiting for Kelly and Clem to emerge.

"Clem! Text Riley and tell her to get the girls the fuck out of here *now*," Kelly yelled as she nailed one of her attackers hard in the balls with her stiletto, slamming her fist and the butt of her gun into the back of his neck when he bent over, and put him on the ground, unconscious.

Motherfucker, she seethed, as the other attacker started toward her. She didn't dare shoot with a crowded bar just down the hall, nor did she dare go out the back door without knowing how many more hostiles might be out there.

She kicked off her stilettos for more stability, holstered her pistol, and crouched low. When the hostile reached her, she threw a few hammer fist punches straight to his abdomen before he even knew what hit him. Then, blindingly fast, she launched a front kick to the groin that completely incapacitated him as well, before she knocked him out cold with her knee.

Kelly looked around, saw no more hostiles, unholstered her gun again, and screamed for Clem to get out and run while she covered the back door.

When Clem was out, she went to the back door and stood to the side for a moment, waiting to see if anyone would try to breach the door. When no one did, she slid on her heels and went to the main part of the bar, which had descended into chaos, leaving the two unconscious hostiles behind.

She slid around confused patrons and pissed-off badasses, and made her way outside, where Clementine, Rowan, and the rest of the girls were already being covered by APS protection.

Riley came running outside, gun drawn, with a look of extreme anger on her face. The anger morphed rapidly into a look of relief, however, when she spotted Kelly, unhurt. She opened her mouth to say something but was interrupted by a supremely pissed-off Clementine.

"God*damn* it, Kelly!" Clem yelled, arms flailing in an absolute fury as she lost her mind in front of God and everyone. "This happens *every* time we go out! *Every. Fucking. Time*! Have you ever thought about switching careers to become a pet groomer, or do some other goddamn shit that *isn't* the C-I-fucking-A…which—let me remind you in case you have forgotten—means *every* fucking LBD night we have ends up with your posse getting *chased, stalked,* or motherfucking *shot at*?" She stomped across the parking lot, one of the APS associates in tow.

"Shot at?" Riley tensed and tightened her grip on Kelly, then pushed Kelly behind her so that her body was between Kelly and the parking lot. "Jesus Christ, Kelly," Riley ground out, livid, her eyes scanning the dimly lit expanse, her gun in her hand. "Those fuckers shot at you?"

"Uh…no. Well, not this time. She was talking about last summer's clusterfuck," Kelly muttered, then wrenched her arm from Riley's grip, using the element of surprise to get free.

She ran across the parking lot after Clementine, drawing up the hem of her sexy black dress as she ran so she could put her gun back into her thigh holster, giving everyone a glimpse of her long, shapely legs.

Riley took off after Kelly with an expression of determination on her face, clearly intending to get to the bottom of this mystery, no matter what it took.

Chapter 4

"Kelly!"

As Riley reached the edge of the parking lot and caught up with Kelly, she swung her around and grabbed her firmly by her upper arms. Before Kelly had time to react, Riley wrapped her arms tightly around the beautiful redhead so that she couldn't move and kissed her.

Kelly froze in shock for a moment, then softened in Riley's arms and kissed her back.

After a long minute, Riley released Kelly's mouth. "*Princesa*," she murmured intently, running her mouth over the side of Kelly's throat. "We need to talk privately about some of what's been going on. You know we do, Red. Come with me to my apartment so we can talk, just the two of us. Yeah?"

When Kelly started to demur, Riley shushed her. "I'm not asking you to share anything you don't feel you can share right now, *princesa*. But I need some reassurance that you're going to be safe when you return to Langley tomorrow."

Kelly looked at Riley for a long moment, then nodded. She softened further in Riley's arms, signaling her agreement to far more than just going to Riley's apartment with her.

Riley's apartment was on the top floor of the massive APS complex and was a mirror image of Bryn's apartment, which was on the opposite side: same private entrance, same electronic keypad entry, same layout. Inside, however, instead of the black, dark chocolate, and cream palette of her twin, Riley's space combined a color scheme of caramel, bronze, and navy blue that was just as striking and powerful as Bryn's.

Kelly's heart was pounding rapidly when she entered Riley's apartment. She felt Riley move very close behind her; then, Riley drew Kelly's long, dark red hair aside and nuzzled the back of Kelly's neck lightly, her breath drawing erotic patterns on Kelly's skin.

Riley's strong hands caressed Kelly's shoulders and slid down her arms to momentarily capture her wrists. Riley turned Kelly around, slid her powerful arms around Kelly's body, and seized Kelly's mouth in an unmistakable show of dominance. Kelly whimpered, feeling herself submit to Riley in a way no one had ever made her submit before. Even as she tried to regain some measure of control, Riley mastered her until Kelly could do nothing but surrender to Riley's will.

Fuck it, Kelly thought, lost in a haze of desire. She was leaving in the morning, going back to Langley, and there was no telling how long it would be before she saw Riley Armstrong again. If ever.

She wanted to belong to Riley, Kelly realized with a shock, if only for one night. She wanted to be just like every other femme she knew who belonged to a strong alpha butch. For once in her life, she didn't want to be the strong one, or the one who took the lead. She wanted to be the one who was mastered, controlled, captured, and dominated.

For this one night.

Riley slowly let her go and looked deeply into Kelly's eyes.

"Come," Riley said simply, taking Kelly by the hand and leading her to a short staircase that ascended to an open bedroom loft.

Kelly climbed the stairs, feeling the laser focus of Riley's gaze as Riley ascended the staircase behind her. When they both reached the top, Kelly felt herself being turned around once again.

"Take off your shoes, *princesa*," Riley instructed her. When Kelly kicked off her stilettos, her heart hammered as she realized the over four inch difference in their height made her feel utterly vulnerable.

Riley ran her hands down Kelly's body, caressing every feminine curve in her path. With a heated gaze, Riley cupped Kelly's full breasts, thumbing her nipples through her dress, and making Kelly shiver with desire.

"You're mine, *princesa*," said Riley, leaning forward to gently bite the side of Kelly's throat. "You need to be aware I've claimed you, and there's nothing in this world that will make me let you go. If you think for even one minute you can ever escape me, Red, you'll find out what being prey really means."

Kelly felt her breath freeze in her lungs with Riley's pronouncement.

With assured movements, Riley swept off Kelly's dress, leaving her clad only in a lacy black bra and a tiny black thong. Riley's fiery amber gaze ran possessively over Kelly's pale skin. She wrapped Kelly's long red hair around her powerful fist and firmly pulled Kelly's head back, baring her throat to Riley's scrutiny.

"I'm thinking you've never in your life been claimed and fucked by an alpha butch, *princesa*." Riley dipped her head, then ran her tongue over the pulse in Kelly's neck. Kelly moaned as a wave of wetness slid out of her body, soaking her thong.

"I'm going to pin you down, put my hands and mouth all over your body, and make you come with my mouth until you scream yourself hoarse. Then I'm going to fuck you so long, and so hard, you'll be feeling me inside of you until the next time I fuck you."

Another flood of moisture cascading from between her legs had Kelly almost faint with desire.

"No one has ever taken control of this little tough girl, now have they?" Kelly heard the amusement in Riley's voice.

"Hasn't anyone ever tied you down, *princesa*—tied these beautiful legs open, tied these delicate hands up over your head, and eaten that delectable pussy until you've screamed yourself unconscious?"

Riley reached behind her and unsnapped her bra, Kelly's full, rose-tipped breasts falling right into Riley's waiting hands. Riley pinched Kelly's nipples, causing her to moan again, then Riley's head came down, and she captured one of Kelly's erect nipples in her mouth.

Riley suckled and nibbled and licked her rigid nipple until Kelly thought she was going to lose her mind. When Riley switched her attention to Kelly's other breast, she slid her hand into Kelly's soaking-wet thong, and eased one long, strong finger into Kelly's tight pussy.

Kelly cried out and involuntarily clenched Riley's finger, as Riley gently penetrated her and worked on opening her channel for a moment. As she nipped and nibbled Kelly's other nipple, Riley stroked her finger in and out of Kelly's clenching body, until Kelly felt herself soak Riley's hand in her juice.

Riley pulled her finger out of Kelly, eased her sopping wet thong down her legs—leaving her completely bare—then swept Kelly up into her arms and laid her on the bed. Riley paused for a moment, then pulled off her own T-shirt and undid her jeans, before pulling them off as well. Kelly's eyes finally focused as she looked at the powerful, mythical form before her.

Riley Armstrong was pure muscle, with broad shoulders, and sinewy corded arms that tapered past a black sports bra to a flat, taut belly with six-pack abs. Her long, muscular legs and tight rear in a pair of snug boxer briefs finished off a physique that clearly showed her serious commitment to fitness. Kelly shivered when she saw a bulge in Riley's briefs that clearly showcased what she was packing.

Riley Armstrong was every single butch fantasy Kelly had dreamed about her entire life.

Riley knelt in front of Kelly, pushed her legs apart with her hands, and gave Kelly a fierce look before she lowered her mouth between Kelly's legs. Kelly cried out as Riley ran her tongue around Kelly's labia and drew it up slowly through the wetness flowing from Kelly's body. Riley held Kelly's hands firmly, keeping her legs open as well; then she sharply spanked Kelly's pussy when Kelly tried to clamp her legs shut from the intense pressure.

"I will flip you over and spank that ass if you *ever* try to deny me access to this body again, *princesa*," Riley growled, a menacing note running through her voice. "You are mine, this body is mine to do with as I please, and you will *never* pull yourself away from me again, do you understand?" When Kelly nodded, shaking a bit, Riley reprimanded her. "I need to hear the words, *princesa*, so I know you understand my command."

"I will n-never deny you again," Kelly gulped, shaking more as Riley's steel dominance wrapped itself around her. "M-my body is yours to command as you see fit."

Riley licked Kelly's clit and nibbled it, making Kelly shriek. Her pussy gushed again. "Very good, Red. Now, because you've been such a good girl for me, you get a reward."

She drew Kelly's clit into her mouth, and began to slowly suck and nibble her harder, until Kelly was screaming with the sensation. Riley worked her faster with her lips and her tongue, the pressure becoming more agonizing, until Kelly felt herself balance on the edge of the precipice. She fell over, shrieking, as her body exploded, and she came harder than she ever had in her life.

In a haze of after-shocks, Kelly felt Riley crawl up her body, inserting the tip of her cock into Kelly's wet, swollen pussy. Kelly gasped in shock with the feel of her, as Riley slowly worked herself in and out of Kelly's pliant body.

Desperate, Kelly wrapped her long legs around Riley's waist, clutching her powerful shoulders as Riley moved in and out of her. Riley moved slowly at first, making sure Kelly could take her; then, she started moving faster and harder, until the two of them were climbing toward the peak together.

Kelly threw her head back and screamed as she exploded, feeling Riley stiffen and freeze, groaning, as she reached her climax as well. Kelly collapsed, limp from the intensity of her orgasm, as she dimly felt Riley gently roll to the side before she pulled Kelly into her arms. The two of them lay together in a quiet, comfortable silence, until Riley rolled on top of Kelly, making her gasp again.

"Catch your breath, *princesa*." Riley bit the side of her neck, spiking Kelly's desire as she slid her muscled legs between Kelly's slender ones. "The night is still young."

* * * * *

Kelly stared at the phone in her hand, still trying to make sense of what Alan McAllister, her handler at the CIA, had just told her before he'd abruptly hung up on her.

She'd been burned.

A burn notice was a document issued by various intelligence agencies, such as the CIA, to discredit or announce the dismissal of agents or sources who were determined to have become unreliable.

It had been established, McAllister had stated tersely, that Kelly's "gift" might increasingly lend itself to more instability than the CIA liked to see in their agents. As a result, her reliability had been called into question.

Given where Kelly's talents had historically been directed during her tenure with the CIA, McAllister said, the agency now felt Kelly and her gift were too big of a risk to their covert and clandestine operations.

"You're just deciding this after eight fucking years? Especially when my performance has been nothing short of exemplary?" Kelly asked him dryly. "Damn, McAllister, I knew the government was a bit slow on the uptake, but this seems somewhat plodding, even for you guys. No matter," she said carelessly. "I'll catch you on the flip side." She heard a tiny beep as McAllister ended the call.

First things first, she thought, her cool mind whirling rapidly. She needed to get out of here, and she needed to trigger her exit plan.

She'd *always* had an exit plan.

After hours of dominant and passionate sex, Kelly had fallen asleep, exhausted, wrapped in Riley's arms. After only a couple hours of sleep, Riley had gotten up, telling Kelly she ran every morning with Bryn and the Seven. She would be back in about three hours, she'd said as she kissed a groggy Kelly goodbye, since it was their monthly long-distance run day.

Kelly had been on the verge of falling back asleep after Riley had left, when the phone call from McAllister had shattered her feelings of peace and safety.

Now, a wide-awake Kelly quickly pulled on her clothes, then let herself out of Riley's apartment. Last night—on their way in from the elevator-access private entrance they'd used from the parking lot—Riley had pointed out the secured door to the visitor's staircase, which was right next to the steel keypad and key card secured door that led into Riley's apartment.

Riley controlled access into her apartment's little vestibule from the visitor's staircase, she told Kelly, through an app on her phone. Anyone was permitted to exit, however, without a key card. Kelly went through that door to hit the visitor's staircase and swiftly descended the stairs.

She let herself out of the APS complex using the military-grade remote control she had swiped from Riley's apartment to open the huge steel access door. She realized she'd probably been caught on camera, but she needed to get far away from the APS complex as quickly as possible.

After slipping through the steel door, she hit the remote again to make sure the facility was re-secured before moving east and then north as fast as she could. She would return the remote to Riley via snail mail, using a trusted middleman she had used on more than one occasion, who would repackage the remote for her and mail it to APS, using an anonymous, untraceable return address.

After moving briskly and silently through the quiet, still-dark city streets for about fifteen minutes, walking in a random pattern so that her trail was hard to follow, she activated the burner phone app on her phone, chose a new temporary phone number, and called for an Uber.

Kelly took the Uber to Tampa—paying with cash—found a 24-hour Walmart, and bought non-descript clothes and sneakers, a warm hoodie that zipped up the front, a shoulder holster for her Beretta, a roomy backpack, and a prepaid phone.

She changed in the store's bathroom after she'd checked out, wound her long, red hair into a tight bun, then stuffed her LBD clothes, her thigh holster, Riley's remote—taking the remote apart and disabling anything that remotely looked like it could emit a location signal—and her purse into her new backpack.

When she was ready, she pulled the hood from her new hoodie up over her red hair and casually left the store with her new backpack slung over her shoulder.

No one gave her a second glance.

In the Walmart parking lot, she unobtrusively removed the SIM card from her real phone and smashed it with the heel of her sneaker until it was obliterated, then turned off her phone and stashed it in the backpack as well.

Jumping on a bus, Kelly went to a car rental agency that wasn't far away and rented a car with a bogus ID from one of her personal false identities—one that wasn't connected to either the CIA, or to her real private life with Rowan. She drove south on I-75 to Sarasota, finally pulling into a busy Wawa just off the highway that was catering to the area's early morning rush hour.

After she set up and activated the burner phone app on her new prepaid phone, she called Rowan.

"Ro-Ro, I need you to wake up and listen to me, honey," Kelly said calmly when Rowan answered the phone sleepily. "I only have a few minutes, and what I'm about to say to you is excruciatingly important. I'm fine, no worries there, but something happened and I need you to get a message to Riley or Bryn for me. Okay?"

"Okay," Rowan whispered, immediately awake, her heart thumping.

"I've been burned by the CIA, honey. In layman's terms, it means I've been fired, although it's a little bit more complicated than that. When my handler, Alan McAllister, called me this morning, he handed me some kind of bullshit story about how the CIA is worried that my gift has all of a sudden made me 'unreliable,' and now I'm a risk to their operations. It's total bullshit and, frankly, I know exactly why I was burned, but it has nothing to do with the story they're circulating. You've always been a *champion* at keeping my ability a secret, Ro, but now, more than ever, you need to swear to me you won't tell anyone anything about what I can do."

"You know I won't." Rowan started to cry.

Kelly paused for a brief minute with tears rolling down her own face, heartsick, then continued. "Don't cry, honey. I need to go underground for a little while, Ro-Ro, and drop out of sight. You won't be able to call or text me because I'm using an untraceable burner phone, but I promise I will get in touch with you whenever I can. Okay?"

"Kelly!" Rowan cried, sobbing with emotion. "*Why*? Why can't you come to APS and let them protect you? Bryn is going to be *so* mad, and Riley is going to lose her freaking mind if you just up and disappear. Why do you have to do this, Kel?"

"Because it's safer for everybody this way, Ro." Kelly's voice was quiet. "I can't, in all consciousness, put Bryn or Riley or the Seven in the kind of danger I know I would if I go to them now. I can't explain any more than that but trust me when I say it's better and safer for everyone if I just disappear. The Armstrong twins and the Seven took care of you for me when that motherfucking psychopath was up your ass. Now, I need to take care of them and keep them safe for you. I love you so much, Rowan, and I know in my heart that everything is eventually going to be just fine. Please tell Bryn she has my undying gratitude always for being your shield and your protection now. And Riley… Riley…"

Kelly paused to steady her voice as it faltered for a moment.

"Tell her sometimes little tough girls have to depend on themselves, but there's no one I'd rather have at my back than her. I have to go, honey. Please don't worry about me. I know you will anyway, but I promise you I'll be safe where I'm going, and I will come home to you just as soon as I can. I love you, Ro-Ro."

Kelly gently disconnected and took a minute to wipe her eyes and compose herself before pulling a hard mask over her features.

Then she went shopping.

Chapter 5

"Kelly?" Riley entered her silent apartment and frowned when she didn't see Kelly right away. Just then, her phone rang.

"Yeah," she answered, starting down her hallway to see if Kelly was maybe in the bathroom taking a shower.

"Riles?" It was Bryn. "I already know the answer is no, but just in case...is Kelly there?"

Riley's stomach started to churn. "I can't find her in the apartment. Why?"

"I came back from our run and found Rowan hysterical. Apparently, Kelly called her while we were out." Bryn couldn't hide the anger in her voice. "Kelly's gone on the run, *mano*. Her handler called her right after you left. She's evidently been burned by the CIA."

"*What?*" Riley's anger hit the stratosphere.

"The CIA burned Kelly. Rowan immediately asked her why she didn't come to APS so we could protect her. Kelly said she knew the real reason she was burned, not the bullshit lie her handler gave her, and she refused to put us in danger, she said."

"I'm going to blister her ass when I finally find her." Riley's voice was deadly.

"She also had another message for you, Riley," Bryn said quietly. "She told Rowan to tell you that sometimes little tough girls have to depend on themselves, but there's no one she'd rather have at her back than you."

Riley was silent for a long minute.

"We have to find her, *mano*." Riley blew out a huge breath. "I don't know exactly what the fuck is going on, but I'm positive it has something to do with Percutio and Kelly's mysterious ability, whatever that is. What has Rowan said?"

"Nothing. Kelly made her swear she wouldn't tell anyone anything about her ability and Rowan swore she wouldn't. Until she gets Kelly's permission to share it with us, she'll take that secret to the grave. That's just how the Holland girls roll." Bryn blew out her own sigh of exasperation.

"Jesus fuck. They're just like us. Is this how pissed off other people feel when they deal with us two?" Although Riley was angry, she totally understood why Rowan was refusing to tell anyone. You protected your tribe and you honored your word, always.

Clearly, the Hollands were just like the Armstrongs. *Fuck.*

"I called Trill and I'm going to take Rowan down to the Recon Room. My little predictive analytics master is going to start mining data and slicing through it, seeing if she can draw a bead on Kelly's location."

Bryn was quiet for a moment, before she said, "Rowan said the one thing she could probably swear to was that Kelly wouldn't want to be too far away from her. She'd want to be in a location where she could get to Rowan fairly easily and quickly if she had to. Trill suggested we use a parameter of fifty miles to start. That will cover the beaches and as far south as Sarasota. If we have no hits, we'll start moving more north."

Riley nodded, calmer now that they had a plan.

"Drew's been down in Purgatory, seeing if she can trace Kelly's footsteps from when she left," Bryn continued. "I don't know, *mano*—the woman can be a fucking ghost, which is just one of the many reasons we all want her at APS so much."

"I claimed her last night, Bryn," Riley said abruptly to her twin. "I claimed her, and I told her there was nothing in this world that would make me let her go." Riley's voice hardened. "I also told her if she thought even for a minute she'd ever escape me, she'd find out what being prey really meant."

There was silence for a moment, until Bryn said, "Then I guess we need to tell the Seven we're going hunting."

Suddenly, Drew tried to call in to Riley, who answered and connected them on a three-way conference.

"I've tracked her as far as Tampa. She called an Uber here in Whimsy from Dunbridge Street, then the next time she pops up on radar is at a Walmart in Tampa. From their camera feed, it looks like she bought clothes, a backpack, a shoulder holster for her gun, and a new prepaid phone. She changed before she left the store, and then destroyed the SIM card from her real phone in the parking lot. We can send an associate up there to get the pieces and see if Trill's team can get anything from it, but I can already tell you our chances of that are either *no* or *fuck no*."

Drew was grumpy.

"Then she completely falls off radar. There is motherfucking *nothing* past that point so far. She's fucking ghosted us big time. Riles." Drew's voice filled with ire. "I've got to tell you, cuz—if you don't, I'm going to wear her ass out for this when we find her. I'm torn between admiring the fuck out of her on one hand and wanting to tear her ass up so hard she can't sit for a week on the other."

"No worries there, *broki*." Bryn and Drew heard the cold smile in Riley's voice, even as she used the Puerto Rican slang for "buddy." "My woman is going to learn we don't run off, unprotected, to take care of ourselves here at APS. Especially," Riley emphasized, the volume of her voice raising a bit, "when organizations like Percutio are fucking chasing your ass."

"Teag is trying to help Trill connect the dots there." Drew blew out a deep breath over the phone. "Why in the *motherfuck* would an organization like Percutio be interested in an analyst like Kelly in the first place? There are probably more than a few other analysts in the covert ops realm who do what she does, so why is *she* special? Why was *she* targeted? Even if Kelly is as brilliant as Rowan is because of this mysterious ability she has, the CIA now fucking having her burned and thrown out of covert ops? It doesn't make the first bit of goddamned sense."

"Which could possibly mean the CIA has a Percutio mole who set all this up so Percutio had an easier path to Kelly," Bryn speculated slowly. "That would make sense. The only thing we still don't know is, *why?*"

"Let's all meet in the Bunker as soon as Rowan is set up and doing her thing," Riley said, referring to the huge group office shared by the Seven. "We can whiteboard out what we know so far. We'll also go back on comms 24/7 until Kelly is back with us."

Riley managed to keep her voice even. "I don't know if Kelly is aware of what happens when one of our own is alone and being threatened, but she's about to find out."

*****

Kelly looked around the comfortable rental on the very north tip of Anna Maria Island, about twenty miles due south of St. Petersburg.

After buying a cheap black wig from a discount beauty supply store and twisting it up, popping in a pair of non-prescription colored contacts she'd bought that made her dark green eyes appear an ordinary brown, then perching a pair of black-framed glasses on her nose, she'd made a trip to a decent-sized, local mom-and-pop hardware shop she'd found. It looked like it had been in its location for a hundred years but still thankfully had everything she needed.

It clearly didn't have any cameras outside of one pointing at the register and one at the entrance of the store, which she was careful to face with only three-quarter or half profile views—even with the wig, the contacts, and the glasses. She bought a new laptop and a small printer at another local store, then food and other household supplies from yet a third.

When she got to the rental, she changed out the hardware on the doors and windows, after discreetly setting up a portable outdoor motion sensor and security alert system, with a half-mile wireless transmission range. It would emit considerable light and sound when vehicles or pedestrians approached within a thirty-foot radius—in other words, when anyone trespassed on the property itself.

After her security was taken care of, her first order of business was to clandestinely dig deeper into the Percutio organization, so she could see if there was any way she could extract herself from this mess.

She knew that Grigor Reizan, the jackass head of Percutio, was the one who wanted her—and she also knew *why* he wanted her. "Not in this motherfucking lifetime, asswipe," she muttered as she started to set up her inside electronics.

She stopped.

For the first time since she'd left Whimsy early that morning, she acknowledged she could finally sit down and take some time to reflect on what had happened between her and Riley Armstrong last night.

"Fuck it," she said out loud to herself as she pulled on her new hoodie, wandered outside to the lanai, and sat in a comfortable deck chair, looking out across the turquoise waters of the Gulf of Mexico.

There was so much to think about.

First of all, Riley was spell-binding, earth-shaking, freeze in your tracks gorgeous. That thick, dark brown hair, her crazy impressive height, a wickedly formidable body to die for, and pure amber-colored eyes that could fix on a femme and make her drop her panties without realizing what she was doing.

No wonder women like that Clarissa chick were so desperate to do everything in their power to score a round two.

Second, Kelly had never been as introverted as Rowan and had more experience with women than Rowan did. But she admitted to herself that, regardless of the amount of women Kelly had slept with, Riley was the first honest-to-god alpha butch she'd ever been with in her life.

She'd always assumed she'd *hate* being with anyone harder than a soft butch, even though she'd always been extremely attracted to the *thought* of an alpha butch.

Kelly knew, however, that she had serious control issues. Giving up even one iota of control to someone else had never been on her list of fun things to do. One look into those controlling, passionate amber eyes last night, however, and Kelly had melted like a snowflake in July.

Kelly knew she was in for it for running, if Riley ever managed to catch her—which Kelly had no intention of letting her do. She also suspected that, should she be caught by any one of the Seven or Bryn, they would turn her over to Riley without a second thought.

From the little Rowan had told her so far, and from what she'd seen herself, alpha butches were…different. Protective. Possessive.

The APS alpha butches also had a fierce code that said if you were tribe and belonged to them, there was nothing in this world they would let touch you.

Then there was Riley in bed.

Remembering last night, Kelly admitted to herself that she had never been taken, controlled, dominated, and claimed like she had been with Riley Armstrong.

Kelly had the uneasy feeling Riley had meant every word she'd said when she told Kelly she would feel like prey if she ever tried to run from her.

As much as Kelly longed to run back to APS and to Riley's arms, however, she couldn't bring herself to do it. Grigor Reizan would cut a swath through the APS management team if he perceived they were interfering in his efforts to get her. The thought of being responsible for one—or all—of their deaths was enough to make her want to vomit.

Having already been responsible for someone else's death once in her life had been more than enough for her, thank you.

A huge wave of sadness passed over her without warning. She would have so loved to have told the CIA to fuck off and joined the APS team. To practice martial arts with Casey, sneak into buildings with Jaime, tear through the sim with Blake, run through her skill drills with Kennedy—her heart broke thinking about everything she was going to miss.

Whimsical Princess

The more she thought about it, though, Kelly knew there was no way she could stay in Whimsy. It was too dangerous to both the people she loved and the people she was coming to respect.

And, she admitted honestly, to love as well.

She had rented the cottage on Anna Maria Island for a week, just long enough to make sure everything was peaceful and settled in Whimsy. She knew she couldn't go back to Woodbridge and that her CIA career had been destroyed—by both Percutio and by whoever the motherfucking mole was in the CIA who did this to her.

So, she'd learn to live life on the run and maybe, in some small way, this would be her atonement for her part in Robyn Braswell's death two years ago. Sweet Robyn, who'd had no idea what she was getting into when she fell in love with Kelly.

Kelly sighed and stood up to go back into the house.

"Welcome to the first day of the rest of your life, motherfucker," she told herself resolutely.

Chapter 6

It was day three since Kelly had disappeared. Rowan was sitting with Trill in the Recon Room, sifting through more data, while Bryn and a few of the Seven waited silently next to Riley.

Rowan, Trill had told them in utter awe, was the most glorious, brilliant, unbelievable data analyst Trill had ever seen.

"And she makes it look so motherfucking *easy*," Trill had reported incredulously. "She'll take some data, run it for a bit, sit there and think about it for a minute, and then carve data slices in a completely new way. You're left sitting there, holding your dick, thinking, '*Why the fuck didn't I think of that?*' She's fucking unbelievable."

As far as the search for Kelly was going... If it had been anyone else she was chasing down, Rowan had told the twins and the Seven, she may have had an answer by now. *There is no one else in this world who could ghost or bury data the way Kelly can, however*, she had said.

"If I'm ever at liberty to tell you everything Kelly can do, I for sure want to be the one who gets to do it, if only to see every single one of you pass out cold," Rowan had informed the Seven earnestly. "My one advantage is that I'm her sister, and I know the way she thinks. It doesn't mean she's made this easy for me on any level, though. Kelly is not only beyond brilliant, she's been a part of CIA covert and clandestine operations long enough to know how to hide freaking *anything*."

Then, Rowan fidgeted.

"Honestly, and no offense to any of you, but she was also probably out-gunning the Seven by the time she was eighteen years old," she muttered, turning back to her analysis. "She's an almost perfect shot, you know."

Riley felt her patience waning the longer time went on. She knew they would have had no chance of finding Kelly at all if it wasn't for Rowan, however, and Riley was grateful her future sister-in-law had at least given them a fighting chance.

But she wanted her goddamn woman. When they finally found Kelly, Riley was going to hold her and kiss her until she couldn't breathe, then blister her ass until she couldn't sit down properly, and then fuck her until she couldn't walk for two days.

Suddenly, a loud gasp from Rowan broke the silence in the Recon Room.

"What is it, *dulzura*?" Bryn went swiftly over to her fiancée.

On the large screen in front of Rowan was a single entry: *P. Bass Enterprises, Fishing Equipment Importers, Anna Maria Island.*

"Okaaay." Trill was puzzled. "This was one of the entries we'd already checked out, and it looked fine. I don't understand what's setting off red flags for you on this."

Rowan's face was white.

"When Kelly and I were little, Kelly already had that Disney princess look of hers," Rowan explained, still in shock. "Dad used to tease her all the time and nicknamed her Princess Badass, because he said even though Kelly *looked* sweet and innocent on the outside, she was anything *but* on the inside. When Kelly and Robyn, her fiancée, started dating, we told Robyn that story, which she loved. She started calling Kelly Princess Badass herself, which she then shortened to *P. Bass*, because she said that saying Princess Badass all the time was too much of a mouthful."

Riley felt the hair on the back of her neck stand on end and an electric shock raced down her spine.

"Trill, can you dig deeper into this identity to see if you can find anything behind it, *broki*?" Riley asked calmly.

"Already on it." Trill's hands were flying over her keyboard.

The room was deathly quiet, only the clicking of the keys on Trill's keyboard making a sound.

After five agonizing minutes, Trill finally said, "Goddamn. There it goes," shaking her head in disbelief. "Ro, we've found her. Her cover splintered when I dug deep. If it wasn't for you, sweetheart, we would have *never* found her."

Trill stared at Riley. "She had everything buried deep enough that it would pass inspection by virtually everyone, unless someone had it in their mind to dig deep. If Rowan hadn't known that 'P. Bass' meant something to Kelly, we would have just cruised on by and she would have stayed hidden forever."

Bryn blew out a huge breath and looked at her twin. "As soon as this fucking bullshit with Percutio is at an end, I can think of five million places we could put Kelly, where she would be a fucking *extraordinary* associate."

Riley nodded, but it was clear she was thinking about Kelly and starting to outline what she needed to do to bring her back to Whimsy.

Bryn gathered Rowan in her arms and murmured, "Thank you, *dulzura*," just as Riley said, "Thank you, little sis. Now, it's time for all of us to get together and work out a plan to bring your sister home."

* * * * *

Casey Christiansen, Jaime Quintero, Teagan Malloy, and Riley Armstrong sat in a black SUV in the dark of the Florida night, motor running soundlessly, eyes on the unlighted cottage at the end of Anna Maria Island. Over the last two days, several members of the Seven had made nighttime trips down to Anna Maria Island, scoping out the kind of security Kelly had established at her rental cottage.

Tonight, after two solid days of planning, they were ready to go in and extract Riley's woman.

Unlike Rowan, Riley had said when they'd all met in the Bunker to start crafting an extraction plan, Kelly was a fighter—and a very well-trained one at that.

"Kelly was with my dad *constantly* while we were growing up," Rowan had explained to Riley and Bryn. "She and Dad practiced a ton of different martial arts: kickboxing, karate, judo, I don't even know what all. All I can tell you for sure is that Kelly is *more* than capable of defending herself."

"We'll need the element of surprise on our side then. We have to decide the best way to render her unconscious and retrieve her quickly, but we need to be very careful we don't injure her," Riley said.

Casey, their MMA and Krav Maga expert, had nodded comfortably. "There are more than a few vital pressure points that can be used to induce unconsciousness, as long as you know what you're doing and are very careful. It's one hell of a better option than using drugs, in my opinion, if you're adept at it. She'll be asleep," Casey further mused. "That will buy us a few seconds, but I wouldn't count on having any more of a head start than that. We need to make sure she's restrained, until we can engage her pressure points and put her out."

Riley drummed her fingers on the table. "When Teagan has all of the security systems, the Wi-Fi, and the electrical disabled, Jaime, you'll be on. You'll get us into the cottage."

Jaime nodded thoughtfully.

"I wouldn't doubt the least little bit that Kelly bought all new hardware for the doors and windows. As a matter of fact, I would be fucking shocked if she hadn't, *ese*." Jaime paused for a moment, thinking some more.

"The cottage will be a dead zone when everything is disabled," Teagan interjected. "Once I shut it all down, especially all wireless devices, we'll be good to go."

Now, the APS extraction team waited until the clock showed it was two a.m.

"It's go time," Riley said softly.

The extraction team functioned just like a well-oiled machine. Teagan went first, making sure all communications, electrical, and wireless systems were completely disabled. Jaime was up to bat next, soundlessly breaching the cottage before gesturing to the rest of the crew that it was safe to enter.

The team crept noiselessly across the floor and into the single bedroom, where they saw Kelly as she quietly slept.

When Riley first saw her woman, she felt a rage she hadn't ever known it was possible for her to feel.

Kelly was lying on her stomach, in a tank top and panties, her right arm outstretched and resting on a weapon as she slept—just in case she had to wake up in a hurry and come to her feet, fighting.

Never. Never fucking AGAIN will my woman EVER find herself alone and in a position to have to defend herself like this, Riley vowed with absolute fury.

NEVER.

Casey held up a fist and got ready to signal everyone to surround Kelly and restrain her. The crew got into position and waited.

When Casey gave the signal, they struck. They were so fast, Kelly barely had a moment to start to fight before Casey had her disabled and unconscious.

Riley carefully lifted Kelly in her arms as Casey, Jaime, and Teagan swept through the cottage, collecting everything they could find to take with them.

Within ten minutes, the APS team was gone, as if they had never been there.

"Casey. How long will she stay out?" Riley asked in a low voice, holding her unconscious femme securely in her arms.

"We should at least be good until we get back to headquarters, cuz." Casey sighed. "Honestly, I doubt she's been sleeping well, so she just may stay asleep. The dark circles under her eyes are goddamn alarming."

Yeah. Riley had noticed.

"With the fucking shit this poor woman has been through, her nerves have probably been rubbed raw." Casey was pissed. "What I did tonight incorporated an acupressure technique that will help her to sleep. With any luck, she'll stay asleep for a few hours until morning, because she's so fucking exhausted."

Riley nodded her thanks.

"Kelly and I will use the overnight suite at headquarters for the rest of tonight. I'll text you all when she's awake, and we'll make arrangements to meet in Conference Room 2. Rowan packed an overnight bag for Kelly so she should have everything she needs when she wakes up. And then, we'll *finally* get to the bottom of all this bullshit, and find out what's had Kelly so scared, she thought she had to cut herself off from us to keep us safe."

Chapter 7

Kelly slowly opened her eyes, feeling a bit fuzzy as her body started coming back online. She frowned as she tried to remember where she was, and why there was a deeply tanned, corded arm slung around her waist.

As memory flared, her eyes widened just as Riley Armstrong rolled on top of her and pinned her to the bed she was sleeping on.

"Good morning, *princesa*," Riley said noncommittally.

Although her tone was casual, her amber eyes had hit a level of pissed Kelly didn't think she could reach on her best day.

"I don't know what you were thinking," Riley continued in the same relaxed voice, with the same dark fury in her eyes, "but running away is not how we do things here at APS."

"Good thing I'm not APS then," Kelly snarked, unable to help herself.

"Oh, but you are, *princesa*." Riley smiled a cold smile as she brushed back the curls from Kelly's face. "You were APS even before those asshole dimwits at the CIA decided to burn your ass. Their loss, our gain, actually."

"You have no right to do this." Kelly's anger burned.

Riley's cold smile deepened. "The night before you ran, baby, you blacked out with my fingers in your pussy, and my mouth on your clit. I'd say that gives me all *sorts* of rights." She rolled off Kelly and stood up. "We have a meeting with Bryn and the Seven in thirty minutes. Rowan has packed you a bag with fresh clothes, and there is a bathroom with a shower right through that door."

"Where are we?" Kelly asked, sitting up, her stomach roiling with nerves.

"APS headquarters. Which means, there's no way to escape me this time, *princesa*." The corner of Riley's mouth tilted up slightly. "No more running. No more secrets. You are no longer obligated to the CIA for *anything*, Red…including keeping their confidence."

Riley strode to the door. "I'll be back in twenty-five minutes, *princesa*, so be ready. There'll be coffee and fruit at the meeting." Then she was gone.

Maybe I'm no longer obligated to the CIA, Kelly thought as she stared after Riley, *but they don't understand I still need to keep APS safe from Percutio.*

Kelly jumped in the shower, then pulled on fresh clothes when she was done, braiding her wet hair away from her face. She shoved everything back into the bag Rowan had sent her, just as the door opened and Riley reappeared.

"Ready?" Riley was still matter of fact.

"So, you said no way to escape you this time." Kelly was equally matter of fact. "I should take that to mean I'm a prisoner and being held against my will, then?"

Riley's amber eyes chilled. "Take that any way you'd like, *princesa*. At the very least, you're going to hear us out, if only for Rowan's sake."

Kelly followed Riley silently through the long hallways until they reached a closed door. Riley punched a code into the electronic keypad set into the doorframe, then opened the door when the indicator light turned green.

Kelly kept her face impassive when she discovered Bryn and the Seven were all there, waiting for them. She was disconcerted to realize the same look was in everyone's eyes—simultaneously both pissed off and protective.

Kelly took a seat, still keeping all emotion off her face, and sat quietly until Riley began.

"Everyone here knows you've been burned by the CIA, Kelly," Riley said without preamble. "What we don't know is why, nor do we know how Percutio figures into all of this. We know those fucks from Percutio are chasing you. Again, what we don't know is *why*."

Kelly took a minute to answer, leaning back and steepling her fingers. "You act like you and your crew here have a right to know that, Armstrong. Maybe I missed the memo, but last I checked, I didn't report to you. As a matter of fact, despite your insistence to the contrary, I don't work for APS. I owe you all *nothing*." Her smile was unfriendly. "And if the purpose of this little charade was to strong-arm me into discussing things I don't much feel like discussing, just so a bunch of badass butches can piss all over their territory, I'd stick this one into your Epic Fail folder. Because I'm not feeling too cooperative right now."

"What are you running from, Kel?" Bryn's hard voice whipped out.

Kelly looked at Bryn consideringly for a minute.

"Because you're my sister's fiancé, and because you've extended APS protection to her, I'll give you this much," she finally answered. "It's too dangerous for you to get involved in this…for *any* of you to get involved in this. You need to turn and walk away, right now, for your own safety."

Kelly looked at Bryn with hard eyes.

"How would you feel, Bryn, if Percutio dumped Riley's bloody body on your front doorstep as a warning? Or the body of one of your Seven? I personally couldn't live with myself if that kind of harm came to one of you, so I left to keep *you* safe, not myself. I don't know any of you well, but I'm not about to give those fuckwits at Percutio a reason to come after you—if only for what you've done for Rowan. You have no goddamned idea what you are playing with here. Grigor Reizan won't kill me, because I have something he wants, but he'll damn well kill you or one of yours if you don't. *Back. The. Fuck. Off.*"

Kelly leaned back in her seat and crossed her arms, signaling she was done with this discussion.

But Riley leveled a hard look at Kelly. "You have *no* fucking idea who or what we are, *princesa*. You don't have the slightest clue about what we're capable of, or of what our reputation is, do you?"

Kelly looked a bit startled as she let her glance fall over the Armstrong twins and the Seven. She saw nine hard faces looking back at her, each one promising a walk through hell to anyone who dared to cross them.

"You may want to deny it, but you are *mine*, Kelly. I protect what's mine. Bryn and the Seven protect what's mine, too. Meanwhile, you were out there, all alone, *unprotected*," Riley gritted out, "having no fucking idea that Grigor Reizan, the omnipotent head of Percutio, probably shit his pants in fear when he found out you now belong to one of the Armstrong twins."

Dead silence hung over the room.

"Now." Riley crossed her powerful arms over her chest as her stare bored into Kelly. "We've asked you a question, *princesa*. You need to tell us exactly what the fuck kind of trouble you're in, so I know what we're up against. What is it you have that he wants, Kelly? Why are you so goddamn important to him that he would launch this kind of an effort to take you?"

Riley handed a folded cream notepaper to Kelly. "This is the note Percutio sent to Rowan." She opened the note, her eyes widening when she saw what was written inside.

Tell your sister the eyes of Percutio are everywhere and its "memory" is very long.

"Reizan, you motherfucking asshole," Kelly muttered, closing her eyes as she pinched the bridge of her nose.

She looked at Riley, and then looked down at the table for a long time, thinking hard. The APS management team saw the internal war she was waging with herself and waited patiently for her to finish her silent machinations.

"Fine." Kelly finally blew out a deep breath and regarded the Seven with a stoic expression. "Do any of you know what eidetic memory is?"

"Eidetic memory." Riley thought for a minute. "It's the ability to recall an image from memory with almost perfect precision after only seeing it one time. People with eidetic memory can remember an image in so much detail, with so much crispness and accuracy, it's as though the image was still being viewed in real time, not as a memory."

"Wait." Bryn's eyes widened. "Are you saying *you* have an eidetic memory, Kelly?"

"A lot of people refer to it as a photographic memory. But there's technically a difference between an eidetic memory and a photographic memory, although both terms are often used interchangeably. Eidetic memory usually focuses on recalling more visual-type memories, like photographs, while photographic memories actually involve recalling lists or pages of data, or numbers," Kelly explained. "Plus, an eidetic memory typically does not last for more than a few seconds in the vast majority of people. A person who has a photographic memory has memories that can be retained for a lot longer, however. Some researchers don't believe true photographic memories even exist, although people like

Leonardo da Vinci and Nikola Tesla and Teddy Roosevelt demonstrated the ability easily enough."

Kelly paused for just a moment, then informed them, "I have an extreme eidetic memory. Actually, I can recall both images *and* data, plus perform serial recalls of memories—sort of like playing a streaming movie in my head—in virtually perfect detail, after only seeing any of them once. My mind can also retain these memories for years, an ability that is exceedingly rare."

The Armstrong twins and the Seven were flabbergasted.

"We didn't exactly pass out cold, like Rowan said we would, but pretty goddamned close," muttered Blake as she and the other members of the Seven looked at each other with incredulity.

"One of the reasons I was recruited by the CIA's covert and clandestine operations was because of my *gift*," Kelly continued calmly. "As you can imagine, it's an ability that's rather handy in espionage situations. Somehow, however, that information was leaked to Grigor Reizan about five or six months ago, which means there's a Percutio mole within the CIA. Reizan then decided I needed to be an asset for *his* criminal organization, instead of for the CIA, which…no fucking thank you, asshole. I'm not interested in playing human audio and video recorder for a bunch of common thugs.

"I suspect the mole found a way to have me burned to open the path for Percutio to recruit me, even though my handler gave me some bullshit reason—that the CIA felt my gift had too much potential to make me 'unstable.'" Kelly traced quote brackets in the air with her fingers as she rolled her eyes.

"Because, you know, it takes eight years to make that determination, which is how long I was with the CIA before I was burned. My eidetic memory… It's genetic in my family. Three things happen with all the female descendants in my line: One, we all inherit the gift, without exception. Two, getting pregnant is extremely hard for us, as if the gift itself doesn't like to propagate for some reason. Three, if we do manage to have a child, it's always a girl."

"Rowan doesn't have an eidetic memory, Kel," Bryn stated, a bit bemused. "So, how is that possible?"

Kelly went silent until she finally looked at Bryn with a look they'd never seen on her before.

"Bryn," Kelly said gently. "Rowan is adopted."

Chapter 8

Electric shock raced around the room at the news.

"You do realize she hasn't been trying to hide anything from you either, right?" Kelly continued, just as gently. "To tell you the truth, she probably forgot. It's something the Hollands have always forgotten, until shit like this bubbles up."

"How do you forget you're adopted?" Bryn wanted to know.

Kelly sighed. "My mom and dad met in college when my mom was a sophomore and my dad was a senior. To hear Dad tell it, he took one look at Mom and knew she was it for him. They got married right after Mom graduated and they tried to get pregnant right away. They tried for literally years with no success, even with medical interventions, until they eventually resigned themselves to being a childless couple after twenty years of trying. Has Rowan ever said anything to you about Dad's family?" Kelly asked Bryn.

"Just that he'd cut off all communications with his family because of what he called their *brainwashing fuckery*," Bryn said dryly.

Kelly snorted. "Dad's family was Holy Roller, hellfire and brimstone, batshit crazy Pentecostal. There was no love in the house he grew up in, just punishment and harsh judgment. The minute he turned eighteen and went to college, he was out. Never talked to them again. But he did still talk to a couple of cousins who were okay. One day, one of the cousins told Dad she'd just found out her daughter was pregnant. Jane was seventeen, had plans to go to college, and a baby didn't fit into those plans. Mom and Dad talked about it for all of a minute, offered to pay all of Jane's expenses as part of a private adoption arrangement, and nine months later?" Kelly smiled with tears in her eyes. "Along came Rowan."

The Armstrong twins and the Seven softened with thoughts of the woman they all loved so much.

"Then, when Ro was two, Mom unexpectedly discovers *she's* pregnant. Totally out of the blue, almost twenty-five years after she and Dad were married." Kelly laughed and shook her head. "And then, here comes me. It was the biggest shock of their lives. Mom said Dad was fucking *ecstatic*. Here he thought he'd never have any kids, but instead he ended up with the two most perfect little girls in the world, he said."

Kelly paused for a moment to wipe the tears from her face, then focused on Bryn, who was still trying to make sense of everything.

"There was no biological or adoptive distinction in our house, Bryn. Rowan and I were just the Holland girls, the pride and joy of Bill and Amanda Holland's life. We never remember that Rowan is adopted because we've never fucking cared. It's just not important."

Kelly gave a soft laugh. "Do you know when she'll think to finally tell you? May 22."

"May 22? That's her birthday." Bryn looked at Kelly quizzically.

Kelly nodded with a soft smile. "When Rowan was eighteen, she expressed interest to my mom and dad in meeting her biological mother, so they set that meeting up. Rowan and Jane have been in touch ever since. Jane is almost fifty now and has her own family. They don't talk all the time, but every year on Rowan's birthday, Rowan calls Jane and they talk for about three hours—giggling like a pair of teenagers and catching up on each other's life."

The love and amusement in the room was palpable.

"Jane is awesome people, and I wish every adoption story in the world could end like theirs has. But…the point of this whole story was to let you know why Rowan doesn't have an eidetic memory like Mom and me, and to explain why she's never thought to tell you she's adopted."

Kelly's face went hard as she looked around the room.

"One of Rowan's greatest horrors is when people treat her differently and act like she's not a 'real' Holland kid because she's adopted. I've beaten the shit out of more than a few assholes who've dared to suggest it over the years, and I'll have no hesitation about throwing a beating to anyone who hurts her feelings about it in the future."

"Stand in line, little sis." Bryn's voice was mild as the rest of the APS management team narrowed their eyes in agreement. Kelly relaxed.

"Back to you, *princesa*." Riley changed the subject. "When did your eidetic memory start to manifest?"

"That I can remember, when I was about six. Mom had to teach me a lot of different ways to control the gift…let alone try to make me understand that not everyone could do what I could and we needed to keep it a secret. Then, when I was older," Kelly paused for a slight moment before she continued, "Dad explained to me I couldn't join the Marines like him, even though that had been all I ever wanted to do. Having an extreme eidetic memory like I do means your reactions and reaction time are often…flawed, shall we say. Not the most optimal state in a combat situation, so I have a permanent medical disqualification." Kelly was emotionless.

"Fucking hell, little sis. I would have wanted to kill someone." Teagan shook her head, acknowledging Kelly's anger and despondency during that time.

"Although the thought of you dealing with that still sucks giant balls, you clearly found a way to leverage your gift if the CIA snapped you up." Everyone nodded in agreement.

Kelly was surprised at their reaction but felt oddly validated. "Dad was actually the one who figured it all out. He talked to some superior about my abilities, then his superior contacted someone he knew in the intelligence community. After about a thousand discussions and a fucking *barrage* of tests, they decided to put me in the CIA as an information analyst after I finished college. It was and is the perfect cover. As my value grew and the agency learned more ways to use my gift, however, the assignments started getting riskier."

Kelly arched her brow at Bryn. "I don't *ever* lie to Rowan, but there is a lot of sin by omission with this job. She would worry herself to death if she knew half the shit that goes on in my life, so it's always been better to protect her by keeping quiet."

Bryn dipped her head in acknowledgment.

Kelly pursed her lips. "I still don't know exactly how anyone outside of a few key people in the CIA found out about my gift. All indications point to an unknown mole within the organization who leaked the information. I just don't know who the fucking mole is."

"Any suspicions?" Drew asked. Kelly shook her head no.

"In the last few months, Reizan's had me tracked constantly." The strain on Kelly's face was becoming more apparent now that Kelly was relaxing in their presence. "There have been a couple of attempts to detain me, like those assholes that night at Seashells, but I've managed to avoid them. My handler recently got word that Reizan was making some kind of final play, but the intel was thin. However, lo and behold, now I've been burned…which means I no longer have CIA protection and I've lost Alan as a resource."

The Armstrong twins and the Seven were pissed to the point that a low rumble filled the room.

"Kel." Casey's voice was quiet. "You're Riley's. I would never presume to tell you what to do because that's for the two of you to decide. But I think you need to hear directly from the Seven that we will motherfucking *annihilate* anyone who dares to touch you. We know you can take care of yourself, but *you* need to know you've got family at your back now."

Kelly felt a catch in her throat.

"*Chula*, I'm thinking the time for being alone is over. You need us. We need you." Jaime looked at her kindly. "First your sister, and now you. You two have been alone too fucking long."

"We're family now, Kel. Rowan is Bryn's and you are Riley's, which makes you our *hermana*, our sister. We'll find this fucking mole. And, news flash, Grigor Reizan is fucking scared to death of those two Armstrong fuckers over there." Jaime waved her hand toward the twins. "So, I'm thinking if he wants to keep his dick attached to his body, he'll back the fuck off."

Riley, who had been extremely quiet up until now, finally spoke up.

"I will kill anyone who so much as even looks at you funny, *princesa*," Riley said with her intense amber eyes. "Yes, you can handle yourself, but it's *my* right as your butch to defend you and destroy any threat to you."

Kelly looked down at the table again with deep concentration, silent once again.

"Well, then," she finally said wryly, lifting her head and scanning the group, "before we all sing *kumbaya* together, there's maybe one more little thing I should probably mention."

The team waited, not liking the vibe coming from Kelly.

"Reizan found out about the hereditary part of my gift from whoever the mole is as well."

Kelly paused for a minute, mumbled a frustrated "*fuck*" under her breath as she massaged the back of her neck with one hand, then finished her sentence in a detached tone, looking directly at Riley.

"The word Alan got was, Reizan's intention was to try and force me to bear his children—create his own army of girls with the gift. When they got old enough, he'd have them bred, too. Rinse and repeat."

* * * * *

CRACK! One of the arms on Riley's chair snapped off. The Seven, along with Bryn, surged to their feet, ready for anything.

"*Mano*. What's your temperature right now?" Bryn's tone was even and calm, but she and the Seven were poised to lock Riley down if they needed to.

Riley held up one hand, signaling she had control at the moment, as she slowly rose to her feet. She fixed her inscrutable laser stare on Kelly, who looked back at Riley with a hint of defiance.

"And you ran away to face all of this by yourself?" Riley's voice was without emotion. "Being burned by the CIA and losing your protection, dealing with Reizan's goons every time you turned around, and knowing you were going to be raped and forced into pregnancy against your will if you were ever caught by Percutio at some point?"

Kelly wisely kept silent.

Riley put her hands on her hips and looked down for a couple of minutes, seeming to stare at the floor without seeing anything. Kelly held her breath, aware of the dead silence in the room and not daring to look at anyone else.

Finally, Riley raised her head.

"Okay," she said unhurriedly, in a noncommittal tone. "I think maybe Kelly and I have some things to discuss on our own right now. While we're having our discussion, can we dig for some intel on Reizan and his band of thugs as it relates to Kelly?"

"You want radio silence on the dig or should we make Captain Grigor Fucktard sweat a little bit, Riles?" Teagan's smile was cold.

"Let's run with radio silence for now. Let that fucker wonder what we're up to." Riley held out a hand to Kelly. "Come, *princesa*. We need to talk and the Seven have some work to do."

Kelly looked frozen, but Riley saw her gaze drift over the cryptic faces of Bryn and the Seven before she rose to her feet and made her way to the front of the conference room.

Trill gave her an intrigued look.

"Was that an eidetic memory thing you just did?" she asked curiously. "Like using an old-fashioned Polaroid camera?"

"I…I guess so," Kelly said slowly, uncomfortable. "It's something I do unconsciously sometimes. I'm not always aware of it."

Trill smiled shrewdly. "I think sometimes you're also *quite* aware of it, Kelly. When you deliberately want to preserve a moment so you can dissect it and analyze it later."

Kelly didn't acknowledge Trill's comment as she waited for Riley.

"I'll touch base with you all later on tonight." Riley ushered Kelly unceremoniously out of the conference room door.

As they walked down the hallway, Kelly said, "Isn't there an inn of some kind here in Whimsy? I need to get my bag, I need to book a room there, and I also need to make arrangements to have my rental car brought up from Anna Maria Island. You know, since I wasn't exactly given a choice about coming here without it."

"*Princesa*...I am riding a very thin line of control right now." Riley's voice was mild. "What you do *not* want to do at the moment is throw me any attitude or snark."

An uneasy look crossed Kelly's face. She stopped when Riley continued toward the elevator that led to her apartment.

"Reception and the front exit are this way." Kelly's voice was as mild as Riley's had been, although she drew in a deep, steadying breath.

"We're going to my apartment, Kelly." Riley looked at her calmly with her hands on her hips again. "I said we had some things to discuss and I don't plan on doing that either in reception or on the front sidewalk. Now, are you coming or do I have to carry you?" Riley arched an eyebrow in Kelly's direction, her hands still on her hips.

* * * * *

Kelly slowly followed Riley down the hallway, feeling scared for the first time in a very long time. It's not like she felt she was in any danger from Riley or anything like that. She just didn't know what to expect from Riley in this strange mood.

When the elevator opened up into Riley's apartment, Kelly braced herself, but Riley merely gestured for Kelly to sit on the large sofa in the living room.

Kelly immediately regretted sitting the minute she did it. Riley's tall, commanding, almost six-foot body towered over her, making her feel submissive and controlled.

"There are two things the alpha butches of APS do not tolerate when it comes to their femmes." Riley's tone was still calm, although far more unyielding than it had been previously. "The first is when they bring emotional or mental harm to themselves—such as when they call themselves names or refer to themselves as worthless or useless. That's Sin One, which is absolutely unacceptable."

Kelly's heart was thundering in her chest.

"Sin Two?" Riley looked at Kelly and paused consideringly for a moment before she continued. "Sin Two happens when an APS femme puts herself into a dangerous or potentially harmful situation. To me, Sin Two is the bigger sin because, while Sin One has the potential to be extremely harmful on a more subconscious level…" Riley abruptly leaned down to look Kelly directly in her face from about three inches away and ground out, her eyes suddenly ablaze with fury, "…you don't get fucking beaten or raped or *dead* like you can with Sin Two!"

Kelly was frozen.

"You are *mine*, Kelly, and I do not *ever* fucking want to hear you say you are not mine or you are not part of APS. *Ever. Fucking. Again.*" Riley's fury had not abated.

Before Kelly knew what was happening, Riley had pulled her up from the couch, sat down herself, pulled Kelly down, and flipped her around so she was lying face down across Riley's knees.

"What in the motherfucking *hell* do you think you're doing, asshole?" Kelly shrieked as she fought to get free.

Riley had pinned her legs down with her own long legs and wrapped one unyielding arm across Kelly's back to pin her arms to her sides. She used her free hand to undo Kelly's jeans and pull them down, baring her ass.

"You goddamned motherfucker!" Kelly was still screaming in an absolute rage. "You have no motherfucking right to do this, you jackass! I am going to fucking *kill* you the minute I get free!"

Cr-ac-kkk! Riley smacked Kelly's ass hard. Kelly lost her breath from the pain and squealed as the intensity of the smack penetrated.

Riley continued to rain hard swats down on Kelly's ass as she unleashed a severe reprimand filled with heavy, corrective discipline.

"You don't *ever* fucking run away from us, Kelly. You don't *ever* try to fucking fix things yourself or take on a motherfucking army of bad guys. *On. Your. Own.*"

Swat! Swat! Swat!

"Don't you understand that I could have *lost* you?" Kelly heard a note of fear in Riley's voice, mixed in with the rage. "Do you not get that I and Bryn and the Seven were fucking *terrified* something would happen to you before we could get to you?"

Kelly felt the tears start to pour down her face as the meaning behind Riley's words started to register.

"There isn't one of us that doubts your ability to take care of yourself, *princesa*. But the odds you were facing? *Fuck*."

Swat!

"Then to hear that piece of shit fuckwit from Percutio wanted to kidnap you and force you to bear children for him? Are you fucking *kidding* me? *Every. Single. One. Of. Us.* Was simultaneously enraged and in a motherfucking *panic* when we heard that.

"I'll tell you this right now. If I hadn't been the one to give you this spanking, each one of the Seven would have lined up to do the exact same thing."

Swat!

"No femme in APS world would *ever* be allowed to put herself at risk like you have."

Kelly started to cry in earnest, the pain from her backside almost more than she could bear as Riley continued to spank her. She went limp with submission, emotionally and physically overcome, and her anger seemed to drain away to nothing as a fundamental truth hit her like a lightning bolt.

Except for Rowan and Clementine, no one had cared about her like this since her mother and father had died.

Riley was absolutely furious with her, but she was also fiercely protective of her woman, and she was going to do everything in her power to make sure Kelly never put herself into an unsafe situation again.

When Riley felt Kelly yield, she stopped the spanking and pulled Kelly up into her lap as Kelly continued to cry. Riley reached down and pulled up Kelly's panties, took off Kelly's boots and jeans, then wrapped her arms tightly around her woman and rocked her.

Riley murmured words of affection and comfort as she stroked the top of Kelly's head while Kelly cried. She unbound and unraveled Kelly's braid, combed her dark red curls out with her fingers, then uncapped a bottle of water Kelly hadn't seen and made Kelly drink some.

"We are going to talk more tomorrow, *princesa*." Riley kissed the top of Kelly's head, her voice gentle now. "But for right now, you are so exhausted, you can't see straight, baby. It's been too goddamn long since you've had a good night's sleep, since you've been in a place where you've felt safe enough to truly sleep without fear. Somewhere you don't have to clutch a weapon while you're sleeping in order to protect yourself. As long as I live, *princesa*, I don't think I'll *ever* forget the sight of you like that." She smoothed Kelly's curls back from her face. "I am going to take you up to the loft, finish undressing you, and tuck you into bed. I won't leave you until you're asleep, but I want you to go to sleep knowing you're safe and warm and cared for."

Riley looked solemnly into Kelly's still tear-filled eyes. "I didn't like spanking you like that, *princesa*. I don't know that any of us who's ever had to discipline a femme that way has enjoyed it. But sometimes, it's part of what's necessary in alpha butch world to keep our women safe.

"We'll talk more tomorrow, *princesa*. I promise."

When Kelly was safely in Riley's bed, securely held in Riley's arms, she fought against the exhaustion that was taking her over, determined to say something before sleep swept her away.

"Except for Rowan and Clementine, no one has cared about me since Robyn died." Kelly's voice was faint as she hiccupped with emotion. "As far as the CIA was concerned, I was just another asset, albeit one with an unusual ability. As far as Percutio was concerned, I was just a means to further their criminal empire. But you…this doesn't even make any fucking sense, but you spanked me because you cared about *me*, Kelly the person. You see *me*, not the memory freak or the fighting machine. I don't know what to do with that yet, Riley."

Riley gently kissed her and then ran her mouth down Kelly's jaw.

"Right now, the only thing you need to worry about is going to sleep and getting some rest, *princesa*. We have time enough to figure all the rest of it out. But right now, your job is to sleep."

As Kelly felt herself sink into unconsciousness, she heard Riley's fierce whisper.

"You're mine, *princesa*. I will *never* let you go and you will *never* be alone or unseen again. This, I swear."

Chapter 9

When Kelly woke up, she was astounded to discover it was ten a.m. the next day. By her estimation, she had been asleep for almost twenty-four hours.

She smiled when she discovered one of Riley's clean shirts neatly folded at the end of the bed, along with her still-clean panties. She slipped them on, raked her hands through her messy hair and hastily braided it, then went downstairs to see if she could find some coffee somewhere.

After she went down the loft stairs and walked down the hall into the bathroom, she smiled again when she found a brand new unwrapped toothbrush and a tube of toothpaste on the bathroom sink.

When she was done taking care of business and brushing her teeth, she paused in the bathroom doorway on her way out when she heard the sound of clicking computer keyboard keys coming from further down the hallway.

The second door revealed Riley in what was obviously her office, typing with blinding speed on a high end, very sophisticated desktop computer.

"Hi." Kelly stopped at the entrance of the room, feeling shy.

"*Princesa*." Riley rolled back away from her computer and patted her lap. Kelly winced a bit when her still sore bottom made contact with Riley's jeans, but she gingerly wiggled into a comfortable position and looped her arms around Riley's neck.

Riley looked breathtakingly handsome in a clean T-shirt and jeans with a concealed carry shoulder holster strapped under her arm. She leaned down slightly, then kissed her woman deeply, running her hands up and down Kelly's back until Kelly melted.

"Did you sleep well?" Riley ran her mouth over Kelly's jaw as she seemed to like to do.

"Better than I have in a long time," Kelly admitted. "I don't think I moved at all. Where did you sleep last night, since it seems I hogged your bed?"

"Right next to you, *princesa*. I went to bed about 10:30 p.m., got up this morning at four-thirty for my run like I usually do, had a meeting with Bryn and the Seven at six o'clock, and then came back up here so you wouldn't be alone when you woke up."

Kelly sighed and put her head on Riley's shoulder. "Would there be any chance of getting some coffee?"

"Absolutely, *princesa*. Give me another couple of minutes to enjoy my woman and I'll go make you some."

Kelly stayed curled up in Riley's lap, enjoying the comfortable peacefulness between the two of them.

"Your rental car has been returned to the rental agency, Red." Riley kissed her on top of her head. "We can go and buy you a car whenever you feel you're ready. I have three parking spaces of my own here at APS headquarters—so does Bryn—and your house has a circular drive leading into a three-car garage. Parking should never be an issue for us." Riley raised her eyebrow at Kelly. "Dare I ask where my remote control to the complex is, Red? I seem to have misplaced it."

Kelly actually blushed. "It should be along any day now. I, um, I kind of had it mailed back to you through an anonymous shipper, so that you couldn't trace the departure origin."

Riley's brow elevated further.

"I have a new one now, so we will just re-enable that one for you when you get your new car." Unable to help herself, Riley smirked. "Damn, baby. I'm starting to wonder what kind of tricks are rattling around under those beautiful red curls."

Kelly blushed again.

"Rowan is working on getting your house finished, so you can have all your shit delivered and get yourselves unpacked, *princesa*," Riley continued. "Teagan is ready to start the wiring for your security system as soon as Ember says the word."

"I have a tiny apartment in Langley I rented after Rowan moved down here, but I only have some clothes and a coffee pot there. No big loss if I don't get any of that stuff back."

"We can send a couple of associates to get your stuff." Riley nuzzled her temple. "You should know Trill had already planned to send someone up to look a little more closely into this CIA burn situation, *princesa*. She said the whole situation stinks to high heaven, she's not happy, and she wants a closer look at the whole mess. She'll keep us posted."

Kelly nodded thoughtfully.

Riley smiled. "Speaking of your house... Bryn wants a boat, especially since you and Rowan have that huge dock out back. She and I are going to go in together and buy one." Kelly's eyes rounded. "I'm going to warn you just like Bryn warned Rowan: You're a Floridian now. We spend our lives on the water, so be prepared. Bryn and Rowan have pretty much agreed they'll probably spend half their time at the APS complex and half their time at your house. Quite frankly, I can't see that we'll do much different."

"I'm glad you and Bryn are so close," Kelly whispered quietly. "Rowan and I are pretty much joined at the hip. That's always been a problem for the people we've dated, for the most part. Especially Rowan's fuck of an ex," she said, snorting with derision.

"I know the feeling. I'll be honest with you, *princesa*. I've dated a fuckton, even though I've never been serious about anyone. The extreme closeness that's shared by twins has led to an awful lot of jealousy problems."

Kelly scoffed. "Jealous bitches are the worst." Riley threw back her head and laughed.

"We're just as close to the Seven, so we spend a shitload of time with them as well. Bryn's already said we're going to have to buy a boat that's at least thirty-five feet long to accommodate all of us."

Kelly sighed with contentment at the thought.

Riley gently slid Kelly off her lap and stood up. "Let me go get you your coffee. I'll be right back."

When Kelly was resettled on Riley's lap with her coffee, she sipped the amazing brew and then tried to articulate some of her thoughts.

"It feels weird not having a schedule right now," Kelly said. "No office to go into, no boss to check in with. I usually run in the mornings myself, although not quite as early as you. I don't know my way around yet, so I'm not really sure how to put all that together. If you can recommend a really good gym for me and a shooting range I can go to, I'd appreciate it, Riley.

"I've lived in Woodbridge my entire life, except the last few months I've spent in Langley. Being a Florida girl and getting used to a whole new area is going to take me some time."

"The Seven now have your schedule completely filled, *princesa*." Riley laughed at the look on Kelly's face. "Those assholes are already fighting for the privilege of being your running partner in the morning. And we have a huge, fully equipped gym and a five-lane shooting range here at APS. The Seven have a new playmate, Red, so they are completely fucking excited."

Riley smirked as Kelly's mouth dropped open.

"Each one of them has loved every single minute they've spent with Rowan…because, well, Rowan. I doubt there's ever been a little sister in history who's been so protected and so loved. But I want you to know, baby, they already know they're going to come to love you just as much. In some ways, they already do. And knowing what they do about your skills, they're over the moon and already making book on who's going to kick whose ass."

Kelly rolled her eyes, then paused.

"Are they going to…you know…about what happened yesterday…?" Kelly stopped, uncertain how to continue.

"*Princesa*." Riley tilted Kelly's face up and looked into her green eyes.

"They are each going to hug you, exchange a few private words with you, and that's going to be the end of it. It's over, it's done with, there's no reason to drag it out any further. Yeah?"

"Okay." Kelly felt relieved.

"I also know Trill really wants to spend some time with you going over your ability. She's absolutely fascinated. However, she's also adamant we not push you in any way until you feel ready to talk about it."

Riley ran her hands up and down Kelly's back again.

"Trill being Trill, she's already had a pretty good idea you've felt exploited on some level for a long time…as if your worth has only ever been tied to your gift, which has totally pissed her off. I'd feel sorry for your CIA handler if I were you, *princesa*, because if Trill ever meets him, it's not going to end well for him, trust me."

"Wow." Kelly was quiet. "I don't know what to say."

"We are a family here at APS, especially Bryn and me and the Seven. I've known those fuckers since I was five years old—in Trill's case, since we were three years old." Kelly's eyes got huge. Plus, Whimsy is a really tiny town, only 13,000 residents, and everybody knows everybody. We all have each other's back and always have. Oh, and before I forget...we are going to dinner at my parents' house this Sunday with Bryn and Rowan."

Kelly's eyes got even bigger.

"Meeting my mother is an experience." Riley grinned. "Every single associate at APS is scared to fucking death of Rosario Reyes Armstrong, including Bryn and me...although she is a kind and absolutely amazing woman. Everyone loves her to pieces, and each one of the Seven is just like one of her own kids. However, she is also a hot-blooded Puerto Rican woman. My dad, who is English and was raised in London, spends a great deal of his time keeping the bloodshed to a minimum when anyone pisses her off."

"Hoo boy." Kelly blew out a huge breath.

"No worries, *princesa*. She already loves Rowan like she's her own daughter, and she's excited to meet Rowan's little sister...especially knowing how close you and Rowan are. Plus, also knowing what you and Rowan have each been through? Add the fact that both of your parents have passed on, and Mama will fucking murder anyone who dares to touch a hair on your heads herself."

Kelly's eyes were huge again.

"I have two younger brothers named Noah and Keenan, and my sister, Daniela, is the baby. Bryn and I are the oldest, although she's an asshole and tries to pretend she's so much older than the rest of us because she was born nine minutes before I was." Riley rolled her eyes as Kelly snickered. "After you finish your coffee, then you can take a shower. I'll take you down to APS headquarters and we'll give you the grand tour. Tonight, however, is mine."

Riley kissed Kelly deeply for a good couple of minutes before she released Kelly's mouth.

"I need to claim my woman again so she understands she's mine in every way. There truly is no escaping me now, *princesa*. You're mine forever."

* * * * *

Feeling a little shy and a lot guarded when she first saw Bryn and the Seven, Kelly paused for a moment as she came into the small conference room with Riley.

She saw nothing but affection and relief on their faces when they saw her. As Riley had predicted, they each pulled her aside privately and put their arms around her in a big hug. They spent a few minutes individually assuring her how relieved they were that she was now safe among them and pledged their support to her.

She knew they were all aware of the serious spanking she had taken from Riley the previous day, but she also realized in the next breath it was over and done with as far as they were concerned. It was clearly time to move on and focus on more important things.

"*Princesa*," Riley said when everyone was finally seated, "what we did for Rowan was give her a very brief overview on what everyone does. Then she spent individual time with each one of the Seven so she could focus exclusively on their role and responsibilities. I want to do that with you, too. I know we've already done introductions once on a much more superficial level, but I'd like to do it again. That way, you can start focusing on our skill sets and start thinking about where you might want to contribute."

"That sounds perfect." Kelly smiled at all of them.

One after another, each one of the smoking hot butches of the Seven formally introduced themselves and told her what they did for APS.

"Teagan Malloy. I'm the Chief Communications Engineer. My crew and I focus on things like the internet and network security." Teagan—like all of the Seven—was tall, with red-gold hair that was a lighter shade than Kelly's, intense green eyes, and an easy, gorgeous smile.

"Good, because I don't know nearly as much about that kind of stuff as I would like to. Lead the way, Teacher." Her eyes twinkled at Teagan, who grinned at her.

"Casey Christensen," said the platinum-haired, blue-eyed butch who was next. "MMA and Krav Maga team lead. My crew and I deliver martial arts and Krav Maga training to all of the APS associates."

"That's awesome, because Krav Maga isn't something I've done for long and I would love to practice more." Casey gave her a big smile and a thumbs up.

"Kennedy Weston. Everyone calls me Kenn, Kelly." Kennedy had dark brown hair and dark blue eyes. "I'm the APS Armory

Master. My team and I oversee the shooting range and the Cage where our weapons are kept." She looked at Kelly and smiled slowly.

"According to your sister, you can shoot a 392 out of 400 in USMC pistol qualification simulations. She is so immensely proud of you, little sis. I personally can't wait until you come to the range and we can work on drills together." Kelly beamed.

"Trillian Dacanay," said the handsome butch with dark blond hair, light brown eyes, and deep dimples. "Information Security Analyst. My team is known as the Geek Crew. We focus on a fuckton of shit, but mainly things like cryptography, computer forensics, and ethical hacking, in addition to data and technical security. Once you feel you're ready, Kel, and I mean when *you* feel you're ready, I'd like to sit with you and Riley in my office. I want to learn more about your ability with eidetic memory and how it works."

Trillian then looked at Kelly intensely.

"I'm feeling more than a little protective over you, little sis. I don't care how long it takes for you to feel comfortable….none of us will *ever* push you to talk about anything until you feel it's right for you. Those useless fucks at the CIA used you for too goddamn long, as if your only worth was as one of their fucking assets. And I'll slaughter that miserable piece of shit at Percutio myself for even daring to plan what he had been for you." Trill's light brown eyes darkened and flamed.

Kelly's mouth dropped open at the sheer menace on Trill's handsome face.

"Temperature, *broki*." Riley's voice was mild, but her body was alert. So, Kelly noticed, was Bryn and the rest of the Seven.

Trill breathed for a minute, looking down at the table, until she finally relaxed and said, "I'm chill, cuz."

"Trill." Kelly paused for a moment before she continued, trying to articulate her thoughts. "You have no idea what it means to me that you feel the way you do. How you *all* feel and especially how you feel about Rowan."

Kelly let her grateful face drift around the room.

"Except for having Clementine, we were both kind of adrift for a long time after our parents died. Riley tells me you all knew my dad, so I know you understand why the two of us miss him so goddamn much." Kelly took a deep breath. "Mom was awesome, too, although I suspect you'd know that someone who was married to Bill Holland was her own kind of special."

The soft looks on the faces of the Seven made her breath catch in her throat for a minute before she continued.

"I owe you all an apology." Kelly was frank. "We could have saved ourselves a whole lot of trouble in the beginning, but I, unfortunately, wasn't in a place of trust. I didn't trust *anybody*, except for Rowan and Clementine. That's not an excuse, just an explanation. It's not your fault, any of you, and I take full responsibility. If I'm honest, I should admit I might still have a little crisis of faith here and there. I am still processing the fact that I was burned by the CIA, even though my record there was exemplary and I rose through the ranks pretty quickly. But again, that's on me, not on you."

"*Princesa*." Riley squeezed the hand she had been holding as the rest of the team regarded Kelly in perfect understanding. "I don't think any of us expects you to sail into this perfectly. Of course you're going to have a crisis of faith here and there. The only difference now is that you can come to me—you can come to *any* of us—if you need to talk or vent or curse. You aren't alone anymore. You no longer have to balance the world on your shoulders solo."

Kelly nodded and swallowed.

"Can I ask you a question before Jaime has the floor?" She smiled at the handsome black-haired butch with dark brown eyes who clearly came from the same ethnic background as Bryn and Riley.

"Of course, *princesa*. What is it?" Riley caressed her arm.

"You keep asking each other, *'What's your temperature?'* What exactly does that mean?" Kelly asked slowly.

"We have a lockdown room here at APS. It doesn't happen that often—as a matter of fact, it happens rarely—but we've had situations where an associate was not able to control their emotions and was a danger to themselves and to others around them."

Kelly sat and quietly absorbed the information as Riley continued.

"In those situations, we send two of the Seven to extract them, remove their weapons, and secure them in the lockdown room until they can get themselves under control."

Kelly's eyes widened.

"Here at the management level, if we see that one of us is getting to a place where control may be an issue, we simply ask them, *'What's your temperature,* broki?' It gives us a chance to get ourselves back under control, *princesa*, before others of the Seven need to take us to lockdown."

Riley smiled without humor.

"Typically, there's a woman involved when we run into these situations at the management level, Red. I don't think it's any surprise to you that I was holding on to my control yesterday by the skin of my teeth. Bryn hit the nail on the head when she told Rowan a testosterone-fueled male has *nothing* on a hard butch whose femme has been threatened, or if a woman under her protection is endangered."

"Oh." Kelly's voice was very quiet.

"So," Riley smiled at her gently, "I appreciate every single thing you know how to do for yourself, Princess Badass, and we're all in awe of your strength and knowledge. Every single one of us. But protecting our women is just how a hard butch is wired, and I'm afraid that's never going to change. I hope you understand your strength and our protection can exist simultaneously, *princesa*."

Kelly looked down at the table and spent a minute in quiet contemplation before she looked at everyone.

"Okay," she said simply. "I can live with that."

"Good. Because I think this fucker is about to spontaneously combust if we don't get on with it and get to her part." Riley smirked as Jaime gave her the finger, and Kelly laughed, the tension broken.

"I'm Jaime Quintero, *mi hermana,* which means *my sister* in Spanish…before your head explodes like your sister's did."

Kelly burst out laughing, knowing Jaime's penchant for speaking Spanish when Rowan didn't understand probably drove her big sister nuts.

"I'm the Physical Security Risk Assessment Expert. My team conducts penetration testing, which is aimed at finding physical security vulnerabilities and risks. We get to break into buildings to steal things and data, pick locks, and even try to con people so we're granted access…all in the name of engineering physical security in a particular location in a way that makes it impenetrable."

"Ooh, fun!" Kelly couldn't help herself.

"Consider yourself recruited then, *hermana.*" Jaime's grin was wicked. "The best part of my job is driving Trill out of her fucking mind and circumventing her security." Kelly laughed again as Trill shot Jaime the finger this time.

"I'm Drew Hollister," the gorgeous butch with light brown hair and hazel eyes said quietly as she smiled gently at Kelly. "One of my roles is as the team lead for counterintelligence operations."

"Wait." Kelly's voice was hushed as her eyes grew huge and her breath caught. The look she gave Drew was one of a deer caught in headlights.

Whimsical Princess

"I think…I think I know who you are, actually."

Chapter 10

"And how would you know that, little sister?" Drew asked mildly, her tone easy and clearly not upset with Kelly at all.

"You're *the Shadow*," Kelly whispered almost inaudibly and closed her eyes, unwilling to look at Drew. "The CIA's been looking for you for years, which I'm sure is no surprise to you. I... I... I think... I think maybe it's better if I actually demonstrate how I know, not just explain it. I want you to know this is something I've never told another living soul. Please don't...don't..." Kelly opened her eyes and actually looked a little ill.

"Beautiful girl." Drew's voice was still easy and kind. "I think maybe you didn't understand when Riley told you we were family. Family means *family*, Kel. The fact that you're telling me you've never told another living soul what you're about to tell us, means you sensed we were family even before you actually knew who we were. Riles?"

"Baby." Riley actually lifted Kelly up out of her chair and put her in her lap, banding her arms tightly around Kelly's body and kissing her on the forehead. "Drew is absolutely right. Just like she would protect you with her last breath, it's clearly evident you would do the same for us. We have no secrets between each other, *princesa*. Whatever you need to tell us, you need to feel free to do so without any worries whatsoever. Okay?"

"Okay," Kelly whispered. She took a deep breath and settled herself more firmly into Riley's lap, then closed her eyes and let herself go limp as a look of extreme concentration crossed her face.

"It was December of last year." Three months prior. "I'd just found out that Mary-Kate Villin from Grayson Financial, where Rowan used to work, had been attacked and beaten. I suspected that fuck, Dino Coravani, had been involved, but I didn't know for sure, so I went up to the hospital to see what I could find out. When I got there, I saw this really handsome butch at the end of the hallway by the nurses' station. For some reason, I knew she wasn't just an ordinary visitor. She was there for Mary-Kate, but she didn't seem inclined to visit. It's like she was on a fact-finding mission, just like I was."

Kelly opened her eyes and smiled tentatively at Kennedy.

"It was you, Kenn. You had on gray wool slacks, a black button-down shirt, a black winter coat with a gray scarf around your neck, and black boots. Your coat was unbuttoned and your scarf ends were hanging down. You were carrying a pair of black leather gloves in your left hand, and there was a bandage on the index finger of your right hand, as if you had cut yourself."

You could hear a pin drop.

"Jesus fuck," Kennedy muttered, running a hand through her short, dark brown hair in shock. "Right on the money, little sis."

"Since it was winter and the weather was freezing, I had my hair all stuffed up under a plain stocking cap—so you couldn't see the color—and a nondescript jacket, with jeans. I had colored contacts in so my eyes appeared brown. I was standing in the hallway, pretending to read the notices on a bulletin board, when you passed me by. You glanced at me, then continued on down the hallway without stopping. You went right around the corner into one of those little rooms where the vending machines were. There was no one in there, except you, and I could hear you pull out your phone to make a phone call. I slipped across the hallway to listen right outside the vending machine area. I sensed that, for some reason, what you were going to say was important."

Kelly looked directly at Kennedy. "Teagan had called you, so you called her back. You told her that Mary-Kate had been beaten up pretty badly by Dino Coravani so he could find out where Rowan had gone, but they expected her to make a full recovery. And you were *pissed*, Kenn. You still didn't know for certain what exactly had happened, but you made the comment that maybe Drew—*the Shadow*—also needed to descend down into Purgatory and start digging from her end. At that point, I didn't want to get caught eavesdropping by you, so I moved much further up the hallway to a spot where it would have been impossible for me to overhear your conversation. I pretended to read the notices there until you came out and retraced your steps down the hallway.

"You stopped about ten feet past me to wrap your scarf around your neck, button your coat, and put on your gloves. You got even more pissed because the Band-Aid on your right index finger got caught on the lining of your right glove as you were trying to put it on. So, you ripped the Band-Aid off, put the glove on, and continued making your way down the hallway.

"I left because I didn't want to hang around anymore, and I figured I would just come back the next day when I knew you were gone." Kelly blew out a huge breath. "I spent the rest of that night in my hotel room, doing some research through some clandestine channels so my forensic trail couldn't be traced. I wanted to know who the Shadow was. What I found didn't exactly convince me to let those numbfucks at the CIA in on the secret."

The room was deathly silent.

"Little sis," Drew said soothingly. "Everything is perfectly okay, I promise you. Other than the fact that Trill might have a fucking heart attack because of what we've just seen you do, it's all good, honey. And you are beyond amazing. I hope you know that."

"Okay," Kelly whispered again. "As long as you're sure, Drew. I never want you to feel like the Seven can't trust me."

"On the contrary, Kel. If anything, this has proven to me exactly what kind of a woman you truly are. We're really lucky to have you, don't you know that?" Drew's gorgeous smile held affection and trust. Then Drew turned and looked at Blake. "Top that, motherfucker," she said, smirking. The entire team roared, the tension broken again, and Kelly shook her head in amusement.

"I'm Blake Seibert." Blake had auburn hair, pale green eyes with flecks of gold, and a mischievous smile. "Since these grandstanding fuckers had to steal my thunder, we'll keep this low-key. Be prepared to be amazed anyway." Kelly laughed as Riley and the rest of the Seven groaned.

"My team and I run Utopia, which is our lab simulator. We've designed realistic combat simulators with full-size, first-person shooters that allow us to simulate weapon-based combat in a first-person perspective. Our associates run through mock drills in our lab. We test their speed, their reaction time, and their accuracy against the sim models. We've also been able to simulate marksmanship qualifications using Utopia. I have to tell you our beloved Rowan almost crapped her drawers the first time the sim went hot and she was standing smack dab in the middle of it."

Kelly snickered with love for her big sister, wishing she could have been there to see that.

"But Rowan rallied nicely and even surprised the shit out of Bryn and me with a move Teagan and Remy had shown her." Blake looked suitably impressed. "Incidentally, Remy is the APS associate from Teagan's crew who guarded Clem during all the shit with that asshole, Coravani. She's also Teag's second."

Kelly nodded, already aware that Clem and Remy were dating.

"That's it for the short version of what each crew does, *princesa*. Now, we just need to schedule long visits with each one of these assholes. I don't think the order makes any difference."

"I'm going to volunteer to be Kelly's running partner for now," Casey said. "I think we need two or three of us in rotation so that we can switch off on our long-distance days.

"Kel, I suspect you don't typically do half marathon-length runs and prefer to keep yours under ten miles, right?"

"Uh, try more like six to eight miles, dude. I'm not a masochist like you all clearly are." Kelly rolled her eyes. "Whoever is running with me is just going to have to keep going when I'm ready to quit."

"No, those will just be the days we do a short run because we've got MMA or Krav Maga or other gym work planned." Casey paused, considering. "That'll work. We usually start around 4:30 in the morning, but I'm not going to subject you to that, Kel. Is six a.m. too early for you?"

"Crazy people," Kelly huffed under her breath, sounding so much like Rowan that Riley and the Seven burst out laughing. "No, actually six o'clock is fine. Five-thirty or six o'clock is typically what time I start myself, depending on what's going on. I can even do five o'clock every day if that will be better for you."

"No, *princesa*, we'll give these lazy fuckers a vacation and make six o'clock our start time." Riley smirked as the Seven simultaneously flipped her off. "Now, I believe we have a tour to complete. We'll start in the employee lounge and take it from there."

Chapter 11

Casey, Jamie, and Blake followed Kelly and Riley to the employee lounge. In the lounge, which was filled with associates, Riley asked for and received everyone's attention.

"This is Kelly Holland, Rowan's little sister and Bill Holland's youngest daughter," Riley said, her arm around Kelly. "She's also mine and you'll be seeing her quite a bit around the complex. She's now part of APS, and the management team is working with her to determine where she'll best fit into the organization."

Kelly was warmed by the welcoming smiles she saw everywhere.

"I'm going to warn you," Riley smirked, "my woman has some serious skills in covert and clandestine operations, so we're definitely going to need to keep on our toes around her."

Kelly rolled her eyes with a smile and the associates in the lounge laughed.

"We're taking her on a tour right now, but feel free to say hello and introduce yourselves when you see her."

Kelly smiled at everyone and waved as she, Riley, and the other three members of the Seven left the lounge.

"So much of the APS complex consists of areas you'll see in your one-on-ones with the Seven, *princesa*, like Hades and Utopia." Riley thought for a moment.

"Hades?" Kelly asked, puzzled.

"Hades is our gym, which that fucker there named," Riley said, gesturing at Jaime, who smirked. "You already know Utopia is Blake's sim lab. You'll be spending some time in Hades with Casey, in addition to Utopia with Blake. You'll also get the opportunity to hang out in Trill's Recon Room, and Kennedy's Cage and shooting range as part of your one-on-ones. Probably the Bunker with Teag and Jaime, and we'll discuss Drew later. You'll be spending time with everyone in the coming weeks."

Riley slid her arm around Kelly.

"I think probably the best thing to do today is to go take a look at the Bunker, which is the office of the Seven, and the back office. Which," she raised her eyebrow at Casey, Jaime, and Blake, "I know is exactly the reason these motherfuckers wanted to tag along."

The three of them grinned.

"Cuz. Do you blame us?" Blake gave an evil smile. "Please don't ruin our fun. Twenty bucks says little sis here takes home the gold." She and Jaime gave each other a high five.

"I am so fucking confused." Kelly looked at Riley for clarification.

Riley sighed. "One of the women who works in our back office has been, shall we say, on the hunt for a senior APS management butch. She originally had her sights set on Bryn until Rowan smacked her down."

"Trill said it was fucking *legendary*," reported Jaime with a huge grin. "Our sweet little Rowan now has the entire complex making book on the survival rate for any bitch who dares to look at Bryn the wrong way."

"Well...*yeah*." Kelly smirked. "She may be sweet, but she's not a fucking pushover. I, however, am not sure exactly what this has to do with me."

"Now that Bryn is off the table, Riley is next in line in her crosshairs," said Casey. "You should prepare yourself, little sis. When Gracie finds out you've taken Riley out of circulation, she is liable to go batshit crazy."

"Riley is a big butch and I'm sure she can defend herself without any help from me." Kelly shrugged. "And frankly, I stopped worrying about bitches like that in middle school."

* * * * *

After a stop to look at the Bunker, the huge office shared by the Seven, they all went into the back office.

The back office was a large, warm room shared by the three women who took care of the back office operations.

The first associate, Daniela Armstrong, was Riley and Bryn's sister—a sweet firecracker of a woman, whom Kelly liked immediately and looked forward to getting to know better.

Effie Jacobsen, another member of the back office team, was an older woman whom Riley told Kelly had been with APS since they had opened the doors ten years prior. Kelly liked her and her warm personality immediately as well.

The third member of the back office team, Gracie Kavanaugh, left Kelly not so impressed. When Gracie saw Riley, she immediately fluffed her hair, adjusted her blouse so her cleavage was evident, then looked down her nose at Kelly.

Kelly rolled her eyes internally. *Jesus. Middle-school bitches.*

"Riley," Gracie purred suggestively and made sure her long, lean legs were visible under her very short skirt. "It's been so long since I've seen you."

She flipped her hair, then looked at Kelly as if she might look at a piece of gum on her shoe.

"Is this one of those temp girls or whatever? Do I need to take her to Trill so you aren't bothered by something so…mundane?" Gracie batted at her eyelashes at Riley while giving Kelly a snotty look.

Seriously?

Kelly's brows raised. *Okay, bitch. It's on. If my new family wants a show, then a show they'll get.*

She smiled without humor at Gracie. "Kelly Holland. CIA." Kelly's voice was crisp. Gracie's eyes widened as Kelly's words registered, and her face paled a bit.

Kelly leaned against Riley and deliberately turned her back on Gracie. "Riles, I appreciate your time and attention today, lover, but

I don't know that interrupting your staff while they're trying to get their work done was the best thing for us to do."

The corner of her mouth tilted up in an icy smile that didn't reach her eyes as she turned to look down her own nose at Gracie, who paled even further despite her tan.

"It's bad enough that people hear 'CIA' and get completely freaked out. Then again, we have a pretty…well-deserved…reputation for being scary, don't we?" She turned back to Riley. "Maybe we should just continue our discussion at home, yes? I need to unpack anyway and find a dresser drawer in your bedroom I can steal." Kelly ignored the slight choking sound she heard from behind them.

"As you wish, *princesa*." Humor colored Riley's voice. She wrapped her arms around Kelly, gave her a hard, dominant kiss, then let her go and caught her by the hand.

"Effie. It was lovely to meet you." Kelly beamed warmly at the sweet older woman. "I would love to have lunch with you one day when I'm all settled in, okay? I just moved down here from the Washington, D.C. area, and things are a little chaotic at the moment, but let's make that happen soon."

Effie agreed eagerly, her face filling with pleasure.

"Daniela, I'll see you on Sunday at your parents' house for Sunday dinner. Bryn and Rowan are coming too, so it will be a relaxing and fun family day." Kelly lowered one eyelid in a hidden wink, knowing she was twisting the knife in Gracie's back, as Daniela fought to keep the amusement off her face.

Ignoring Gracie completely, Kelly headed toward the door.

"We'll let you guys get back to work. All of us have more CIA business to discuss anyway, so I think the best thing will be for us to head back to the Bunker. Have a great day, everyone. Toodles." She waggled her fingers as she waited for Riley to open the door.

After they had all filed out of the back office and the door shut behind them, Kelly stopped, put her hands on her hips, and regarded Riley with one eyebrow raised.

"Riles. Do you, by chance, happen to remember that whole 'I wouldn't fuck her with your dick' discussion we had the other night?" Her eyebrow elevated further as Riley gave her a lopsided grin.

Casey, Jaime, and Blake howled and slapped each other's backs as Kelly shook her head and started down the hallway.

"I. Am. *Dead*." Casey tried to catch her breath. "Trill and Teagan are going to be *so* goddamned mad they missed this…not to mention Kenn and Drew."

Blake was already busily texting on her phone, still laughing. "Life has gotten a whole fuck of a lot more interesting since the Holland girls came to town," she whooped and sent the text. "The Seven are now officially in the loop and they can eat their fucking hearts out because they missed the *epic* Kelly Holland Beatdown."

Kelly burst out laughing, unable to help herself.

"Can we go back to the Bunker?" she asked Riley after she subsided. "I would really like to put together a schedule for my playdates with the Seven. Any order, whatever makes sense to you, but I'm excited to get started and learn as much as I can. One thing, though." Kelly paused for a minute and looked at them all seriously. "I don't know that I'm going to be able to choose just one area to work in. I mean, I love *everything* about MMA and Krav Maga, for example," she gave Casey a bright look, "but I want to do other stuff, too, not just that."

"I don't think any of us expected you to stick to one thing only, *princesa*." Riley drew her woman to her side. "Besides, I'd have a riot on my hands if I stuck you in just one area."

"Damn fucking skippy, *broki*," Jaime muttered as the corner of Riley's mouth tipped up.

"I want a playdate with Drew, too," Kelly said firmly. The APS team went quiet.

"I know Bryn and Drew wouldn't let Rowan go down into Purgatory, and I agree one hundred percent with that decision. As a matter of fact, I would have been pissed as hell if they would have let her. However," she smiled coldly, "I was CIA clandestine and covert operations for more than a few years. I know who the Shadow is. I also think I've proven my ability to ghost when necessary. I'm the last person you need to worry about being down there. Plus, I really don't have any interest other than observing," she told them. "I'm not a fan of the dark web, and I've only spent time there when necessary. Frankly, I can find plenty of assholes on the surface. I just want to see Drew do her thing."

"Noted, *princesa*." Riley walked with her down the hallway, the other three APS associates trailing behind them. "I doubt she'll have an objection, knowing how well you can handle yourself. I'll talk to her about it the next time I see her. In the meantime, we'll get to the Bunker and get your playdates all scheduled. When that's done, it will be a good day for us to go and hang out with Trill."

Riley smirked. "That motherfucker is going to spontaneously combust if she doesn't get some alone time with us soon." Kelly snorted in amusement. "Then I think we're going to call it a day, *princesa*. You're still tired and you still have rest you need to catch up on. Tomorrow is another day, yeah?"

"What Riles said," Casey agreed with a decisive nod. "I don't mind telling you, little sis, the dark circles we saw under your eyes had all of us a little less than happy."

Blake was uncharacteristically serious. "I wasn't part of the extraction team, Kel, but Jaime filled me in when they got back. You need rest, lots of it, and—lucky for you—you now have eight bossy older siblings, and one extremely bossy significant other, who will definitely make sure you get it." Blake smiled kindly, but there was a definite glint in her eye.

Kelly huffed, but a tiny dimple appeared in the corner of her mouth.

"Okay. First stop, the Bunker," said Riley. "You assholes can help us put together Kelly's playdate schedule. Then she and I will head to the Recon Room to meet up with Trill. I think a very short run for you in the morning, maybe five miles, would be beneficial, *princesa*. Case, you got her?"

Casey gave Riley and Kelly a thumbs-up.

"To the Bunker we go then, Red."

Chapter 12

Kelly screamed as she fought to get free of the restraints around her wrists and legs that Riley had bound her with.

After Kelly and Riley had finally arrived back at Riley's apartment after spending the afternoon with Trill, Riley had barely let Kelly in the door before she'd plastered Kelly up against the wall and started to devour her mouth. When Kelly was in a haze of desire, Riley led her up the short flight of stairs to the bed loft, stripping her as they went until Kelly was bare when they got to the top.

"You're fucking mine, *princesa*," Riley growled, running her hands over Kelly's naked body, cupping her full breasts. "I'm going to take you right now and fuck you until you can't breathe. I've waited too long to have you again and I refuse to wait even one minute longer."

Riley tossed Kelly on the bed and followed her down, pulling her T-shirt up over her head and stripping off her boots and jeans. She pulled Kelly's hands up over her head and pinned her down, pushing her legs apart with her own strong thighs until Kelly was helpless.

Riley kissed Kelly, controlling and domineering, until Kelly felt like she was on the verge of passing out from the feel of Riley's muscled body on top of her. Lost in a sea of passion, Kelly didn't realize at first that Riley had bound her hands up over her head after she restrained her, then slid restraints that had appeared from under the mattress and bound her legs open.

In shock, Kelly gasped and pulled at the restraints until Riley lowered her mouth between Kelly's legs with a low, wicked laugh.

Riley began to lick and nuzzle her pussy, with Kelly crying and trying desperately to close her legs and pull her hands down over her head, but she was completely under Riley's control.

"Look at this wide-open, pretty pink, delicious pussy. Such pretty red curls. Such a luscious feast."

Kelly screamed again, yanking on her bonds, as Riley nibbled her clit, then sucked the swollen, sensitive button into her mouth.

"Look at you, *princesa*." Riley's amber eyes glowed with lust. "This gorgeous red hair. These beautiful dark green eyes. This soft, delicate skin, the color of moonlight."

Riley ran her hands over Kelly's body.

"These long, luscious legs and these curvy hips that were made to be gripped as you're fucked to within an inch of your life."

Kelly's pussy gushed from Riley's erotic words.

"First time I saw you? You reminded me of those ethereal women who were painted by the Renaissance masters. Those delicate, voluptuous creatures who seemed like they were created just for passion and sensuality. Tell me you're mine, Kelly," Riley suddenly commanded her. "Tell me you're mine to command, mine to take, mine to own. Tell me you are mine in all ways."

"I'm... I'm..." Kelly's voice shook as she cried out, unable to speak.

Riley gave another quiet, wicked laugh. "You call me lover, *princesa*," she said, amused, as she worked a couple of fingers from one strong hand into Kelly's pussy. "But did you know I'm your demon lover, my beautiful captive? I'm the captor in the night who sees her beautiful prey and comes out of the darkness to take what belongs to her. There is no escaping me, *princesa*. Not now. And not ever."

Riley took Kelly's clit into her mouth and sucked hard as she thrust her fingers deeply into Kelly's tight channel. Kelly shrieked as she exploded and kept screaming, as Riley showed her no mercy and continued to fuck Kelly with her fingers.

When she was only half conscious, Kelly felt Riley release her wrists and legs, then she felt Riley slide her hard strap-on cock into Kelly's wet, swollen pussy.

"Tell me you're mine, *princesa*."

"I'm yours! I'm yours!" Kelly screamed, submitting completely to Riley's possession.

As Riley started to fuck her, slowly at first and then faster and faster, Kelly cried out, feeling Riley take her higher and higher toward the peak.

As she exploded for a second time, Kelly felt her world go black as her body went limp and Riley's loud groan filled the room.

When Kelly came to, she realized she was lying on clean sheets and that Riley had bathed her. She was being held in Riley's powerful arms as Riley stroked her, running her mouth gently over Kelly's throat and jaw.

"You are so beautiful when you come for me, *princesa*." Riley ran her hands down Kelly's body as she nuzzled her woman. "You come hard, then your face goes calm and your eyes soften. I've never seen anything more beautiful in my life."

Kelly sighed and sunk deeper into Riley's embrace as they both lay there for a while in contented silence.

"*Princesa?*" Riley's voice was gentle. "I want to ask you something, something I'm quite sure is a very upsetting subject for you. It's something that I'm positive we need to discuss, however."

"Okay," Kelly whispered after a minute with a sinking heart, knowing instinctively what Riley was going to ask her.

"Tell me about Robyn, baby. I know you two were engaged, and I know you said she was killed about two years ago. I'd like you to tell me what happened." Riley nuzzled Kelly's jaw and ran her strong hands gently over her femme.

Kelly stiffened and was silent at first. Riley waited patiently for a long time until Kelly slowly started to open up.

"Robyn and I met about four years ago. We were both CIA, and we met when we were assigned to the same project. She was a sweet, fun person, a *great* analyst, and I enjoyed getting to know her. She…she surprised me, though, because she got really serious about me, really fast, when I thought all we were doing was hanging out at first."

Kelly was quiet again for a while.

"Robyn didn't know about my eidetic memory because no one did, except for my handler and a select few within the CIA organization. I wasn't allowed to share the information with anyone. Robyn was a little puzzled at first—especially after we started dating—because I was sent out on assignments a lot more than she was, even though we were both analysts. She kind of shrugged it off, though. She figured it was because I was in a different directorate, or because I had some kind of different skill set or something. Yeah. Or something."

Kelly's voice was bitter.

"Percutio was a big problem even back then. Grigor Reizan had no fucking clue what or who I was at that time, but we all still had to be careful. If he even had a suspicion someone was part of the U.S. intelligence community, it would cost them their life. After Robyn and I had dated for about a year, one night I came home, and…and she asked me to marry her. I knew I wasn't *in* love with her, but I really, truly loved her, so I said yes. She was absolutely ecstatic and I was happy, too—even though I couldn't get past the feeling that knowing me was going to end up costing her.

"And it did. One day that next year, as I was getting ready to leave the office for the day, my boss called me into his office. I didn't report to Alan McAllister then… My old boss was an asshole named Harvey Stich, who was getting ready to retire in a year or so. I go into Harvey's office and it's like wall-to-wall people in there. No one would look me in the eyes and I knew, I motherfucking *knew*, that something bad had happened to Robyn."

Kelly was emotionless.

"Long story short…Robyn had been more suspicious than usual about Percutio in recent months, because so much of what I did with my eidetic memory gift was aimed at them. She didn't know why I was so heavily involved with the CIA's investigation into them: she just knew something was funny and she didn't like it. We had fights about it and I told her to stay away from them. I didn't tell her *why*, though, because I wasn't supposed to share information about my gift with anyone. She didn't listen, and Harvey called me that day to tell me Robyn had been ambushed and murdered by Reizan's goons."

Riley's arms tightened around her.

"The worst part was when Stich, a total motherfucker who hated queers, told me—after dismissing everyone else who was in his office so no one could see what a chicken shit pussy he was—that he was going to have Robyn posthumously censored for 'acting outside of allowable boundaries,' as he sneered at me. I told him to go ahead." Kelly's voice and smile were ice cold. "That I would be *more* than happy to demonstrate to his superiors how my gift worked.

"So, unless he wanted to be censored himself, lose his pension, and have a huge shitstain that looked just like him on his record, he'd back the fuck off…because I could recite—chapter and verse—every single sleazy motherfucking thing he did while he was in the CIA that wouldn't exactly be approved of by his superiors."

Kelly's voice was like granite.

"I told him I'd make goddamn sure I cost him *everything*. He turned purple with rage, called me a queer fucking cunt, threw me out of his office, and that was it. I never heard another word about them posthumously censoring Robyn. Her service record is exemplary, with awards for dying in the service of the United States. That motherfucker, Stich, retired about ten months later, and I haven't seen or heard of him since. Hopefully, he fell head first down a fucking latrine in the dark somewhere. However..."

Kelly was quiet again for a while.

"It's my fault that Robyn is dead, Riley," she said, again emotionless, when she finally spoke again. "If I had just told Robyn about my gift, she would have understood why the CIA had me so focused on Percutio and backed off." A tiny break appeared in her voice. "She would still be alive. I'll carry the guilt and the blame for her death for the rest of my life because *I. Didn't. Fucking. Tell. Her.*"

"*Princesa.*" Riley held Kelly's body tightly to her. "Because she sounds like she was an extremely honorable human being, I suspect Robyn would say the exact same thing to you that I'm about to. She was grown, she made her own choices, and *you* are in no way responsible for the consequences of *her* actions. She knew what she was getting into, she chose to take the risk because she was worried about you, and those consequences had the most tragic outcome possible. But you can in no way blame yourself for what happened. I have a feeling Robyn would be absolutely fucking furious with you if she knew this is how you've felt."

Kelly choked on a sob and tears started to fall.

Riley held her tighter. "You've never let yourself mourn, baby…not about Robyn, not about your career, not about your parents, not about *anything*. You've been so busy protecting Rowan and Clementine and everyone else, there's been no time for you to take care of yourself. You've kept everything hidden and buried, just completely locked down, for such a fucking long time."

She kissed Kelly tenderly on the forehead.

"It's destroying you on the inside, Kelly. Let it *go*, baby. You need to let it all go and release yourself from the anger and the blame and the guilt you've carried—far too fucking much of it, for far too fucking long. You're safe with me and I'm here to catch you, *mi princesa*, I promise you. *Let. It. All. Go.*"

At Riley's words, a great gush of emotion came bursting out of Kelly without warning.

For the next hour, Kelly screamed and sobbed and cursed and ranted as she splintered wide open about *everything*.

About Robyn and how goddamned angry Kelly still was with her, because Robyn had put herself into the position she did and had gotten herself killed.

About Percutio, and how Grigor Reizan and his bitch ass had one of the best women she'd ever known in her life murdered in cold blood.

About how fucking Reizan now arrogantly thought he had the motherfucking *right* to try and take her, someone who didn't belong to him, just so he could use her to further his own criminal empire.

About the CIA being so blind and stupid, they had permitted a fucking mole to destroy her career, when every evidence to the contrary pointed to her being one of the best fucking assets they'd ever had.

About how those CIA fuckers had also selfishly prevented Kelly from being there for her sister when Rowan was being stalked by a fucking psychopath but had then callously thrown Kelly away like she was garbage when they fell for the word of an unknown liar.

About her parents and how they'd left Kelly and Rowan behind to fend for themselves, and deal with these fucking shit shows without them.

About her motherfucking *gift*, which wasn't a gift at all, but a freak ability that had cost Kelly almost more than she could bear throughout her entire life—including destroying her dream to become a Marine like her father.

Through it all, Riley had held Kelly while she screamed and cried and raged, until the storm had finally passed and she lay in Riley's arms, spent and absolutely exhausted.

Riley leaned over to her nightstand drawer, pulled out a clean handkerchief to wipe her woman's eyes and face, gave Kelly the handkerchief so she could blow her nose, and uncapped a fresh bottle of water.

"I'm so sorry, Riley," Kelly quavered faintly after a while as she hiccupped with residual emotion. "I didn't mean to lose control like that."

Riley kissed her tenderly. "You have *nothing* to apologize for, *princesa*. I think this was a long time coming and I, for one, am fucking glad as hell you finally found release and let that shit the fuck out. You didn't say anything that didn't need to be said. Let me take care of you for now, baby." Riley nuzzled Kelly's jaw. "I want you to sleep, eat, play with the Seven, and hang out with your new friends and Rowan. Fuck everything else. It's time for me to take care of you for a little while, instead of you trying to take care of the world. Yeah?"

"Yeah." Kelly's voice was drowsy as she went limp and peaceful in Riley's arms, completely drained from her emotional meltdown.

"Sleep, my baby." Riley nuzzled her beautiful woman again. "You won't ever have to fucking worry about anything anymore. I'll burn the fucking world down before I'll let it hurt you again."

Chapter 13

The Bunker was dead quiet.

When Kelly had finally gone into a deep, healing sleep after her cathartic and emotional release, Riley had made sure she was tucked in and comfortable, then texted Bryn and the Seven, telling them to meet her in the Bunker.

Once there, Riley had filled them in on everything Kelly had shared with her about Robyn's death, and then told them about Kelly's subsequent meltdown in detail.

Casey had eventually been the one to break the deadly silence that had fallen over the group when Riley was done.

"I need to fucking beat something. Or rather, someone," she said matter-of-factly, her words and her calm bearing completely at odds with each other. "Preferably that piece of shit, Reizan, or Kelly's useless handler at the CIA. Either will do."

"First, we had to watch our Rowan deal with that asshole prick, Coravani." Trill was seething. "Now, that mangy Percutio fuck thinks he's going to put his filthy paws on Ro's little sister? On *our* little sister? Oh, *fuck* no."

"Say the word, Riles." Jaime smiled a cold, lethal smile. "We haven't had a good dick hunt in a while." She and Blake high-fived each other, identical expressions of malice on their faces.

"It may well come to that." Riley stretched out her long legs and blew out a deep breath. "Right now, though, my woman is fucking exhausted and emotionally spent. I told her she didn't need to do anything right now outside of play with the Seven and hang out with her friends and her sister."

"Good. Since I assume we're going to let her sleep instead of run in the morning...?" Casey arched a brow until she saw Riley's nod of acknowledgment, then continued. "Why don't you bring her to Hades when she's awake and ready to move a little bit, Riles? We'll get her on the mats so she can burn off any residual emotional backlash she might have stored in her body. I'll get Jess down there with us and let her know Kelly is a bit emotionally depleted right now but needs to move. Jess will jump right on it. She'll work with Kelly on blowing out any remaining bullshit, restoring her balance, and she'll also tell Kelly all about our community outreach program for teaching local women self-defense using Krav Maga."

Jess was Casey's number two, a caring, compassionate butch who was in charge of their community self-defense program, as well as an absolute beast with Krav Maga.

"I like that," Riley mused. "Jess is fucking awesome, and she and Kelly will get along great. Kelly said she wants to learn more about Krav Maga anyway, and I'll be honest: I can see Kelly helping out with the community outreach program eventually."

Jaime looked at Trill. "I hate to tell you this, *broki*," Jaime's eyes twinkled at her friend despite the gravity of their conversation, "but Red was fucking losing her mind at the thought of breaching our security with my crew and me. I owe Rowan one as well, so I think getting the two of them involved together with a penetration test would be a damn fun playdate for Kelly right now. Rowan, too."

"I know, fucker," Trill groused half-heartedly as she whipped an eraser from the Bunker whiteboard at Jaime's head. Jaime grinned as she caught it and whipped it back.

"Seriously though, Jaim, that's a great idea," Trill said thoughtfully, reflective again. "I'll tell my crew to prepare for a breach and you can get your team onboard to do pentesting with Kel and Rowan." Jaime nodded at her.

"We're going to stay away from doing anything that involves her gift for now since those motherfuckers at the CIA have her so fucked up over it." Trill and Jaime looked at each other and growled in disgust, eyes dark.

"Any one of the Seven who wants to be part of a team sim test in Utopia with Red, let me know," Blake said next. "I think it would be fun to let her test the sim for the first time with all of us, or at least with as many of us that can be there. I know her pistol skills are in the fucking stratosphere, Riles, but how is her knife work?" she asked Riley next.

"We'll have to ask her," Riley replied. "Whatever weapons she wants to use for the first time will be fine, though." She regarded her twin. "Rowan already warned us that playing in the sim would be one of the first things Kelly would want to do when she got here." They smirked at each other.

"Skill drills at the shooting range with her will be fucking easy," said Kenn. "Rowan said Kelly loves to shoot and do pistol/rapid reload drills, so we're already there. You just say when, cuz." She nodded at Riley. "I'm sure she'd love a tour of the Cage as well."

"I think I want to hold off doing any telecommunications stuff for a while," mused Teagan thoughtfully. "Christ knows she's more than fucking intelligent enough to grasp it, and she wants to learn, but it's not exactly playful. I really want her to relax and have some fun and feel more settled in her skin before we start throwing shit like that at her."

"I agree," said Drew. "I feel the same way about my shit. It's not exactly playful either." She drummed her fingers on the table. "And I really don't want Kel down in Purgatory when she's so fucking tired and emotionally drained. There's some scary-ass shit that goes on down there, and I don't know that she's emotionally equipped to handle it yet. Riles?"

"I think we can find more than enough to keep her occupied elsewhere for a while," Riley concurred. "I also texted Rowan and asked her to get the girls together this Friday night at Seashells. She and Clem are already on it. Any of you want to show up, that's great, but don't worry about it if you can't. Mama is going to have Bryn and Rowan's engagement party soon, so we'll all have a chance to hang out together then."

Riley was contemplative for a moment.

"I'm a bit on edge, *mi corillo*," she admitted, rubbing the back of her neck with one hand. "My woman has been through so goddamn much because of these dickheads. I'm fucking *done*. At the very least, Grigor Reizan is going to understand what he can expect to have happen if he or his goons so much as touch one hair on her head. Unfortunately," she took in a deep breath, "he is a motherfucking dumbass whose greed for Kelly's gift just might override his sense of self-preservation. I wouldn't put it past him to try and sneak her out of the country."

"Then we kill him, *mano*." Bryn's voice was like ice, her eyes hard. "All of them—Reizan *and* his entire Florida crew. They live now because they keep their sleaze out of APS territory. Instead of worrying about Kelly's gift, they need to remember the air they breathe is our gift to them."

Riley nodded slowly.

"As far as the CIA goes," Riley said, "we know Kelly has said Reizan and Percutio have a mole planted. She's also said they have no fucking clue who it is. Her handler, Alan McAllister, sounds like a bit of a dip shit, frankly…someone who's constantly behind the eight ball."

"Maybe we need to do some digging," Trill observed. "Jaim, you still got your shovel handy, cuz? If Riley can get the names of who is actually authorized to know about Kelly's ability, maybe we can extrapolate from there and back into the names of those who aren't supposed to know but do." Jaime gave her a thumbs-up in agreement.

"In the meantime, I need to have words with Grigor." Riley's voice was forbidding. "He's going to understand, in no uncertain terms, that if he or his goons come within a mile of Kelly, there are going to be some dickless wonders wandering the streets. Trill, you and Jaime get to digging on this bullshit burn situation with the CIA. Casey, give Jess a heads-up that Kelly and I will be down sometime tomorrow morning."

Riley paused for a minute, considering.

"I'm calling Reizan tonight and letting him know what he can expect if he or his army of fucks come anywhere near Kelly. Drew, let's make sure we have Purgatory wired for sound." The corners of Drew's mouth tipped up without humor. "Let's also make sure we all have our ears to the ground."

There was silence for a moment.

"She's a brave little soul," Kenn said suddenly. "And so goddamn strong, it's unbelievable. The shit she's been through would have fucking destroyed almost anyone else. I'm thankful beyond words that she's safe with Riley and with us now."

Bryn unexpectedly laughed in amusement and shook her head. Riley and the Seven looked at her questioningly.

"The first time I ever talked to Kelly on the phone, I was struck by how amazingly well she had mastered her voice inflection," Bryn said. "Her mastery over her voice control was and is virtually perfect. I was also blown away with how easily she was able to manipulate Rowan into thinking playing their point-counterpoint game was Rowan's idea, so Kelly could 'crack' a little way into the game and tell Rowan all about Coravani—which then gave Kelly a wide-open path to persuade Rowan to come to Florida from Virginia."

Bryn snorted after explaining the point-counterpoint game Rowan and Kelly had played with their mother for years, when they would each take an opposing side on something and debate the pros and cons between them.

"I remember deciding right then and there Kelly was either going to end up being one of my best friends or my worst nightmare."

"What's your conclusion?" Riley raised one eyebrow and smirked at her twin. "I'm sort of thinking it's both."

"I'm sort of thinking you're right, *mano*," Bryn shot back, still clearly amused.

"I don't look for Kelly to wake up until tomorrow morning. She was fucking wiped out," Riley said, getting ready to stand up and depart. "But I have the sense she's going to wake up feeling lighter than she has in years. That burden she was carrying around had some heavy shit in it and she purged a lot of it today."

Riley's amber eyes were cold. "Let's get done what we need to get done tonight while she's sleeping. I'm going to call Grigor and put some murderous fear of APS into that fucker while you all do your thing."

Then she rolled her eyes.

"I still think Reizan's too greedy to heed the warning long term, but I've long looked for a reason to put a bullet hole into that stupid son of a bitch, so there's that. Status update here at 0600 tomorrow, *mi corillo*. Let's keep getting to the bottom of this shit, shall we?"

* * * * *

Kelly looked at the window cling on one of the enormous glass doors at the entrance of Hades—the APS gym—and started to laugh.

It was edged in vicious-looking flames with the word "Hades" in big red and black Gothic letters at the top, and the phrase "Abandon hope all ye who enter here" in smaller black letters below it.

"Rowan had that made for Jaime, since Jaim was the one who named the gym Hades." Riley rolled her eyes, which made Kelly laugh even harder.

"That's my Ro." Kelly wiped tears of laughter from her eyes. "She's always had the most incredible sense of humor."

When Kelly had woken up that morning, she'd found herself being cradled securely in Riley's muscular arms, warm and safe.

She'd still felt tired and a little depleted from her massive emotional breakdown the day before, but she'd also felt peaceful—as if someone had turned a firehose on the great ball of inflammatory sludge that had been sitting in her chest for the past few years and blown it out of her.

Riley had kissed the tip of Kelly's nose when her eyes had fluttered open. "Good morning, *princesa*." Riley's eyes and voice were gentle. "How do you feel this morning?"

"Peaceful." Kelly let the sense of calm wash over her as she sighed and curled up even closer in Riley's arms.

"Good." Riley stroked her back. "I have a feeling you've probably had enough of sleeping for right now, though, yeah?" Kelly laughed and nodded in agreement.

"I think we're going to have some coffee first, *princesa*. I'd like you to eat some fruit so we can make sure your glucose level is where it needs to be, then you can take a quick shower before we meet up with Casey at Hades. But we're in no rush." Riley cocked her eyebrow at Kelly. "I normally wouldn't worry about showering *before* we went to the gym, but I'm guessing you'd probably appreciate it."

Now, in their fight wear, they went through the door and started toward the back of the gym. Kelly was surprised when she heard a chorus of "Hi, Kelly!" coming from associates working out in different areas. She beamed happily and waved to everyone, then continued on with Riley to the mats in the rear of the gym.

On the back mats, Casey was talking to another handsome APS associate, who was dressed in the blue and black colors of Casey's team. She was about Kelly's height, with light blond hair cut in a fade, intense gray eyes, and was just as insanely muscled as Casey was.

"Hey, Kel." Casey hugged Kelly for a long minute and kissed her on the cheek, then continued to hold her by the shoulders while her sharp blue eyes scanned Kelly's face and eyes intently for a minute. Casey was evidently happy with what she saw, because she nodded once and then let Kelly go, turning to give Riley a high five.

"Red, this is Jess, one of our Hades associates and my number two." Casey introduced Kelly to the butch she had been talking to. "She's our Krav Maga expert, and she's also in charge of our community outreach program to teach women in Whimsy self-defense."

Jess shook Kelly's hand, smiling kindly. "Kelly, it's wonderful to meet you. Everyone at APS has been very excited to meet Rowan's little sister. I understand from Casey and the twins that you're quite the martial arts expert yourself."

"I've studied a lot of martial arts, especially with my dad when I was younger," Kelly said, feeling unaccountably shy. "However, I'm not really that well versed in Krav Maga. I understand from the twins and the Seven you are an absolute beast when it comes to that." Jess laughed and shook her head. "I am looking to learn anything you're willing to teach me, Jess. Maybe you can give me some more details on your community outreach program, too?"

"Be happy to. You know, it was your sister who came up with the idea for us to offer self-defense classes to the community in the first place."

Kelly raised her eyebrows in surprise.

"Seriously, Rowan was here one day watching Bryn and Casey do a demo, and then Case showed her some Krav Maga self-defense moves," Jess informed her. "She found them so easy, she said it would be great if we could teach basic self-defense like that to any woman in Whimsy who would be interested in learning."

"That's my big sister," Kelly whispered softly, pride shining in her eyes.

"I understand from Riley and Casey you've been a bit run down lately, Kelly, so I'm going to suggest we do some basic mat work with Krav Maga for now just to get you moving," Jess suggested. Her gray eyes twinkled. "Then, when you're feeling better and you've built your stamina back up again, you can go ahead and kick my ass."

Kelly burst out laughing as Casey and Riley chuckled.

As Jess and Kelly started to do some stretching, Casey and Riley stood back, watching them as they talked.

"I called that sleaze bucket, Reizan, last night," Riley told Casey. "Pussy motherfucker was all, 'Oh no, Riley, we would *never* disrespect you like that,' when I warned him about Kelly. Fucking bullshit, he wouldn't. The asswipe was practically salivating when her name came up."

"If you need someone to do for you what Teag did for Bryn, and be Kelly's sidekick for a while, just say the word," Casey responded. "Jess is my number two, she can run Hades just about as well as I can, so I can cover Kelly during those times you need to put your undivided attention elsewhere."

"Appreciate it, *broki*, and I'm going to take you up on that." Riley slapped Casey on the shoulder. "Reizan's definitely planning a move. When Kelly and I go home tonight, I'm going to fill her in on everything that's going on with Reizan. She needs to be prepared for anything, and she needs to understand why she'll have 24/7 coverage going forward for now."

"Rowan was a lot more stationary because she was having the Dream Creamery and the Arts Center built when all the shit with Coravani was going down," Casey mused, still watching Kelly carefully. "Kel will be more mobile, so that's a different challenge."

"But," Riley reminded her friend, "Kelly will be doing a lot either at APS itself or as a playdate with one of the Seven, so there's that.

"When Kelly and Rowan go out with Jaime and her crew to do the breach test, for example, Reizan and his goons will have to get past six mean-as-fuck APS associates to get to Kelly." Riley's smile was icy. "Good luck with that, asshole."

"I'll fill the gaps then. When Kel's not with you or another one of us, I'll step up and grab a couple of my crew. Maybe she'll want to hang with her sister and her friends one afternoon." Casey wrinkled her nose at the thought of hanging around a femme get-together.

"Jesus fuck. The shit I fucking do for you, asshole." Riley burst out laughing and slapped Casey's shoulder again.

"You know I appreciate you, fucker." The two of them watched Jess and Kelly as they worked on some Krav Maga drills together.

"She has an incredible sense of timing, Riles." Casey broke the silence eventually. "You can tell she's new to Krav Maga itself, but her foundation of martial arts training is clearly evident and damn near professional level. Fuck, I wish we all could have spent time with Bill Holland on a more personal level. I already knew he was a fucking brilliant sniper instructor, but there was a lot more under the hood there than we ever knew." Casey shook her head in regret.

"I know." Riley continued to watch Kelly closely. "When she's back at full strength, I want to do a martial arts demonstration with her here in Hades. Either you and her or me and her, jiu-jitsu or karate or judo, whatever she wants."

Riley's voice went ice cold.

"Those numbfucks at the CIA made her think she wasn't good for anything but as a fucking asset because of her gift. Fuck them and fuck that. She is worth so much more than that and I don't give a shit if she ever uses her ability again."

"Fucking A," an equally icy, but scarcely detectable voice said behind them. It was Trill. "Motherfucking useless assholes. I'm going to annihilate that pussy-ass mole when I find him or her."

Her voice calmed and she spoke louder. "Bryn told me you were in Hades, Riles. I came over to ask you and Kelly if she wants to run through some pistol drills with Kenn and me at the shooting range when she's done here. Maybe she wants a tour of the Cage while we're at it?"

"I heard that! And *yes!*" Kelly didn't take her attention off her sparring with Jess even as she excitedly yelled. The APS crew grinned at her enthusiasm.

"Fucker. Do I come into the Recon Room and interrupt your geeky-ass shit?" Casey groused, but her eyes twinkled at her friend. Trill lowered one eyelid in a barely perceptible wink.

"Someone needs to save her from this Cro-Magnon man bullshit." Trill smirked and ducked as Casey aimed a punch at her arm. "But she's doing spectacularly well and she's having fun, so I guess that's the important part."

They all watched Kelly again for a while until Jess called a halt to the Krav Maga drill for the day.

"Kel, you're amazing." Jess put her hands on her hips and grinned. "For someone who is pretty new to Krav Maga, you are picking it up damn quick. When you are back to full strength, there will be nothing that can stop you."

Jess' grin grew broader. "You should know I also love the nickname Red, so Red you will be in Hades from now on." Kelly rolled her eyes, then snickered.

"So original, new friend," she teased Jess, switching her dark red ponytail over her shoulder as Jess laughed outright. Kelly turned to find Riley, who was right behind her. "Can I do this again soon, Riley? If Jess has the time?"

"I will always have time for you, Red, so you and Riley and Casey get together and decide the best schedule for you and we'll make it happen." Jess spoke kindly. "If you're up for it, maybe you three can come to the next community self-defense class, too." Kelly's face brightened.

"Thank you, *broki*." Riley gave Jess a high five, then gave Kelly an intense look. "Now, to the shower with you, *princesa*. I hear a shooting range calling your name."

Chapter 14

"This range is clear."

"Holy shit, Trill!" Kelly's eyes were still enormous as she, Riley, Trill, and Kenn made their way out of the shooting range. "Even my *dad* couldn't shoot like you."

"I will take that as the incredibly humbling compliment it is, little sis." Trill's dimples peeped as they all left the range. "Marksmanship has always fascinated me, even as a child. When I was five, my dad bought me my first BB gun. He filled milk cartons with sand and set them up against hay bales in our backyard so I could practice shooting. That was it for me—I was hooked." Trill's dimples deepened. "Besides, you're no fucking slouch yourself, Kel. Rowan told us you shot a 392 in pistol qualification simulations with your dad and I think you proved your skill today as well."

"Yep, 392 is awesome. 400, however, is fucking legendary," Kelly groused at Trill as the APS crew snickered at her pique. "Just you wait, Trill. I'm going to catch you one day."

"I don't fucking doubt that one bit, Kel." Trill smiled at her. "Your eye and your aim are virtually perfect. Your dad was a Marine so you already know this, little sis. Marines are riflemen first, before anything else, so good marksmanship is the most important skill of all." Trill smiled reflectively. "From the time we were really young, we all knew none of us had any interest in being career military. I think something like APS was already starting to be a dream for us by fifth grade. But I'll admit that, if I'd stayed in, I might have gone the sniper route like your dad." She winked at Kelly.

They all continued on in silence down the hallway toward the Bunker.

Riley touched the comm in her ear. "Kelly, Trill, Kenn, and I are headed toward the Bunker if any of the rest of you are around."

"Already here, fucker," Teagan said as they entered the office of the Seven. She stood up from her desk and went over to Kelly as Drew looked up from her own desk and smiled.

One by one, Bryn and the rest of the Seven joined them. Each one of them went to Kelly to hug her and kiss her on the cheek; then they each looked her over with sharp, assessing eyes, just as Casey had done to her in Hades.

"I need to talk to Rowan." Kelly's eyebrow was arched even though her eyes were soft. "She'll tell me if this is what it's like to have a bunch of bossy older siblings and an extremely overprotective butch in your life."

"This is exactly what it's like, *chula*," Jaime assured her. "Even though we've all agreed you know how to take care of yourself, it doesn't mean *tus hermanos*, your siblings, aren't going to look out for you."

Kelly's eyes grew softer.

Teagan patted the edge of her desk for Kelly and Riley helped her to jump up. Riley leaned against the desk next to her and wrapped one muscled arm around her waist.

"I was going to talk to Kelly when we got home tonight to update her on the situation with Percutio," Riley started. "I also wanted to talk to her about why we all want her to have 24/7 protection for right now." Kelly's eyes rounded.

"I decided that was a better conversation to have when we were all here. I got a chance to talk to Case this morning while Kelly was working with Jess in Hades, so I was able to update her about the conversation I had with that miserable fuck, Reizan, last night."

Casey growled and the rest of the Seven's eyes narrowed at her reaction.

"However, I haven't seen the rest of you until now, and since I also needed to bring Kelly up to speed, I figured we should just do it all at the same time."

Riley's arm tightened around Kelly as she turned to look directly in Kelly's eyes. "Baby, you know more about covert and clandestine operations than just about anyone else here at APS. You also know who Reizan and Percutio are, on a much deeper level than most people will ever know. As much as I want to protect you because you're my woman," the corners of Riley's mouth tilted up slightly, "and as much as your siblings here want to wrap you in cotton wool and put you on a high shelf somewhere to keep you out of harm's way, we know we can't do that."

"The fuck we can't," muttered Blake savagely before she sighed. "But we won't."

Kelly let her soft eyes drift over each face.

"I promise each of you, from the bottom of my heart, I will never do anything reckless or foolhardy, nor will I ever do anything that might put myself in danger in any way if I can possibly avoid it," Kelly said from her heart. "I will always make sure I have one of you—or associates from your crews—around me for protection unless I am with Riley. When I left because I'd found out I'd been burned by the CIA, and I thought I was keeping *you* all safe from Percutio by leaving," Kelly hesitated for a moment before she continued, "I told Rowan that you'd kept her safe for me when I couldn't be here with her...so, I was going to return the favor and keep you all safe for her."

"*Princesa*," Riley murmured, rubbing her shoulder as Bryn and the Seven looked at her with eyes filled with respect and a new love.

"I didn't understand then that I don't have to do that alone anymore. I can be a viable and contributing member of this team *without* putting myself in danger solo." Kelly's eyes grew shiny, then she grinned impishly. "Or without giving my sister a heart attack."

The entire APS management team burst out laughing, the tension broken.

"Also," Kelly's eyebrows lifted, "I suspect there has been more than one conversation recently about staying away from any mention of my gift, or never discussing how my ability can be leveraged in APS operations."

The room was dead silent as everyone froze.

"Guys." Kelly sighed. "There is a *big* difference between being used as an asset as if your memory ability is the only thing you're good for and being valued for *all* of your abilities because you as a person contributes to the success of your team as a whole. I know you all understand I'm way more than just my gift. You honor my ability to fight, and you acknowledge my experience in clandestine and covert operations. You can't wait to teach me how to do things from an APS perspective, like breach a physical location," she grinned at Jaime, who grinned back at her, "or teach me Krav Maga, or explain telecommunications and how it relates to what we do here at APS…

"I am *so* much more to you than just an eidetic memory dump like I was for the CIA. Or a womb so some pansy-assed, piece of shit motherfucker, like that numbfuck at Percutio, can try to create an army for his own greed." Kelly snorted. "Good luck with that, asshole, because my family will fucking *annihilate* you if you dare to touch me."

She looked around at each one of them as they nodded at her with cold, resolute faces.

"Just like Trill is a fucking godsend with technical security, or Blake can sharpen our crews and their fighting abilities because she fucking *owns* that sim, or Drew can track anything in Purgatory while scaring the shit out of anyone who has even remotely heard of the Shadow, etc. I simply have my own ability to contribute." She smiled and shrugged. "Let's use it when and where it makes sense, just like we do with the rest of you." Kelly's face was bright. "It doesn't have to be the elephant in the room. Bryn, let Ro know she can talk about it with us however much she wants, okay?"

"Thank you, Kel." Bryn nodded at her. "Rowan would have never in a million years betrayed your confidence and I know you know that."

"Let's talk about that miserable Percutio fuck, then. Riles, I'm turning the mic over to you." Kelly put her head on Riley's shoulder, glad to be done talking now that everything was out in the open.

"Thank you, *mi princesa*. I, for one, am glad as fuck we have no more secrets between us. Welcome to APS, baby." Riley kissed her hard as everyone clapped and hollered.

"I haven't had the opportunity to talk to my twin yet," Riley began when the moment was over, "but I'm liking the idea of having you float between the teams for now, Red. I think you'll get a good overview of the entire APS structure better that way."

"I like it, too. Plus," Bryn added dryly, "that way, none of these fuckers gets the monopoly on your time and attention, Kel, and Riles and I won't have to put up with any goddamn whining." Kelly snickered as seven middle fingers shot into the air in perfect sync.

"I called Reizan last night to let him know Kelly is now mine, she belongs to me and APS, and that he and Percutio had best keep their distance if they want to keep their lives." Riley rapidly got down to business. "Reizan kept assuring me they had no intention of being a threat to Kelly in any way. However, I call bullshit, *mi corillo*. I told Casey that motherfucker was almost salivating when I brought her name up."

"Riles also said it's evident Reizan and his gang of fucks have some type of plan regarding Kelly and her gift," Casey chimed in. "Trill and Jaime are digging for info. Red?"

"Yes?"

"Can you get us the names of the CIA individuals who are aware of your ability? I imagine there aren't many."

"I could," Kelly answered slowly, thinking hard, "but with the way my directorate did things, I guarantee you I was given maybe seventy percent of the agency names. The rest of the names were kept hidden by the higher-ups. However…"

Kelly interrupted the cursing that had started. The management team subsided, listening.

She looked at Riley with sorrow in her eyes. "I told you Robyn was a great fucking analyst. And she was, one of the absolute best. She was like a dog with a bone once she got her teeth into something. One day, right before she was murdered, I came home and found her working on a document, being all secretive. It was handwritten, like she didn't even trust it to be available electronically. When I asked her what it was, she kind of stammered a little bit and said it was nothing."

Kelly smiled, her eyes glassy.

"Robyn couldn't lie for shit, but I decided not to press her on it. We'd been getting along better after all the fighting we'd been doing over Percutio, and I didn't want to shatter the peace. She put the document away, we went out to dinner, I forgot about it, and then she was killed a few weeks later. That document was in Robyn's personal papers, which I have." Kelly took a deep breath and her voice quavered slightly. "They're with the stuff Rowan and I had shipped directly to our new house a couple of months ago. I've never looked at any of Robyn's papers since the day I got them right after her funeral. It was… It was just too hard."

"*Princesa.*" Riley's voice was extremely gentle as she stroked Kelly's back soothingly. "Would this document be the only one of Robyn's that would have been handwritten?" Kelly swallowed and nodded.

"Robyn never wrote *anything* by hand. She always used her laptop."

"Do you know where the document is now?"

"I do, actually, because Robyn was very organized. At my new house, there's a manila file folder in the box with all my papers that's labeled *Personal Correspondence*. That hand-written document was in there."

Blake and Drew were already moving.

"Umm, I don't have the keys to my house yet." Kelly stopped, then rolled her eyes. "Wait a minute. What am I fucking thinking?" she muttered as the two of them vanished out of the Bunker. She shook her head. "Anyhow, there's no guarantee this is even related, but my spidey sense says it just might be. I don't know what she was working on or why she was being so fucking secretive. But," Kelly's eyes were cynical, "I guess since I wasn't exactly being forthcoming, she was entitled to keep her own secrets, right?"

Chapter 15

About forty-five minutes after Blake and Drew had left, Kelly was starting to tell the APS crew the details around how she'd been burned by the CIA when their comms went off.

Kelly froze as black, enraged thunder hit every face. The APS crew listened for several minutes to whoever was on the other end of the comms.

"What's her status?" Riley's voice was calm, although filled with wrath. Kelly pulled in a horrified breath.

They silently listened for another minute. Muscles relaxed infinitesimally, which Kelly took as a good sign, although she still didn't know what had happened.

"But you have it?" Riley paused for a moment. "Good." She blew out a deep breath and pinched the bridge of her nose. "I guess this means we need to call Vince and a motherfucking cleanup crew, though. Tell Drew to hit the infirmary when she gets here."

Kelly felt her eyes get huge.

"Report in when you get here as well, Blake. I know you have to wait for Vince so you can tell him what happened, and then wait for our cleanup crew to get there, too. Tell Vince I'm going to call him later about this entire clusterfuck. And tell that fucker, Hollister, I'm tired of her taking hits to the same goddamn arm. The least she could do is change it up every once in a while and make it fucking interesting."

Bryn snorted and the entire crew relaxed.

"I'll see you shortly." Riley touched her comm, then looked immediately at Kelly. "Baby." Riley's voice was extremely gentle and she rubbed Kelly's shoulder. "She's just fine, but Drew was the target of some gunfire when she and Blake went to leave your house after they found Robyn's document."

Kelly nodded impassively, waiting for more details.

"They grazed her upper right arm, which totally pissed her the fuck off, and she and Blake returned fire. There is now a dead motherfucker in your side yard, unfortunately. The other assholes fled on foot." Riley pinched the bridge of her nose again. "We have a couple of APS associates guarding the body already just in case some fucking asshole decides it's a good idea to play David Copperfield and make the body disappear. Vince, our police chief, has units coming on scene and Blake is waiting there to give a statement."

Suddenly, Riley laughed with relieved humor and shook her head.

"Blake is going to give Drew such a fucking rash of shit for this. Drew gets to ventilate some dickhead and Blake gets stuck with the admin piece of it." There were equally relieved chuckles around the room.

"But she's okay?" Kelly asked tentatively, still a little worried about Drew.

"She's absolutely fine, baby, I promise. She's going to add another interesting scar to the ones she already has, but it won't even be enough to brag about." Riley caressed Kelly's cheek.

"Blake has Robyn's document safely sealed in a waterproof pouch and zipped away in the side pocket of her cargo pants." Riley frowned. "I'd like to fucking know how they found out about that document, considering there was never even a digital footprint, but we'll unravel all of that when Blake gets back. I also want to know who the fuck 'they' are who's causing all this bullshit. Is it solely Percutio? Is it the CIA mole and their friends? Is it a joint venture between the two? Is there another player we aren't yet aware of? Why is Robyn's document so fascinating all of a sudden?"

"Maybe because no one knew about its existence for a long time," said Kelly slowly, thinking hard. "If Percutio's involved and I'm the attraction because of my gift, it would make sense it's only bubbling up now, since Reizan didn't have the first fucking clue about what I can do until about five months ago."

"Which is probably why Robyn's document lay undisturbed for so long," Teagan mused thoughtfully. "No one even knew it existed back then."

"But what triggered the avalanche? How did Reizan even find out about the document? How do we know there's anything of value in it at all, considering Robyn—to my knowledge—didn't know the first thing about my eidetic memory ability? *I* certainly didn't tell her because I was ordered not to tell *anyone*." Kelly drummed her fingers on the table.

"Robyn's document had been tucked away in a manila folder in my Virginia bedroom for almost two years. As far as I could tell, no one knew I had it. I would have been willing to bet no one even fucking knew it existed except for me."

"Someone else knew about it, *princesa*. Even if they didn't, they were able to connect the dots well enough to suspect Robyn had created such a document." Riley steepled her fingers. "It apparently took them this long to figure out where a document like that might be. You were in Woodbridge, then you were in Langley, now you're down here in Whimsy. They had a lot of tracking to do." Riley was pensive. "My money says they want to know what's in it just in case it contains something above and beyond what they've always known or suspected."

"Robyn could have told whoever this person is herself." Trill threw that speculation out. "I know she was your fiancée, Kel, and she was clearly as honorable as all get out. But could she have been worried enough about you that she would have confided in someone else without your knowledge?"

"My initial reaction would be to say no fucking way, but... I guess maybe she could have, if she was worried enough." Kelly thought about it. "Actually, I can think of a handful of people we both worked with for years whom she might have felt comfortable confiding in. Honestly, I think Robyn's document is going to prove to be a dead end, though. If Robyn finally did figure out my eidetic memory ability two years ago, her document probably details all of that information. That document would have been fucking *explosive* two years ago, when Reizan was still in the dark about my gift." Kelly sighed. "But today? When I've known for almost six months that Reizan already knows every fucking detail about what I can do?"

"I hate to say this, baby, but I think you're right." Riley continued to soothingly stroke up and down Kelly's back. "I'm betting Reizan wanted Robyn's document just to make sure he wasn't missing anything."

"However… What we don't know? Who is the motherfucking mole that's been planted?" Casey was steaming. "Because that son of a bitch is feeding intel to Reizan about Kelly's movements, and we know that motherfucker is scheming to get his filthy paws on her."

"Or, at least he or she *was* feeding Reizan intel," Kenn pondered. "Wanna bet he was the asshole responsible for having Red burned, thinking she'd end up being alone and vulnerable? Making it way too fucking easy for Percutio to snap her up…or so he thought."

"When, in fact," Teagan smiled, not a very nice smile, "our intrepid girl reporter here has been safely surrounded by miles and miles of metaphorical barbed wire fence." Kelly laughed at Teagan, unable to help herself.

"Let's wait 'til Blake gets here and I can finally read Robyn's document," she suggested. "It will point us in the direction we need to go once we know what's in it for sure." Everyone nodded in agreement. Then Kelly smirked. "First, we'll give Blake a minute to whine and snark and cuss Drew out, of course."

There were snickers of agreement.

"Oh, and I want one of those ear comms, too," she stated firmly. "Being out of the loop while all this was going down was no fun. If I'm going to be scared to death because one of you has stepped in some shit, I want to know why on the spot."

"I got you, little sis." Teagan rapidly sent a text. "Remy, my number two, is going to take care of it." Kelly smiled at her gratefully.

Riley caressed Kelly's shoulder. "Why don't you finish the story about your handler calling you and telling you you'd been burned by the CIA while we're waiting for Blake, *princesa*."

"Oh. Right," Kelly remembered. She leaned more securely into Riley's side. "Where was I? Oh yeah…so McAllister, my handler, tells me there had been growing concern in the upper ranks of the CIA about my gift and its potential to make me 'unstable,' as he called it."

"Wait. What the fuck?" Trill was pissed. "Do those fucking idiots even understand how an eidetic memory works? Yeah, okay… Kelly was given a permanent medical disqualification so she wasn't eligible to join the Marines or any branch of the armed services. It absolutely fucking sucks, but you can, unfortunately, understand why having an extreme eidetic memory like Kelly does might possibly interfere with a soldier's ability to engage in combat when a situation has gone hot."

Kelly nodded begrudgingly.

Trill was growing angrier. "But in a position such as that of an information analyst? Even if you're engaging in covert or clandestine operations, the idea of someone with an eidetic memory—in those circumstances—becoming unstable is so remote as to be laughable."

"Not to mention the fact it took the CIA eight years after I was hired to come to that conclusion," Kelly said dryly. "Especially since I'd spent months upon months taking a fucking battery of tests and going through numerous psychological evaluations before the CIA would even begin the actual hiring process."

"Something's fucking rotten with that whole situation." Casey was still heated. Rumbles began to fill the room.

Suddenly, Trill put up her hand and everyone fell quiet.

"Jaime. Maybe we've been going about this the wrong way, cuz," Trill said slowly. Jaime looked at her with a question in her eyes as Trill paused and regarded Kelly thoughtfully.

"Kel…we originally thought that if we could get the names of the individuals who were actually authorized to know about your ability, we could then back into the names of those who aren't supposed to know but do."

"And that would have been a great thought if I could tell you the name of every single person who knew about my ability." Kelly sighed, frustrated. "But I can't."

"Maybe it doesn't matter now, especially since the dumbass cut the CIA off from you completely by burning you."

The APS team listened to Trill closely.

Trill explained. "The mole expected he was going to leave Kelly vulnerable by isolating her like that, but she surprised the hell out of him by becoming a part of APS instead. That probably pissed him off to high heaven and put him in a really bad position to boot. He's probably losing his mind, trying to figure out a way to reestablish contact with Kelly before APS contacts the CIA—or so he assumes we will—and his higher-ups find out he fucked up in a big way."

Riley's voice was like ice. "What are the chances he's been making up a bunch of bullshit about Kelly's performance over the past six months? And he finally accumulated enough false reports to be able to go to her superiors and say, *Hey. I hate to say this, because she's been a damn fine operative in the past, but it appears Kelly Holland has become unstable over the past several months. We can't, as a matter of national security, have an operative we can't trust undertaking covert and clandestine operations.* So they burned her."

"I'll fucking kill him." Kelly was livid.

Calming herself, Riley kissed her femme's temple and stroked her back soothingly. "The CIA can't have you back anyway, *princesa*, but we will make sure your name gets cleared and that fucker gets buried in a twenty-foot deep pile of shit."

"Thank you, *mi amante*." Kelly kissed Riley's surprised face, then whispered into Riley's ear, "I figured learning how to say *my lover* in Spanish was appropriate, don't you think?" Riley wrapped her muscled arms around Kelly and kissed her temple again.

Trill smiled slowly, a smile full of menace. "Maybe we should create a tiny, tiny breach so numbnuts thinks he's found a way to contact Kelly then. I'm assuming your handler would report the breach, Kel?"

Kelly snorted. "Alan is so fucking by the book he probably consults our corporate manual so he can follow proper procedure on how to take a shit."

Teagan was already swiftly texting instructions to various associates. "You needed an APS phone anyway, Red. We'll set it up so any CIA contact—or any contact at all, really—will simply think they were downloaded from your old contacts list. Remy and my crew are on it. The only thing anyone will be able to do is call or text that number. Any other attempt at access of any kind will be denied. They'd be too suspicious otherwise." Teagan grinned at Kelly. "I should be having you do this, Wonder Girl. I still remember scanning Rowan's phone deep the first time she came to APS. Trill and I lost our shit over how secure it was."

Kelly winked at the two of them.

Just then, the door opened and Blake came in.

"Fucker is just finishing up in the infirmary. She'll be right in. Turns out she needed two stitches." Blake rolled her eyes as she made her way to her desk. "I told her that was some pansy-ass shit. Two goddamn stitches? She might as well have been bitten in the ass by a dog."

Kelly ducked her head and tried not to laugh as the rest of the team snorted. When she straightened up, she found Blake's twinkling eyes on her.

"Got something for you, Red." She unzipped the side pocket of her cargo pants and extracted a handwritten document in a waterproof pouch, several pages thick.

Kelly took the document from Blake and pulled it out of the pouch. Her heart contracted as she recognized Robyn's small, neat penmanship and her eyes grew shiny. Riley tightened her arm around her in support.

"Little sis?" Casey's kind, gentle voice reached her. "You take your time, okay? There's no pressure. We're all here for you, for as long as you need."

Kelly blew out a deep breath and visibly pulled herself together.

"I could never bring myself to read this." Her voice was sad. "It was in one of Robyn's personal files that I was given after her funeral and I... I just couldn't. Everything was too much of an emotional minefield then. The thought of reading through her personal papers when we had just buried her? There was *no* fucking way." She sat quietly for a moment, then said, "I'm going to read this straight through. I don't want to digest too much the first time around, if that makes any sense. I just want to absorb it on a more superficial level first."

"Makes perfect sense, *princesa*." Riley kissed her temple again. "You read, we'll wait, and then we'll all try to make sense of it together."

Suddenly, the door to the Bunker opened again and Drew came in. The edge of a white bandage showed under the right arm of her T-shirt, which was apparently new.

"Dickhead bastard ruined my favorite T-shirt," Drew said in greeting, clearly still pissed, as she made her way over to her desk. "Now, the numbfuck gets to push up daisies as payback."

Kelly's eyes widened.

"Little sis." Drew looked at Kelly speculatively as she sat down with a slight grunt. "Are you doing okay?"

Kelly was speechless for a moment, then her green eyes narrowed. "*Broki*," she said, repeating the Spanish word she'd heard often from Riley. "What the fuck? *I'm* not the one who took a goddamn bullet to the arm."

"*Two. Stitches,*" Blake mouthed silently at Kelly with a smirk as she caught the whiteboard eraser Drew launched like a missile at her head with her left hand.

"Pfffttt." Drew rolled her eyes after Blake subsided. "That useless piece of shit couldn't hit the broad side of a barn. He barely grazed me. It's all good, little sis." Drew narrowed her eyes in turn. "Now, let's try this again. Are you all right, Red?"

"I was just about to read Robyn's document," Kelly admitted after a small pause. She sighed and rested her head on Riley's shoulder for a moment before she straightened up again. "I'm glad you're here and okay, Drew." Kelly's voice was calm as she looked down at Robyn's document. "Now, we can all find out what Robyn wrote together."

There was dead silence in the Bunker as Kelly settled herself, took another deep breath, and quietly began to read.

The longer Kelly read and the deeper she got into the document, however, the paler she grew. The twins and the Seven looked uneasily at each other as Kelly continued to read, and her hands eventually began to shake a bit.

"*Princesa.*" Riley folded her own large hands over Kelly's smaller ones when she reached the end of the document and stared unseeing at nothing. "Your hands are like ice." She caught a bottle of water that Kenn tossed to her and uncapped it. "Drink this, baby."

Riley helped Kelly to hold the water bottle as she drank deeply. When Kelly was done, she closed her eyes and dropped her head in disbelief.

"Everyone is very worried about you right now, *princesa*. Can you let us know what has you so disturbed so we can all walk through it together?" Riley held her woman tightly and rubbed the backs of her arms with a comforting gesture, warming her.

"Riley." Kelly's voice choked. She raised her head and stared at her butch incredulously. "I can't… I can't believe it. I just…"

She looked at Riley with eyes that were slightly shell-shocked and swallowed.

"It's Alan McAllister, Riley. Alan McAllister is the Percutio mole. He has to be."

Chapter 16

"Alan McAllister? That makes no goddamn sense, baby." Riley continued rubbing Kelly's arms as she clearly tried to understand. "Robyn died two years ago. McAllister has only been a CIA handler for what, six months?"

Kelly's head was spinning as an avalanche of information hit her like a ton of bricks. She held up a finger as she took a couple of minutes to put her thoughts in order.

Finally, she said, "Follow me here, okay?" She closed her eyes again. "Robyn died two years ago. Harvey Stich, my boss and handler at the time, retired about a year after she died. Then I had an interim handler for about five or six months before Alan was assigned permanently to me."

Kenn stood up and went over to the whiteboard. She started diagraming the timeline as Kelly talked.

"It looks like McAllister wasn't even in the picture when Robyn wrote her document, Kel." Casey gestured to the whiteboard. "From every standpoint I can see, he was never aware that document had been created at all. You said yourself that the document has been stored in your bedroom for the last two years." The platinum-haired team lead was struggling to understand.

Kelly's face was pale. "We thought no one else knew about it until five or six months ago, right? But we've also said there was a very real possibility Robyn had found someone to confide in, trying to make sense of things. In her document, she mentions talking to her good friend *Alan* on several occasions, someone who was a fellow analyst." Understanding started to dawn across everyone's face. "At the end, Robyn *had* figured out that I had an eidetic memory, and a pretty extreme one at that. She'd also determined the CIA was using me and my ability to gather information that could be used against Percutio."

"Wouldn't you have known McAllister was also an analyst back then?" Trill asked curiously.

Kelly blew out another deep breath. "Not necessarily, Trill. There are seven different known CIA directorates—or divisions—and hundreds of analysts at Langley. Robyn and I had only ever been assigned to the same project one time, which was how we met. After that project was over, however, we never worked together again because we were in different directorates—plus our skill sets were just too different. The fact that we even had that one project together was a complete fluke."

"I'm sorry, little sis. I'm still not following." Drew was patient.

Kelly steepled her fingers. "Robyn and Alan knew each other because they worked in the same directorate—the DA, or the Directorate of Analysis. The DA is the analytical branch of the CIA, responsible for the production and dissemination of data. As a result, their skill sets were so similar, they were often assigned to the same projects and worked together a lot. Okay?"

The APS management team nodded.

"In contrast, I was in the DO, or the Directorate of Operations. It's also known as the Clandestine Service, and is one of the smallest components of the CIA. We were responsible for clandestine operations. Alan and I didn't know each other back then because we were in *completely* different directorates. Plus, our skill sets were dissimilar enough that the chances we would ever be assigned to the same project were between slim and none ... even in the unlikely event of another cross-directorate project. Still with me?"

The crew listened intently, nodding again.

Riley laughed under her breath and rubbed Kelly's arm. "And here my twin and I were betting on you belonging to the Special Activities Division, *princesa*."

The entire team grew still and alert when Kelly's body abruptly reared up on the desk where she was sitting and her face grew paper white. "Who's been talking to you about SAD, Riley? Where in the fuck did that come from?" Kelly's body started to shake as her eyes widened into enormous pools of panic.

"Whoa, *princesa, whoa*. Simmer down, baby." Riley wrapped her arms tightly around Kelly and rubbed Kelly's arms again in an effort to calm her femme. Kelly buried her face in Riley's throat as Riley gently shushed her and tried to still the heartbeat that was thundering against her. The rest of the team stayed alert, keeping a close eye on Kelly with worry on their faces.

"Kel." Bryn's voice was quiet, looking at her twin in concern. "Riles and I were just speculating before you even got to Whimsy, and we talked to the Seven about it a little bit. No one's said anything to anyone, I promise you. And we aren't going to fucking say anything now. You're our sister, you're my twin's woman, and it will be a cold goddamn day in hell before we betray any of your secrets."

Riley loosened her grip when she felt Kelly relax a bit, but she continued to rub Kelly's back. "*Princesa*, are you trying to tell me you were a part of the covert operations branch of SAD?" She dropped a calming kiss on the top of Kelly's head, then rubbed her woman's arms some more.

"N-n-not exactly." Kelly spent a minute breathing and bringing her heart rate down, before finally taking in a huge breath. "SAD operatives are typically former military, which you know I am not. But I do—did—have a dotted line to the covert branch of SAD, because of my ability, and because of the mission they were planning—to launch a full-scale attack on Percutio."

She lifted her head and turned to face everyone again. Seeing the concern on everyone's face, Kelly tried to smile.

"You all need to understand that the CIA had absolutely *no* idea what to do with me, especially as I got deeper and deeper into covert and clandestine operations. I am, for lack of a better term, one of a kind. They didn't have any experience dealing with anyone who could do what I did and, in some ways, they were just making it up as they went along. Some of the higher-ups at the CIA weren't exactly supportive of using my gift in covert or clandestine operations at first, either. One of the directors flat-out told me he didn't believe in any of my 'woo-woo' shit." Kelly's smile was not nice. "He was transferred overseas when I casually let his remarks slip to Harvey Stich, who was my handler at the time. I told Stich maybe I needed to think about going elsewhere if that was the general perception of my abilities."

Jaime snorted. "Good for you, *hermana*."

"Asshole," Drew muttered under her breath, her pissed-off expression matching everyone else's.

"I was technically an analyst in the DO, though. Very, very few people knew I was involved with SAD in any way." Kelly looked abashed. "I'm sorry, guys. I didn't mean to freak out like that, but it was so unexpected."

"Don't you *dare* apologize, little sis. That would have been enough to fucking knock anyone for a loop," Kenn said vehemently, and the rest of the Seven rumbled in agreement. Kelly drew back, astonished at their protectiveness.

Riley continued to stroke Kelly's back. "Continue, *princesa*. You were telling us that Robyn had figured out your eidetic memory ability."

Kelly nodded and resumed her story. "Robyn sees I'm being sent out of town way more often than she is—than virtually any other analyst is—and she eventually grows suspicious. At first, she had no idea I'm being leveraged for my eidetic memory gift. But she doesn't like anything about what she's been seeing. The only thing I was ever assigned to was Percutio projects, which was highly irregular. She decides she's going to get to the bottom of whatever's going on. So, she starts investigating. Along the way, she confides in her good friend Alan because she doesn't have me to talk to and she needs an outlet."

Kelly's eyes were sad.

"At the very end, she *did* figure out I have an extreme eidetic memory ability, and that I was being leveraged as a big fucking asset because of it. But she's murdered by Reizan's goons before she can confront me about it."

Kelly paused for a couple of moments to get herself back under control.

"Reizan, that useless fuck, had Robyn murdered because he saw she was getting too close to Percutio secrets. It had nothing to do with me personally because Reizan didn't have a fucking clue who I was or what I could do back then."

"McAllister knew, though, because Robyn had confided in him." Drew's voice was ice cold. "What I don't get is why he sat on the information for eighteen months before doing anything about it."

"Because he was nothing more than a low-level analyst back then," Trill said slowly, thinking hard. "You think Reizan would have risked accepting an overture from a dime a dozen grunt like McAllister, especially one from the CIA? There's no fucking way."

She continued speculating. "Robyn's figured out Kelly has an eidetic memory that's head and shoulders above what a typical eidetic memory is…but then Robyn is murdered by Percutio.

McAllister knows Kel's secret as well, but he's not in a position to do anything about it without potentially putting his own life at risk for attempting to establish contact with Reizan. McAllister saw what happened to Robyn. He knew Reizan was a ruthless son of a bitch, so McAllister wasn't about to put his own cock on the line."

"Until," Riley's voice went arctic, "McAllister is promoted into the position of CIA handler, a pretty big fucking jump. I'll bet you any money he contacted Reizan then—since he had more juice at that point—and spilled his fucking guts about Kelly and her ability, including the hereditary piece of it."

Riley looked directly at Kelly, a dark look in her eyes. "He most likely assured Reizan that if *he* could be assigned as your handler, he could make sure Reizan had a clear path to you so he could grab you and use you for himself."

"That's why none of this shit bubbled up until about five months ago." Kenn was clearly unhappy. "McAllister didn't contact Reizan until after he was promoted to handler, and then it took Reizan a little while to get his ducks in a row."

"I imagine Reizan thought he'd hit the motherfucking jackpot." Bryn exchanged an icy glare with Riley. "An asset with a goddamn solid gold eidetic memory capability he could steal for himself to further his criminal empire. Plus, an asset who also has genetic reproduction potential, so his empire can just keep going on and on and on."

"That asshole was probably jacking off with happiness." Blake was savage.

"But McAllister fucked up." Teagan's tone turned malignant. "He'd set Kelly up to be burned by the CIA, by making it seem as though she had become unstable and was no longer trustworthy. He figured by doing that, he would leave her unprotected and vulnerable, and then Percutio would have a clear shot at her."

"The fucking dickhead didn't count on APS bringing Kelly into our fold and surrounding her with our protection so they couldn't get to her." Jaime, who had been quiet up until now, gave a slight, chilling smile. "He has to be pissing in his pants, *mi corillo*. Reizan knows for sure that Kelly belongs to Riley and APS now, especially because Riles called Reizan last night and threatened his life if he so much as dares to look at Red funny."

Trill nodded. "If McAllister can't find a way to reestablish any type of direct contact with Kelly—considering he was the one responsible for having Kelly burned and officially disowned by the CIA in the first place—Reizan will have McAllister's dick whacked off."

"Small job," muttered Blake cynically. The crew snorted.

Kelly was pensive. "I'd like each of you to read Robyn's document, if you would. That way, we'll all be on the same page, and I'll be confident we didn't miss anything because we'll all have had eyes on it then. We'll also keep it here at APS so it stays safe and those dickheads can't get their hands on it."

The entire crew nodded in agreement.

"That's a great idea," Kenn said.

Kelly relaxed against the comfort of Riley's muscled arm around her. "What in the hell would I do without you guys now?" She smiled at them all with emotion in her eyes. "I mean… of course, I know how to bury myself and wipe my trail." Her eyes shone with humor as she tried to inject a little levity into the situation. "If it wasn't for my smart-ass and way-too-intelligent big sister, you would have never found me the first time."

Kelly looked at Bryn and smiled as everyone laughed, then she looked around the room.

"But I'm thinking I like being safe with you all a lot better." She beamed at the soft, caring faces being aimed in her direction.

"Speaking of Rowan, *hermana*, she is chomping at the bit to see you." Bryn smiled at her future sister-in-law. "I know you are both going out with your friends Friday night, but maybe Riley and I can take the two most beautiful women in the world out to lunch that day."

"Flatterer." Kelly laughed at Bryn, touched, and felt herself completely relax for the first time in hours. "We can do that. In the meantime… Teag, let me know when my APS phone is ready and we'll set our trap."

"Remy's on her way with your new phone and your ear comm right now, Red," Teagan informed her. "I don't remember if you've met Remy yet, but she's my number two in the telecommunications crew. She and Clementine have been dating for a few weeks."

"I know, God help her." Kelly rolled her eyes. "Don't get me wrong. I love Clem to absolute pieces and I'd do anything for her. But I'd probably kill her if I had to date her."

Teagan smirked. "No worries, little sis. Rem has it all under control. You weren't here, but when all the shit with that dickhead, Coravani, was going down, Remy taught Clementine a very valuable lesson on what happens when a femme puts herself in danger around an APS alpha butch."

Kelly felt her jaw go kerplunk. "And Clem didn't kill her?" she asked, looking at the twins and the Seven in total amazement.

"Apparently, Clem responds to alpha butches. Many strong femmes do." Teagan crossed her muscular arms and looked pointedly at her.

"Moving right along," Kelly muttered, avoiding Riley's eyes but feeling her amusement. "Anyhow," she decided to ignore her butch, "since we're in *Ask and thou shalt receive* mode—and I'm taking total advantage of that right now—I want a desk here in the Bunker." Her smirk at Riley and Bryn was flippant. "And a laptop and whatever else all the badasses get. Oh, and some APS polo shirts would be nice, too."

"*Yassssss.*" Blake and Jaime grinned and gave each other a high five. "Little sis is moving in! This is going to be so fucking epic."

Riley arched an eyebrow at her femme. "Why do you think you need all that, *princesa*?" she asked Kelly in surprise. "What are you envisioning as your role here?"

Kelly quickly became serious.

"I'm not used to being idle, Riley," she said quietly. "I've either had school or a job since I was eighteen years old. And then one day, in the blink of an eye, it was all gone. Everything I had identified with in my adult life had disappeared without warning."

The Bunker was quiet.

"I can't live without a purpose, *amante*. I know I can be useful here, given time, even if my usefulness doesn't mean much initially." Kelly paused for a minute until she was sure her voice was steady. "I like your idea of having me rotate between the crews so I can learn about APS. I don't expect access to anything major, Riley. Just basic information, enough so I can learn and grow."

"Baby." Riley's voice was equally quiet. "There isn't a thing the Seven has access to that we wouldn't trust you with. Only personnel records and things like that will be restricted, like they are for everyone, simply because of legal and privacy concerns. My hesitation is only because I don't *ever* want you to feel we are expecting too much from you." Riley caressed her arm. "I know you are a hard worker, *princesa*, and you have already been extremely useful. I've also seen how goddamn fast you learn."

Riley tilted Kelly's chin so she could look fully into her eyes.

"But I want to make sure you know the one thing we will *not* do is take advantage of you the way the fucking CIA did." Everyone else voiced their unanimous consent.

Kelly smiled. "I already know that," she assured Riley and the others in the Bunker. "But it's important to me that I pull my own weight, just like everyone else does. If you think Bill Holland didn't drill *that* into my head, you didn't know him as well as you thought you did."

"I don't think there's a person in this room who will ever fucking forget *anything* Bill Holland drilled into their head," said Bryn dryly as everyone laughed.

"Fair enough, baby," said Riley. "We'll get maintenance to put an extra desk in here for you, have Daniela order you a new laptop, and Teag will have someone from her crew wire you in. Then you and I can spend a day going over our systems so you can start learning where everything is."

"We're running at six a.m. tomorrow, then meeting with Jess in Hades right after, Kel," Casey reminded her.

Trill tapped a few keys on her laptop. "My primary home is in the Recon Room, little sis, although I do have a desk down here," she told Kelly. "After you're done with Jess, we'll meet here and figure out a new rotation schedule for you."

Just then, a knock came at the door.

"It must be Rem." Teagan got her feet. "Just as an FYI, Red, only the twins and the Seven have access to the Bunker. Now, you will, too." She opened the door to reveal a dark-haired butch, about Kelly's height, with striking blue-green eyes and a pleasant smile standing there.

"Hey, Rem." Teag ushered her number two into the Bunker.

"Kelly, this is Remy. Remy, Kelly." Teagan introduced them and they shook hands. "Beware, Rem. Kelly is one of Clementine's best friends, along with Rowan, so you'll have all three of them to deal with."

Remy laughed, comfortable and clearly unperturbed. "I think we'll be okay, Teag. I like girls who are as fierce about their friendships with each other as these three are, from what I've heard from Clem. Kelly, I have your ear comm and your phone." Remy handed a small box to Teagan. "Teag and Riley can check them to make sure they're set up the way they want, then they can pass them along to you. You should be all set.

"I've already downloaded the phone numbers for the Armstrong twins, the Seven, me, and Jess—because I know you've been working with her—and Clem and Rowan. Beyond that, I'm going to leave it for you guys to figure out." Remy smiled. "It was good to meet you, Red. I need to run to a meeting, so I have to bail, but you make sure you call me if you need anything, okay?"

"Nicknames travel fast in this place," Kelly muttered as Remy laughed.

She left after Kelly had thanked her for setting everything up for her. Kelly tried unsuccessfully to stifle a yawn, her body still worn out, which everyone in the Bunker caught immediately.

"Okay, *princesa*, you're done." Riley swept her off the desk and tucked her into her side. "You're still healing, and we aren't going to risk you getting sick because we pushed you too fast. We're going home, we'll order something for dinner, then we'll make sure you have a really good night's sleep. Teag can make sure your electronics are fully wired—which, knowing Remy, they're already perfect—then Teag will set the breach tonight. Casey can give you your phone and your ear comm in the morning when you meet up for your run."

Riley kissed Kelly's temple. "We'll meet her in the reception area at six o'clock tomorrow morning. After you run, she can bring you to Hades so you and Jess can work on your Krav Maga training. I'll bring you back up to our apartment so you can grab a shower and then we can meet Trill back here in the Bunker to talk about our rotation schedule."

Kelly huffed. "Rowan was right. Bossy." A wicked grin crossed Riley's face as Bryn and the Seven snickered.

"That's right, baby." Riley looked at Kelly intently and smirked. "All the APS butches are bossy as fuck. And don't you ever forget it."

Chapter 17

"Ro-Ro, this looks spectacular."

Kelly and Rowan stood in the middle of their house with Ember, their architect, and Nia, their contractor, watching as Nia's crew finished up the final changes Rowan had requested.

Teagan, Remy, and Shelby—who was also from Teagan's crew—were there as well, talking to Bryn and Riley about the security system APS was going to install.

Earlier, Riley and Bryn had taken Kelly and Rowan out to lunch as promised, opting to go a bit farther afield than Whimsy, and taking them to an amazing little beachfront cafe on St. Pete Beach.

* * * * *

"Bryn took me here for lunch last week and I loved it," Rowan had informed her little sister as they were driving to a favorite APS place called Cafe Vinales. "They have real food, too, not just protein and rabbit food like these two eat." She cast her eyes heavenward as Kelly snickered.

Bryn had caught Rowan's eyes in her rearview mirror, her own eyes promising all sorts of delicious retribution. "I don't hear you complaining about my body while we're in bed, *dulzura*," she said, smirking as Rowan blushed.

"What does that mean? *Dulzura*?" Kelly asked, changing the subject in an effort to help her sister out. "It's not a stretch to figure out that *princesa* means princess, but *dulzura* doesn't seem to have an English equivalent, phonetically speaking."

"It doesn't. *Dulzura* means 'sweetness' in Spanish." Bryn glanced at her fiancée again in the rearview mirror. "I've called Rowan that from the moment I met her, Kelly. That's just what she is for me."

Rowan reached up from her position in the back seat and rubbed Bryn's shoulder tenderly, her face filled with love.

"While you were on your way to the Dream Creamery from MacDill when you first got here, Kel, Clementine told Bryn and me, the Seven, and all of your girls that you looked just like Ariel, the Disney princess." Riley turned around in the front seat so she could look directly at Kelly. "And damned if you don't, baby, so that's why you became *princesa* to me." The corners of Riley's mouth tipped up. "Although I definitely agree with Clem's assessment that you are more of a Disney princess gone badass."

"So says one of the badass twins of APS, who has the head of Percutio crapping his pants right now," Kelly snarked back playfully. She reached over and held her sister's hand tightly, rapidly becoming serious. "I know you and Bryn talked last night, Ro, and I know she told you some things that were hard for you to hear."

Before Riley and Kelly had left the day before, Bryn had pulled them to the side and told them she wanted to tell Rowan about Kelly's breakdown, including the details behind it.

"She's stronger than you think she is, Kel," Bryn had told her firmly. "I also never want there to be any secrets between the four of us. We're family—we share the good *and* the bad with each other." Kelly nodded, even though she was a little worried about Rowan's reaction.

As Bryn pulled into a parking space at the cafe, Kelly squeezed her sister's fingers comfortingly. "I promise you, I am more than fine now, big sis."

They had continued their conversation after they'd gone into the cafe and were seated.

"I just wish I'd have known you were going through so much, Kel," Rowan fretted. She'd cried when Bryn had shared Riley's story of Kelly's breakdown with her.

"It was my choice not to lay all that bullshit on you, Ro-Ro. Frankly, that would have made everything worse for me, you know?" Rowan nodded in reluctant understanding.

Then, Kelly looked at the twins gravely. "I am so glad we have this opportunity to talk, just the four of us. I think if Ro and I explain what life was like for us after our parents died, you'll understand a bit more."

She paused for a moment, not quite sure where to begin.

Rowan jumped in. "As you already know… Five years ago, Mom died from an aortic aneurysm that burst unexpectedly. She was here one day, gone the next. I don't think words can describe how absolutely horrible living through that was." She shut her eyes in remembered grief.

Kelly continued, her voice a little wobbly. "Two years later, Dad has a massive heart attack and *he* dies. He had tried so hard to hold it together for Rowan and me. But Amanda Holland had been the love of his life for over fifty years and he was completely lost without her."

The sisters clutched hands tightly, fighting against the tears that were threatening to fall.

"We were just…adrift. We had Clementine. Kelly had Robyn at first, but Robyn was murdered the next year, so that was another tragedy piled on." Rowan was quiet before she went on. "I think moving to Whimsy was the best thing that could have ever happened to us, despite that idiot, Coravani, and this crap Kelly is dealing with now. And," Rowan smiled slightly, "despite my initial resistance to the idea of moving down here." She shook her head wryly.

"We were trying to survive this horrible hell all alone and now, we aren't." Kelly looked at Riley and Bryn, who had been watching them steadily. "I'm not going to say the pain of losing Mom and Dad isn't with me every day, because it sure as fuck is. I will miss them every day for the rest of my life." Kelly's eyes were glassy. "But it seems easier to bear somehow because of the amazing people we've met in Whimsy."

"It hurts, but it hurts differently." Rowan tried to articulate her thoughts as well. "Kelly and I have this enormous family to share our pain with now, and the burden seems…diminished, in some respects."

"*Princesa*," Riley began, just as Bryn said, "*Dulzura*," and they both stopped. Kelly and Rowan laughed, the moment made a little bit lighter by the relief of humor.

"*Princesa*," Riley began again after Bryn had nodded to her. She slid her muscular arm around Kelly from her seat beside her woman. "My twin and I are absolutely blown away with your strength and your courage. Both of you. There are few women in this world who could have survived what you two did and still came out fighting."

Bryn concurred, kissing her fiancée on the cheek. "We'll talk about this more later, *dulzura*. I think Riles and I both want to hear more about your parents, the happy *and* the sad, and your mom and dad deserve better than a quick discussion at lunch. In the meantime, we are going to have a good lunch together, then go and check the progress on your house. Riles and I are meeting Teag, Remy, and Shelby there to finalize the security system plans while you two meet with Ember and Nia. And then, Holland girls, I think it's time to pick a move-in date."

* * * * *

"We'll be completely done with our part in the next couple of days. We only have some last-minute finish work to complete." Ember was looking at her iPad.

Nia was looking at hers as well. "You can tell your APS people they can come in and start to wire any time, Em. I have a couple of very minor things still on my punch list, but they honestly shouldn't take more than a day to finish up."

"What's a punch list?" Kelly asked curiously.

"A punch list is the list that tells me the final work items I have left remaining before a construction project is considered complete," Nia said. Her eyes twinkled at Ember. "This picky bitch lays awake at night and dreams up shit to throw on my punch lists, I swear."

"Don't let her fool you. She has it easy because her work is always virtually perfect," Ember assured Rowan and Kelly. "If she wants to see a picky bitch, she should jump on some of my other projects."

"Ember and Nia have worked together for years," Rowan informed Kelly. "We've been so lucky to have them. I'm going to miss them like crazy when this is done and they're gone."

Nia smiled at her and ran a hand through her short gray hair. "We still have Clementine's apartment to do, Ro. And even when the entire project is over, it won't mean we can't meet you for a beer or a glass of wine at Seashells."

Ember tapped on her iPad. "I'll schedule the cleaning crew when Teagan tells me she'll be done with the security system. Then we can get you unpacked and moved in, girls."

"I love this house already." Kelly sighed. "I love Riley's apartment at APS, too, don't get me wrong. But here we have a pool and an outdoor kitchen and…Rowan?" Her eyes widened. "Riley says she and Bryn are buying a boat to keep at our back dock."

"I think we need to have a housewarming party at some point, Kel." Rowan's face glowed. "Bryn says the weather is perfect here in April. Maybe we should have a pool party and a barbecue to celebrate the new house. Rosi is planning our engagement party for the beginning of next month, but the housewarming would be a lot smaller and a lot more casual. We've decided to have the wedding at the end of October, when hurricane season is just about over, although I don't think Bryn is too happy waiting that long. I told her *she* could fight it out with Mama, however, because I sure as heck wasn't getting in the middle of that one. So, I'm thinking having a small pool party at the end of April will be just fine."

Kelly nodded, then flapped her hand at her sister, shuddering at the thought of planning a party. "Then make it happen, Ro-Ro. It sounds fun, but you know I suck at doing that kind of shit and you are amazing at it. From what you've told me about Riley's wonderful mother, I'm sure she would be more than happy to help you."

Suddenly, she was engulfed in a pair of hard, muscular arms that wrapped around her from behind.

"You'll have to excuse us, Ember. Nia." Riley nodded at them over Kelly's head. "My woman has been a bit worn down lately and we're going out tonight, so I'm going to take her home to rest before we do that." She kissed Kelly's cheek.

"Bossy," Kelly mouthed to Rowan as Teagan, Remy, and Shelby joined them. Rowan's eyes closed in an expression of total resignation as Bryn pulled her into her side and looked at Kelly consideringly.

"Oh, Kel." Rowan kept her eyes closed and waited.

Teagan's eyebrow arched. "What was that, Red? Bossy? I don't think we could quite hear you." She cupped her ear and smirked. Kelly realized Teag had deliberately told on her and rolled her eyes.

"It's not anything I haven't called her a million times already and she knows it." Kelly relaxed back into Riley's arms, unperturbed. "Don't be a brat, Teag. Jesus, and you all say femmes are bad."

The APS crew burst out laughing as Rowan's eyes rounded.

"When it's telecommunications' turn to play with Kelly, I goddamn well better be invited." Shelby shook her head, still laughing, then punched Teagan in the arm.

"It's definitely not a secret that Kelly calls me bossy a lot." Riley kissed Kelly behind her ear, then released her and tucked her into her side as well. "However, I know someone who's already had a big day and needs to rest before we go out tonight. She did a short run this morning with Casey. She worked on some Krav Maga moves with Jess. I spent some time with her, starting to teach her our systems, and then she worked on her rotation schedule with Trill."

Rowan's eyes were huge.

"Holy cow, Kelly. Please don't make yourself sick by doing too much, okay? Not that Riley will let you, but I worry." She looked at Kelly with love. "I'm your big sister. It's my job to worry."

"No worries, big sis. I promise you I'm being careful. Now," Kelly cut her eyes sideways at Riley, "I think we're going to get going so I'm not in trouble for real."

"Good call, *princesa*." Riley kissed Kelly again, then took her hand. "We'll see you all tonight."

* * * * *

Kelly didn't think she'd ever laughed so hard in her life.

A considerable number of APS associates had come to Seashells to hang out with Kelly and her new friends. They'd all heard about Kelly joining APS as a working associate and wanted to take the opportunity to introduce themselves and give her a warm welcome.

Clem, Nova, and the rest of the girls were extremely excited for her and Kelly was happy to have another chance to get to know them all better.

Nova, she had already discovered, had the same type of snarky, sarcastic humor she herself did. Alyssa and Brooke weren't far behind Nova, and Clementine was a perfect match for them as well.

In contrast, Delaney seemed quiet, shy, and exceptionally sweet, although she laughed at the ribald banter just as much as the rest of them. According to Nova, Delaney was an extraordinary pastry chef who had just returned to Whimsy after many years away.

Kelly noticed that Teagan's eyes never seemed to leave Delaney, who would flush every time she happened to catch one of Teagan's looks. Curious, Kelly wondered if there was a story there and made a mental note to ask Rowan about it at the first opportunity.

"Red." Casey and Jaime appeared on either side of her and they each kissed her on the cheek. "Are you having fun? Can we get you anything?" They both looked around with a frown.

"Where is your butch, *hermana*?" Jaime asked. "Is everything okay?"

Kelly was amused to realize they'd both unconsciously assumed protective stances.

Kelly smiled at them both. "I'm fine, *hermanos*, I promise. Riley got a phone call and it was so noisy in here, she stepped outside just a second ago to take it."

She looked at them both with her eyebrows raised.

"There are about fifty gazillion APS associates in here keeping an eye on me for her right now. Fifty gazillion, plus two, now that you're both here." Kelly pursed her lips and tried to keep the amusement off her face. "And surely you didn't expect me to be sitting here unarmed, did you?" She shook her head in mock disappointment.

Casey smirked. "Not a bet I'd take, little sis." She looked at Kelly appraisingly. "Clem was absolutely fucking right, though. You totally have that Disney princess vibe going on."

Kelly had on a deep purple dress with a fitted, dropped waistline and cap flutter sleeves with her black stiletto heels. Her dark red curls were pulled back from her face with a purple headband and left to fall down her back, while her makeup was soft and understated.

"I told you all before," Clem interjected, leaning over so she could hear the conversation. "This bitch looks like she should have her gorgeous ass parked in a cottage somewhere, singing and cooking for fucking dwarfs."

Kelly rolled her eyes and flipped Clem off.

Casey looked at Jaime. "Not that we would *ever* let it happen, but fifty bucks says Kel could pound the absolute fucking shit out of any Percutio scum while wearing a dress and high heels."

"Do I look like I throw my money away, *ese*?" Jaime punched Casey in the arm. "Besides, you weren't here the night Kelly got together with the girls for the first time and two Percutio scum showed up. That's exactly what she fucking did, *broki*. Unfortunately, I didn't get a chance to see her do it firsthand, but I saw the aftermath and it wasn't pretty." Jaime high-fived Kelly.

All of a sudden, Kelly's new phone buzzed from the depths of her purse, which was lying on the table in front of her.

"That's odd." Kelly frowned. "No one really has this number yet. I haven't even had a chance to give my new number to the girls yet or set up my voicemail."

Her eyes widened.

"Oh, fuck," she blurted out. "What if it's…?" She abruptly snapped her jaws shut.

"Let's go, kiddo." Casey held out her hand calmly and helped Kelly off the barstool. "We need to find Riley and let her know someone is trying to contact you. Give me your phone, Red."

Kelly dug in her purse and handed her phone to Casey.

"I'll be right back," Kelly said casually to the girls, acting as if there was nothing wrong. "Riley went outside to take a phone call because it was too noisy in here, but I need to go and find her for a minute. Don't have too much fun without us!"

Casey handed Kelly's new phone to Jaime, who looked at the missed call as they were walking to the front entrance.

"It's a private number and they didn't leave a message." Jaime pulled out her own phone and rapidly texted Riley. "*Hermana*, I want you to stay inside the front doors with Casey until I can talk to Riley, okay? I have a feeling it's that motherfucking piece of shit, McAllister, attempting to make contact with you."

They were suddenly surrounded by a half dozen APS associates, most of whom Kelly recognized from her visits to headquarters.

"Hey, Kelly. Hey, you two." The speaker—a striking butch with long, black dreadlocks, stunning dark hazel eyes, and beautiful mocha-colored skin—smiled gently at Kelly before turning to look at Jaime and Casey with sharp eyes. "Anything we can help with, dudes?"

First of all, Kelly thought with a mental eye roll, the APS employment application must have a requirement that only good-looking butches need apply. Every one of the associates surrounding them clanged the hotness bell loudly.

Second, it was apparent that, unless you were sharp, observant, and protective—as well as ridiculously muscled—you clearly didn't have a place at APS either.

"Thank you, *mi corillo*." Jaime nodded to them. "If you could keep Red company until Casey and I get back with Riley, we'd appreciate it." She turned to Kelly. "Kel, this is Desi, my number two. Des, stay with her until we all get back, okay?" She and Casey walked rapidly outside.

The handsome butch nodded at her affably. "Kelly, it's good to finally meet you. It seems like every time you were at headquarters, I missed you by like five minutes." Desi shook her head wryly, but Kelly noticed her sharp, hazel gaze never stopped scanning their surroundings.

"Is there a concern?" Kelly asked slowly. "Or is this just precautionary?"

"Mainly precautionary, Red. Riley had already told us she didn't want us to play when it came to you, because of your former employer or those other dickless wonders, so we aren't." Desi was relaxed, yet alert.

"My hero," Kelly muttered dryly. Desi grinned.

"My new APS phone rang, but no one should have the number yet," Kelly explained. "Casey and Jaime were hanging out with me at the girls' table when it rang. Riley had stepped outside to take a phone call because it's so noisy in here, so we went to find her. I swear to Christ, you all must have an umbilical cord connected to one another. Casey was going to have to stay with me herself until, all of a sudden, you all psychically showed up."

"Seems that way, doesn't it?" Suddenly, Desi pulled her phone out of the back pocket of her cargo pants and looked at it. Her handsome face went hard. The other APS badasses caught her look immediately and went on full alert.

"Code 8. Let's be discreet," Desi muttered softly but clearly to the crew. A couple of them departed swiftly toward the back, while the others formed an inconspicuous protective shield around Kelly. "Kelly." Desi slid noiselessly to Kelly's left side.

"There were shots fired outside, Red. Riley, Jaime, and Casey are all fine, but Riles wants you the fuck out of here ASAP in case there are hostiles in here, which there, unfortunately, might be. Jaim will meet us right outside the back exit. Riley and Casey went to get Riley's SUV."

A glance across the crowded bar revealed Bryn and another bunch of APS associates discreetly positioning the girls at a corner table where they would be more protected.

"Hey, Kelly." A strawberry-blond with gray-green eyes took up a position on Kelly's right side. "I'm Dara, Drew's second. Hell of a way to meet for the first time, isn't it?" She grinned briefly but was busy scanning the crowd as she, Desi, and a few other APS associates started heading toward the back of Seashells, Kelly in tow.

After they went down the back hallway, Desi cleared the exit, then gestured at Kelly to step out of the back door. Kelly saw Riley's SUV idling in the back alley in the darkness.

Riley and Casey were covering the back entrance, guns drawn, while Jaime quickly bundled Kelly into the backseat. Within thirty seconds, everyone was back in the SUV and they were gone.

"The *fuck*?" Kelly exploded, her heart hammering rapidly. "Don't tell me that useless motherfucker, McAllister, actually had the brains to pull off something like this?"

"*Princesa.*" Riley glanced at her in the rearview mirror as she drove. "This get-together with all of us was casual and it wasn't exactly a secret. A lot of people in Whimsy heard about it. McAllister, that fucking rat bastard, had called Reizan first thing when he fell for the fake breach we put on your new phone. That wasn't exactly a shocker to us." The disgust in Riley's tone was apparent. "When the two of them found out about the get-together, they planned to lure me outside with a bogus phone call, which they did, and would immediately call your new phone when I left the bar. They theorized you would then go straight outside to find me."

"And then what were they planning to do?" Kelly was horrified. "Shoot you and snatch me?"

"Pretty much." Riley was unperturbed. "What those dumb fucks didn't realize was that there would be no way I would leave you unprotected or in a position where you would have to come outside by yourself."

"Dipshits," Casey muttered from the front passenger seat.

"But they fucking shot at the three of you when Casey and Jaime went outside to find you." Kelly was ballistic.

"When Jaime and Casey walked out, the thugs from Percutio were probably waiting for you to make an appearance right behind them. By the time those numbnuts figured out you weren't coming outside, we'd already realized this was a setup and took cover. There was no danger, *princesa*."

"Oh, Jesus. I have to call Rowan, she's probably going insane. If I can find my fucking phone, that is. And Clem is going to fucking kill me for ruining another get-together." Kelly pinched the bridge of her nose and closed her eyes.

"I have your phone and Bryn has it all taken care of, baby." Riley turned the SUV in the direction of APS headquarters. "Everyone at Seashells is safe, Rowan is calm, and Bryn said they'd see us Sunday at my parents' for dinner."

Jaime grinned. "As far as the girls go, Clem might be pissed, *hermana*, and Delaney might be a bit bewildered…but I guarantee you Nova, Alyssa, and Brooke are busy making book with the APS crew on how long it takes you to rip McAllister's balls off." Her grin widened as Kelly cursed softly under her breath.

Jaime checked her phone. "Desi is going to meet us at headquarters to pick Casey and me up and take us back to Seashells. Good thing too, because I'm sure as fuck not missing the opportunity to get my bet in."

"*Broki*," Kelly growled, punching Jaime in the arm.

"Get used to it, *chula*." Jaime rubbed Kelly's arm with affection in return and grinned even more. "Welcome to APS."

Chapter 18

Kelly, Riley, Bryn, and Rowan stood in the front entranceway of the senior Armstrong home in the Marina Bay Club, saying hello to the twins' fair-haired father, Oliver.

Oliver Armstrong was extremely tall at 6'4", with the same lean, muscular body type as Riley and Bryn. His blue eyes twinkled at Kelly as he shook her hand, then gave Rowan and his twins a hard, warm hug in greeting.

"So, this is the infamous Kelly Holland, I presume," he said in his deep British accent, turning back to Kelly after he had let Rowan go. "It's wonderful to meet you, love. Can I offer you something to drink before Rosi takes off my head?"

"I heard that," a pretty Hispanic-accented voice said from the top of the stairs. "Oliver, honestly. You're going to have that child thinking this family is nothing but a bunch of bloodthirsty ghouls." Light footsteps started to descend.

Oliver looked at Kelly with his eyebrows raised, prompting her to smack her hand over her mouth to keep from giggling out loud. She could already tell she was going to adore the Armstrong family.

"Oh my goodness. Another beauty." A petite, dark-haired, dark-eyed woman rounded the end of the staircase. She hugged and kissed

Rowan and her twins fiercely before coming to stand in front of Kelly and peering at her intently. "My Riley told me you looked exactly like Ariel, the Disney princess, Kelly. And it's true, I can see why people would say that. Although," she reached up to the much taller Kelly and hugged her, too, "there is a strength of character in your face that an animated cartoon character could never hope to achieve."

Kelly fell in love on the spot.

"Thank you, Mrs. Armstrong," she said gratefully. "I've been compared to Ariel my entire life and I don't think anyone has ever said anything so meaningful to me."

"It's Rosi, *querida*, and I didn't say anything that wasn't true. Your sister, by the way, has already honored me by starting to call me Mama like my children do. I hope that someday you and I get to the point where you feel comfortable doing so as well."

Rosi took another look at Kelly in her proper dark-green sheath dress with matching cardigan, her dark red curls pulled back into a half-up, half-down style.

"My twins certainly have good taste," she admired, looking from Kelly to Rowan, who wore a silky gold pantsuit with embroidered sleeves, her blonde curls loose.

"That we do." The heat of Riley's eyes touched Kelly as she slid one strong arm around her waist.

"Let's get you girls something to drink, find out where the rest of my children are, and make our way to the table, shall we?" Rosi motioned toward the dining room. "We can chat and get better acquainted over dinner."

* * * * *

Kelly relaxed in the comfortable family room with Oliver, Rowan, and the twins after dinner, replete.

It had been a wonderful meal, filled with good food and laughter. Kelly, much to her surprise, found herself fitting in naturally and easily with the Armstrong family right away.

Daniela, the baby, was just as sweet and funny as Kelly remembered. Noah and Keenan, Riley and Bryn's younger brothers, were a hoot, bickering and snarking at their siblings in an absolutely hysterical way—although Kelly noticed it only took one quelling glance from Riley or Bryn to get them to settle down.

When they were done, Rosi had refused to accept her or Rowan's help in cleaning up, shooing them both out of the dining room. She kissed them on the cheek before she ordered them to go into the family room and enjoy themselves.

"That was amazing, even though my stomach is groaning." Kelly sighed as she leaned contentedly against Riley after they sat on a comfortable couch. "I don't much like to cook myself, although Rowan is a fabulous one. I used to grill with my dad, but that was about it."

"When you move into your new house, *princesa*, you and I can man the grill while Bryn scrubs potatoes for Rowan then." Riley smirked at her twin as Bryn flipped her off.

"I can't wait to move in and have all of our stuff delivered," said Rowan, who was curled up against Bryn. "And then go shopping, because we got rid of so much when we moved down to Florida. We need to replace a lot."

Kelly shuddered and flapped her hand at her sister. "You and Clem have fun. Take Rosi with you since, judging from this house, she has amazing taste. Try not to set the credit cards on fire, and I'll see you when you get back."

Riley, Bryn, and Oliver laughed.

"Since the prospect of going shopping seems to fill you with just as much horror as it does me, I have a proposition for you, Kelly love," said Oliver, holding a glass of after-dinner cognac. "I don't know if Riley or Bryn or Rowan has had the opportunity to tell you yet, but I was a Royal Marines sharpshooter before I moved to America to go to law school."

Oliver sipped his cognac.

"When I was born, my mother was an American living in England and my father was a British citizen. I was born and raised in London, but I've had dual citizenship since birth because of my parents. I didn't actually move to America myself until I was in my later twenties, though."

"Rowan told me all about your Royal Marines career." Kelly's eyes turned sad for a moment. "Our dad would have so loved to have met you, Oliver."

Oliver's eyes were sympathetic. "I feel the exact same way, love. I think your father and I would have had a lot in common, although we served two very different military forces. That said, Riley probably hasn't had a chance to share this with you yet, but APS and I co-own a sniper training range." Kelly's eyes grew big.

"The range is located inland, over the Sunshine Skyway Bridge in a very remote area, about an hour from here. I've been privileged to help out with some of the APS long-range weapons training over the years. Riley and Bryn tell me you are an expert shot, and I'm going to assume your father taught you some standard sniper training protocols along the way since Rowan tells me you spent so much time with him growing up."

Kelly nodded.

Oliver smiled. "Then why don't we let Rowan and Clementine and Rosi go shopping, and the rest of us will make a day at the sniper range our play date."

"Yes!" Kelly squealed excitedly, making everyone laugh. "I would *love* that. I still have all of my dad's rifles, which are packed along with the rest of our Virginia possessions." The corner of her mouth quirked up as she looked at Riley.

"We better ask Trill to come with us or she'll shoot *me* for having that kind of fun without her. And probably Kenn, too." Riley kissed her temple and laughed as she tightened her hold around her woman.

"Trillian would have made an exceptional sniper," Oliver agreed. "Her marksmanship is excellent, plus she has the mental fortitude to handle the challenges and the stress of that position."

"Trill told me that if all of them hadn't already had the dream of APS when they were so young, she probably would have stayed in the Marines and taken the sniper path," Kelly told him. She looked back and forth between Riley and Bryn. "I still don't understand how all of you knew so early that forming an organization along the lines of APS would be what you wanted to do," she said slowly. "I think Trill told me you knew you wanted to make something like APS a reality by the fifth grade?"

Kelly's voice grew sad again.

"Come to think of it, though, I always knew I wanted to be a Marine like my dad. I can't remember a time when I didn't want that. So, I guess I do get it after all."

"Baby." Riley rubbed her back and looked deeply into her eyes. "Bryn and I don't have any secrets from our parents, so I would like to tell them about your magic." She smiled and kissed Kelly's temple again. "But that's *your* secret to tell, there's no pressure here for you to say *anything*, and Mama and Dad will respect that."

Kelly smiled and turned fully to Riley, cupping her handsome face in her hands. "Do you remember before the four of us had lunch the other day, Bryn told me she was going to tell Rowan about my difficulty processing everything that had happened, because we were family and we didn't have secrets from each other?"

Riley nodded, wrapping her arms around her.

"Your mom and dad are family too, *amante*. Neither you nor Bryn should *ever* feel you need to pick between your parents and the Holland girls. That's not how we were raised and that's definitely not how we operate." Kelly raised a semi-teasing brow. "For better or for worse, your family is stuck with mine."

"For some reason, I don't think that's a hardship, love." Oliver looked at her affectionately. "Rowan is already extremely dear to us and I know it's not going to take long at all for you to get there as well." He paused for a moment. "Riles, is this discussion something your mother needs to hear?" Oliver looked at his youngest twin.

"It is, Dad. It's a really long story and I think it's best shared by Kelly. Or by me, with Kelly sitting right here so we make sure we cover all the bases."

"Well, then." Oliver stood up. "I'd better go get Rosi and bring her in here so we can talk. I'll be back shortly." He walked out of the room.

"Are you okay, Kelly?" Rowan asked worriedly from the shelter of Bryn's arms. "I know Bryn has shared everything with me, but it wasn't all at one time. This is going to be a lot in one sitting."

"It is," Kelly agreed. "Luckily for me, I have someone sitting here beside me who can do most of the talking." She put her head down on Riley's shoulder.

"Whatever you need me to do, *princesa*." Riley kissed her forehead and caressed her back. "I'll talk, you steer the conversation when necessary, and make sure I don't forget anything."

Kelly snorted and raised her head. "Right, because people with minds like steel traps forget so much." She rolled her eyes for good measure, then gasped as Riley's muscled arms banded tightly around her.

"*Princesa?*" Riley nibbled seductively on her ear. "Snarking at your butch is a spanking offense. A *gentle* spanking offense, true, but it's still a good way to end up over my knee."

"Riley!" Kelly hissed. "Hush! What if your parents hear?" She tried unsuccessfully to wiggle away.

The corners of Riley's mouth tipped up as she tightened her arms even more. "Mama would ignore it and Dad would approve." Her grin widened as Kelly's eyes rounded. "That's what happens when you get involved with an alpha family, baby."

"I *realllly* didn't need to know that," Kelly groaned as she hid her face on Riley's shoulder. She heard Bryn chuckle from across the room.

Just then, Oliver and Rosi entered the room, hand-in-hand. Oliver took a seat in his large, comfortable armchair again, and then pulled Rosi down next to him, wrapping his arm around her. Rosi sighed and leaned against her husband.

"I understand from Oliver you all have a story to tell us," Rosi said, settling herself a bit more comfortably. "Kelly, you need to know that anything you share with us will not go any farther than this room, *querida*."

"I know that." Kelly was decisive. She looked at Riley. "I'm just not exactly sure where to start, *amante*, so why don't you go ahead?" Out of the corner of her eye, she saw Rosi smile with soft eyes at Kelly's nickname for Riley.

"Kelly originally came down from Langley to spend a couple of days leave with Rowan because of the shit that happened with that dickhead, Coravani," Riley began. "Kelly was an information analyst for the CIA and seemed to be assigned primarily to Percutio-focused operations."

Both Oliver and Rosi's eyebrows hit their hairlines.

"The night before Kelly was supposed to go back to Langley, Rowan and Clementine arranged a night out at Seashells for all the girls—Kelly, Rowan, Clementine Martin, Nova MacLeod, Brooke Marino, Alyssa Riker, and Delaney Sedgwick. Some APS associates were there to provide protection for them because Bryn, the Seven, and I were feeling seriously off about the vibes Kelly was putting out. Even though she wouldn't say anything." Riley looked pointedly at Kelly.

"Bossy," Kelly muttered under her breath, making Rosi snicker.

Riley tightened her arms infinitesimally around Kelly again. "*Princesa*," she warned calmly and Kelly subsided.

"Anyhow," Riley continued, "at one point during the evening, Kelly and Clem went to the ladies' room. While they were in the restroom, Kelly heard an odd noise coming from the hallway, quietly went to investigate, and found two Percutio fucks right outside the door, ready to grab her."

Rosi growled, her dark eyes aflame, as Oliver's blue eyes turned positively arctic.

"Kel yelled at Clementine to text me and let me know what was going on, and also to tell me to get the rest of the girls out. She put those assholes on the ground so Clem could escape, cleared the back entrance, and then made her way out the front to the rest of us." Riley caressed Kelly's back. "My woman is skilled in covert and clandestine operations, so subduing those dicks wasn't much of a challenge for her."

Rosi looked proud. "Both my girls are a force to be reckoned with then," she stated, nodding in satisfaction. Kelly felt a flood of warmth hearing Rosi describe her as one of "her" girls.

"Kelly came home with me even though she still wasn't much inclined to say anything about either the CIA or Percutio," Riley said. "The next morning, I got up early to do my usual APS run. Kel was still sleeping. It was our monthly long-distance run day, so I was gone for about three hours. When I came back, Kelly was gone." Riley kissed Kelly's temple.

"Bryn called me just as I had started to search my apartment, and told me when she got home, she found Rowan hysterical. Kelly had called her, told her that her handler had called her right after I'd left, and said she'd been burned by the CIA."

"*What?!*" Both Rosi and Oliver were outraged. "That meant all of her CIA protection and support was gone, correct?" Oliver asked, his voice coated in ice.

Riley continued to caress Kelly's back soothingly. "Correct. Turns out there is a Percutio-owned mole in Kelly's division. He made it look as though Kelly was becoming unstable, so he was able to have her burned as a result. And he did it so Percutio had a clear shot at taking Kelly for themselves."

"Oliver." Rosi's teeth were clenched. "Someone needs to pay for this, *cariño*." Oliver rubbed Rosi's back just as Riley was doing to Kelly in an attempt to calm her down.

"You'll have to get in line behind Trill, Mama." Bryn spoke up wryly. "She's beyond pissed and she's already vowed massive bloodshed over this."

Rosi smiled coldly with threatening eyes. "I am sure my Trillian will not deny her Mama Armstrong a chance to play." The twins shook their heads in amusement as Rowan and Kelly looked at Oliver with huge eyes. Oliver shrugged, noncommittal and not in the least surprised.

"My woman had absolutely no idea Grigor Reizan is quite familiar with APS and is, shall we say, a wee bit leery about getting on our bad side," Riley went on. "But she is quite familiar with Percutio, and she knows exactly what they're capable of doing. So, she told Rowan she was leaving to keep *us* safe. Then she disappeared."

"Kelly, love." Oliver shook his head, then rubbed the bridge of his nose. "You should have never done that. No one has ever been able to hide from either of my twins."

"It took us three days to find Kelly, Dad." Again, Oliver and Rosi's eyebrows hit their hairlines and they both gaped in astonishment. "Drew is *still* pissed because, when Kelly fell off radar, no one could pick up her trail. Even the Shadow was stymied."

Kelly put her head down and smirked a little bit, knowing she and Drew were just fine, but that Drew was still feeling a little bit stung.

"If it wasn't for Rowan—because she's a fucking phenomenon as a predictive data analyst and she also understands how her sister thinks—we would have never found Kelly. Kel's that goddamn good, which is why she is now an APS associate." Riley nuzzled Kelly's temple. "Bryn and I and the Seven are fucking ecstatic to have her on board."

"Explain this to me, please. Why does Percutio want her so much?" Rosi's eyes were sharp. "It is clear to everyone how smart she is, but there is something extremely odd about how hard they are pursuing her." Rowan and Kelly looked at each other, wondering exactly where Rosi's on-target perceptions came from.

Bryn caught their look and answered, smiling slightly. "Mama's been married to a former Royal Marines sharpshooter and a state's attorney for almost forty years." Her grin broadened. "Plus, since he retired, Dad has other outside interests Mama has been involved in as well. She doesn't miss much."

"Thank you, my child." Rosi blew a kiss across the room at Bryn before she turned back to the entire group. "Now, I would really appreciate a fucking explanation as to why Kelly is being pursued so hard by those thugs before I start throwing things."

"Including throwing them at her husband." Oliver raised an ironic brow as Kelly and Rowan fought to contain their giggles.

Riley grinned and then rapidly sobered. "Kelly has an extreme eidetic memory," she told her parents. "Not only does she have virtually perfect recall with photographs—any kind of image, really—*and* data, including serial recall, she can retain those mental images in her mind for *years.*

"Kelly would be a huge fucking asset in Reizan's criminal organization if he ever got his hands on her. He'd use her to memorize blueprints and maps, take inventories, access schedules…there's no fucking telling what all he'd force her to do."

Oliver blew out a slow, deep breath while Rosi looked back and forth between Riley and Kelly, speechless.

"No wonder those maniacs want you so much," Rosi pronounced finally, still slightly in shock. "Now I understand why Riley has been so convinced Grigor will eventually break his vow not to touch you."

"There's another piece to the puzzle, Mama." Riley stopped, visibly struggling to bring herself under control. Oliver and Rosi were clearly taken aback at their child's uncharacteristic struggle and looked to Bryn for an explanation.

Bryn calmly stepped in. "I got it, Riles." She held Rowan's hand tightly. "Kelly inherited a hereditary component to this gift through her mother. Rowan, as you know, is only biologically related to their dad, so this doesn't affect her."

Rowan smiled serenely at everyone, plainly comfortable with the discussion.

"The gift, as Kelly and Rowan call it, is always passed down to the female descendants of the line, although it's extremely hard for them to get pregnant. Kel says it's as though the gift itself doesn't want to reproduce." Bryn's eyes glittered and her voice turned icy. "Apparently, though, that soon-to-be-dead shitheel, Reizan, thinks he's going to kidnap Kelly and force her to bear his children, so he can build himself an empire of female eidetic super assets."

"He's. *Dead.*" Remarkably, Rosi kept her composure and uttered the words quietly, recognizing that her youngest twin was balancing on the very edge of control.

Feeling the danger in the room, Kelly decided to take matters into her own hands.

"*Amante*," she said patiently and wrapped her arms around Riley. "Look at me." She kept her composure even when she saw the ice cold look of death on Riley's handsome face.

"That piece of shit is going to learn one hell of a lesson if he doesn't uphold his promise to leave me alone." Kelly lifted one of Riley's hands and kissed the knuckles. "I'll save you and Trill some scraps if you want me to, but I make no guarantees, handsome." Kelly smirked wickedly, running her fingers down Riley's cheek. "Sometimes, I like playing with my food before I eat it, and I've never been big on sharing those kinds of snacks."

Riley noticeably relaxed at Kelly's playful words, then rewarded her woman with an equally wicked smirk. "Don't make me threaten to turn you over my knee in front of my parents, *princesa*." She raised a mock-stern brow at Kelly. Kelly's jaw went kerplunk and her eyes rounded.

"*Bossy*." Kelly was only half kidding in her outrage. "You do *not* get to have all the fun, Riley Armstrong. As a matter of fact," she smiled slyly, running her hand suggestively up and down Riley's arm, "I think we need to establish the Covert-Clandestine Games at APS and see who whips whose ass. Let everyone make book on *that*."

Rowan choked in an effort to subdue her laughter and hid her red face against Bryn's shoulder, while Oliver, Rosi, and Bryn laughed outright.

Riley's amber eyes heated. "Keep on, *princesa*," she murmured as Kelly smirked. "I have absolutely no objection to tying you to my bed and leaving you there until you learn your lesson." Kelly's jaw dropped again.

Then she huffed and decided to ignore Riley's comments before she got herself into even deeper hot water with her butch.

"The point is," she said, rapidly becoming serious and looking at Oliver and Rosi, "Reizan and his merry little band of thugs think they have the right to take what doesn't belong to them. However, Riley, Bryn, and Rowan will tell you I am *more* than capable of taking care of myself. Not that I even have to, though. I have nine of the biggest, meanest badasses in existence at my back, who will utterly destroy anyone who thinks they're going to raise one finger against me."

Kelly smiled coldly, then her face relaxed and she nodded reassuringly at the Armstrongs.

"So don't you worry." She sighed and leaned back against Riley again. "However, there is still a lot more to this story, unfortunately, if you two are up to hearing it now."

Chapter 19

"You can't stop now, *querida*," Rosi said, shifting next to Oliver. "I take it you were exclusively given Percutio-related assignments then because of your gift, yes?"

Riley resumed the narrative after Kelly gestured to her. "She was. Unfortunately, though, Kelly's fiancée at the time—who was also an analyst for the CIA—got increasingly suspicious, because Kelly was never assigned to anything that didn't involve Percutio, which was unusual."

"Even though I begged her not to, Robyn wouldn't leave it alone. She didn't know about my gift because I had been instructed by my bosses not to tell anybody." Kelly's voice faltered.

Riley wrapped her arms securely around Kelly and kissed her on the forehead. "I got this, baby, okay?" she murmured gently.

Kelly nodded and closed her eyes as Rosi and Oliver looked at her with concern.

"Two years ago, Robyn was murdered by Reizan's goons." Riley stroked Kelly's arms soothingly as her parents went completely still. "Robyn spent too much time delving into Percutio on her off time, trying to discern why the CIA had assigned Kelly to them exclusively, and she apparently got a little careless."

Kelly's voice became very quiet. "I kept begging Robyn to leave it alone and she wouldn't. It ended up costing her her life." She wiped at the tears that were streaming down her cheeks. "I carried guilt for the longest time…thinking that Robyn's death was my fault because I didn't tell her about my gift but should have—even though I had been ordered to keep quiet about it."

Riley caressed her gently. "Kelly was finally able to purge a fuckton of grief and guilt and anger the other night, all this bullshit she's been carrying around for years. Not just about Robyn, but about a ton of other shit, too. Like her parents' deaths, for one." She kissed Kelly again on the forehead, then looked at Oliver and Rosi. "She is one of the strongest women I've ever met in my life. Anyone else carrying around a burden like she was would have imploded a long time ago."

"It wasn't pleasant," Kelly admitted. "I was exhausted when it was over, slept for a solid twenty-four hours, and have been spending the last few days just getting some strength back. I honestly didn't realize how tired I'd gotten."

"*Because*," Rowan uncharacteristically snarked to the room, causing both Oliver and Rosi's eyebrows to fly up into their hairlines again, "she's always protected Clementine and me, so she decided to do all of this crap on her own rather than ask her *big sister* for help."

Riley and Bryn grinned as Rowan lovingly glared at her little sister, who looked a bit abashed.

"No more, Kel." Rowan's voice turned gentle. "We aren't alone anymore." Kelly ducked her head and nodded, struggling to keep her composure.

"Kelly, love." Oliver was equally gentle as he smiled at her warmly. "Rosi and I can never take the place of your parents. Not would we ever want to. But we'll always be here for you and Rowan, and you need to know that." Kelly wiped her tears and nodded again with a grateful look.

"Getting back to Robyn…" Riley kissed Kelly's temple again and continued, knowing Kelly was at her emotional limit. "Kelly had been sitting on a document she was given right after Robyn's funeral, a handwritten document that contained all of Robyn's notes and speculation about what was going on with Kelly and Percutio. It was in Robyn's personal correspondence folder. Kelly didn't read it for a long time because Robyn's death was too raw."

Kelly sighed. "Turns out she had figured everything out about my eidetic memory gift. Robyn had written about everything she'd learned—by hand, not electronically—but no one else ever saw that document except for me. Well, me and the twins and the Seven, but that wasn't until a few days ago when I finally read it. Robyn's document sat in my bedroom in Virginia for over eighteen months, isolated, until we packed it with the rest of my important papers and shipped it down to Clem at the Gulf Breeze Inn—separate from the bulk of the house stuff. Then Clem brought it to our new house, where it continued to sit, undisturbed."

"That is, until two fuckwits from Percutio showed up. On a long shot, Reizan had decided to try and look for such a file in their house the exact same night Blake and Drew went to get Robyn's document." Riley was still pissed. "We had all been in the Bunker discussing Robyn's document and all of the shit surrounding it, so they took off to go and get it."

"Gunfight?" Oliver's voice was clipped.

"Drew's right shoulder was grazed, but she and Blake dropped the son of a bitch." Riley's tone was filled with malicious satisfaction. "Blake called it in to Vince and handled it while Drew reported to our infirmary. Turns out she needed two stitches."

"Hell's bloody bells," Oliver muttered under his breath. "Drew's all right then?"

"She's fine and Blake is giving her a rash of shit about it." Suddenly, Riley smirked. "Said Drew might as well have been bitten in the ass by a dog."

Oliver burst out laughing, the tension broken.

Rosi, however, was not amused. "I don't like to hear about one of the Seven getting hurt," she lectured them with angry eyes. "I'm just thankful Drew is okay. What I want to know is, how did Reizan find out about Kelly's gift if this document Robyn wrote was in Kelly's bedroom in Virginia for most of the time?" Rosi speared them with a direct look.

"When I read the document, Robyn kept referencing her close friend, Alan—another analyst she worked closely with at the CIA," Kelly said. "Since she couldn't talk to me about any of this, that was apparently who she was confiding in. Even though Robyn and I both worked for the CIA, we were in different directorates—or divisions—because our skill sets were so different. We both carried the title of analyst, but I was in Operations because I did field work encompassed by the clandestine arm of the agency. Robyn was in the actual Analysis directorate. I really didn't know any of the other analysts she knew," Kelly said, shrugging. "There are literally hundreds of analysts at Langley, so that's not unusual. We originally met because we were assigned to the same project in a very rare cross-directorate venture, but it was a total fluke. We were never assigned to the same projects again."

Riley's eyes were icy. "Since she did field work, Kelly was assigned a new CIA handler named Alan McAllister about six months ago after her old handler retired. Coincidentally, that's when the interest in her from Percutio started to manifest.

"Alan was the CIA analyst Robyn thought was a friend, until he chose to sell Kelly's secret to that piece of shit, Reizan, for his own gain." Rosi hissed in anger.

Riley kept rubbing Kelly comfortingly. "From what we can determine, Alan was too far down the totem pool to risk contacting Reizan prior to his promotion. He sat on the information about Kelly until he was in a position to use it. That's why things were quiet for so long. When McAllister was promoted to handler and went to Operations—which gave him a considerable amount of juice—he then contacted Reizan, told him all about Kelly and her gift, and arranged to be assigned to Kelly as her handler. End game: Alan would be extremely well rewarded if he maneuvered Kelly into a vulnerable position so Percutio could take her for their own use."

"Fucking Percutio mole." Oliver was pissed. "No wonder they've been able to track Kelly so well."

"Alan has probably been having a fucking heart attack, though." The corner of Kelly's mouth tilted up. "He was responsible for having me burned, thinking that would leave me alone and vulnerable. He probably shit his pants when he heard APS had taken me under their wing instead. He was undoubtedly panicking, believing he'd completely lost all contact with me, and he knew Reizan would put a bullet in his head if he found out how badly he'd screwed up."

"So, we created a tiny breach in Kelly's new APS phone. It looked like McAllister was one of many who was simply added to Kelly's phone as a contact," Riley informed them. "We kept the rest of her phone locked down tight and completely inaccessible. The only thing McAllister was able to do was call or text Kelly. Even though Kelly was burned by the CIA, the logical assumption would be that her entire contact list had been copied to her new phone."

Oliver nodded. "Smart."

"Friday night, I was at Seashells with some of the girls and my phone rang. I mentioned it was odd because no one really had the number yet," Kelly revealed. "Riley had just left to step outside and take a phone call because it was so noisy. Jaime and Casey happened to be with me, and they had me wait inside the front door with Jaime's second, Desi, while they went outside to find Riley."

"When I answered my phone, there was no one on the line," Riley said. "When Jaime and Casey came outside, we realized immediately it was a setup, and that whoever was behind it expected Kelly to come outside right behind the two of them. We got her out safely, and it was real fucking apparent that McAllister had fallen for the breach on Kelly's phone." Riley played with the dark red curls falling down Kelly's back. "There hasn't been any further contact from McAllister, but it's just a matter of time."

"It looks like McAllister and Reizan have no idea we're on to them, which is good," said Kelly. "I personally think they've fallen back to regroup. They're aware the girls and I have 24/7 APS coverage, but I bet any money they think it's because APS perceives a general Percutio threat, not because my former CIA handler is dirty."

Riley looked at Bryn, then at her parents, and smiled coldly. "You should know Grigor is not long for this world if he doesn't heed my warning to leave my woman alone. And I'm going to burn McAllister's life to the ground for what he's done to Kelly."

Chapter 20

"Motherfucker. Blake, you fucking asshole."

Kelly, Riley, Bryn, and a few of the Seven had been spending the afternoon running drills in Utopia. Rowan was watching breathlessly from the control booth as the APS team faced off against a menacing enemy combatant team.

Kelly—Rowan had discovered with pride and not a small amount of trepidation—was every bit as dangerous as her new APS siblings were. Her virtually perfect marksmanship, coupled with her talent as an MMA fighter, made her a force to be reckoned with.

Kelly had just narrowly missed being tagged by one last huge enemy by diving to the side, shooting as she dove. She caught him right between the eyes and the enemy combatant disappeared, leaving the sim clear.

Blake smirked, wiping the sweat from her brow as she cleared the sim. "Good job, Red," she praised as she called the sim clear and shut it down. She kissed Kelly on the cheek and handed her a towel. "It's almost as if you've been playing with us for a long time."

Rowan burst out of the control booth and laughed as she clapped her hands. "Kel, that was freaking *amazing*. Dear Goddess, I had no idea you could fight the way you do. I mean, of course I know you can, I saw you and Dad work together lots of times, but that was unreal."

"I'm totally impressed with your skills, Kel." Bryn smiled at Kelly, her hands on her hips.

"Seriously, little sis, for your first time in the sim, that was phenomenal," added Teagan as she wiped her own face.

Kennedy gave her a high five with a big grin. "This was almost as impressive as your performance out on the sniper range last week, Red. These fuckers would have shit their pants if they could have seen you in action out there."

"As much as I hate to admit it, the CIA also gave you some seriously good training, baby. Then again," Riley raised an eyebrow, "a huge part of why you're as good as you are is because Bill Holland was your father. You're determined to be the absolute best at what you do, just like he was."

Kelly shrugged, a faint grin on her face. "Everything I've done here so far has been amazingly fun. APS headquarters is like Disneyland for badass adults." She blotted her face with the clean towel Blake had handed her, then tossed it to Riley. "Tomorrow night, Ro and I get to attempt a breach of APS with Jaime and her crew. I cannot *wait*." Kelly and Rowan beamed at each other. "And I think Casey wants to talk to me about doing some kind of a demo or something?"

"You and I are doing a Muay Thai demo in Hades, *princesa*," Riley informed her. Kelly's eyes got huge. "Casey wants to meet with us to schedule it." The corners of Riley's mouth lifted in a wicked smile. "This will give you an opportunity to hand me my ass like you've been threatening to do, baby." After she wiped her own face, she tossed the towel back to Kelly.

Kelly squealed and punched her fists in the air. "Yes! Your ass is *so* mine, Armstrong." Everyone burst out laughing as Kelly threw a few mock punches in Riley's direction. Riley smirked at Kelly, a glimmer of amusement and not a small amount of heat showing in her amber eyes.

"Someone also needs to set up a proper betting pool for this one. Rowan fucking torched our credit cards when she, Clem, and your mom went shopping for our new house. I need to get some of that money back." Rowan huffed and rolled her eyes at her little sister.

"Now you know how a butch feels when her femme goes shopping," Blake snarked at Kelly with a wicked grin, ducking as Kelly threw her towel at her.

Suddenly, they all stopped as their comms went off.

"Go." Riley activated the comm in her ear and the rest of them followed suit.

"There's been another attempt to communicate with Kelly." Trill's voice came over the comm. "Darcy intercepted a text message sent to Kelly's new phone from an unknown caller." Darcy was Trill's second.

"The message reads '*Kelly, it's Alan. Please give me a call at 703-555-2032 so we can talk.*' Remy is already working on tracing the text right now. Rem and Darcy are together in the Bullpen." The

Bullpen was the large, open office space shared by all APS associates who were not part of management.

"That's not Alan's regular number, but it's a Langley one," Kelly observed. "Not that it's definitive proof it's really Alan."

"Tell Rem I'm on my way, Trill." Teagan kissed Kelly on the cheek, then headed out of Utopia, tossing the case with her sim weapon to Blake. "I'll keep you all updated. I'm sure we want to have Kelly call McAllister as soon as Remy has the trace going. I'll meet you back in the Bunker when she has it set up." Teagan disappeared through the door.

"I'm going to have one of the crew take Rowan back over to the WAC, then I'll catch up with you all in the Bunker," said Bryn, kissing Kelly on the cheek as well and taking Rowan's hand. Rowan also kissed her sister, murmuring, "I'll talk to you later," and left Utopia with Bryn.

"Riley." Kelly tapped her chin after they'd all put their sim weapons away and re-armed themselves, a considering look on her face. "Alan knows me well enough to be damn sure I'm going to be pissed and hostile when I call him back. So I'm going to propose I hang up on him this time around, but not before I plant a few mental seeds first."

"What kind of mental seeds do you suggest, *princesa*?" Blake and Kennedy walked with Kelly and Riley out of Utopia, and the group headed toward the Bunker.

The corners of Kelly's mouth curled up in a devious smile. "I think I should lord it over good ol' Alan, gloat that I was 'rescued' by APS when the CIA threw me away oh-so-callously. And I should brag that the work APS has me doing regarding Percutio is *so* much more explosive than what the CIA was having me do. Then I'll tell him to suck it and hang up on him."

"Way to bait that hook, baby." Riley checked her phone. "He'll definitely contact you again in a day or two after he's given you a bit of time to simmer down. That will give us time to plan our next steps. Bryn's on her way to the Bunker. As soon as Rem is ready to start the trace, Kelly can call McAllister." Riley hit her comm. "*Mi corillo*, Kelly is going to contact McAllister as soon as Remy has her trace set up. ETA, about ten, fifteen minutes. We'll be in the Bunker."

When everyone had finally met up and Remy had a trace active, Kelly put her phone on speaker and dialed her former handler, nodding confidently at the twins and the Seven.

"You rang, asshole?" Kelly infused her voice with sarcasm and a tiny bit of defensiveness when Alan answered her call.

"Kelly." Alan couldn't mask his relief. "Thank you so much for calling me back."

"I almost didn't, McAllister." Kelly was hard and unfriendly. "Frankly, I don't know why I'm fucking bothering now. In case your memory needs jogging, the CIA *burned me*. For no apparent reason, just left my ass hanging out in the wind like I was nothing. That's okay, though." Kelly's tone changed, becoming heavy with gleeful malice. "It took all of you being the fucking dumb shits you are for me to realize there are *much* better deals and organizations out there. I guess I may actually owe you fuckers a big thank you for that."

"What do you mean?" Alan pushed, clearly taken aback. "Who have you found that's better?"

"I've been rescued by APS, McAllister. When the CIA burned me like I was so much fucking trash and APS found out about it, they couldn't offer me a job fast enough. They were thrilled to bring me on board, actually."

Kelly winked mischievously at the twins and the Seven, each one of whom wore a look of amusement on her face.

"Do you want to know what the most interesting part of it all is, Alan? I've learned more about Percutio in the last three weeks I've been with APS than I have in the last three *years* with the CIA. Fucking eye-opening stuff about them, dude. Stuff I would have given my right arm to know when I was with the CIA." Although Alan couldn't see her, Kelly's mouth quirked up in a devilish smile. "APS is fascinated with my gift, Alan. They think *I'm* a gift because of what I can do. I'm already on their Percutio team and, the general consensus is, if you were stupid enough to throw me away, they'll leverage my abilities accordingly."

"Kelly," Alan cajoled. "I know how angry you must be. Trust me, I have done nothing but try to fix this since the day I had to call you and tell you the CIA decided to burn you. You are an extremely valuable asset. I don't know who was responsible for having you burned, but I'm trying to get to the bottom of it."

Kelly rolled her eyes at the APS management team, cynicism clear in her expression. "Save it, McAllister. APS has offered to find Grigor Reizan for me. With their help, I can neutralize his ass and de-fang Percutio once and for all. Robyn will finally be avenged and the CIA will be nothing more than a bad memory for me. So, unless you can trump *that* offer, my friend, you and the CIA can fuck right the hell off."

There was a faint beep as Kelly hung up on McAllister.

"Fucking *stellar, princesa.*" Riley caught Kelly up in her strong arms and kissed her fiercely as Bryn and the Seven applauded. "You were pissed, you were smug, and you taunted him just enough to make him wonder what you truly do know about Percutio. Excellent job."

"I give McAllister forty-eight hours, tops, before he contacts Kelly again." Trill was busy on her laptop. "I want to propose we create an APS Percutio task force, with one associate from each of our teams. That way, we can start seriously digging to figure out what Reizan has up his sleeve."

"Reizan and his goons have historically been forbidden to operate in the Tampa Bay area because this is APS territory," Casey said next. "That doesn't mean, however, that the sneaky fuck isn't laying down plans to violate that order now. He wants Kelly too much."

"Agreed." Riley looked at her twin. "Do you want to bet Reizan is busy trying to figure out a way to infiltrate APS? Good luck with that, asshole, because our people have been with us for a long time and they are beyond loyal. But that doesn't mean he won't try to penetrate our outer fringes."

Bryn drummed her fingers on the tabletop. "That's not a bet I'd take, *mano*. When we get the task force set up, we can task some of them with finding out what new peripheral players have come on our scene within the last six weeks. Girlfriends, new friends, vendors, etc. Our people can check them out and seal any leaks there if we have to."

"Can we also get a list of known Percutio associates who live in Tampa Bay?" Kelly sat at her desk and fired up her own laptop. "Where they hang out? Who they might know? I'm assuming your order to Reizan was just for conducting Percutio business in the Tampa Bay area, and it didn't prohibit one of their associates from actually living here as long as they follow the rules?"

Riley nodded. "That's correct, *princesa*. We keep a constantly updated list of local Percutio members. It's a big organization, but we're only interested in keeping a close eye on those who live in our backyard. What are you thinking?"

"Let me get my thoughts straight before I say anything further, *amante*, okay? I have an idea, but I want to make sure it's feasible first so I don't sound like an idiot." Kelly logged into the APS system.

They all scoffed. "One thing you are *not* is an idiot, little sis." Drew raised her eyebrow at Kelly. "As far as I'm concerned, you figure out what you need to figure out, and you let me know if I can help you." There was a rumble of agreement in the Bunker.

"Each of you pull an associate—not your number two's—from your team who will be assigned full-time to Percutio until further notice. Let them know about their new assignment and kick the names over to Trill so she can set up the task force." Riley was texting notes to herself.

"Kel, I just sent you the list of Percutio members in the local area, with all the information we have on each of them." Trill's fingers flew over her keyboard. "When the Seven has chosen who they want to be on the Percutio task force from their teams, their first assignment will be to investigate the new APS peripheral players. I know we trust our own people implicitly, but we want to make sure no one is trying to slither in through the back door."

"That should take a few days. In the meantime, *mi hermana*, you and Rowan and I have a date to breach APS headquarters with my crew tomorrow night." Jaime smirked at Trill. "Be prepared to weep, *broki*, because I have a feeling the Holland sisters will have you crying like a baby before it's over." Kelly threw her head back and laughed as Trill flipped Jaime off.

"We'll finalize the task force, make sure our operations are completely secure, then discuss next steps. *Princesa*, do you need more than a few days before you can share your thoughts with us?" Riley asked.

"No, that should be plenty of time. Actually, I probably don't need more than a day before I'm ready to pitch my idea to you and Bryn and the Seven," Kelly said, already deep into the file Trill had sent to her.

"Excellent. We can all give an update at our regular management meeting the day after next." Riley looked at the back of Kelly's head with amusement. "I hate to interrupt your beauty sleep, baby, but we meet every morning at six a.m."

Kelly flipped Riley off over her shoulder without turning around. "I am not some wilting flower, Armstrong. If staff meetings are at six a.m., then staff meetings are at six a.m. Casey, I'll be ready to run at 4:30 going forward."

Kelly then looked over her shoulder at Riley with her eyebrow raised. "Little tough girl, remember?"

"I remember," Riley said softly, her amber eyes glowing with heat as they rested on Kelly's beautiful face. "I don't think any of us could ever forget exactly what you're made of, Kelly Holland."

Chapter 21

Kelly waited quietly with Riley, Bryn, and Rowan—plus Jaime's crew—in front of the large eight-unit apartment building located on the west side of Biscayne Street South, directly across the street from the APS complex. Jaime was due to make an appearance at any moment.

While Riley and Bryn had apartments within the APS complex itself, each of the Seven had an apartment in this building, which had been built especially for them. The eighth apartment was not occupied and was used for extra storage.

The two-bedroom, two-bathroom apartments were large, comfortable, private, and allowed the Seven to return to APS headquarters quickly when necessary. The security was unparalleled, and each apartment was wired with state-of-the-art communications technology and wireless failover, which allowed them to seamlessly switch from a disrupted connection to an independent, high-speed connection if necessary.

Kelly had handed Bryn a bag as they'd left the Bunker the day before, telling her the clothes inside were for Rowan for the penetration test tonight.

Thanks to Kelly, Rowan was now clad in the same tight dark blue leggings and long-sleeved dark blue rash guard that Kelly had on, her blonde curls tucked into the identical dark blue knitted cap that Kelly had on over her own dark red curls.

"Clothing in dark blue is better than black for stealth at night, Ro," Kelly had explained to her sister when she saw her. "Dark blue actually blends into dark backgrounds in no-light conditions more readily than stark black does. Something in black will form a harsh, solid outline, whereas something in dark blue intermingles with its surroundings and melts more invisibly into the darkness."

Upon hearing Kelly's explanation to Rowan, Riley had wrapped her muscled arms around her femme and squeezed her tightly.

"You excite me, *princesa*," Riley had breathed quietly into Kelly's ear. "It will take me years to uncover all of your layers. I've only barely scratched the surface of everything you are." Kelly felt her core clench at the desire in Riley's voice.

Jaime came quietly out of the apartment building. "Are we ready, *mi corillo*?" she asked in barely audible tones, adjusting the comm in her ear. Kelly signaled in the affirmative with the rest of the crew, waiting for Jaime to indicate they were ready to move out.

Earlier that day, Jaime and her physical security crew had met with them in one of the conference rooms to go over their penetration test—*pentest*—plan.

"The first thing we'll do is a technical surveillance countermeasure investigation," Jaime told them. "I know I like to give Trill a rash of shit over security because she's one of my best friends, and that's what we do with each other. But make no mistake, *hermanos*. Trill is a fucking technical security *legend* and getting the best of her is all but impossible.

"First, we'll need to search for radio frequencies and infrared energy capable of transmitting a signal from the entire area of investigation. We'll also need to check for the presence of any covert cameras, unauthorized Wi-Fi, multimedia, and Bluetooth devices. We need to look for *anything*, no matter how small or seemingly insignificant, that could give our position away or alert others to our presence."

Jaime smiled without humor. "I guarantee you that fucker will have tricks up her sleeve we will never see coming unless we are very, very alert. APS is the secure facility it is because of her skill, and she doesn't *ever* play when it comes to security."

Desi, Jaime's number two, began their countermeasure investigation by running a power line scan on the power lines surrounding the APS complex, looking for what Jaime had explained were called carrier current devices. *Those types of devices could utilize the power lines as a transmission path*, Jaime had said, *connecting to a conductor which could send outside audio or video transmissions to Trill's crew.*

Morgan, whom Rowan remembered had been instrumental in helping to bring Dino Coravani down, was using a thermal imaging camera to search for heat sources from hidden devices.

"Thermal imaging cameras have the ability to sense infrared light in low- or no-light conditions," Morgan had told them during their meeting. "Thermal imaging devices can 'see' you. They create images based on differences in temperature by detecting infrared radiation—in other words, heat—that emanates from objects, such as your body, and the surrounding environment."

"Running reconnaissance is the very first thing we do during a countermeasure investigation," Jaime then informed them. "We have all possible exits and entrances already mapped. We have some existing security barriers that don't change, like our outside doors, but some that do. For example, Trill and her crew like to move our security cameras around before a known pentest, just to fuck with us."

"All of our outside door locks are electronic. They require not only a card key, but also a PIN code." Morgan's sea green eyes had smiled at them. "Pin code pads for facilities like ours are typically connected to a central access control system. Some of our inside doors, like the ones that give access to extremely sensitive areas, however, are stand alone. That can make our job that much harder if we are running an internal penetration test. Of course, we all typically have the correct card keys and pin codes to the complex, but Trill and her team will change our access and lock us out of everything when we're running a pentest."

Both Kelly and Rowan had been breathless over the skill and knowledge displayed by Jaime and her team. Rowan especially had been blown away by Jaime's uncharacteristically stern demeanor as she taught them how physical security worked at APS.

Kelly, however, was less surprised.

"I caught a very, very brief glimpse of Jaime when she, Riley, Teagan, and Casey came to extract me from Anna Maria Island, before Casey rendered me unconscious," Kelly told Rowan. "Needless to say, Jaime Quintero is *not* someone I'd want to face in a dark alley if she was after me."

Desi had continued when Morgan was finished. "Whether a door's keypad lock is integrated into a larger security system or not, it still requires an electrical current to release its lock bolt. The current is generated and triggered as soon as the user enters the correct code into the keypad lock system to unlock the door." Desi mimicked entering a code.

Then the handsome butch had smiled with a trace of humor. "I'm still working on triggering the current without having to enter the code. Darcy, Trill's second, has me blocked and keeps me locked out, so I haven't been successful so far. That fucker." The rest of the crew had snickered.

Kelly and Rowan had looked at each other, realizing at that moment that *all* of the associates at APS were extremely close and had a deep respect for each other—not just the Seven.

"Are you from Whimsy, Desi?" Kelly had asked curiously, changing the subject for a moment. "What about the rest of you? Did you all grow up together like the Seven did?"

"I'm the only one on the physical security team who's originally from Whimsy," remarked Angel, another one of Jaime's crew. "Des is from Miami. Morgan is from Cleveland, of all fucking places, but she moved here to Whimsy when she was in high school. TJ is from Orlando, and Chris is a native of Naples."

Desi's face went uncharacteristically soft. "Overall, the APS associates—outside of the Seven—are from everywhere, but fate or whatever the fuck you want to call it, brought us all together. School, family, general relocation… There are a million reasons why every one of us ended up in Whimsy and eventually became part of APS. All we know is that this is where we were meant to be and none of us would *ever* want to be anywhere else, or around anyone else."

A slightly menacing shadow then fell over Desi's face. "We might bust each other's balls a lot, but I'd slaughter *anyone* who dared to mess with one of my homies."

"We have the best goddamned crews in the world," Riley had stated flatly as Bryn nodded her head in agreement. "Their talent and loyalty are beyond measure. You and Rowan should feel free to go to any of them at any time if you need something, and we or one of the Seven are not available for some reason. I'd trust any one of them with you implicitly."

Now, Kelly and Rowan noticed Angel and TJ, another APS physical security crew member, were scanning the building perimeter with binoculars after the physical security crew had finished disabling the devices they'd found. When they were done, Angel soundlessly signaled that the perimeter was clear, and the entire crew moved seamlessly to surround the huge complex.

"*Hermana*, I want you to stay with Riley, and Rowan can stay with Bryn," Jaime's voice whispered in her ear. Jaime had changed the frequency on Kelly's comm to accept transmissions from her own crew. She had also blocked any outgoing transmissions to the rest of the Seven for the duration of the pentest.

"Copy that," Kelly touched the comm in her ear and whispered back. She crept with Riley around to the north side of the APS complex, which covered a full city block, staying well back from the well-lit exterior of the building.

She looked at the huge headquarters, her eyes sweeping thoroughly over the north side of the premises. She recognized the huge, galvanized steel door set into the side and knew it was operated by the military-grade remote controls owned by each associate.

The secure entrance led into an associate parking area, an employee entrance to APS, Riley's reserved parking spaces, and the private elevator to her top-floor apartment. Bryn's apartment access with her reserved spaces, additional associate parking, and another employee entrance were located through an identical steel door on the building's south side.

Kelly knew the visitor's entrance that led to APS reception was on the west side of the complex, facing the apartments across the street where the Seven lived. After taking a moment to orient herself, she spent some time scanning the north side of the building more deeply. She grumpily came to the conclusion there was no way to force a breach through the steel door. Additionally, there were no other windows or doors on the north side they could use for access either.

"Trill, I absolutely adore you, but I'm going to kick your ass, *broki*," Kelly muttered, suddenly realizing as she heard soft laughter that her comm was still open and everyone could hear her. She shook her head and cast a playful glare at a grinning Riley before gesturing toward the front of the building.

Just as she was about to walk with Riley to the west side of the complex, however, she spotted something at the bottom of the building that made her frown.

Kelly touched the comm in her ear again. "Wait a minute. What the fuck is that? That thing there, right up against the bottom of the building, just east of the garage door on the north side? I can barely see it, but there's something there."

She peered again more closely at the tiny, scarcely visible gleam she could see in the grass at the building's base. She crept closer to the complex, making sure she still stayed well back from any light source, and looked again. From her new position, she saw what appeared to be a miniscule steel grate all but invisibly hidden by the grass. It was so tiny, she had almost missed it.

"It's the outside part of a raised access floor, *princesa*. The actual raised access is inside the building itself. It creates a hidden void used for the passage of mechanical and electrical services, as well as data cables." Riley's low voice filled her ear through her comm. "This tiny outside piece allows the system to breathe without letting water in. Why?"

Kelly thought for a minute, then clamped her lips against a victory squeal as she activated her comm once more. "What do you want to bet Jaime and her crew could push some type of signal interference up through the grate that would unlock the doors? Maybe introduce some static or magnetic noise that would interrupt the signal? I'll wager these cable pass-throughs have never been tested, at least not from out here anyway.

"I'm positive the cables have standard shielding from end-to-end that limits any type of signal interference, but it's maybe not as robust as it probably is past the initial void. As long as you know what frequency the doors use, which I'm sure the crew either knows or can easily find out, we can disable them without affecting the rest of the building. At least we can if the wiring was done correctly when the facility was built, which I'll also wager is true."

There was a long silent pause. "Son of a fucking *bitch*," Jaime finally swore vehemently through the comm, joining an added chorus of cursing. "She's absolutely right, *mi corillo*. There would be nothing here in the pass-through outside of standard signal shielding that would block a signal if the data cables were accessed externally. The outside grate is so fucking tiny and invisible, it's never occurred to any of us to attempt a breach from here. Especially through the raised access floor from the outside."

They could hear Jaime blow out a deep breath. "*Hermana*, you are absolutely a fucking gift to us. Although this has never been an issue in the over eight years since this facility was built, this could have potentially resulted in a major breach to APS someday. Des, let's work on accessing the facility with the team, then do what we need to do to seal the break immediately."

She chuckled without humor. "Trill is going to lose her motherfucking mind, *hermanos*. Red, I'm sure you also want to see her face when we all come strolling in. This is definitely a critical situation, but I have to admit I'm liking the *gotcha!* aspect of it. Even though I'm pissed as hell this has never occurred to me before."

"I'll look through our files and pull the facility information on that particular frequency, Jaim," Angel volunteered. "I'll send it to Desi and you two can launch when everyone is in position. This is going to unlock *every*-fucking-thing on that frequency, so we need to make sure we have manual security until we've breached the building and relocked the doors."

Kelly felt Riley's arms wrap around her from behind as they waited while Jaime and her crew got to work.

"If I *ever* hear you say you don't feel useful to us, *princesa*," Riley whispered in her ear, "I will turn you over my knee and blister your ass until you can't sit down for a week." Kelly felt her eyes grow huge.

"What you did for APS just today alone has earned you a place here for the rest of your life." Riley nuzzled the soft skin behind Kelly's ear, making her shiver. "Not only are you beautiful, you are so goddamned brilliant, it takes my breath away. I can't imagine living life without you now. Not now, and not ever."

Kelly felt tears prick her eyelids as she relaxed back against Riley's strong body. "I can't imagine living life without you either, *amante*." She gulped as she tried to keep hold of her emotions. "I'm so happy to be a part of APS. So grateful and thankful for how all of you have taken Rowan and me under your wing, especially you and Bryn. We found our tribe right when we least expected it."

"The two of you are easy to love, baby." Riley caressed the side of Kelly's face. "You both are a living testament to the amazing people that Bill and Amanda Holland were. They would be so incredibly proud of their girls." Kelly rubbed her cheek against Riley's hand, feeling too full of emotion to speak.

They stood together quietly until their comms flared to life about thirty minutes later.

"The signal interference works, *mi corillo*. We're ready to complete the breach," Jaime said quietly. "The second we finish disabling the locks and open the door, however, be aware that Trill and her crew will automatically know someone has accessed the complex. We will all breach the facility through the front visitor's entrance just as soon as the door is unlocked. Angel and Desi will immediately proceed to the north entrance to stand guard, and TJ and Morgan will proceed to the south entrance, while I find Trill to let her know what's happening. Chris," the fifth member of Jamie's five-person crew, "will continue to cover the visitors' entrance. Bryn, Rowan, Riley, and Kelly will proceed straight to Conference Room 1 and wait for the rest of us there. I'll confirm when the facility has been re-secured."

Kelly felt her heart pounding as the entire breach team met on the front sidewalk.

"Des. Hit it," Jaime ordered. They all moved swiftly to the front door as Desi pressed some buttons on her iPad Mini. Everyone heard a faint click as the door unlocked.

Like lightning, Jaime's crew executed their roles like clockwork. As Kelly moved with Rowan and the Armstrong twins into Conference Room 1, after the rest of the team had already disappeared down the hallway, she saw Trill and her crew pouring out of the Recon Room.

While Trill's associates immediately scattered, chasing after the physical security team, Kelly saw Trill stop to talk to Jaime, hands planted ominously on her hips.

"Oh, fuck." Kelly felt ill as the four of them moved into the conference room.

Rowan sat down heavily into one of the conference room chairs, eyes wide, as Bryn sat down beside her. "Trill looked like she was about to spontaneously combust, Kel. I have *never* seen her that mad. Holy crap."

Bryn easily lifted her fiancée up and resettled her on her own lap. "That's because you didn't see her when you were taken, *dulzura*. Don't let those dimples fool you." She kissed Rowan softly. "Trill can be meaner than a snake when she wants to be, just like the rest of the Seven."

"Yeah, Ro. You also weren't with us when Trill threatened to slaughter Grigor Reizan." Kelly shuddered at the remembrance. As her sister's eyes widened even more, Kelly fixed her own eyes anxiously on the conference room door.

After about twenty-five minutes, Jaime and her crew came into the conference room. "The complex has been re-secured and all of the doors have been locked again," Jaime reported. "Teagan and Kennedy have their seconds coordinating 24/7 coverage between their crews for the entire complex, until we can fix the weakness in our outer perimeter."

She raised one dark brow and braced herself against the back of a conference room chair, propping one of her boots up against it. "Trill's on her way, incidentally, and she is *pissed*." Kelly looked uneasily at Riley, then turned her attention back to the conference room door.

Just then, the door opened and a clearly furious Trillian Dacanay walked into the room, followed by Darcy.

Chapter 22

Kelly felt her lungs freeze as Trill's unsmiling face zeroed in on her, her usually gentle and twinkling light brown eyes dark with fury, her deep dimples nowhere in sight.

Kelly slowly stood up, hands flexing nervously, as Trill approached her. Although Trill was the shortest one of the Seven, she still stood eye level with Kelly, although her anger at the moment made it seem as though she was ten feet tall.

To Kelly's utter surprise, however, Trill wrapped her arms around her and held Kelly with obvious affection, hugging her gently. Kelly all but collapsed against Trill in sheer relief.

"Are you mad at me, Trill?" Kelly's voice was muffled against Trill's shoulder as she fiercely returned her friend's hug.

Trill just tightened her arms, then carefully cupped the back of Kelly's head with a strong hand. "I am fucking *livid* right now, Red, and I seriously want to kill something. But I'm not mad at you, little sister. *Never* at you. As pissed as I am, I know with absolute certainty that you did APS a great service today."

The two of them hugged for a couple of minutes more, and Trill nodded at Riley over Kelly's shoulder when she finally felt Kelly ready to step back. Riley took her woman back from Trill, tucking Kelly into her side.

"Before Trill decides to beat the fuck out of herself anymore, *mi hermana*, let me just say this." Jaime's expression was somber as she cut Trill off before Trill could open her mouth again. "Every single fucking one of us missed that weakness in our security. *Every. Single. One. Of. Us.* Me, the rest of the Seven, the Armstrong twins—hell, the entire APS organization, Red. Almost fifty associates total. Over eight years since the APS complex was built, through fucking countless penetration tests, technical challenges, you name it. *We. All. Fucking. Missed. It.*"

Riley took over from Jaime, soothing her still-nervous femme with gentle strokes of her back and arms. "It took you and your experience as a covert and clandestine CIA operations agent to catch this, *princesa*. I'm just as fucking pissed as Trill and Jaime and the rest of us—and just as responsible—for missing this. But I also don't know that I've *ever* been prouder of an APS associate as I am right now."

Bryn regarded Kelly from where she sat with Rowan on her lap and chimed in with her own thoughts.

"Kel, you and Rowan both have gifts that have held us all in complete awe. No, Rowan isn't a full-time APS associate like you are, but she's still on our books as an independent contractor. She's one hundred percent come through for us when we've needed her, as you well know." Bryn smiled reassuringly at Kelly. "Exactly like you did yourself tonight."

Chris, the black-haired butch with ice blue eyes from Jaime's team who'd been introduced to Kelly earlier, spoke up next. "Kelly, one of the reasons APS has the reputation it does, and why we're as good as we are, is because we're all committed to learning from our mistakes so we'll do better the next time. That's what the Armstrong twins and the Seven teach us, every single damn day. And they don't exempt themselves from those lessons either, which is one of the reasons why their crews will follow them down into the depths of hell without thinking twice."

TJ nodded in agreement. "You're part of that now, Red." She looked at Kelly intently. "If you're like us, and I'm suspecting you are, you'll kick your own ass harder than any of us *ever* could when you do make a mistake." Kelly huffed out a laugh and nodded an agreement, finally relaxing a bit.

"As far as this particular situation goes, we're all on the hook for it because none of us caught that weakness." Desi, who had been quiet up until now, put in her own two cents. "But we'll all work together to fix it, too. As a matter of fact, I volunteer to lead a cross-team effort to inspect every inch of this facility—inside and out—to make sure the APS complex is totally sealed."

Just then, the door opened again to admit the rest of the Seven, all of them plainly in a pissy mood.

"The *fuck*?" Drew was not happy, her hazel eyes almost as dark as Trill's. "How come we never fucking saw this before? Someone seriously needs to kick my ass for this."

"Holy fucking shit. I cannot fucking believe I've missed it all this time." Teagan's voice was as dark as Drew's eyes as she entered the conference room behind Drew, running her hands in aggravation through her red-gold hair.

She and the other members of the management team, who all looked just as pissed as they filed in, searched everyone's face in confusion, as the entire conference room burst out laughing, dispelling the tension.

Chuckling and shaking her head in amusement, Riley filled the newcomers in on what had just transpired. "And that fucker over there," she gestured at Trill when she was finished, "needs to stop beating herself the fuck up and admit we're all at fault here.

"That goes for you, too, Darcy." Riley raised a brow at Trill's second, who had stayed silent through it all. "You're Trill's second, you wouldn't be if you weren't a fucking superstar, and shit happens sometimes." Darcy nodded at Riley's words and her muscles released infinitesimally.

"We all fucked up. Now, let's fix it."

Trill blew out a deep breath and nodded, too. Kelly was relieved to see Trill's eyes return to their normal light brown color, and her deep dimples peeped as she finally smiled at Kelly.

"Des, I think I'm going to take you up on your offer to oversee the breach inspection since we deliberately excluded any of our seconds from being on the Percutio task force." Desi gave Riley a thumbs up. "Actually, I think I'd like to see everyone's second as a part of this effort. I want Kelly in on it because she can bring that

CIA operations experience to the table. *Mano*?" Riley looked at her twin.

"I'm totally on board with that," Bryn agreed, her arms still wrapped around Rowan. "Teag, Kenn—are we set as far as security coverage until we can get the void signal interference plugged and tested?" The two nodded.

Riley stood up. "It's getting late, and I can tell Kelly and Rowan have just about had it." Kelly leaned against Riley as she suddenly felt exhaustion sweep over her. "You, *princesa*, are excused from both our morning run and our staff meeting. Case, let Jess know Kelly will meet her in Hades about eight o'clock to work on her Krav Maga."

"I got you, Kel." Casey surveyed Kelly critically before she started to text Jess, then grinned as Kelly rolled her eyes at her.

"You won't miss much in the staff meeting, baby. Bryn and I will be making sure everyone is up to speed as far as our plans to move forward with this breach assessment. If anything else happens to come up, I'll fill you in when I see you." Riley kissed Kelly on the forehead and they prepared to leave.

"And stellar job, Red." Blake gave her a thumbs-up as the whole room started to applaud. Uncharacteristically, Kelly blushed scarlet and waved her hand in dismissal.

Riley took her hand. "We give each other credit whenever it's due, *princesa*. As fucked up as this situation is, we found it thanks to you, we can fix it, and now we can make sure it will never happen again."

Whimsical Princess

* * * * *

Kelly and Rowan looked around at their new home with wide, emotional eyes.

In the past few weeks, there had been a flurry of activity finishing the house. Ember and Nia had completed the finish work, Teagan and her team had installed their state-of-the-art security system, the contents of their Virginia home had been delivered, and all of the new furnishings Rowan, Clem, and Rosi had purchased had arrived.

Kelly had left most of the organization and decorating of the house to Rowan and the rest of their friends, while she, Riley, Bryn, and the Seven focused on setting up the pool area, the fire pit feature, and the outdoor kitchen/grill.

Thanks to Riley and Bryn, a beautiful boat Riley said was an Offshore Voyager 3500 also floated serenely at their back dock. Kelly and Rowan's mouths had fallen open when they saw it for the first time.

"It's so *big*." Kelly's eyes were huge.

Riley put her arms around her woman. "It's 39' long and has a seating capacity of twelve. Between my twin and me, the Seven, and you two, there are eleven of us, *princesa*. Add your girls and now, we're up to sixteen. We won't all be able to go out together at the same time, but Bryn and I wanted something that could accommodate most of us whenever we could, without getting too huge.

"As far as Bryn, the Seven, and I go, we all have boat licenses and can pilot this boat. Although I should tell you Blake is a fucking machine when it comes to maritime knowledge. She actually has her U.S. Coast Guard captain's license." Riley grinned at the look on Kelly's face. "Blake's dad was a bona fide master mariner with an unlimited master's license until he retired, and she inherited her love of boating from him. If you or Rowan ever have any questions about seamanship, Blake is definitely who you want to ask."

Kelly's new pride and joy was stashed in the garage next to Rowan's Audi. When she and Riley had gone car shopping to buy Kelly a new vehicle, Kelly had somewhat shyly admitted to Riley what her dream car had always been. The corners of Riley's mouth had quirked up before she'd immediately headed to a Jaguar dealership in St. Petersburg.

When they returned to the house, Riley following Kelly in her SUV, Bryn and the Seven were outside waiting for them, since Riley had texted them when they'd left the Jaguar dealership. Bryn smirked as Kelly pulled up, having been thoroughly briefed by Rowan. The jaws of the Seven had dropped open in astonishment as Kelly pulled into the circular driveway.

"Fucking *hell*, little sis!" Kenn had whooped as she raced to help Kelly out of the car. "Are you fucking shitting me? This is *outrageous*!"

Kelly's new car was a gorgeous blue Jaguar F-Type R, a V8 eight-speed automatic. Kelly had actually giggled as she accepted Kenn's assistance, then sighed as Riley wrapped her happy woman securely in her arms when she reached her.

"600 horsepower, all-wheel drive. Annnnd…this baby can drop 60mph in 3.5 seconds." Kelly giggled again, radiating sheer joy. "Since I love you all to pieces, I think each one of you should take her out and test her. Just to make sure your little sister will be safe, you know." She beamed happily at her new siblings, who whooped and high-fived each other in excitement.

Now, Kelly and Rowan were in the living room of their finished house, staring at the beautiful family collage Bryn had given to Rowan for Christmas, which hung in a place of honor. They stood with their arms around each other, tears streaming down their faces, as they looked at the faces of their beloved parents.

"They're happy, Ro. Can you feel them?" Kelly's heart was in her eyes and on her face, even as she cried tears of both sorrow and peace.

Rowan nodded, her own tears matching her sister's. "Oh, Kelly… I miss them so freaking much. But I do feel them. I feel such a sense of peace from them, because they know we're somewhere we can be safe, and we're with people who love us."

The Holland sisters then looked around for the Armstrong twins at the same time. Riley and Bryn, who had stayed back out of respect, immediately came and took possession of their women.

Bryn, with Rowan tucked securely in her arms, looked at the Holland family collage.

"Bill. Amanda," she said quietly. "We've got your girls. As long as Riley and I are around, there is nothing in this world that will ever touch them."

Riley's quiet voice echoed her twin's. "We promise you that from the bottom of our hearts. You gave us all such a gift in them. Every single one of us here will treasure and protect them always."

Kelly turned around, still crying, and gestured to the Seven and the APS femmes, who were clustered unobtrusively by the front door. At Kelly's request, all of them—Teagan, Kennedy, Blake, Jaime, Casey, Drew, Trill, Clementine, Nova, Alyssa, Brooke, and Delaney—came forward and surrounded Kelly and Rowan, their faces full of enormous respect and feelings too deep to put into words.

The entire group stood together silently for a few minutes, looking at the beautiful Holland family collage, until Kelly raised her head from where it had been laying on Riley's shoulder.

"For the first time since my mother died, I feel totally peaceful. Rowan and I will miss them both desperately for the rest of our lives, but I know we feel in our hearts they're together again and happy—wherever they are."

Even with the emotion coursing through her, though, Kelly couldn't help but notice just then that Teagan had her arms around Delaney, Trill held Nova, Alyssa was in Jaime's arms, and Brooke rested against Blake. Her spidey sense prickled and her senses reeled, wondering if there was more to this than just the emotion of the moment.

However, Riley broke into her thoughts as she nuzzled Kelly behind her ear.

"Welcome home, *princesa*. You and your sister both. No matter where we go or what we do, this house will always be a place of rest and sanctuary for you, Rowan, and our family. Forever."

Chapter 23

Every eye hit the tall, hot, sexy blonde who had just walked into Club Infinity, one of Tampa's premier nightclubs.

Long, straight platinum blonde hair hung down her back, swinging from side to side as she strutted through the entrance, until it reached a curvy backside. Crystal blue eyes that were rimmed seductively in dark navy and silver tones—crowned with thick black lashes—swept over the other patrons a little anxiously, as if she was looking for someone.

She wore a short, tight, sleeveless white dress that hit her mid-thigh and looked as if it had been poured on her. Her long legs ended in stiletto heels with a sexy ankle strap, her clearly expensive jewelry was heavy hammered silver, and her full pouting lips were painted a deep red.

She continued through the entranceway just like she was taking a runway, pausing every few feet to look around her again, before sighing in exasperation and moving on.

When she reached the huge front main bar and had walked a short distance down the line of barstools, she paused, smiled absently at the group of men who were standing beside her, then turned to the bartender and dismissed them immediately. "I'd like a white wine spritzer, please," she requested in a smoky voice with a Midwestern cadence, turning around and scanning the bar again as she waited for the bartender to make her drink.

"You look a little lost, *jan*," said the man closest to her in an accented voice, leaning over with obvious interest. He was a big guy, stocky, with a swarthy complexion and cold, black beady eyes. "Are you looking for someone?"

The blonde sighed in irritation, tapping one of her stilettos, and finally gave him her attention. "Apparently, my stupid boyfriend stood me up *again*. This is the second freakin' time this week and I just don't know what's wrong with him. Unless it's that stupid redhead who lives upstairs in his apartment complex." She rolled her big, blue eyes and shook her head, sending her platinum blonde tresses swinging.

The bartender arrived with her drink and, as she was about to pull money out of her small clutch purse to pay for it, she gasped as the man laid one of his big hands over hers. "Allow me, *jan*," he said, gesturing to one of the other men with him, who leaned over the bar and told the bartender to put her drink on their tab.

"Well, gee, thanks." The blonde flashed him an effervescent smile. "I was startin' to think I got all dressed up and came out for nothin'." She batted her eyes at him flirtatiously.

The man turned to look at his friend. "Rook. Why don't you and Striker go find us a table in the back? We need to make sure this lovely lady is taken care of and is comfortable. It looks like her boyfriend doesn't know the proper way to treat a lady." The man's eyes looked the blonde up and down in a perusing fashion as Rook went to do his bidding. "What is your name, *jan*?"

"Misty." The stunning blonde giggled as she sipped her wine spritzer. "Gee, Harold is gonna be *so* mad if he finds out I talked to another man. Then again, he hasn't bothered to show up *again*, so he probably doesn't even care. What's *your* name, handsome?"

"You should call me Parrot, Misty*jan*. My full name is too hard for Americans to pronounce. And I wouldn't worry that pretty little head about your boyfriend anymore if I were you." The cold black eyes looked at her with a definite glint. "Any idiot who leaves a woman like you alone deserves to lose her." Misty giggled again.

Misty's expression didn't alter as a tiny, hidden comm in her ear flared to life.

* * * * *

Kelly Holland—aka, Misty—had argued fiercely with the Armstrong twins and the Seven when she'd brought them her plan of gathering intel on Percutio, by using some of the same methods she'd used in the CIA's covert and clandestine operations directorate.

Riley especially had lost her shit when she learned the details of what Kelly was proposing.

"Have you lost your goddamn *mind, princesa*?" Riley's voice was the closest thing to a shout Kelly had ever heard. "You expect us to agree to let you walk smack dab into the middle of a group of

Percutio scum, dressed as provocatively as all fucking get out, just so you can scramble their brains and see what you can draw out of them?"

Bryn and the Seven were also seething at the thought, their faces and their vocal assessments plainly expressing what they thought of Kelly's plan.

"There is no fucking *way* any of us are *ever* putting you at risk like that." Riley was livid. "I know you were a fucking hotshot CIA operative, *princesa*, and were involved in a lot of dangerous operations, but *motherfucker*. No. Fucking. Way, Kel. Not on *my* watch."

But Kelly yelled back even louder, her green eyes on fire.

"This is what I fucking *do*, you assholes! For eight fucking years, I did shit like this for the CIA all the time—most of which was *way* beyond what I'm proposing to do here. This is fucking *nothing* compared to some of the operations I've been involved in. I have a shitload of identities and disguises I've used over the last eight years. I've never been caught, never even been *made* on an assignment."

Suddenly, all her anger dropped away, her voice becoming ice cold, tempered steel.

"If this is how you all feel, then I would like you to accept my resignation, effective immediately." Kelly calmly stood up and gathered her things, refusing to look at any one of them. "If this is the level of respect you have for my abilities and my experience, then I have no place at APS. I'm not going to sit here and fight with you, or *beg* you, every fucking time we have a mission and I want to do my part and bring my experience to the table. *Not. Doing. It.*"

"Kelly—" Riley began, but Kelly held up her hand.

"No. I'm fucking *done*, Riley. I'm done with all of you right now." She pulled her comm out of her ear, tossed it on the table, then stalked to the door. "I'm going to my house and I would appreciate it if you would allow me my space. I'm far, *far* too angry to even be in the same room with you assholes right now." She left without a backward glance.

"*FUCK.*" In an uncharacteristic burst of temper, Riley kicked the conference room chair next to her. Every single one of them looked at each other, ready to commit murder.

Until Kennedy sighed, still pissed off to no end, but resigned. "She's right. We disrespected the *fuck* out of her." Kenn then turned her anger on herself. "We treated her like some brainless, incompetent airhead who needs protection, instead of the *extremely* capable professional she is."

"*Fuck*," Trill echoed Riley, rubbing her hand over her eyes. "We've stepped in some fucking shit this time, haven't we?" She gritted her teeth. "It's anybody's guess at this point if she'll ever forgive us. Fucking morons, all of us."

The group was silent, each one of them engrossed in her own dark thoughts.

"Riles." Through sheer force of will, Teagan's voice was even. "I take it texting or calling her right now to apologize would be a bad idea, wouldn't it?"

Riley laughed without humor. "She's liable to blow the whole fucking APS complex up right now rather than talk to any of us. Especially me." She looked at her twin with irony.

"If I were you, *mano*, I'd get ready for the lecture of my life when I got home...because you *know* Kelly has called Rowan, and Ro is going to blow your ass the fuck up when you see her." Bryn glared at her twin, then suddenly slumped back in her chair, resigned as well.

As it was, none of them heard from Kelly until the next morning. To make matters worse, an agitated Bryn discovered when *she* got home that Rowan had chosen to spend the night with her sister in their new house, rather than stay with Bryn in their apartment.

Kelly texted Riley the next morning and requested that Riley, Bryn, and the Seven meet with her in Conference Room 1. When they all arrived, they found both Holland sisters seated side-by-side at the end of the table, coiled like rattlesnakes with their arms folded. Rowan had a distinctly unhappy look on her face, while Kelly refused to look at them at all, instead staring down at the table.

After they were seated, the Armstrong twins and the Seven waited quietly, the silence eventually growing awkward. To their surprise, Rowan spoke first.

"I don't think I need to explain to you all the level of disrespect you displayed toward my little sister yesterday. At least I hope I don't," Rowan said quietly.

The APS crew shifted uncomfortably.

"I don't always understand this world of yours, how Kelly fits into it, or even everything she does. What I *do* know, however, is that my sister is a consummate professional in anything she undertakes. I also know that it's critically important to have teammates you can trust at your back when you're doing this kind of work."

Rowan continued her lecture. "Unfortunately, now she doesn't feel she has that. And it's no wonder she doesn't. Instead of you all sitting down and acknowledging the danger in what she was proposing, but then working as a team to identify all of the risks and plugging the holes to see if this approach was even feasible, you all freaked out like a bunch of knuckle-dragging cavemen and made Kelly feel 'less than' by your responses."

The room was deathly quiet.

Rowan shook her head sadly. "I love you all, but I've never been as disappointed in you as I was yesterday when I was told about your actions."

Blake clenched her fists when Rowan fell silent. "Kelly. Ro." She paused for a moment, trying to articulate her thoughts. "I can't speak for the rest of the team. I know without a doubt we fucked up and fucked up bad. I am sorrier than you know that I overreacted the way I did. But…" Blake paused again, searching for the words.

Drew spoke up next. "What we did was wrong. So fucking wrong, there isn't any excuse for it. Like Blake, I'm not speaking for anyone but myself.

"But, Kel… I'm sorry, but when you outlined your plan, the very first thing I felt was the type of fear I'd *never* felt until the day Rowan was taken. Unfortunately, my hair-trigger response to what you were proposing reflected that."

"I'm afraid logic didn't play a part in how I reacted either." Trill's voice was dry. "I *know* who you are, Kel. I *know* what you're capable of, and what your proficiencies are. But logic meant fuck-all when the only thing I could picture was those slimy Percutio fucks touching even one hair on your head."

Jaime was quieter than they'd ever seen her. "I watched you blow the fucking doors off the security at the APS complex, Kel, and I *still* acted like, as Ro said, a knuckle-dragging caveman. Like the others, my fear made me stupid." She shook her head in self-recrimination.

Riley stared steadily at the top of Kelly's bent head. "*Princesa*," she said in a low voice, wishing she could hold her femme. "I have no excuses here. None. What I did was beyond inexcusable, and I am sorrier than you know. I would have never done that to Bryn or any of the Seven, and you should be treated no differently.

"But I hope you can understand just how much we've all come to love you, and why it's so important to us for you to be safe. That's why we overreacted, and why we need to work on the knuckle-dragging." Her voice was wry. "Me, more so than anyone.

"Baby." Riley waited patiently until Kelly finally raised her head and looked at all of them.

The entire room was stricken by the hurt they saw on her face, her puffy, bloodshot eyes telling them the story of her sleepless night.

"*Princesa*, I am giving you my heartfelt apology and asking for another chance to prove to you that you are worth far more than what my behavior yesterday displayed. I love *and* respect you, Kelly Holland, and I will spend the rest of my life proving that to you."

Kelly drew in a deep breath, angrily swiping at the tears that started to fall down her face, as everyone waited for her response.

"I appreciate what you've all said today," she said finally. "I believe you understand how hurtful and harmful your words yesterday were, and I do trust you have the intention to not let this happen again. I know you all are protective, and I appreciate that, too. But if I'm ever going to feel like an integral part of this team, you have to let me bring my experience and my capabilities to the table, even if you don't like them.

"If you don't like something I've proposed and you think it's too dangerous, you have every right to say that. I *expect* you to say that, when that's what you feel." Kelly looked around the conference room at each of them. "However…it's not like I ever plan to run an op without you guys at my back. And I don't think it's asking too much for the courtesy of a discussion about a proposal, rather than an immediate negative proclamation from on high."

Casey was frank. "You're right, Red, it's not asking too much. I, for one, am going to do my damndest to make sure this clusterfuck never happens again. I *hated* this and what we did to you. But…I'd still really like to hear from you that you do understand where we were coming from, no matter how wrong we were in how we chose to express it."

Kelly nodded. "I do understand. And as I've said, I appreciate your protectiveness. You'll forgive me if I'm a bit skittish for a little while, though, and it takes some time before I'm completely comfortable this won't ever happen again. I'm sorry, guys, but I can't help it. Yesterday was too hard and I need some time to get over it." They all nodded, not happy, but realizing where she was coming from. "You also need to thank Rowan, because I was totally ready to walk yesterday and she talked me down off that ledge. I'm not saying that to make you all feel bad either."

Kelly let her eyes rest on each face, sad at the stress she saw there but knowing that she needed to be honest.

"If we're going to be a team, then we all need to learn how to work together as a team." She sighed but was resolute as she finished her thoughts. "I love you all, too. So much. But if we can't trust and depend on each other without even thinking about it, then we have nothing."

Now, "Misty" sipped her drink and gave no indication Trillian Dacanay was feeding her intel on the tall, swarthy man she was with.

In addition to her now-restored ear comm, a tiny transmitter was also hidden in one of her long, dangling earrings, so the APS team could hear exactly what was going on around her.

"That's Aram Hakobyan, Kelly, one of Reizan's lieutenants," Trill said softly through the comm. "They call him *Parrot* because he likes to chatter a lot. He's Armenian like Reizan, although Reizan is also one-quarter Filipino on his father's side. Hakobyan is in charge of Florida for Reizan."

Trill's voice dropped even lower. "Hakobyan is extremely dangerous, Red, so please be careful. For backup, Kenn is sitting at the bar on the far left, black fedora and black blazer. Drew is about thirty yards behind you, button-down shirt, suspenders, leather jacket, fitted leather baseball hat worn backward. Teagan, Casey, and Blake are in Club Infinity's front parking lot. Riley is with Bryn, me, and Jaime in the parking lot of the bar next door."

Kelly lowered her eyes while Trill was talking, as if she was shy, then she lifted her eyes and focused her big, baby blues on Parrot's face.

"Yes, Parrot. Thank you," she whispered, acting as if she was overwhelmed by his attention, but letting the Seven and the Armstrong twins know she'd heard Trill and understood.

"And where do you live, Misty*jan*? Are you close by here?" Parrot's eyes were intent.

"Oh, I don't really live in the Tampa area, Parrot. Not yet anyway, although I plan to move here. At least I *did*." Kelly looked crestfallen. "I met Harold online late last year, and we seemed to get along so perfectly together. We decided I would come and stay for a while, so we could really get to know each other in real life…although I insisted on stayin' in a separate hotel, instead of with him at his apartment. He wasn't too happy, but I told him it would be better if we both had our own space. Besides," Kelly straightened up primly, "I told him I wasn't that kind of girl."

She fixed her blue eyes earnestly on Parrot's face.

"There's also this girl who lives in his complex who's made it *super* clear she's into Harold, too. He keeps tellin' me not to worry about her, but I just don't know. She's very aggressive, and Harold doesn't seem to want to put her in her place and tell her he has a girlfriend. He's also been different since I got here last weekend." Kelly let her voice tremble a bit and her eyes grew a little glassy. "Now, he's blown me off two times this week, and I don't know what to do about it. Thank goodness I've been using Uber to get around and not depending on him, or else I'd really be stuck." She sipped her drink despondently, all effervescence gone.

"You are not to worry, Misty*jan*, because I will see you safely home tonight." Then Parrot regarded her cynically. "I also hate to tell you this, and please forgive me for being so blunt, but your Harold sounds like a weasel whose sole aim was to take advantage of you. When his expectations didn't pan out the way he wanted them to, he immediately washed his hands of you and moved on." He patted her hands with a seemingly compassionate look. "He is a fool who doesn't deserve such a beautiful woman."

Kelly heaved a big, dramatic sigh and let a few tears fall. "He seemed so different when we talked online, too. I don't know why I'm surprised, though. It's the story of my life." She sniffled and gave another sad sigh.

"I guess now I should go back across the bridge to St. Petersburg and pack. I have an open return ticket back to Milwaukee, so I'll try to catch a flight home tomorrow."

Kelly's eyes then narrowed with pretend anger. "I wish I could remember how to find Harold's apartment so I could give him a piece of my mind in person before I go. I've only been there once, on the day I got here actually, because we've been meetin' up at my hotel. All I remember is that he lives in some cutesy little town right next to St. Petersburg named Whisper or Whistle or somethin' stupid like that."

She slid off her barstool and picked up her clutch, tucking it under her arm.

"Thanks for the drink, Parrot, and for listenin' to my woes, but I should go. It was very nice meetin' such a gentleman. Maybe I'll meet someone like you someday."

"Do you mean Whimsy?" Parrot's voice was dark.

Kelly snapped her fingers and turned back toward Parrot as she was preparing to walk away. "Whimsy! That was it." She rolled her eyes again. "Harold always droned on constantly about what a great place it was, even though I don't think he ever mentioned the name more than two or maybe three times. Why? Don't tell me you live there, too?"

Parrot burst out laughing, not a very nice laugh. "Let's just say the boss of the organization I work for and his rivals don't exactly see eye-to-eye, *jan*. Whimsy is where their headquarters are located and, in the interest of keeping the peace, we stay on this side of the bridge and keep to ourselves. Our own headquarters are in Miami. The only reason I live in the Tampa Bay area at all is because my ailing mother has lived here for forty years, and she refuses to move anywhere else."

Kelly could just imagine the snorts from the Armstrong twins and the Seven upon hearing that.

She let her eyes round. "You're not in any danger, are you? Oh, Parrot, what horrible people they must be." She let her hands flutter helplessly in distress.

Parrot took her hands again. "Calm, Misty*jan*. There is no danger to us. We avoid trouble whenever we can, but you can be sure in the unlikely event there *was* any confrontation between the two sides, we would end up winning."

Kelly barely refrained from snorting herself.

"Now, Rook is signaling to me that we have a table in the back area where they serve food. It is quieter and we won't have to shout. Let's go and get comfortable, maybe have something to eat, yes? The food here is surprisingly good. At the very least, it would be my pleasure to show you a very nice evening out before you go back home to Milwaukee."

Kelly twirled a platinum blonde strand shyly. "Well, if you're sure, Parrot. I'm positive the last thing you expected tonight was to pick up a stray. I feel just awful buttin' into your evenin' plans."

Parrot lifted one of her hands and kissed the back, then offered Kelly his arm. "My friends and I came out for a drink and to have a relaxing evening, no more. You are *butting*, as you say, into nothing."

"Okay." Kelly dropped her eyes and blushed. "Thank you, Parrot."

When they were settled at their table, Kelly shyly asked their server as he was taking their drink orders where she could find the ladies' room. She excused herself and told everyone she would be right back. Fortunately, there was a line to use the ladies room, so while Kelly was waiting, she held her phone up to her ear and pretended she was talking to a friend as she spoke into her comm.

"I think I'm going to be here for a little while longer, Kayla. It's kind of noisy in here, so I can't talk much. Wait 'til I tell you the story about how Harold blew me off though. What a meanie. Anyhow, how are you?"

"You're doing great, Red," Trill said over her comm. "It's unlikely you'll learn a whole lot, but this Parrot likes to talk and he seems to be taken with you. See if you can draw him out and maybe he'll let it slip about Reizan's plans."

"All I know," Riley's dark voice came over the comm, "is if that motherfucker doesn't keep his hands off my woman, there's going to be bloodshed before the evening is over."

"Silly goose." Kelly's voice was light. "I'll call you when I get back to my hotel tonight and we'll talk about it. Anyhow, I'm almost at the front of the line. Can everything else wait until I get back?"

"Same exit plan strategy we have in place, Kel," Trill confirmed. "When you're ready to leave, drop your earring, then go to the ladies room again after you've picked it up. Kenn or Drew will get you what you need to get out undetected."

Kelly nodded as if she was still listening to her friend. "Okay, Kayla. I'll be able to text you my flight information tomorrow when I know what it is for sure. In the meantime, I'll give you a call later on tonight."

She pretended to end the call, then went and used the ladies' room. When she got back to the table, Parrot stood up and pulled out her chair for her.

"My goodness, what a gentleman you are, Parrot. And a white wine spritzer? Boy, you really were payin' attention, weren't you?" Kelly blushed, pretending to be completely overwhelmed.

"I told you, Misty*jan*, it is our way to treat our women well." Parrot looked at her with complete focus. "I took the liberty of ordering our appetizers while you were gone. I hope you like antipasti, since it's the closest thing they have here to what we call *mezze* in Armenia."

Kelly smiled at him. "I do, very much." She sipped her wine spritzer. "Parrot, what does that mean? *Jan?* You keep using it with my name and I don't know what it means."

Parrot gave her a slight smile. "It means *dear* in Armenian, Misty*jan*. We use it with people's names as a term of endearment."

"Misty" blushed.

Parrot subtly shifted toward her, his own drink in his hand. "Now, tell me about yourself, Misty*jan*. I know you live in Milwaukee, and you are clearly a beautiful, innocent girl whom vultures like to prey on." Kelly stared at him, wide-eyed. "What else should I know?"

"Well, I'm a hairdresser and I'm an only child." Kelly took another sip of her white wine spritzer. "My mom passed away last year and my dad has never been in the picture, so I'm pretty much on my own now. I left a long-term relationship in the summer of last year—my high school boyfriend, actually. We were together for a long time. He moved to California, and I was kinda happy to see him go, to tell you the truth. We didn't have much in common anymore."

"And then you met this Harold person." Parrot's tone was dry. Kelly blushed and nodded sheepishly. "*Jan*, family is everything to an Armenian." Parrot looked at her with heat in his eyes. "We take care of our families, we take care of our women. To be a wife and to be a mother is the greatest blessing a woman can have in my culture."

Oh, fucking barf, Kelly thought to herself in disgust. But she nodded submissively.

Parrot patted her hand in sympathy. "You are so alone, Misty*jan*. You deserve a good man, one who can support you so you can be happy raising your children without care. Without worries about dirty business dealings, or nasty rivals. That *khiyar*, Harold, or those other useless fools across the bay do not understand what it means to treat a woman with honor."

Kelly saw her opening and took it.

"Parrot?' She lowered her smoky voice and whispered timidly. "Can I ask you a question?"

"Of course, Misty*jan*."

"I don't want to pry into things that are not my business, Parrot. Besides, business talk confuses me." Kelly twisted her fingers, letting it appear as if she was very nervous. "I'm just a hairdresser. I can admit I'm a simple girl, and that I'm not crazy smart. I guess I don't understand why you and those people across the water hate each other so much, though. I mean, hate each other to the point you each stay on your own side of Tampa Bay? That's *crazy*," she burst out, blue eyes wide.

Parrot sighed. "This might be disturbing for you to hear, Misty*jan*, because you are such a delicate little thing." He paused for a moment as the waiter served their appetizers. When he had gone, Parrot continued. "But I am going to share this with you so you understand."

Kelly nodded.

"There is a woman within their organization who has been completely ensnared by them, Misty*jan*. She is a pretty little girl just like you are. They call her *princess*—because she supposedly looks like one of the Disney princesses, with her red hair and green eyes. I have never seen her for myself, although several of my associates have, and they say that this is true."

Kelly nodded, acting absorbed in the story, even as she felt the hair on the back of her neck stand up on end.

"She also knows quite a bit about the security industry and is *extremely* talented, from what I understand…so my boss would very much like to talk to her about coming to work with us. He knows we can offer her much, much more than they are giving to her, most likely. Unfortunately, however, those fools have her locked up so tight, and she is so hidden away from everybody, we have no way to initiate any type of contact with her. But," Parrot's mouth seemed suddenly full of shark's teeth, "my boss has a plan."

"A plan?" Kelly echoed, looking confused and acting bewildered, even as her heart was thundering in her chest.

"He thinks he has figured out a way to reach her, Misty*jan*. A way to actually have a private discussion with her without anyone's interference. If Grigor's plan goes as it is expected to and we finally—*connect* with her, shall we say—she will be with us before too long."

There was a moment of silence, Parrot abruptly seeming to consider if he had said too much.

"Well." Kelly's spidey sense went off, warning her to terminate the conversation immediately. "Like I said, all this business stuff goes completely over my head. I wish you luck, and I hope you can rescue that poor, dear girl and talk some sense into her."

She gave Parrot an exaggerated shiver, then deliberately turned her attention to her appetizer.

"Mmmm." Kelly used her fork to break into an admittedly decadent-looking arancini. "I just *love* Italian food. Tell me about Armenian food, Parrot. I'm embarrassed to admit I don't know the first thing about it!" Parrot relaxed at her cheerful words, clearly dismissing any misgivings he might have been having, to Kelly's relief.

The appetizer course passed with light chatter and mild flirting. Kelly continued her role as the naive, charming Misty, letting her clear giggles ring out often, and asking all sorts of questions about life in Armenia.

Parrot's interest obviously kept deepening. Kelly didn't discourage his attention, knowing she was safe as long as they were in public and she was surrounded by APS protection like she was. When their appetizer plates had been cleared away and their server had finished taking their main course order, Kelly became distraught when one of her earrings, the one without the transmitter, suddenly fell on the floor.

"Oh! Oh, darn! I cannot *believe* I dropped my earring!" Kelly pretended she was going to stoop to get it until Parrot placed his hand on her arm. He gestured to one of the other men to get it for her, and she thanked him profusely when he handed it to her.

"I think I'm going to run back to the ladies' room before our dinner gets here and wash it off before I put it back in my ear. This dirty floor." Kelly wrinkled her nose in disgust. "Parrot, would you mind pourin' me a glass of that wonderful-lookin' red wine for when I get back?"

"It's my pleasure, Misty*jan*." Parrot kissed the back of her hand again, his eyes focused with deliberation on her, as Kelly giggled and blushed again.

"I'll be back. Hopefully, the line isn't as long this time," she purred throatily as she walked away from the table with a switch of her hips.

When Kelly finally made it through the line and into the restroom door, she found Kenn waiting for her inside, a small black duffel bag slung over her shoulder.

Kenn slid in front of Kelly with practiced ease, as if she'd been waiting for the large handicapped stall that opened up at the end. After Kenn had entered the stall, Kelly did the same as Kenn had, waving the others in line ahead of her, until Kenn came out of the handicapped stall without the duffel bag.

Kelly entered the stall, finding the duffel waiting for her in there, and she promptly flew into action. She kicked off her stilettos, took off her jewelry, and shimmied out of her tight white dress—careful not to disturb her inner thigh holster—then yanked the platinum blonde wig off her head, revealing her own dark red tresses hidden under a wig cap.

She popped out her blue contact lenses, rapidly scrubbed off her heavy makeup, put in a pair of brown contacts, pulled out a short black bobbed wig from the duffel and put it on, outlined her mouth in a pale peach lipstick, and perched a pair of black horn-rimmed glasses on her nose.

Kelly then pulled on a sedate black knit skirt with a black-and-white striped long-sleeve T-shirt, a black cardigan, and a pair of black flats. She stuffed everything into the duffel bag, then checked herself once more in the mirror, took a deep breath, and exited the stall to find Drew waiting for her.

"Hey, baby." Drew kissed her lightly and took the duffel from her, careful not to bump anyone in the busy restroom. "Do you mind if we go ahead and skedaddle on home? I can't seem to shake this headache tonight, no matter what I do."

"No problem, honey. Work wore me out today and I could use an early night anyway." As they exited the ladies' room, Kelly saw Drew discreetly hand the duffel bag to Kenn, who had reappeared outside the door.

Drew took Kelly's hand and they leisurely walked toward the outside exit. Out of the corner of her eye, Kelly saw Parrot staring toward the women's bathroom, oblivious to the fact that sexy, platinum-haired "Misty" now looked like a cute, geeky, brunette librarian.

Drew unlocked the doors of an unfamiliar dark blue SUV and helped Kelly into the passenger side. As Drew climbed into the driver's side and started the engine, Kenn unobtrusively slid into the passenger side next to Kelly, tossing the black duffel bag behind the seat, and the trio took off.

"Fucking *hell*, little sis. You about gave me ten fucking heart attacks with that shit in there." Kenn blew out a deep breath and touched her comm. "We're clear and on our way back. ETA, approximately forty-five minutes."

"Copy that," Trill's voice responded. "Teagan, Blake, and Casey are following you and we're right behind them. We'll all meet in the Bunker when we get back to APS."

When they arrived, jaws dropped in disbelief when they saw Kelly in her librarian gear. She smirked as everyone went into the Bunker, still speechless at her transformation. She took off her horn-rimmed glasses, popped out her brown contact lenses, took off the black bobbed wig, then freed her own dark red curls from the wig cap.

"Time to debrief," she said, a shrewd look upon her face as she ruffled her hair.

Chapter 24

Barely forty hours had passed since shit had blown up between her and Kelly, but Riley couldn't give two shits less, she decided.

After they'd all met with Kelly and Rowan yesterday—after what Rowan had termed the knuckle-dragging fiasco—and had come to a mutual understanding, Kelly had spent the entire day at APS headquarters with the Seven in the Bunker.

Despite her lack of sleep, she'd detailed her proposal to make contact with the Florida Percutio crew, and the APS management team got to work discussing it.

"The Florida Percutio crew chiefs often hang out at a place called Club Infinity in south Tampa. Looks and sounds like a swanky place," Kelly had mused, looking at her laptop.

She'd then quirked an ironic brow at them.

"Because you all *clearly* have never run chick infiltrations before, there are some things you need to be aware of. Men think with their dicks. Now, I *know* that isn't news to any of you, especially in light of what you do here at APS. But, because badass butches don't do chick infiltrations, you may not be aware that appealing to the dick is the *easiest* fucking way to get information from a target. *If* you know what to do."

Kelly steepled her fingers. "A chick infiltration involves more than just flashing boobs or leg, though. When you act a little helpless, but not completely incompetent, when you pretend you're a bit dingy and naive, but not stupid, most men gravitate toward that shit. *Especially* men like these assholes. If a female agent wants to blow an op, she'll look and act like a total slut. Men know they can hit that and move on in 3.2 seconds. There's no mystique there, she's an easy capture, so why would they bother putting any work into it? Plus, a guy usually isn't going to introduce that type of girl to his mother."

Despite themselves, the Armstrong twins and the Seven were fascinated by Kelly's information.

"So, you send in an agent who's a real looker—sexy, but not slutty." Kelly leaned back in her chair and continued. "She's shy. She's naive. She isn't stupid, but her priorities are things like children and puppies and rainbows and making sure her man is happy. She's looking for someone she can depend on, and with whom she can feel safe. You want to hit a guy's protection button *hard*. You want to be someone he envisions himself bringing home to Mama. You also want to be pretty enough and enticing enough so that his friends will just die of envy. He'll blow up like a pufferfish and eat that shit up."

"Jesus Christ, Kelly." Casey's bright blue eyes grew dark. "We're supposed to be your wingmen on this, not your royal assassins. Because I can guarantee you that's exactly what will happen if these fuckers hit on you too hard. *Especially* around Riley."

Kelly spoke calmly as she looked directly into Riley's eyes. "Which is why I'm going to suggest that Riley sit this one out. Wait." She held up her hand, cutting Riley off as she started to speak. "I trust that you can handle yourself, even in a situation where you're unprepared and you're blindsided. Because that's something that can happen sometimes, and you have to be prepared for that possibility. However…number one, I need backup who can blend into their surroundings on something like this. You are the *farthest* thing from someone who blends in that I can think of, especially in an environment like Club Infinity, Riles."

Kelly was blunt.

"And number two, this Aram Hakobyan, this Parrot I'm targeting… I can't afford to be distracted, and I will be if I know you're right there. Particularly with what happened yesterday. I'm not saying you can't be there at all. You *should* be there, but not on the front lines, Riley." Kelly's voice dropped to a near whisper. "I hope you can understand where I'm coming from. An op like this—working together on a pretty significant chick infiltration—it's brand new to all of us. Frankly, we don't know exactly how things are going to play out. We need to minimize the risk to keep us all safe."

When it came time to actually execute the operation, Kelly had taken an Uber alone from her Whimsy home. She had it drop her off a few blocks from a hotel in St. Petersburg, where she had rented a room under the name of Misty Schroeder, making sure she hadn't been followed.

She had changed her clothes and donned her Misty persona in the hotel room, then called another Uber to take her to Club Infinity in Tampa as Misty. Except for Kenn and Drew, who were already waiting at Club Infinity when she arrived, no one had seen her in her Misty disguise.

Dara, Drew's second, had gone and collected Kelly's personal belongings when Kelly had left the hotel, making sure there was no trace of Kelly left behind.

Now, the entire team shook their heads in awe of Kelly's ability to transform her appearance and couldn't stop staring at her as she dismantled her guise as a sedate librarian.

"You should have seen her as Misty, too," Kenn said wryly, looking at Drew with an arched brow as Drew nodded in agreement. "You would have sworn they were two completely different women, with absolutely no trace of the Kelly we all know and love. Fucking unbelievable."

"Her skill? Jesus Christ." Drew blew out a deep breath and looked at Riley. "Her experience in this area is going to be a godsend to us, Riles, although I'm going to have to warn you—it was all I could do to keep my position and not introduce Hakobyan to my fist when I saw his blatant interest in Misty. And Kelly's not even mine. I'm certain we can all do this, especially because Kelly is such a professional, but fuck me. It's going to be harder than hell sometimes and we all need to be prepared."

When Kelly had finished shaking out her hair and faced the team, Riley decided she couldn't stand it anymore.

Kelly had returned with Riley to their APS apartment at the end of the previous day, after they'd completed their infiltration plan with the rest of the team, but it was a quiet, awkward evening. When they went to bed, Riley pulled Kelly into her arms as usual, but neither of them spoke, both of them unsure of how to broach the subject of their rift.

When Kelly awoke, Riley was gone—out on her daily run, Kelly guessed—so Kelly had brushed her teeth, got dressed, made herself a big travel mug filled with coffee, and left to get everything ready for the infiltration planned for that evening. She and Riley exchanged a couple of short texts during the day, but that awkward silence still lingered between them.

Now, Riley swept Kelly up into her arms and kissed her with a forceful, all-consuming passion, letting her mouth, her hands, and her body say everything she wanted to say to the beautiful femme who had rapidly become her life.

"I'm so sorry, *princesa*," Riley murmured when she had released Kelly's mouth, cupping a strong hand on the back of Kelly's head and resting her head against Riley's shoulder. "I'm rapidly learning these kinds of ops are going to be some of the hardest fucking things I'll ever do in my life. But your skills in covert and clandestine operations can't be denied.

"You have my full support, now and always, baby. I apologize for being such a knuckle-dragging asshole."

Riley released Kelly so she could look into her eyes as she addressed the room at large. "With any luck, we won't ever have to do this shit too often. I sure as *fuck* hated the thought of anyone else's hands on you in any way, but I did feel that you were at least as safe as we could possibly make you. You were surrounded by APS protection, you were doing what you needed to do, and I'm surprisingly okay with that now. Was it hard? *Fuck*, yeah. But can we do this? Absolutely."

Kelly nodded in gratitude, with relief and love in her eyes. Riley smiled at her woman and touched her face, then continued on with a dark look as she glanced around at everyone else.

"Thank fuck for two-way radio communications, because from what I heard, Hakobyan the Parrot flatly confirmed that fucker, Reizan, has a plan to take Kelly. And I want to know what the fuck that plan is."

* * * * *

Casey excused herself as they were all getting settled at their desks, returning with a cooler filled with chilled water bottles. Kelly accepted one gratefully.

"You good, *hermana*?" Jaime, who was sitting at her desk next to Kelly, asked in a low tone as Kelly uncapped her water and drank deeply. "You need anything else?"

Kelly smiled at her. "I'm good, *broki*, thank you. Just a little thirsty. And not loving the thought of this conversation we're about to have." Jaime concurred.

"The biggest takeaway I got from the whole infiltration is that Hakobyan was smugly positive Reizan had a plan to get to Kelly," Riley began from where she was sitting on the top of Kelly's desk, holding her woman's hand. "Hakobyan admitted to Kelly that APS has *the princess* locked down currently, so they haven't been successful in establishing any type of communication with her to date. However, why is he all of a sudden so sure Reizan can break through now? What's so different?"

Trill was rapidly typing on her laptop. "Follow me here for a minute because I'm coming up with one *hell* of a theory about this whole thing." She stopped typing and turned to look at the rest of the team. "Even though Percutio operates all up and down the eastern seaboard, Florida is the state where they have the strongest hold. Since Reizan has a top lieutenant in every state where he operates, and Aram Hakobyan is the lieutenant who runs Florida for him, it stands to reason he's also Reizan's second-in-command overall."

The team agreed.

"So, as Reizan's second, Hakobyan would theoretically know about *everything* that goes on within the Percutio organization, more so than any other associate," Trill continued. "At least, you would *think* he does." The Armstrong twins and the Seven cocked an inquiring eyebrow at her.

Trill drummed her fingers next to her laptop, organizing her thoughts.

"Hakobyan would have had *every* reason to lie to 'Misty' about Kelly, given Kelly's eidetic memory abilities. As a matter of fact, he wouldn't have even brought Kelly up himself in the first place, wanting to keep her a secret, and limit knowledge of her to the Percutio brass. Despite being known as the Parrot, Hakobyan wouldn't have talked about Kelly—even when he truly believed Misty was just an unsophisticated, uncomplicated woman who was content with surface explanations, and who wouldn't look too deep into anything he told her. But he *didn't* keep his mouth shut. Hakobyan was actually the one who brought Kelly up and told 'Misty' that Percutio wanted her."

"Hakobyan also couldn't resist the urge to brag a little bit to Misty—painting himself, his boss, and Percutio as these superhero rescuers who were going to liberate this poor, misguided girl from the axis of evil." Drew snorted as she rolled her eyes.

"Yes, but," Trill considered her words for a moment before she continued slowly, "if you knew your boss was targeting a super asset with a very rare, potentially very *lucrative* eidetic memory gift—like Kelly has—don't you think you would be a little more, I don't know, *secretive* about her? Even when you're talking to someone as naive as Misty? Even when you're someone like Hakobyan, who admittedly likes to talk a lot normally?"

"Holy *fuck*. Hakobyan doesn't *know*," Teagan realized, shocked, as the same stunned awareness swept over everyone else's face.

"Reizan hasn't told any of his own people *jack shit* about what Kelly can really do. He's keeping the real knowledge of her and her abilities all to himself. He plans on using her for his *own* personal gain, not for Percutio's. Mother*fucker*."

Casey stared down at her hands, splayed out on the table, thinking just as hard as the rest of them. "When Misty disappeared on him and couldn't be found, I bet Hakobyan figured out real fucking fast who she really was then. He was probably *furious* when it finally dawned on him, not to mention a little concerned. But it wasn't because he knew *what* she was. Just *who* she was. The only thing Hakobyan knew was that Reizan had been frothing at the mouth to get to Kelly for months, and his cock would be in a vise if Reizan ever found out Hakobyan had her and then lost her."

"Plus, if Reizan found out Hakobyan had potentially created another barrier between Kelly and Percutio because of his loose lips on top of it all, it would definitely mean his dick," Blake threw in. "Couldn't happen to a nicer guy," she added cheerfully.

"So, what are our next steps?" asked Bryn. "Keeping an APS guard on our favorite hotshot covert operative at all times goes without saying. Sorry, Kel," Bryn told her, clearly not sorry at all. Kelly rolled her eyes at her sister's future spouse as the corner of Bryn's mouth quirked.

"Circling back around... Regardless of the eidetic memory thing, I'm bothered by the fact that Hakobyan was so fucking *sure* Percutio could get to Kelly now." Kenn was deep in thought. "Why is he so fucking *sure*? What's changed? They have to know we have Kelly protected 24/7."

Jaime tapped the keys on her own laptop. "There isn't a leak anywhere in our organization that we can find so far. Our seconds—all of our associates, as a matter of fact—check out and always have. Any peripheral players, even the new ones, are checking out so far." She growled in frustration. "Our seconds have been going over every fucking inch of the APS facility since Kelly found our security glitch, *hermanos*. We've found nothing else outside of the void weakness up until now, and that's being fixed as we speak," Jaime continued, nodding at Trill in acknowledgment.

Teagan pursed her mouth, thinking. "Kelly and Rowan's house is wired to the gills. Trill and Jaime's people threw the pentest from hell at it after my crew had everything finished, and there wasn't even so much as a hairline crack. The fuck *anyone's* getting into that house."

"This is getting uncomfortably reminiscent of the time Rowan was taken and we couldn't fucking figure out what had been setting off our alarm bells." Blake's voice was dark. "Then again, no one had counted on an inside betrayal from that bitch, Astrid Hallifax."

"The good news is, we don't have that risk here," said Drew, "because your girls checked out, too, Red—Clementine, Nova, Alyssa, Brooke, *and* Delaney.

"Not that I think any of us are surprised by that. Except for Clem, we've known them all since grade school, and Clem is Rowan's best friend from up north."

"Tomorrow, I'm supposed to be meeting Rowan and Clem and the rest of the girls at an empty storefront two doors down from the WAC and the Dream Creamery." Kelly's eyes brightened, despite the seriousness of the conversation. "Del and her parents are opening a new bakery there, and she wanted our input on some stuff. Casey and Campbell are coming with me because Riley and Bryn have a client meeting they simply can't miss."

Kelly smirked at Casey, briefly amused despite the gravity of the conversation.

"Ready for a girls' afternoon out, *broki*?" Casey groaned as the rest of the crew snickered. Casey shot them all her middle finger and rolled her eyes.

"Seriously, though." Kelly rapidly grew solemn. "I was going to take the opportunity to ask the girls if they've noticed anything out of the ordinary, no matter how small. Every single one of them is observant as hell and as smart as a whip."

"I agree. It's easy to dismiss someone like Delaney and think of her as just a pastry chef, for example. But not only is she intelligent, her attention to detail is staggering, simply because that's what she *does* in her work." Teagan's voice was matter of fact.

"I don't know if there's much else we can do at this point, except continue to connect the dots. Maybe we can see if McAllister's still involved." Kelly had ignored the last three increasingly desperate voicemails from her old handler.

"Frankly, it's starting to sound as though McAllister and Reizan have hatched some type of secret plan between themselves." Bryn's voice was cold. "Reizan doesn't want anyone else in Percutio to know about Kelly's magic, because he wants her and the profits from her ability all to himself. McAllister's in it for the money, too, and he's expecting a big fucking reward from Reizan for bringing Kel to him in the first place. He's been playing the long game on this for almost two years, and he isn't about to let Kelly slip through his fingers now."

Riley added her two cents to her twin's thoughts. "Reizan has probably given his people some huge bullshit story about how Kelly is bright as fuck, she's part of the APS organization now, and they can get a fuckton of information out of her on the internal workings of APS—intel they could never get before."

"Which is all true," Blake agreed. "The big draw for Reizan, however, is her eidetic memory capabilities. His people just don't know it."

Riley ran her fingers down Kelly's cheek. "I know I don't need to tell you this, *princesa*, but you need to be as fucking careful as possible. Reizan and his goons have *something* up their sleeve and, until we can figure out what the fuck it is, I don't want you taking any chances."

Riley leaned over in front of the entire management team and kissed her with a deep passion.

"I love you, Kelly Holland," Riley said after she'd released Kelly's mouth and held Kelly's delicate face so she could look deeply into Kelly's green eyes. "I swear to you, it will be a cold goddamn day in hell before me or your family here will *ever* let anything touch you."

Chapter 25

"Delaney! Holy shit, honey! This is going to be incredible!"

Kelly was standing with Delaney, Rowan, and the rest of her girl posse in the middle of the empty space where Del's new bakery was going to be. Casey and Campbell, another one of Casey's crew, had accompanied Kelly to Delaney's storefront.

"I know, right?" Delaney was jubilant, as excited as anyone had ever seen her. "My parents have been an absolute godsend in helping to make this happen. And Ro has talked to Ember and Nia about doing this project while they're working on Clem's apartment at the same time!"

She smiled shyly at Kelly. "Nia is Mom's second cousin, you know. Whimsy is like its own interrelated city-state, Kel." Kelly laughed, but then she sighed right on the heels of her laughter.

"I don't mean to rain on your parade right now, Del—because this is so exciting and I'm totally excited *for* you. But Casey and I need to ask you all something really quick while I have this opportunity to see everyone together." Kelly waved Casey and Campbell over from where they were standing by the front window. "I know Rowan has brought you all up to speed on the fucking shit going down at APS with Percutio right now." Her friends growled in tandem, even sweet, mild-mannered Delaney.

"Well, that's fierce," Campbell muttered, impressed, as her eyebrows hit her hairline.

The corner of Casey's mouth quirked before she stepped into the conversation. "We don't want to upset anyone. It would be extremely helpful, however, if you could let either the Armstrong twins or any of the Seven know if you notice or have noticed anything out of the ordinary around town, no matter how small it might seem to you. The assholes from this organization are apparently bound and determined to leverage Kelly's memory gift for themselves. We don't know what they have planned yet, but we don't like the intel and we're trying to stay one step ahead of them."

"Dude." Clem's fist was on her hip as she glowered at Casey. "I may be little, but this fist packs one hell of a wallop. The fuck *anyone* is touching Kelly on *my* watch." The rest of Kelly's friends scowled in agreement, their eyes dark.

"All of this is because of Kelly's magic, isn't it?" Brooke asked, her voice pissed, already knowing the answer but wanting to hear it from Casey directly.

Kelly had already talked to the girls a few weeks earlier, explaining her eidetic memory capability in detail while swearing them to secrecy. She'd then told them Grigor Reizan, the head of Percutio, wanted to use Kelly's ability to further his own criminal empire, so there was a risk to Kelly's safety.

Whimsical Princess

The femmes had gone absolutely ballistic—Nova and Clem, in particular, threatening a fire-and-brimstone reckoning if Percutio didn't stay in their lane and stop harassing their homegirl.

Although Kelly didn't think there was any threat to them, because none of the other girls had anything Grigor would want, she'd still made them promise to stay aware of their surroundings at all times.

Alyssa had given Delaney a vengeful smile while they were talking. "We might not be as used to this shit as the APS badasses, Del, but we still take care of our own."

She continued with a dark look. "You'd just gotten here when that fucking dickhead stalker, Dino Coravani, kidnapped Rowan and was going to rape and kill her." The women could see by the look on Delaney's face that she remembered, her face full of loathing.

Nova's face had then filled with gleeful malice. "But, as we all recall, Rowan fucking *dropped* his ass. Escaped the shit he'd tied her up with and shot the asshole right in the motherfucking head." Rowan had simply shrugged at the reminder, unperturbed.

"We're all family, Delaney, and that now includes you too, homegirl." Brooke's smile held no humor. "So, it will be over our dead bodies that any jackass *ever* threatens one of our own."

Now, Delaney spoke up suddenly when Casey had finished asking the girls to be cognizant of their environment.

"You know, Casey, I think maybe I *did* notice something. I didn't think much of it at the time, but now that we're talking about it…" Everyone listened, intent.

"After my parents and I signed the lease here and picked up the keys, we came over to look at the space again. I noticed something odd when we were coming in here. This storefront is almost at the end of Cedar Key Boulevard, which dead-ends into Beach Bay Drive at the Boca Ciega Bay, right?"

They all nodded.

"So, when you hit the end of Cedar Key, you have no choice but to make a left or a right onto Beach Bay," Delaney continued, gesturing with her hands. "You can't just make a U-turn to come back up Cedar Key, because the boulevard is too narrow.

"You *have* to go around the block if you want to hit Cedar Key again, unless you're kind of an idiot and attempt to do a really freaking ugly three-point turn at the three-way stop. Now, I can definitely see someone going around the block once, if they're new to Whimsy and just learning their way around. Twice at the most, if I'm being generous and really cutting someone some slack."

Everyone nodded in agreement.

"But *four or five times?*" Delaney rolled her eyes, skeptical. "That's unheard of. Downtown Whimsy's not that big. They can't be *that* lost. There was this vehicle… I remember thinking at the time these people were just being weird. It was a dark-colored SUV—maybe dark blue, nothing special—and it looked like there were three people in the vehicle. One driving, one riding shotgun, and one in the back. The windows had a heavy tint, so I couldn't see the occupants clearly, but it was definitely three guys. The SUV had Florida plates and was moving very slowly, too slowly for even

Cedar Key, in my opinion. I could see the vehicle through the windows of my new space, and I saw, plain as day, they came down Cedar Key like four or five times. I didn't think any more about it after they were gone. But, in light of what you've told us, Case..." Delaney's voice trailed off.

Casey leaned over and kissed Delaney's cheek, making her blush. "That's *exactly* the kind of thing I'm talking about, Del. You're right... That *was* weird and it wouldn't be something you'd expect to see on Cedar Key. Now, the question becomes, what were they scoping out and why? The WAC and the Dream Creamery? The Gulf Breeze Inn? Something else? You'd literally just signed the lease on your place, so chances are it wasn't you—although I won't rule that out yet. But that sighting was odd enough that we need to dig into it a bit further."

Casey smiled warmly at Delaney. "We are *so* happy to have you back in Whimsy, Del. You've been gone *way* too fucking long, girl. On behalf of the Armstrong twins and the Seven, I just want to say, *Welcome home.* Teag was absolutely right: Pastry chefs are observant as fuck."

Del turned scarlet as Kelly leaned over and hugged her hard, while the rest of the women applauded.

"I'm going to stop by again a bit later this week, Del, okay?" Kelly beamed at her pretty, black-haired, blue-eyed friend and hugged her. "I really want to hear about your plans for this place, but I don't want to be responsible for causing a butch meltdown by talking about, oh my Goddess, *girl stuff* in front of them right now."

Delaney giggled while the rest of Kelly's tribe snickered. Campbell and Casey's eyes twinkled at Kelly, even as Casey shot her the finger.

"I'll call you in a couple of days, Delaney." Kelly hugged the rest of her friends fiercely, then got ready to leave with Casey and Campbell. "Toodles, girls. I love you all madly and I *promise* you that everything is going to be okay. Trust me."

Chapter 26

Kelly whimpered into Riley's mouth, trapped beneath Riley's strong body, as Riley devoured her femme whole. Kelly ran her hands over Riley's powerful shoulders and back, feeling Riley's strength beneath her fingers and gasping for air as she lost herself to her surrender.

Kelly slid her hands down Riley's body in a haze, searching for the heat between Riley's legs as she gloried in the feel of Riley's response to her. One hand wandered over Riley's muscled thighs and toned ass, as she played in the neat brush of hair with her other hand, rhythmically stroking inside her lover's damp folds.

Kelly felt the arc of Riley's arousal spike and spiral when Kelly moved her hand faster, loving the feeling of taking this butch and her desire so totally into her control. Dimly, Kelly knew her mastery of Riley wouldn't last for long, so she nuzzled Riley's throat as she worked her fingers harder and faster, feeling Riley's body rise to meet her as it reached the pinnacle of her sexual passion.

Riley stiffened and her muscles went rigid as she came, groaning. Kelly captured Riley's mouth, swallowing Riley's orgasm as Riley shuddered and groaned again. After a moment, with Kelly planting soft kisses on Riley's throat and neck as Riley's heart rate slowed, Riley captured Kelly's mouth again with a hard, demanding kiss.

"*Princesa.*" Riley's seductive voice went straight to Kelly's core and she felt a gush of liquid flood out of her. As Riley began to stroke her pussy with those long, wicked fingers, Kelly felt herself open helplessly to her commanding lover.

Kelly's voice shook. "Riley," she moaned, sinking deeper and deeper into Riley's dominance as Riley naturally reasserted control over her yielding woman.

"You're mine, forever and always, Kelly Holland." Riley slid her fingers inside of her femme, making Kelly cry out with her possession. "Until the end of time, I will possess you. I will own you. I will protect you. And I will fucking *kill* anything that dares to try and hurt you, or to take you from me."

Kelly's pussy contracted harder around Riley's fingers as Riley worked her body, until Kelly felt herself hovering on the edge of the most intense orgasm she'd ever felt.

She screamed as Riley finally pushed her over the edge, her body contracting and shaking with the force of her release. Kelly felt Riley's fingers slide out of her, the tip of Riley's hard strap-on cock penetrating her, as she sank into the feel of Riley's muscled body under her hands.

They moved together, first slowly and then more fiercely, finding their rhythm as their bodies and hearts and souls connected. Kelly felt bathed in Riley's love and passion as she hurtled toward an even more powerful orgasm, Riley keeping pace with her, until

Kelly's world exploded in a shower of brilliant light and profound emotion.

When Kelly became lucid, she realized that Riley had already cleaned her up and changed the bedding as she usually did. She also found herself wrapped securely in Riley's strong arms, clean and warm and safe. Kelly couldn't help it; she felt slow tears slide down her face as she tried to articulate her feelings in an emotional, quavering voice.

"I love you, Riley Armstrong," she whispered to her lover from her protected refuge in Riley's arms. "As ecstatically happy as I was for Rowan when she found Bryn, there was a piece of me that was sad in a way. Sad, because I didn't believe that kind of love would ever be possible for me." Kelly's tears fell faster. "But here you are. My rock, my safe place, my mate in every single way I can think of. Just like you said, Riley—until the end of time, I'm yours and you're mine. Forever and always."

Riley tenderly kissed the beautiful redhead, then looked into Kelly's emotion-filled green eyes with a steady gaze. "Marry me, *princesa*." Kelly's eyes widened in shock as Riley smiled at her with enormous love in her own eyes. "I want you to be my wife, baby. I want people to see a ring on your finger and know that you're taken in every way possible. I haven't had time to get you a fancy engagement ring, *princesa*, but I was pretty sure you'd prefer just a flat wedding band of some sort anyway…given your predilection for kicking ass, and the fact that a regular engagement ring would probably catch on everything and piss you right the fuck off."

Kelly laughed even as she started to cry, pulling Riley up beside her so she could fling her arms around Riley's neck. Riley kissed her, then released her mouth. "Will you marry me, Kelly Holland?" she whispered in Kelly's ear, nuzzling her gently.

"*Yes*! Yes, I'll marry you! I love you so, *so* much, *amante*." Kelly cried happy tears with her head buried in Riley's neck. She eventually raised her face and looked at Riley, her heart on her face. "Even though I've never wanted a formal wedding like Rowan's always wanted, Riles, I'll do anything to make you happy. Even marry you out on a remote rock somewhere if that's what you want to do."

Riley stroked her fiancée's beautiful face and kissed her forehead as she pulled Kelly back down into her arms.

"Well…here's the thing, *princesa*. I've never wanted a big wedding either. Hell, I never even pictured myself getting married at all, until I met you." The corners of Riley's mouth quirked up. "So, why don't we have a big open wedding ceremony on Whimsy Beach. Casual, anyone who wants to come can come. We'll have Bryn and Rowan as our only attendants and exchange our vows in front of all our friends and family right on the beach. Then we'll take over Seashells across the street and set up one hell of a wedding buffet in their big back room. Open bar. People can run back and forth across the street to the beach and the volleyball courts."

Kelly's eyes kept getting bigger and bigger.

"My only stipulation is that I want to see you in a wedding dress, baby. I want everyone to know I am marrying the *princesa* of my dreams."

Kelly drew in a sharp breath as tears filled her eyes again. "Oh my Goddess, *amante*. That sounds so absolutely *perfect* to me." Then Kelly squinted her eyes in Riley's direction. "But are you sure Mama won't be mad at us? A wedding like that is only one step up from eloping, if you think about it."

Riley gave her a wicked grin. "Bryn is on the hook for the big fancy wedding, so we can get away with a more casual one and Mama won't be mad. Besides," Riley's grin grew wider and more wicked, "we can easily plan something more informal for the end of April, well before hurricane season—which technically starts June 1—and when the weather is still absolutely beautiful. That way, *I* beat that asshole to the altar, since she and Rowan have to wait until the very end of October to have their wedding—both because Mama needs a lot more planning time for a wedding like theirs, and also because the most active time for west-central Florida during hurricane season is August through October. Let's see her run her fucking mouth about being nine minutes older than me *then*."

Kelly burst out laughing until tears were streaming down her face.

"So much for Rowan's pool party, too." Kelly started laughing again at the quizzical look on Riley's face, explaining that Rowan had also wanted to have a pool party housewarming at the end of

April to celebrate their new house. Riley chuckled, then looked at her smart watch.

"We have five weeks between today and Saturday, April 24, baby. Think we can pull off a beach wedding between now and then?"

Kelly arched an ironic eyebrow at Riley and snorted. "Seriously, Riles…have you met me? Surely you don't think I'm capable of pulling something like that off by myself, and you know you're just as hopeless when it comes to this shit. However…we'll tell everyone about our engagement tomorrow morning. I'll go to the WAC and the Dream Creamery to tell Rowan, while you tell Bryn at the same time. Then you two can come on over while I send out a massive text message to everyone. We'll sit back at the Dream Creamery and wait for the hordes to descend, because you know they will. After all the excitement dies down and we tell everyone what we're planning. Mama and the girls will be so *horrified* at the thought of a reception with just Doritos and beer if they leave everything to me that they'll swing into action and totally take over all the planning. Piece of cake."

It was Riley's turn to throw back her head and burst out laughing.

"My partner in crime," Riley finally said with a chuckle as she kissed Kelly's face again. "You make me so happy, baby. You're bright and you're beautiful and you're wickedly funny and every damn day is an adventure with you."

Whimsical Princess

She became serious and switched gears for a moment. "When Bryn and I got out of the service and headed for college, Bryn knew from day one she wanted to major in psychology. She's always been absolutely fascinated with the human psyche, and she knew having that kind of a background would be irreplaceable when we all finally got APS off the ground. It took me a wee bit longer to figure out what I wanted to major in. But Mama will tell you...I was the Armstrong kid who always wanted to plan and control things, even more so than my twin." Riley smirked at Kelly, who rolled her eyes at her new fiancé with a, *Tell me something I didn't know* look on her face.

"So, I decided to get a degree in operations management, *princesa*. With a company like APS, where our ultimate goal is to make the world a safer place for women, it seemed to make sense. I focus on solving challenges with process and procedure, while Bryn deals with the human behavior part of the equation. Then the Seven bring their formidable skill sets to the table on top of it all. We're a perfect fit."

Riley nuzzled Kelly's temple.

"You're just like a puzzle piece that's snapped perfectly into place with us, *princesa*. You have this amazing covert and clandestine operations background that will now let us manage risky situations to women even better than we already do today. Do I like the potential danger aspect of it? *Fuck*, no. But I've seen you in action, I know just how goddamned good you are, and I know with everything in me that we were meant to be together for always—

helping the world one woman at a time. You're exactly what I've been looking for my entire life, *princesa*, even when I didn't know it."

Riley kissed the tears that were sliding down Kelly's face. "Together, baby, we're going to be unstoppable. I will be grateful to the universe for the rest of my life for bringing you to me, Kelly Holland."

Chapter 27

"Hey, Del?"

Kelly stuck her head in the front door of Sweet Expectations, Delaney's new bakery, and hollered for her friend.

Delaney, a classical literature buff, had decided that Sweet Expectations would be an awesome name for her bakery, in a nod to the classic Charles Dickens' novel, *Great Expectations*.

In addition to Delaney's bakery, the last couple of days had been filled with excitement all around for everyone.

Just as they'd planned, Kelly and Riley broke the news of their engagement via text after telling Rowan and Bryn in person. Within thirty minutes, the Dream Creamery was filled to the brim with excited friends and family who were thrilled at the news and couldn't wait to offer their congratulations.

Bryn, Riley had told Kelly with amusement later, had called Riley six different kinds of a dickhead when she'd found out what Riley and Kelly were planning as far as having a wedding.

To Bryn's chagrin, Riley had smirked at her twin and told her they'd now be even, since Bryn had been born first, but Riley was getting married first. But the twins had then hugged each other tightly in a rare display of physical affection, both of them grinning widely and pounding each other on the back.

"Who'd have ever fucking thought that two confirmed bachelors like us would get reeled in—hook, line, and sinker—by a couple of Virginia girls, who have enough charm and grit between the two of them to sink the Titanic?" Bryn quirked her eyebrow at Riley with wry humor.

Riley burst out laughing. "If you would have dared suggest it, *mano*, I would have aimed a punch at your face, then ran for the fucking hills," she admitted. She looked at her twin with a grateful heart. "But I'm thinking Fate knew exactly what the fuck she was doing after all."

Rowan had squealed with excitement and flung her arms around her little sister when Kelly had told her that Riley had proposed. Kelly had met Rowan at the Dream Creamery before they were open for business, and the two of them had found themselves with a rare bit of time alone.

After spending a few minutes hugging each other and talking about wedding plans, Kelly had mentioned she was going to be spending time with Delaney in the next couple of days—both to find out her plans for the new bakery and to ask her to make Kelly and Riley's wedding cake.

"That reminds me," Kelly had said, leaning up against the front counter of the Dream Creamery with her arms crossed. "I told Riley I was going to send a mass text out to everyone with the news after I let you know. That means we're going to be descended upon when I do. I wanted to ask you something first before I forget again, however."

Rowan looked quizzically at her little sister.

"What's the deal with Delaney and Teagan?" Kelly asked. "I swear to you, the temperature feels about 120° whenever they're together, and Teagan's eyes could probably scorch a hole right through Delaney's clothes. But Del always seems nervous when Teag's around and takes care to make sure they're never alone. What gives?"

Rowan sighed, then told Kelly the story of Casanova.

"I guess Teagan had a huge crush on Delaney when Del was in ninth grade, but Delaney got caught up with this lesbian Nova refers to as Tina the…uh… Tina…oh, heck. As Tina the Twat." Rowan's face colored.

"Delaney moved to Michigan with this Tina person right after Del graduated college." Rowan sighed again. "Tina's mom was very sick and wanted to move back home to Michigan from Whimsy. Tina pushed Delaney's guilt buttons *hard* over Del expecting Tina to take care of her mother all alone, especially since Tina's mom loved Delaney so much.

"Plus, Delaney knew Tina would *never* take good care of her mom if she was left to her own devices, and Delaney didn't want to risk anything happening to her, so she went with them."

"Hence, Tina the Twat," Kelly murmured with a disgusted eye roll.

Whimsical Princess

"I guess Teagan's never gotten over Delaney, even though Del was gone for over ten years. Apparently, Delaney didn't have an easy life with Tina either, but she wouldn't leave Tina's mom, because she was afraid Tina would start abusing her if there was no one else around." Rowan growled in uncharacteristic anger.

"Tina's mom just died maybe a month or two ago, so Delaney was *finally* able to leave Tina. She moved back home to Whimsy right after the funeral."

Kelly shook her head in further disgust. "What a total cluster fuck. So, why didn't Delaney and Teagan just start dating when Delaney moved home again without Tina?"

Rowan raised her eyebrow. "Because after Delaney rejected her, Teagan started dating and hitting on anything in a skirt. Don't get me wrong, Teagan is one of the most respectful butches I know, but she dated so much without getting serious about *anyone*, it earned her the nickname 'Casanova.' Even though she had to keep it hidden from Tina, Delaney stayed in touch with Nova for the ten years she was gone. And Nova could swear that no one has touched Delaney since she was in college…because that's the last time Delaney ever had sex with Tina. Honestly, if even then."

Rowan shook her head sadly.

"Tina was a very controlling person. Nova thinks there was no way Delaney could have ever met or talked to anyone else, especially as hard as it was for even Nova to keep in touch with Del." Rowan's face was grim. "You are talking about one very innocent femme trying to stay away from one very experienced butch…whom that innocent femme just might regard as a player."

"Fuck my life," Kelly groaned, running her hands distractedly through her long, dark red hair. "There's a mess of epic fucking proportions."

Just then, Kelly's phone chimed, interrupting their conversation. Kelly quickly read the text message, then grinned at her sister.

"My fiancé and your fiancé said we could have girl time and talk about wedding plans later, but they're coming over to the Dream Creamery right now." Kelly smirked. "I need to send the announcement text right now so we can prepare for what Riles is calling the invasion from hell." Rowan giggled.

"We'll talk more about this Delaney and Teagan situation later, Ro. Are you ready for the stampede?"

Now, Casey and Campbell entered Sweet Expectations with Kelly, Casey frowning at the unlocked front door.

"Guess Teag needs to give our Delaney a lesson on femme safety and the consequences of committing Sin Two," Casey muttered wryly as Kelly yelled Delaney's name again.

"Maybe she's in the bathroom." Kelly started toward the back of the almost empty storefront. She smiled as her phone rang and Del's name came up on her display.

"There she is." Kelly answered her phone. "Girl, where in the hell are you? Did you forget I was coming by today to talk more about Sweet Expectations?"

"If you want your friend to live, Ms. Holland, you will pretend this is her on the phone and not let anyone with you think any differently." A male, foreign-sounding voice said in Kelly's ear. "I am going to put her on the phone in a second so you will understand that I am not joking, and that your friend's life depends on your actions right now."

Kelly heard a small sound, and then Delaney's shaky voice filled her ears. "Kelly?"

"Where are you?" Kelly kept her voice calm and matter of fact even as her heart thundered in her chest. "Are you far from the bakery?"

"I'm sorry, Kel, they won't let me talk except to tell you to do everything they tell you to do if you don't want me to get hurt."

There was another small sound and then the foreign male voice spoke again.

"I know there is a back exit out of the storefront, down a hallway past the bathroom, and out of sight of the front room, Ms. Holland. You are going to excuse yourself to go to the bathroom and slip out of the back door. In two minutes, a black SUV will pull up around back. You are to get into the backseat when the door opens. Do this quietly and quickly, Ms. Holland, because I assure you…your friend's life truly does depend upon it."

Kelly nodded, pretending she was listening to Delaney on the other end of the line. "Okay, Del. I'll see you in about ten minutes then."

She hung up her phone, then faced Casey and Campbell.

"Del had to run an errand, but she's on her way back. I'm going to go to the bathroom before she gets here." Kelly's mind was racing frantically, but she knew there was no way to signal Casey or Campbell without putting Delaney's life at risk.

"Everything okay?" Casey's sharp eyes rested on Kelly's suddenly pale face.

Kelly smiled casually at Casey. "Too much excitement for one week, I think, *broki*. Let me go to the bathroom so I'm done when Delaney gets back."

Kelly walked normally down the hallway, then tiptoed when she reached the bathroom, slipping past it to the back door, which she unlocked and opened silently. Just then, a black SUV with heavily tinted windows pulled up to the back door and the back passenger door on the driver's side opened.

Kelly quickly slipped into the backseat of the SUV and turned to face the man with glowing, cold black eyes and a dark, swarthy complexion sitting there.

"Hello, *princess*," he said as he raised a hypodermic needle and plunged it into Kelly's thigh.

Chapter 28

"Kel? Jesus Christ, how long does it take one woman to pee? Kelly!" Casey hollered, knocking on the closed bathroom door.

But there was no answer.

Just then, Casey noticed the back door to the store was cracked open slightly. A cold chill ran through her body as she went to inspect it.

"Campbell!" she yelled, flinging the door open and looking out into the empty alleyway. "Text the Armstrong twins and the rest of the Seven and tell them to get their fucking asses over to Del's new bakery *now*," she roared.

Within five minutes, the entire APS management team was there, guns drawn, listening as Casey rapidly explained to them what was going on.

"Kelly was fucking *fine* until Del called. She answered the phone normally, and then, I don't know." Casey was absolutely livid. "She was having a normal conversation, but then her face drained of color and she looked a little sick. She told Del, or *whoever* the fuck was on the phone, that she would see her in about ten minutes, then she told us she was going to run to the bathroom before Del got here. I asked her if everything was okay, and she said it was just the excitement of the last week.

"Campbell had automatically checked the back door when we first came in, because Del had left the front door unlocked for some goddamn reason. We wanted to make sure the store was secure. It was fucking *locked*, Riles. Why in the *motherfuck* would Kelly have unlocked the back door and slipped out without wanting us to know?"

"Because." Riley's rage hit the stratosphere and she willed herself to stay calm, forcing down the fear that almost overwhelmed her. "Someone has Delaney. They called Kelly on Del's phone and threatened Del's life in order to get Kelly to cooperate. I fucking bet—bullshit, I fucking *know*—it's that prick, Grigor Reizan, who took both of them. Only a threat to one of her friends' lives would have made Kelly act like this and put herself in danger."

Teagan's green eyes were almost black with fury even though she spoke calmly as well. "Any idea where they might have taken her and Del?"

"I have a couple of ideas. Even better yet, Kelly now has a GPS tracker on her so we don't have to guess." The management team stared at Riley in surprise, hope dawning as they all rapidly headed back to the APS complex.

Riley gave them a chilling smile after the team reached the Bunker and continued. "We were going to discuss it with everyone at our next staff meeting, since the whole knuckle-dragging episode was over by then, and we were moving on. Kelly had told me she didn't want to be unreasonable about her safety just because she felt like being stubborn. She and I then agreed it wouldn't be a bad idea for her to have a tiny tracker on her body somewhere, given the threat from Percutio."

There were a few deep exhales.

"The second ear piercing with the large gold stud in Kelly's right ear? There's now a micro GPS tracking chip inside the stud. There's also one in her navel piercing as a backup. The GPS receivers in those two pieces of jewelry can always pinpoint Kelly's location, as long as she has them on her and she's somewhere with decent satellite communications."

Riley was swiftly typing on her phone.

"I have Kelly's GPS receiver information, and her receivers are constantly on. She'll need to touch the earring stud or the navel piercing in order to establish connection with a satellite, which she may not be able to do initially if she's been bound or is unconscious." A small tic showed in Riley's firmly clenched jaw as her GPS navigation system started to scan.

"How hard will it be for her to establish a satellite connection if she's been bound?" Trill asked impassively, the light of hell in her eyes. "And what can I do to facilitate any of this?"

"All Kelly will need to do is rub the earring stud against a firm surface to tell the GPS receiver to connect to a satellite," Riley answered, "which she can do even if she's been bound. The challenge, however, will be to have the satellite connection established if Reizan decides to keep Kelly permanently unconscious. Even if Delaney is being kept with Kelly, Del would have no way of knowing there were GPS tracking chips in Kelly's jewelry or how to activate them."

Riley's voice was ice cold, without emotion, solely focused on what she needed to do to bring her woman safely home.

"I don't think there's anything you can do from here, Trill. To be honest, I can't see Reizan keeping Kelly unconscious for long, though." Riley's smile was frigid. "He's going to want to let her know she belongs to him now. Or so he thinks."

Drew's eyes were arctic as well. "Then all she'll need to do is pretend to scratch her ear on her shoulder or on the floor.

"Precisely." Riley's GPS navigation system kept scanning for Kelly's receivers. The entire team sat there rigidly, the long minutes ticking by, until Riley's phone finally gave a beep. Her heart gave a great leap as the system locked on to something and a bunch of satellites flared to life on her phone screen.

"Bingo. They're at the Port of Tampa."

The management team looked at each other with angry, ruthless expressions.

Riley's face also held no mercy. "That dead son of a bitch is going to try to smuggle them out of the country by boat."

* * * * *

Kelly slowly opened her eyes and tried to focus in the soft light as she regained consciousness. She gave herself a few minutes to come back online, breathing deeply until she became more clear-headed so she could assess her situation.

She was lying on a low king-size mattress, in a large room on what was clearly a ship of some kind. Her arms were restrained behind her and her feet were bound together as well. Her boots and socks had been removed, although she was thankful to feel the rest of her clothes were still in place.

Delaney was lying on the mattress beside her, still unconscious, with her arms and legs similarly tied. But while Kelly's arms were secured with handcuffs, most likely double-lock, she was thankful to see Delaney had only been restrained with zip ties.

Her heart thundered in her chest when she realized the two of them were still alone in the room. Hastily, she rubbed her right ear firmly against the mattress, praying she'd connected the GPS satellite in the micro tracking chip in her gold stud earring with the pressure.

With no time to spare, she let her eyelids flutter shut again and pretended she was just stirring awake as she heard heavy footsteps enter the room.

"Well, good morning, my princess," a cheerful male voice with a distinct foreign accent greeted her. Kelly blinked her eyes open and glared at the dark, swarthy man who had jammed the hypodermic needle into her leg.

"Grigor Reizan, I presume?" Kelly asked with hate in her eyes and in her voice as the man started to smile. She narrowed her eyes at the smug, self-assured piece of shit before her. "And I am not *your* princess," Kelly gritted at him, trying to keep her anger level under control. The dark man's cocky grin widened.

"Oh, but you are, my gloriously beautiful asset. You are my princess and my secret weapon and my wealth generator. *All. Mine.* And the future mother of my children, too, so that we can build an army of female super assets together."

"The fuck I will." Kelly was unable to keep the growing rage out of her voice.

"That's where you're wrong, princess." Grigor swiftly lost his smile, revealing the cold-blooded killer he actually was. "Because if you don't, *jan*, your friend here loses her life. Slowly. Painfully."

Kelly felt the hair on the back of her neck stand up on end, both from Grigor Reizan's threat against Delaney, and from hearing him use the same endearment that Aram Hakobyan had used with "Misty."

"Don't listen to him, Kel." Delaney's groggy voice reached her. "Don't let him exploit you like that. Your gift is too sacred to be used by a piece of crap like him. Screw him."

Grigor laughed with menace. "What a brave soul you are, Ms. Sedgwick. Of course, we all know my princess would *never* jeopardize your health and your welfare, no matter what you might say, so you are quite safe."

"She is not *your* princess." Delaney grew angry as she reiterated Kelly's words. "She belongs to Riley Armstrong, not to you. Riley will burn the world down before she'll ever let someone *inferior like you* take advantage of Kelly." From Reizan's lowered brows, Delaney had clearly struck a nerve.

Del gasped in shock as Reizan suddenly smacked her hard across the face, sending her senses reeling with the wrathful blow.

"I find I tire of your theatrics, Ms. Sedgwick." Reizan's voice was cold and forbidding. "However, Riley Armstrong is not here, now is she? Clearly, she does not deserve a woman like Ms. Holland if she allowed her to be so easily stolen away."

Kelly was seething. "If you *ever* touch Delaney like that again, I promise you…you won't like what I do, Reizan. You have to sleep sometime, motherfucker, and I know a dozen ways to make you scream while I'm killing you very, very slowly."

Reizan's wide smile returned. "Now see, Kelly*jan*, this is why we belong together. You are a beautiful, brilliant, ruthless princess—one who belongs on the arm of Percutio's king."

He came closer to the bed.

"We were meant to rule the world together, princess. After dinner tonight, you will indulge me and show me exactly how your gift works. I am sure I do not need to remind you that Ms. Sedgwick is here to help you remember the consequences of any stubborn refusal to give me what I want."

Kelly's green eyes glowed with even fiercer hate.

Just then, a soft knock came at the stateroom door.

Chapter 29

Kelly's eyes narrowed as the stateroom door opened to admit Alan McAllister. He stepped into the stateroom, closing the door behind him as Kelly stared at him with contempt.

"Well, well, well," Kelly snarked, unable to help herself. "If it isn't the head traitor of Traitor's Anonymous. Set up any more CIA colleagues lately, Alan? Get them burned and thrown out of the agency under false pretenses? Ruin their careers? No?"

Alan shrugged, clearly unperturbed by Kelly's glare. "Grigor promised to make me *extremely* wealthy if I would deliver you to him, Kelly. Given the payoff I was looking at, I was going to make that happen by any means necessary. You can actually blame Robyn for getting you into this mess, Kel."

Alan's eyes were cold.

"If the stupid bitch had kept her mouth shut about your gift in the first place and not confided in me, her *good friend*—because her emotional ass needed someone to talk to—I would have never known about you. For what it's worth, I did try to get her to back off after she'd figured out everything about you. But, she wouldn't listen to me and kept digging into Percutio business, so…" He shrugged.

Kelly had been breathing fire at the disrespectful way McAllister was talking about Robyn, but she felt icy fingers trail down her spine at his words as the light bulb went off.

"So, *you* were the one who found a way to anonymously let this incredible piece of shit here know about Robyn." She jerked her chin at Reizan. "That's why he had her murdered…because *you* had made damn sure he found out Robyn was with the CIA. You were already playing the long game, waiting until you had enough juice to talk to Reizan directly…but, in the meantime, also eliminating a CIA analyst who could pose a threat to your plans."

Kelly couldn't breathe for a minute, faced as she was with the depths of McAllister's corruption and betrayal.

Alan shrugged again and looked at Kelly without emotion. "Like I said, if the stupid bitch would have listened to me and backed off, she would still be alive. It's her own fault her nosy, persistent ass is dead."

A red film of rage fell over Kelly's eyes, as she vowed deep within her soul to Robyn's spirit that Alan would pay one way or another for everything he'd done.

McAllister continued, no longer interested in the subject of Robyn's death. "I sat on the knowledge of what you are without telling a soul for *eighteen months*, Kelly. I knew if I was patient enough for long enough, and could get to Grigor to tell my story, the payoff for me would be huge."

Alan smiled faintly, the first breath of animation skittering across his face.

"None of it was easy, but I finally figured it all out myself." Alan's tone was arrogant and boastful. "First, I had to contact Grigor and tell him about you and your gift…patiently waiting for the right time, so I could be sure he wouldn't kill a CIA agent for daring to approach him. Because I was high enough on the CIA totem pole after I was promoted to handler, however, he was willing to listen to me." Alan gestured to Reizan. "Grigor was *thoroughly* intrigued by what I had to tell him about you, Kel. He offered me quite the deal if I could acquire you for him, with the understanding the deal would remain a secret between the two of us alone."

Kelly's rage grew by leaps and bounds the more McAllister talked.

"That deal was precisely what I'd been working toward for two goddamn years, so I didn't give a fuck *how* secret he wanted to keep it," Alan continued. "When we'd agreed upon terms, I had to make a plan: First, I had to determine the best way to leave you vulnerable, and then I had to actually deliver you to Grigor and his associates. Fucking APS almost screwed the pooch on that one, though, didn't they?"

A flare of anger appeared in Alan's eyes.

"I'd come up with a brilliant plan, making it appear to the CIA that you were going off the rails. The oh-so-easily-manipulated higher-ups then burned you because you appeared to be unstable and no longer reliable. Consequently, all of your CIA protection was taken away from you. You. Were. Defenseless."

McAllister's anger started to burn a little hotter. "But those fucking assholes at APS had to stick their noses in where they didn't belong and ride to the rescue. They just had to offer you a job at APS and fuck up my entire plan. However," Alan's bravado returned, "I told Grigor you'd do *anything* for your bitches, so we decided to take one of them as a little bit of insurance, to ensure you would cooperate. We had to do this all ourselves, the two of us, without any help. Grigor's crews thought we took you for the APS intel you possessed. Which we certainly did, in a sense."

Alan leaned against the stateroom door and crossed his feet at the ankles.

"But Grigor didn't want any of his associates to know about you and what you could do. He wanted the profits from using your ability all to himself. So, there is no one outside of the two of us who know the whole story. Never have and never will. Me?" McAllister laughed, a cruel, ugly laugh. "I want all of the money Grigor has promised me, so I can ride off into the sunset and live happily ever after."

He looked at Kelly with a faint touch of regret on his face.

"You were a good agent, Holland. One of the best in the business."

Alan walked across the stateroom and slightly bent over where Kelly was lying on the bed.

"But your ability—your gift—is your ticket to fortune, Kel. Not a bureaucratic agency filled with stuffed shirts who don't understand what's truly important, or a ragtag group of do-gooders like those idiots at APS, who fail to see the opportunity you present."

"Alan," Grigor called from his position behind McAllister.

McAllister straightened up and turned around, his eyes widening when he saw the gun in Reizan's hand. Kelly's heart raced as Reizan fired two shots directly into McAllister's heart.

Alan went down, a look of surprise on his face, and was dead before he hit the ground.

Chapter 30

Kelly briefly glanced sideways at Delaney, who was surprisingly calm in the face of Reizan's violence.

"Well." Reizan was matter of fact, ignoring the body on the floor. "I never did like him. An incompetent blowhard braggart who almost lost you more times than I can count, princess. Make no mistake: That payoff would not have been the last I saw of Alan McAllister. His greed would have always brought him back for more.

"Besides..." Grigor smiled coldly, a sickening satisfaction on his face, "now, I truly *do* have you and your ability all to myself. Except for those fools at APS, your charming sister, and the rest of your little friends, no one else knows exactly what Kelly Holland is capable of."

Kelly felt her rage intensify even more, shaking her with its force.

"You, my princess—with some *incentive* to guarantee Ms. Sedgwick's continued good health—are going to use your gift on my behalf, until my influence, my reputation, and my wealth hit near *mythical* heights. And then, Kelly*jan*? You are going to bear my children for me. Glorious daughters, who will carry the same gift as their beautiful mother. Narek!" Reizan called sharply.

The stateroom door opened once again and one of Reizan's associates appeared.

"Take out the trash, will you?" Reizan gestured casually at McAllister's body. "Get Ilya in here to help you. When you are done, you may release these lovely ladies from their bonds, so they can be more comfortable."

He looked at Kelly, unsmiling.

"I do not think I need to tell you the penalty for your friend by your misbehavior, if you try to do something you should think twice about doing. However, just in case I do… Are you left-handed or are you right-handed, Ms. Sedgwick?" Although addressing Delaney, Reizan didn't remove his eyes from Kelly's face.

"Right-handed," Delaney answered quietly after a moment.

"And so, Ms. Holland. Should you dare to try my patience, your pastry chef friend here will have the forefinger of her right hand cut off."

Delaney couldn't stifle her gasp, while Kelly narrowed her eyes at Grigor Reizan in sheer hatred.

"As you bear my children and we then have no need for Ms. Sedgwick to stay with us as your incentive any longer," Reizan said casually. "It would certainly be a shame if she was unable to resume her career when she is released, would it not?"

"I hate you." Kelly's voice was equally quiet. "You make McAllister look like a boy scout, Reizan. You have no ethics. Certainly no honor."

"Ah, but that is where you are wrong, Kelly*jan*." Reizan came over to the bed once again, then leaned down and caressed Kelly's face. "It all depends on what your definition of honor is, my princess. My definition simply means the winner takes all. Always."

Reizan straightened up, then turned and walked to the stateroom door.

"My associates will be back momentarily to free you. Then, someone will be back to escort you to dinner in approximately five hours. I suggest you two use the time until then to rest." And he was gone.

When Narek and Ilya had returned from disposing of McAllister's body and had freed the girls from their restraints, Kelly and Delaney had spent some time massaging the feeling back into their arms and legs after the two men had left.

"I'm so sorry, Del." Kelly sighed. "But I can't risk putting you into that nut job's crosshairs by taking a chance on trying to escape. I guess we're stuck here for now, honey."

She spent a few minutes connecting and disconnecting the satellite from the GPS receiver in her ear, hoping Riley would see it and know they were okay.

When Kelly finally glanced up, Delaney shook her head at Kelly very slightly, then casually touched her eye and her ear, as if asking Kelly if there were any eyes and ears on them right now.

Kelly frowned, not understanding what Delaney was asking at first, but then used her formidable skills to search the stateroom after she figured out what Delaney was trying to ask her.

After a while of thoroughly searching the entire stateroom, Kelly found two bugs, but no camera devices at any kind. She signaled her findings to Delaney.

"Do you think good old Reizan will have mercy on us and get us something to eat soon?" Delaney quietly dropped to her knees and reached under the edge of one of the chairs in the corner of the stateroom.

To Kelly's utter shock, Delaney extracted a gun from under the chair. Kelly realized the gun must have flown out of Alan's jacket when he hit the floor and disappeared under the edge of the chair before Reizan saw it.

Given her position on the bed at that time, it was a miracle that Delaney had seen it, too. With an enormous sense of relief, Kelly mouthed, "I ADORE you," to Delaney, who nodded in satisfaction.

"I don't know, Del. I don't feel like I could eat a thing. I guess I should think about it, though, if only to keep my strength up. Honestly, all I want right now is some peace and quiet." Kelly quietly scooped up the gun and checked it, finding three rounds and one in the chamber.

Not optimal, but it was better than nothing, Kelly decided.

Delaney silently rummaged through the dresser drawers, pulling out a pad of paper and a pen from one of them.

"Reizan said something about wanting a demonstration of your gift after dinner," she said to Kelly. "With any luck, that means I can try to get rid of this headache for a few hours. He hit me pretty hard and my face hurts."

She narrowed her eyes at her friend as she scribbled, *"If we can lure another one of Reizan's goons in here and you can take him out, we can take his gun, too."*

Aloud, she said, "And don't you *dare* apologize, Kel. It's not your fault he's a sadistic piece of crap. I pushed him, so he had to show us who big man on campus was."

"You're getting one hell of a bruise on your cheek, Del. I wonder if Reizan's generosity extends to a couple of Tylenol. It should. He was the fucker who put the bruise there."

Delaney handed the pad and pen to Kelly when she gestured for it. "Not quite yet, Kel, okay? I hate taking anything, and I'd rather try to shake it off naturally if I can. I'll ask for some in a bit if this headache doesn't start going away."

Kelly rapidly scribbled a note to Delaney. *"When we're ready, I'll knock on the door and ask for some Tylenol. When whoever it is comes back, I'll act really worried and say you lost consciousness. You can be lying on the bed, pretending you're out.*

"I'll hit whoever it is on the back of the head with Alan's gun after he passes me. He won't be expecting it, and they won't have any idea I have a weapon. I'll make sure he's out, then I'll take his weapon.

"They left the zip ties when they freed you. I put them in one of the dresser drawers. We'll use them to restrain him, and then gag him."

Delaney nodded, then took the pad and paper. "*Is there any way to determine how many goons are with Reizan?*" Again, she said out loud, "I'm really feeling a bit woozy, Kelly. I'm going to lay down for a bit, okay?"

"Okay, honey. Sleep tight." She quickly wrote, "*Right now, no, but I'll bet you there aren't many. I'm guessing maybe four. Reizan doesn't want <u>anybody</u> to know he has us or that he's leaving the country, so he's running a bare minimum skeleton crew on this yacht.*

"*If we're right, that means there's a goon outside our door, one piloting the ship, and two seeing to the rest of the ship. I don't know how big this vessel is, but it feels plenty big. It's my guess, however, that we're going to intercept another bigger ship once we're in the Gulf...one that's fully staffed.*"

Delaney nodded again.

"*Do you know how to shoot a gun?*" Delaney shook her head no, looking disgusted with herself.

"*That's okay, Del. It's simply point and shoot, aiming in the general vicinity of your target. Just remember to hold on tight, so the recoil doesn't kick the gun out of your hand.*

"*We'll give it another thirty minutes. I'll lure the asshole in here and take him out, then restrain him. Then you'll stay in here with him, while I go run reconnaissance on the rest of the ship. I don't want to fire my gun if I can help it, because it will be game over with all the noise...but we'll do what we need to do."*

Delaney blew out a deep breath and nodded a final time.

Kelly wrapped her arms around Delaney as Del did the same, and they held onto each other for a long minute.

Kelly scribbled one more note. "*I'm so proud of you, honey. This has been some scary fucking shit, but you are handling it like a trooper. We're going to get through this, Delaney. I swear.*"

Chapter 31

Two fast powerboats pounded north through Tampa Bay on a course to intercept the *Arusiak*, which meant "morning star" in Armenian, a 72' yacht registered to Aram Hakobyan of Tampa.

When Kelly's GPS tracking chip first showed she was at the Port of Tampa, the Seven immediately sprang into action. As Kelly's GPS showed her start to move a short time later, they were subsequently able to determine that Kelly—and, they assumed, Delaney—were onboard the *Arusiak*.

Blake had called her father and rapidly explained the situation to him. Once he grasped the seriousness of what Blake was telling him, Mr. Seibert quickly arranged to have two powerboats waiting for the Armstrong twins and the Seven at Harborage Marina. It was the only full-service mega yacht port on Florida's west coast, Blake told the rest of the management team.

When Rowan asked Blake worriedly if she would be able to pilot the *Arusiak* once they took command of the yacht, Blake had grinned, despite the gravity of the situation.

"Not to worry, sweetheart," Blake soothed. "I think I was about seven the first time my dad let me help him pilot something like that." Rowan's eyes got huge. "Dad will be waiting at Harborage

Marina for me to bring the *Arusiak* in, Ro, and he will kick my ass if I so much as loosen a screw on her bridge. So, no worries."

The APS team held a fast meeting while Mr. Seibert was arranging the powerboats for them. While they met, Mr. Siebert also contacted the Coast Guard on their behalf, to bring them up to speed on the situation. Blake took the twins and the rest of the Seven through the specifications for the yacht where Kelly and Delaney were being held.

"This motherfucker is a big damn boat, dudes. Cost, it runs about 3.5 mil. 72' long, four staterooms, six heads. Cruising speed is 16 knots, and the fuel capacity is 2,800 gallons. There are two inboard engines, each with 1,150 horsepower. I'm going to guess they're keeping the girls together in the master stateroom, which is located amidships on this vessel. That's going to make things even more challenging for us, because it means they're being kept smack dab in the middle of the fucking ship. Another argument for Reizan keeping the girls together is because he doesn't have the manpower to keep and watch them separately."

The Armstrong twins and the Seven agreed.

"He's keeping this kidnapping as hush-hush as possible…even Hakobyan doesn't fucking know. So, you figure he's probably running a four-man crew at best, enough to get him out to sea where he can intercept a bigger yacht with a full crew—one that's not Percutio-related. The more individuals in the Percutio organization know about Reizan kidnapping Kelly and Delaney, the bigger risk Reizan takes in letting his secret about Kelly out. You *know* that greedy motherfucker is not about to do that, because he wants to use Kelly for his own personal gain."

Blake pulled up another set of specifications on her phone. "Our biggest challenge will be taking command of the *Arusiak* while keeping Kelly and Delaney safe. If we estimate a four-person crew, they'll have one guarding the girls, one piloting the ship, and two taking care of everything else."

Next, Blake pulled up a schematic with the *Arusiak*'s layout on it. "They can't have eyes everywhere, and I'd guess that useless fucker, Reizan, isn't one to get his hands dirty and pitch in to help. It will be fairly easy to board the *Arusiak* from the stern. I'm going to suggest we use one of the powerboats as a decoy—to keep their attention drawn up front toward the bow—while those in the other powerboat board from behind at the stern. It's a beautiful day. I've already confirmed there's a ton of traffic on the water, so we won't stand out."

"Fuck, you guys are amazing." Riley blew out a deep breath. "Blake, how many years have we fucking known you? Thirty? It's so easy to forget sometimes just how goddamn much shit you really know. All of you."

Blake nodded at her friend solemnly.

Riley looked at her GPS navigation system, which was tracking Kelly's whereabouts. "That's the third time we've lost the GPS connection and it's come right back on. I'm thinking Kelly is turning it on and off to let us know she's conscious, and that she and Delaney are okay for now."

"If the girls are in a guarded stateroom," Casey drummed her fingers, "what are the chances that arrogant fucker let them loose because he perceived very little risk in doing so? They're unarmed, plus he's using the threat of harm to each of them to keep them under control. But that still means they're unrestrained."

Blake's phone rang and she had a short, but intense conversation with whoever was on the other line before disconnecting and looking at the rest of the team.

"That was my dad. Only six people—all of them males who spoke with an accent, except for one—boarded the *Arusiak* before it set sail. But get this. Four of the foreign males carried two very large trunks aboard with them, and they refused any offers of help from port staff." Blake's face darkened with anger. "What do you want to bet the girls were unconscious and in those trunks?"

"*Mano.*" Bryn's voice was mild, sensing Riley was on the verge of losing her shit. "We're going to find them, Riles. Both Kelly and Del are bright as fuck and they *will* find a way to hang on until we can get there. Count on it." Riley refocused her thoughts with an effort, then nodded calmly at her twin.

"That goes for you too, *broki*," Bryn added quietly, looking at the violence that was resting on Teagan's face.

"Del might be shy, but I personally wouldn't want to piss her off. She fought too long to protect that asshole motherfucker's mom up in Michigan to let something like this derail her." Teagan blew out a deep breath and visibly got a firm grip on herself as well.

Casey continued her train of thought when Riley and Teagan had settled. "The guy with no accent *has* to be Alan McAllister. If McAllister and Reizan are the only two who know the entire plan, the only one hanging around Reizan without an accent would be McAllister."

"So, we've got McAllister, Reizan, and four Percutio goons. We've already speculated that one of them is piloting the ship—probably Hakobyan's regular captain—and one of them is guarding the stateroom where the girls are being held. The last two are going to be moving around."

Blake was making notes to herself as she talked.

"McAllister and Reizan will most likely be together in the salon, which is aft and closer to the stern, but it's completely encased in glass. Their eyes will be drawn forward to the decoy powerboat in front of them once a ruckus starts with that."

"If McAllister's even still alive." Drew's voice was dry. "I can't see Reizan letting him live, now that Reizan has Kelly and no longer has a use for McAllister."

Trill agreed. "Reizan will not only want to nullify that risk, he'll also want to make sure he's the only one left who will profit from Kelly and her ability. McAllister was probably too blind to see that threat coming."

The team nodded grimly.

Blake's phone chimed and she checked her messages. "It's Dad. Powerboats are here and ready," she informed the team. The nine of them swung into action.

Now, after going over everything with Bob Seibert—who was standing on the Harborage Marina dock with Oliver Armstrong, Delaney's father, David Sedgwick, and Teagan's father, Mark Malloy—and solidifying their plans, the Armstrong twins and the Seven jumped into the powerboats and took off.

Since Blake would have to board the *Arusiak* and take command of her once they were clear, Drew and Casey were piloting the powerboats.

Drew and the Red Team—consisting of Bryn, Kennedy, Jaime, and Trill—were in the decoy boat. Casey and the Blue Team—which had Riley, Teagan, and Blake—split off from the Red Team and lost themselves in the traffic on the water once the *Arusiak* was in sight.

Their target sighted, Drew casually pulled ahead of the *Arusiak*, deliberately causing a distraction for those aboard the yacht. The Red Team was in clear sight, their faces hidden by sunglasses, as Drew drove as though they were a group out partying on the bright, warm March day.

Sneaking up behind the *Arusiak* on the starboard side, Casey took her cue, preparing to maneuver her powerboat so the Blue Team could board the *Arusiak* from the stern.

Suddenly, however, the sound of gunshots came from inside the *Arusiak*.

Chapter 32

Kelly nodded at Delaney as Del sank on the bed and pretended to be unconscious.

"Hello? *Hey*!" Kelly rapped sharply on the stateroom door. "I need help in here, dickhead! My friend has been woozy since your asshole of a boss smacked her in the head, and now I can't get her to wake up!"

Kelly pounded on the door once again.

"I fucking swear to Christ, asshole, if *anything* happens to her because you ignored me, I will personally see to it that Reizan rips your fucking balls off!"

The door opened and Kelly let outrage and worry war for dominance on her face. A swarthy guard, whom Kelly had never seen before, poked his head into the stateroom.

"See?" Kelly pointed to Delaney's limp form on the bed. She let a tiny sob escape. "Oh, Jesus, I'm going to fucking *kill* him if she's not okay!"

The guard, gun in hand, entered the room, not particularly wary because he knew that neither of the women were armed. As he passed Kelly, she glared at him in worry, but he ignored her and headed for the bed where Del lay still.

Quick as a flash, Kelly brought the butt of McAllister's gun down hard on the back of the guard's head as soon as his back was to her. He crumpled to the floor, unconscious, his gun flying from his hand.

Delaney scrambled from the bed and went flying to the dresser to retrieve the zip ties, as she said aloud, sounding drowsy, "It's okay, Kel. I'm okay. Just sleeping. Why are you so freaked out?"

Kelly picked up the guard's gun from the floor and placed it on the bed along with McAllister's. Then she quickly and expertly bound the guard with the zip ties, before ripping a wide strip from the bottom of her t-shirt to gag him.

"Because I couldn't get you to wake up, and I was scared to death something was wrong." Kelly went over to the stateroom door, which the guard had left open, and pushed it closed to make it sound like the guard had just left. "Thanks for nothing, asshole!" she yelled through the door for further effect. "Jesus, what a fucking moron."

Kelly then nodded at Delaney silently, and the two of them managed to drag the dead weight of the guard to the other side of the bed, where he couldn't be seen from the stateroom door.

"You should go back to sleep, honey, and rest your head. I think I'll lay down, too. My fucking nerves are shot," Kelly said, heaving a great sigh.

"That's a good idea, Kel," Delaney replied, making her voice sound like it was fading.

Kelly left McAllister's smaller Glock lying on the bed for Delaney and picked up the guard's heavier Luger. "*Leave it to a fucking Armenian to carry a damn German gun,"* she muttered to herself, as she rapidly checked it over and found it fully loaded.

She pulled the pen and paper they'd been using out from the dresser drawer and scribbled a quick note to Delaney. "*Leaving you the Glock, it's lighter. Kneel on the other side of the bed next to dickhead. Hold the Glock with both hands, arms bent to rest your elbows on the bed to support it, finger off the trigger. Don't take your eyes off the door.*

"*Anyone comes in and you don't know them, point and shoot! Don't ask questions. And don't move until me, the twins, or one of the Seven come, k?*'" Delaney nodded grimly.

Kelly gestured silently at the stateroom door, holding the Luger down at her side. Grimacing, she avoided the pool of blood next to the bed again, her bare feet noiseless on the tile, and slipped over to the stateroom door.

She opened it and peeked out, looking out at a short flight of stairs that led to the main areas of the yacht. Listening intently for the sound of boots, she mounted the staircase and paused to look around again when she reached the top. There was still no one in sight.

Kelly took a deep breath, trying to figure out the layout of the boat from where she stood, starting to creep down the outside. The yacht was definitely a big one, but there was a distinct lack of places to hide.

Suddenly, hearing voices speaking in a foreign language, Kelly ducked into a small entranceway that led into a tiny galley kitchen.

Fuck, she cursed silently to herself, as she realized she'd backed herself into a corner.

Kelly waited, motionless, hoping whoever it was would just pass on by and continue on to what she assumed was the salon.

Her soul froze as she heard two sets of boots descend down the staircase she'd just come up and make their way to the stateroom, where she'd been held with Delaney. The sounds of yelling and then multiple gunshots were loud, as was the sound of another pair of boots running toward her.

As the sound of the boots grew louder, Kelly raised her Luger, stepped out of the entranceway to the galley, and shot a man she recognized as either Narek or Ilya. He dropped and Kelly flew past him, her feet thundering down the short staircase to the stateroom where Delaney was.

Kelly froze as she realized Reizan was in there with Delaney, a large knife in his hand, with another man bleeding on the floor. Delaney was still kneeling, paralyzed, on the other side of the bed as Reizan started toward her.

* * * * *

"Go! Go!" Riley yelled at the sound of the gunshots, holding onto the side of the powerboat. Casey swung around in the yacht's wake, trying to get closer so that the Blue team could board the *Arusiak*.

As soon as Casey was close enough, Riley, Teagan, and Blake jumped aboard, guns drawn and crouched low. Out of the corner of her eye, Riley saw the other powerboat with her twin and the Red team approach.

"Kelly!" she hollered, just as Teagan yelled, "Delaney!" They followed Blake to the salon doors. Riley kicked them open, but there was no one in the salon.

As Bryn and the rest of the red team boarded the *Arusiak*, Blake headed for the bridge, finding the captain there and leveling her weapon at him. "Shut up, motherfucker," Blake snarled as the man began to stammer. "Where the fuck are the girls?"

"I don't know!" the man cried. "They were being kept in the master stateroom, but I don't know if they've moved them. I'm only the captain for Aram Hakobyan, I swear!"

Blake kept her weapon trained on him as she touched the comm in her ear. "The captain swears the girls were being kept in the master stateroom," she reported. "I'm on the bridge with him right now. As soon as someone else can get up here and secure him, I can take the bridge and get us the fuck out of here."

Riley and Teagan rapidly but quietly exited the salon and made their way down toward the middle of the ship, hearts thundering as they prayed Kelly and Delaney were okay.

* * * * *

"Ah, Kelly." Reizan stopped halfway to Delaney, an ugly smile on his face. "So glad you could join us. I should have known that useless piece of work, McAllister, would attempt to ruin my plans, even dead. But no matter, princess. I still have you *exactly* where I want you."

Reizan showed Kelly the knife he gripped in this hand.

"It was very clever of you and Ms. Sedgwick to realize that Alan had lost his weapon. It was also equally clever for you to retrieve it and to leave it for her protection. However… Ms. Sedgwick is not much of a shooter, I'm afraid." His cold smile didn't teach his eyes. "She got one of my men, unfortunately, but it appears she is now out of bullets. Now, you get to watch me cut off *all* of her fingers as your punishment, Kelly. It will keep me occupied until the rest of my men get here. You also need to understand that I will stab her in the gut so she bleeds out slowly, if you attempt to interfere, princess."

Reizan started back across the stateroom, still unaware that one of his men was unconscious and bound on the floor next to Delaney, or that Kelly had already shot another one of them in addition to the one who lay dead on the stateroom floor.

"Reizan." Kelly's voice was steady. "I think you forgot one little thing, asshole."

"Oh? And what might that be, my princess?" Reizan paused again and looked at the beautiful redhead.

Kelly gave Reizan the coldest, most malicious smile Delaney had ever seen on anyone's face, before Kelly swiftly brought up the

Luger that had been hidden down at her side and aimed it right at Reizan. His eyes widened in disbelief.

"Never bring a knife to a gunfight, motherfucker." With one perfect kill shot, Kelly watched impassively as Reizan's head exploded.

Chapter 33

"Del! Stay here in the stateroom, okay? I need to figure out what other hostiles are out there." Kelly flew to the stateroom door, checked to make sure the coast was clear, then hit the stairs once again. She crept upstairs, then slid into the hallway, looking toward the bow of the boat for any remaining Percutio men before she turned back around.

Suddenly, a tall figure in black appeared out of nowhere and pulled Kelly tightly into her arms.

"Riley! Oh, Riley!" Kelly threw her arms around her fiancé and started to cry, her relief enormous. She started to shake from her adrenaline rush and she burrowed into Riley's arms.

"Kelly!" Teagan appeared behind her, rage still edging her features, as she looked past Kelly for Delaney. "Is Del okay? Where is she?"

"She's in the master stateroom, Teagan. She's okay, just tired and bruised. She was a fucking fighter, *broki*, jumping in it without any hesitation whatsoever. I couldn't have done this without her." After kissing Kelly hastily on the cheek, Teagan ran down the stairs toward the master stateroom.

Riley captured Kelly's mouth with a brief, hard kiss before asking, "*Princesa.* Where's Reizan?"

"Dead." Kelly suddenly felt exhausted. "His body is on the floor of the master stateroom. One of his goons is bound with zip ties and is behind the bed on the far side, unconscious. I shot the second one right outside the galley, and Delaney shot a third one, who's also lying on the stateroom floor. Del and I were betting there were four, besides Reizan and Alan McAllister."

Kelly struggled for a moment, the events of the past few hours starting to catch up with her.

"Reizan shot and killed Alan in front of us. So, we have six accounted for: Reizan, McAllister, Goon 1—who is bound and unconscious in the stateroom—and Goon 2, whom Del shot and is lying on the floor of the master stateroom, presumed dead. Goon 3, whom I shot, is lying outside the galley, also presumed dead. Goon 4 is the captain. What Del and I *didn't* know was if there were any more hostiles besides them."

"No, baby, that was all of them. We were able to get that intel from Bob Seibert—that there were only six who came aboard." Riley shook her head in awe. "I swear to Christ, *princesa*, you and Delaney were like a two-woman SWAT team on this ship. Un-fucking-believable."

Suddenly, Riley touched the comm in her ear, still holding tightly onto Kelly and kissing her forehead.

"Go." She listened for a couple of minutes before she told Kelly, "Kenn and Jaime are guarding the captain. Casey and Drew are taking the powerboats back to Harborage Marina, and they'll meet us there. Blake has the bridge here, and she's taking us back to Harborage as well. Trill and Bryn are making sure the rest of the ship is clear, and Teagan has Delaney."

Riley finally permitted herself to relax a bit and captured Kelly's mouth more thoroughly, feeling massive relief and love flood through her body at the feel of her woman safe in her arms.

"The Coast Guard is going to want to talk to you and Delaney, *princesa*," she said when she had finally released Kelly's mouth. "Bob Seibert, Blake's dad, has been keeping them informed for us so far. Mr. Seibert is a master mariner, incidentally—which means he holds the highest level seafarer license it's possible to achieve—and he fucking knows *everyone* in the Coast Guard here, plus all the people at the Port of Tampa. The Coast Guard knew we were dealing with a hostage situation and were standing by to provide support as needed."

Despite her exhaustion, Kelly raised her eyebrow. "Do I even want to know what kind of juice APS has in the greater Tampa Bay area that the fucking *Coast Guard* would defer to them in something like this and let them take the lead?"

Riley smirked at her, but instead of answering, she kissed Kelly's forehead again before continuing.

"Needless to say, baby, Grigor Reizan and Percutio have never been popular with *any* law enforcement agency here in Florida." Riley kissed her temple as they headed for the salon. "You and Delaney will both have to give a statement describing what happened from the time each of you were taken, but beyond that, you won't have much to worry about. As a matter of fact, there's going to be a bunch of law enforcement officials lining up to shake your hand for taking Reizan out."

As they passed the stairs leading down into the master stateroom, they met Teagan and Delaney coming up. Teagan's arm was wrapped firmly around Delaney for support.

When Delaney saw Kelly, however, she flew up the rest of the stairs and grabbed Kelly in a huge hug. The two women stood there for a long time with their arms wrapped around each other.

"Nothing like a little hostage situation to get to know someone better," Kelly joked eventually even as she wiped her eyes, prompting Delaney to burst out laughing as the girls finally stepped back from each other.

"Right? I think I'm going to create my first dessert and name it in your honor, Kel." Delaney's eyes gleamed with both mirth and residual tears. "I'm going to call it *Kidnapper's Confection*." They both giggled, exhausted and slap-happy.

Riley and Teagan rolled their eyes at each other, then back at the women. "Femmes," Teagan muttered, even as her eyes never left Delaney.

Then, Riley looked at Delaney's face and her brows lowered. "Reizan?" she asked tersely, gesturing to the large black and blue mark blooming on Delaney's cheek.

Delaney nodded as she touched her face gently. "My cheek looks a heck of a lot better than Reizan's head, though, thanks to Kelly," Del assured Riley and Teagan, who looked similarly pissed.

"We're going to take you two to the salon, so you can rest for a bit before we get to Harborage Marina. Both the Coast Guard and the FBI are there, waiting to talk to you both." Riley rapidly sent a text. "Your parents are also there, Del, plus my parents and the rest of your girls, including Rowan. I just asked my dad to give your parents a heads-up about your face, so it's not such a shock."

Riley got Kelly and Delaney settled in the salon while Teagan found them some cold water. After drinking deeply, Kelly collapsed against Riley and closed her eyes to take a nap.

Teagan gently but insistently seated an equally exhausted Delaney on another couch, sitting down beside her and urging Del to rest. Delaney initially stiffened for a moment, but then relaxed against Teagan, closing her eyes as well. In an instant, both women were asleep.

* * * * *

Almost absentmindedly, Teagan gently stroked Delaney's black curls away from her face, her other arm wrapped firmly around the petite pastry chef. "They're so tired and have been through so much," she said to Riley in a low voice so she wouldn't disturb them. "I look at that bruise on Del's face and I wish I could kill Reizan again myself, the motherfucker."

"I know." Riley had both arms wrapped around her sleeping fiancée. "Kel said she could have never done what she did without Delaney's help. It sounds like Del was pretty fierce." Riley was contemplative as she looked at her friend. "The last ten years have changed her, Teag. She's not the girl we all remember." Riley continued. "She's still sweet as fuck, and she still clearly cares about the people around her. But she's, I don't know, *cautious* in a way she never was back then. Almost as if she's expecting to take damage if she doesn't protect herself."

Teagan's face was cold. "I know. It's not just that, either." She held Delaney closer. "I'm prouder than hell that she was able to do what she did today, Riles. But when Kelly told us how Del jumped in, feet first, with no hesitation? All I could think was, those were *not* the actions of the shy, passive Delaney I remember."

Teagan's face grew colder as she focused on the beautiful, sleeping face against her.

"There is a Michigan asshole motherfucker out there who better hope to Christ I never find out what she put Del through. Or what she did to turn the sweetest, most innocent woman I've ever known into someone so guarded that she won't let anyone get close to her."

Chapter 34

It had been a long, hard day for everyone.

When the *Arusiak* finally docked at the Harborage Marina, and marina personnel had her completely secured under the direction of Bob Seibert, Riley and Teagan led Kelly and Delaney down the gangway.

Delaney was quickly taken possession of by her parents, David Sedgwick gratefully shaking Teagan's hand and thanking her profusely for all of her assistance. Kelly was swept up by a relieved Rowan and Rosi Armstrong, with Oliver wrapping his arms around the three women and hugging them hard.

Clementine, Nova, Brooke, and Alyssa were next, crying tears of joy that their friends were safe. Delaney then faced a *very* unhappy APS team when they all saw the dark bruise on her cheek. Del hugged and kissed each one of the team, assuring them—just as she had Riley and Teagan—that Reizan had gotten the worst end of the deal.

When they were done, Riley and Bryn introduced Kelly and Delaney to two other people who had been standing by patiently: Lieutenant Joshua Hachette, a representative of the sector commander of Coast Guard Sector St. Petersburg, and Special Agent Cassidy Lopez of the FBI.

They both shook Kelly and Delaney's hands, inquired after their welfare, and expressed their thanks on behalf of the United States government for their actions in putting an end to Percutio's malignant head.

"Josh? Why don't we all go inside? Dennis, the harbormaster, said we can use his conference room." Riley took Kelly's hand and started to lead her toward the office.

Kelly looked back at Delaney, who was hand-in-hand with Teagan, and mouthed, "*Josh?*" with a frown on her face. Delaney shook her head, just as clueless as Kelly.

Teagan, the corners of her mouth quirking, filled Delaney in. "Last year, APS helped the Coast Guard and the U.S. Navy bring in a $200 million drug haul they had seized from smugglers."

Delaney's eyes widened.

"APS doesn't typically get involved with that sort of thing, Del, but Drew and her crew had already been tracking the head smuggler. Our intel had informed us the now-dead motherfucker was smuggling local young women and selling them, too." Teagan's brilliant green eyes grew dark before she continued. "Because our missions sort of collided, that's how we met Lieutenant Hachette. We all got to know each other pretty well during the course of the mission."

Delaney was quiet as she mulled over that information, plainly doing some serious thinking.

When they arrived at the main marina offices, they all went into a conference room and found a seat. A few of the Seven made sure there were cold water bottles available, then Special Agent Lopez got started when everyone had settled.

"Again, Lieutenant Hachette and I would like to extend our heartfelt thanks to you both on behalf of the United States government for your roles in eliminating Grigor Reizan, the head of Percutio. I'm sure it comes as no surprise to either of you that we've been after Reizan for a very long time." Agent Lopez nodded at Kelly and Delaney. "Ms. Holland, Ms. Sedgwick, I'm going to ask each of you to tell us everything that happened, starting with your abductions, okay? We'll circle back around and fill in the gaps as needed, but let's just focus on your untainted recollections for now. Ms. Sedgwick, would you like to start?"

Delaney told them she'd just gone into her new bakery when a man she didn't know quickly came in behind her, and she felt a prick on the side of her neck. After that, she didn't remember anything more until she woke up, bound, on the floor in the back of an SUV. Reizan had held her phone to her ear, telling her to only let Kelly know he would kill her if Kelly didn't do as he said. When she'd done as she'd been instructed to do, she felt the prick of a needle again, and again remembered nothing until she woke up in the *Arusiak*'s master stateroom with Kelly.

When Delaney was done telling them what she remembered of their ordeal, including how Reizan had struck her—filling the conference room with rumbles of anger—Kelly started. She told them about Delaney's forced phone call, and how Kelly had snuck out of Delaney's bakery and gone with Reizan because she'd feared for her friend's life.

After Kelly had also recounted the details of their kidnapping from her own perspective, Riley then stepped in, filling in both Lieutenant Hachette and Special Agent Lopez on Kelly's eidetic memory gift.

Their eyes widened as Riley explained the genetic component as well. She made it clear that Reizan had fully intended to rape Kelly and sire a dynasty of eidetic super assets—in addition to using Kelly for her memory ability. Delaney had been taken to keep Kelly in line, to ensure Kelly would follow Reizan's orders to prevent any harm from coming to her friend.

Both Lieutenant Hachette and Agent Lopez were appalled and angered by Reizan's intentions. "Death couldn't come fast enough for that son of a bitch," muttered Josh Hachette in revulsion, sharing an icy look with the APS team.

"We now look for Aram Hakobyan to step into Grigor Reizan's place," Riley said.

Bryn added, "Hakobyan doesn't know about Kelly. Reizan was bound and determined to keep knowledge of Kelly's ability to himself so he could use her for his own personal gain, not Percutio's. Alan McAllister, the CIA mole who gave Kelly up and was the only other person in this clusterfuck besides Reizan who knew about Kelly and her ability, is dead—killed by Reizan—and so is Grigor."

"Which means," Riley stated, looking at her fiancée, "that Kelly is now safe. Neither my twin, any of the Seven, nor I are going to tell anyone else about her. Kelly's sister, who is Bryn's fiancée, plus Kelly and Delaney's few close friends who know, aren't going to tell anyone. You two," Riley gestured at Lieutenant Hachette and Special Agent Lopez, "certainly aren't going to tell anyone. Kelly's secret has died with Reizan's death. Reizan killed McAllister because he was too greedy to share her, then he lost his own life because of his greed."

"His cohorts in Percutio had thought Grigor wanted her simply because she'd been a hotshot covert and clandestine ops agent for the CIA…the best in the business, McAllister had told them." Bryn's eyes were hard. "They had assumed—wrongfully—that Reizan was going to use her to delve deep into any APS secrets she'd learned when she came to work with us, after having been improperly burned by the CIA. They further assumed that would give them a significant strategic advantage."

"None of them knew about her eidetic memory capability or how something like that could be used to further their criminal empire." Riley's wintry expression matched her twin's. "And now, they never will."

* * * * *

A week later, Kelly, Riley, Trill, and Kenn stood in Ballast Point Park in south Tampa, waiting near the entrance to the fishing pier for Aram Hakobyan—the new head of Percutio—and a few representatives from the Percutio organization.

When Hakobyan had called Riley and requested a meeting at a time and place of Riley's choosing, Riley had agreed, picking Ballast Point Park as a neutral location.

Anticipating Kelly's insistence on going with her, she assigned both Kenn and Trill as her bodyguards, knowing their reputations as APS' fastest and deadliest shots would send a *clear* message to Percutio that Riley wasn't about to play any more when it came to Kelly's safety.

When Hakobyan and his associates arrived, Hakobyan spent a long minute looking at Kelly impassively before a fleeting smile crossed his face. "Hello, Ms. Holland," he greeted her quietly. "Or, should I say, *Misty*?"

Hakobyan then turned to Riley, perhaps sensing her slight bristling. "I am sure it is no surprise to you that I have taken over for Grigor, Riley. I thought perhaps it would be best if we spoke face-to-face, so that we could all make sure we had a mutual understanding of our relationship going forward."

Riley inclined her head, her face settling.

"First of all, Ms. Holland," Hakobyan said, addressing her directly. "My organization owes you a deep apology for the dishonorable actions of our deceased former head."

Disgust sat clearly on Hakobyan's face.

"Of course, I would love to have you as part of Percutio. Your skills are quite impressive, and I am sure our admiration of your abilities is also of no surprise to any of you. But I know that you will never leave APS, Ms. Holland, and I am not interested in having anyone in our organization who is not there of their own free will. Yes, again I will be honest and say that I would also be extremely interested to know more about the internal workings of APS. However, kidnapping women against their will to find out is not our way." The disgust on Hakobyan's face deepened. "I do not know what got into Grigor, that *khiyar*, but we do not treat women like that. Or at least we will not as long as *I* am in charge."

"You said that at Club Infinity that night about Harold." Kelly was curious. "*Khiyar*. What does that mean, Mr. Hakobyan, if you don't mind me asking?"

Hakobyan gave her that brief, amused smile again. "It is the Armenian word for *cucumber*, Ms. Holland. In this context, it means a dumb or a useless person."

Kelly nodded in acknowledgment, the shadow of a smile crossing her own face.

Hakobyan addressed Riley again. "You have our apologies for Grigor's disgraceful behavior, Riley, you and Ms. Holland both. You also have my pledge that Percutio will stay out of the seven-county APS territory in Florida, as has always been our agreement. You have my personal word on that. If there is even the slightest doubt in your minds, I would expect no less than for you to take whatever steps you feel are necessary to keep yourself and your organization safe."

Riley again inclined her head in acknowledgment.

"One last thing." Hakobyan looked around at all of them. "I will be moving to Miami immediately, to our own headquarters down there. And so, I will need to appoint a new Florida chief. The associate I have in mind is a man named Hayk Simonyan. He has been one of my own personal crew chiefs for a very long time. I will make arrangements to introduce him before I leave, and I will personally make sure he understands what the expectations of APS will be. That is all I have to say."

Kelly belatedly realized that Riley was deliberately standing back and letting her take charge of the meeting. Her heart swelling with love, she stepped forward to address Hakobyan directly.

"I accept your apologies, Mr. Hakobyan, and I believe you are sincere. I'm also certain you thoroughly understand the penalty for letting something like this happen again." Hakobyan quietly signaled his understanding. "We'll start fresh then, and we'll be ready to meet Mr. Simonyan when you're ready to introduce us. You know how to contact us. I don't believe we have anything further at this time either, so good day to you, Mr. Hakobyan."

Kelly nodded to Hakobyan, then turned and walked away alongside Riley, Kenn, and Trill at her back.

When they had all climbed into their SUV, Riley leaned over from the driver's seat and kissed Kelly deeply.

"Excellent, *princesa*." Riley caressed Kelly's face before letting her go and starting the engine. She touched her comm so that Bryn and the rest of the Seven were hooked into the conversation.

"Aram Hakobyan is not a good man, *mi corillo*, but in this case, I believe he was sincere in offering both his apologies for the clusterfuck with Reizan, and his commitment to abide by our rules going forward." Riley brought everyone up to speed on the meeting with Hakobyan. "Reizan never *did* share the secret of Kelly's ability with anyone else. Since he and Alan McAllister are dead, Kelly and her secret can now be considered safe."

Thunderous applause and whoops echoed through the comm. Kelly grinned, enormous relief on her face.

"Hakobyan is not interested in acquiring Kelly as an asset unwillingly, so it appears Percutio is no longer a threat to any of us," Riley noted. "I can't say that will remain the case if Hakobyan ever *does* find out about her gift...but at this point, I can't see that happening."

Kelly blew out a deep breath and reached over to caress Riley's arm, then touched her own comm.

"Take us home, *amante*," Kelly said, emotion in her voice. "I have a wedding to get ready for, and some APS responsibilities to catch up on. I need to talk to Casey and Jess about my coming to the next community outreach demonstration, then get with Drew to see when I can go with her into Purgatory. Plus, you and I have a Muay Thai demo to put on in Hades. *Normal* shit, my friends. Regular old APS business shit."

Kelly grinned again at her fiancé, who smirked back at her. She glanced over her shoulder at Trill and Kenn, who were grinning as well.

Whimsical Princess

"I love the hell out of each and every one of you. We have some ladies to protect, so let's get home and get the fuck to it."

Epilogue

Delaney Sedgwick paused in the middle of icing some petit fours she was experimenting with for Kelly Holland's wedding to Riley Armstrong in less than a month, and let her mind wander again.

It had been two weeks since she and Kelly had been taken by Grigor Reizan and his crew of thugs. The bruise on her cheek where Reizan had struck her had faded until it was little more than a few yellow and green streaks now, and the tenderness had almost disappeared completely.

Delaney thought about that day.

She was still surprised that she hadn't been that afraid in the face of Reizan's threats, but she supposed that had been because Kelly had kept her that way. Kelly Holland, Del acknowledged, totally defined the word *badass*.

Although, she thought, *I was amazed to discover I had more guts than I'd ever realized.* It was like her mind had gone still and clear, she'd been able to focus and plan—even if she hadn't known what the hell she was actually doing—and she and Kelly had formed an effective, efficient team, almost without thinking.

When she'd finally gotten home after her meeting with the Coast Guard and the FBI after their rescue, her mom had insisted Delaney be seen by a local psychologist recommended to them by Rosi Armstrong. Marsha Sedgwick was adamant that sometimes trauma could lay buried and creep up on you when you least expected it.

Which was true, Delaney had admitted, even as the psychologist had reassured her mother after a few sessions that Del was fine, and there was no evidence of permanent mental damage—much to Marsha's relief.

However, no one knew Delaney had often had more trauma in one day with that asshole, Tina Schaffner, than she'd *ever* had with the entire Percutio mess.

If anything had affected her in the last several weeks, it was the shock of seeing Teagan Malloy again last month after all her years away. Her first glimpse of Teagan at the Whimsy Arts Center grand opening had sent Delaney's senses into a tailspin, from which they hadn't yet recovered.

Teagan hadn't changed much in the over ten years since Delaney had last seen her. That tall, strong, heavily muscled body. That thick, light red hair. Those brilliant green eyes, and the killer smile that still soaked every pair of panties in sight.

Del had learned that Teagan, the Armstrong twins, and the rest of Teag's posse—whom everyone now referred to as the Seven— were closer than ever. Bryn, Riley, Teagan, Trillian, Jaime, Blake,

Drew, Kennedy, Casey—all former Marines now, all University of Florida graduates.

The Armstrong twins and the Seven had each pursued their goals with a single-minded purpose. When they were done with their service and with school, they had banded together to create the most successful security and protection company for women in the Tampa Bay area.

They were amazing, just like she'd always known they would be. *It's ironic*, she thought with a bitter twist of her lips, *that their accomplishments had come too late for me.*

Delaney sighed and threw her spatula into a sink full of hot soapy water. If she was being honest with herself, she'd admit she couldn't ignore the reaction of her body from just the thought of Teagan's body.

Teag had always been able to affect her like that, even when they were in high school and Delaney was dating Tina.

When Teagan had pulled Delaney against her to rest when they were on the *Arusiak*, Del knew she hadn't felt that safe and protected since high school either. She'd felt as though there was nothing in this world that could ever touch her, just as long as she was in Teagan Malloy's arms.

A sharp knock came at the front door, interrupting her wistful musings. Delaney frowned, dried her hands on a towel, then went to see who it was. Her mother was at the grocery store, her father was at work, and none of them were expecting anyone.

To Delaney's complete and utter shock when she opened the front door, Teagan Malloy stood unsmiling on the doorstep—her tall, muscled body clad in jeans, a black APS polo shirt, boots, and a leather jacket. Mirrored sunglasses hid her brilliant eyes.

Teagan slowly pulled off her shades so that her intense, vibrant green orbs were visible. Delaney caught her breath as those hypnotic eyes focused on her face with laser precision and a heat Delaney couldn't ignore.

"Hi, Delaney. May I come in?"

ABOUT THE AUTHOR

Tiffany E. Taylor writes sensual lesbian romance fiction within the passionate butch-femme dynamic in a variety of genres: action/adventure, contemporary, and paranormal. She lives with her spouse and their daughter in an idyllic queer-friendly little town on Florida's west-central coast. You can find out more about Tiffany at www.tiffanyetaylor.com, or you can follow her at:

Facebook: www.facebook.com/tiffany.taylor0627
Instagram: www.instagram.com/tiffanyetaylor_sapphicauthor
Twitter: www.twitter.com/TiffanyE_Author

And before you go… REVIEWS are like rocket fuel for authors. You keep us going when you take some of your precious time and tell us what you think. I know you're busy, but I'm asking you to take just a few minutes to post a review on Amazon. It doesn't have to be long—just a few sentences would be lovely—but I will be immensely grateful.

COMING IN 2022…
Whimsical Angel
(Book 3, The Whimsical Dreams series)

    Teagan Malloy of the APS Seven has long been known as "Casanova" in the tiny community of Whimsy—a magnet for the hordes of women who've fallen for her brilliant green eyes, hard muscled body, and killer smile.

    But Teag has always played the field in an effort to forget the shy, beautiful femme she loved and lost over fifteen years before. She's always resisted attempts by women to become "the one" in her life...because if Teagan can't have Delaney Sedgwick, she isn't interested in having anybody.

    The day finally arrives when Delaney comes home to her after many years away and makes Teagan believe in miracles again. The happy couple soon finds out, however, that Delaney hasn't come home alone.

    A viciously jealous ex bent on revenge is determined to destroy Teagan and Delaney, and wants nothing more than to watch them explode in a shower of hellfire and pain. And Tina Schaffner will do *anything* to make that happen.

    It's the man whom Tina has hired to help her who's the real threat, however—someone who will not only crush Teagan and Delaney for a hefty fee, but who will also stop at nothing to take over the lucrative protection business run by APS. Frank Bellwood is determined to be crowned the undisputed king of protection and come out the big money winner in this game.

Even if it means he must engineer the total destruction of APS itself in the process.

.

Whimsical Haven

(Book 1, The Whimsical Dreams series)

When Rowan Holland of Woodbridge, Virginia lands squarely in the crosshairs of a psychotic stalker, fleeing to Whimsy, Florida might be her only chance of escape.

There, she'll meet the head of lesbian-owned Armstrong Protection Services. Possessive. Protective. Deadly.

Bryn Armstrong, one of the owners of APS, is immediately captivated by an equally-mesmerized Rowan, and vows she will do everything in her power to protect Rowan from this psychopath.

When the stalker follows Rowan to Whimsy, staying hidden in the shadows, it's up to Bryn—along with her twin, Riley, and "the Seven," the butch management team of APS—to cut him down and put an end to Rowan's nightmare.

But, as the stalker draws closer to Rowan and the increased danger to Bryn's woman becomes more real, Bryn and her team know they must find and stop the psychopath, who just may be a killer in disguise.

TW: This work of fiction contains a scene of disciplinary spanking and other instances of light BDSM that some readers may find triggering.

One More Chance
(Book 1, The Dance series)

Seven years after her wife's tragic death, a still-mourning Aimée "Jake" Charron finds herself unexpectedly intrigued by a personal ad sent to her by one of her best friends. It was a femme sucker punch right to the gut, and Jake finds her inner alpha butch responding with an almost predatory desire.

After two failed relationships, Geneva Raineri doesn't believe in fairy tales and happily-ever-afters anymore. Her neighbor posts a personal ad Gen wrote as a joke on a butch/femme romance site—and when a self-professed alpha butch named Jake responds, Gen finds herself swept up into a sensual game of cat-and-mouse that soon has a captivated Gen feeling like Jake's prey.

Jake knows she's already had one chance at a forever love, but lost it when her wife died. She wants Gen with a desire she'd thought was long dead—but Jake believes expecting to find another great love after you've already had one and lost it is a fool's game.

Gen, however, is determined to prove to Jake that anyone lucky enough to be given another shot at happiness needs to grab it with both hands and never let it go.

As Jake and Gen navigate personal journeys that include heartbreak, self-discovery, passion, and courage, they both discover that risking everything to take one more chance on love might ultimately be their salvation.

Painted Hearts Publishing

Painted Hearts Publishing has an exclusive group of talented writers. We publish stories that range from historical to fantasy, sci-fi to contemporary, erotic to sweet. Our authors present high quality stories full of romance, desire, and sometimes graphic moments that are both entertaining and sensual. At the heart of all our stories is romance, and we are firm believers in a world where happily ever afters do exist.

We invite you to visit us at www.paintedheartspublishing.com.

Printed in Great Britain
by Amazon